AMONG THE DANGS

Books by George P. Elliott

PARKTILDEN VILLAGE
AMONG THE DANGS

AMONG THE DANGS

Ten Short Stories by

George P. Elliott

Holt, Rinehart and Winston   *New York*

The author wishes to acknowledge the magazines which
originally published the following stories:

Accent for "Hymn of the Angels" (Fall, 1960)
Epoch for "Love among the Old Folk" (Summer, 1952)
Esquire for "Among the Dangs"—first published June, 1958
The Hudson Review for "The NRACP" (Autumn, 1949), "Children of
    Ruth" (Winter, 1951), "Faq'" (Spring, 1952), and "Miss
    Cudahy of Stowes Landing" (Spring, 1954)
Quarterly Review of Literature for "A Family Matter" (Vol. 7, No. 2,
    May, 1953)
Western Review for "Brother Quintillian" (Fall, 1954) and
    "Beatification of BobbySu Wilson" (Fall, 1957)

A number of these stories have been included in various editions
of Prize Stories: The O. Henry Awards edited by Paul Engle
and Best American Short Stories edited by Martha Foley.

Library of Congress Catalog Card Number: 61–5348

To Mary Emma

Contents

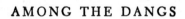

AMONG THE DANGS

A Family Matter

I

In the summer of his thirty-fifth year Bryan Mott, second son of the inventor Gordon Mott, received the following letter from his father.

My dear Bryan,

Ever since Thelma's unhappy death this spring, I have had the growing feeling that her daughter Jessica (I believe I sent you a picture of her, a charming thing) not only does not need me but what is worse does not want me hanging around. In my day, and it is obviously my day no longer, a girl of twenty would have sought the wise counsel of a man like myself in a thousand concerns. There is no reason for her to think I lack wisdom, and I haven't bothered her much; yet everything I say bores her to death (the expression is hers). Now that she's home for the summer vacation I have been feeling superannuated, and besides I abominate the New York heat.

Therefore I have decided to renew my acquaintance with my sons, beginning with you.

According to the ticket I have before me, I shall arrive at the SP station in Oakland at 8:03 P.M. July 11. If I don't see you at the station I'll take a cab on out.

There's a lot more to say, but since I'll be seeing you so soon I won't bother to write it down.

The check enclosed is to cover any extra expenses you may run on my account. I don't eat much but I do cause a lot of trouble. Which Martha will bear the brunt of, so I've made it out to her.

Give my best to her and the children. I hope she is a little mellowed by having had children. A psychoanalyst told me once—I've tried everything, mineral water, body-building, psychoanalysis—that the reason I've had so many wives was that I was seeking a mother-substitute. Which may be so, and if it is then Martha as she was when you first married her is not the one for me. Charming, intelligent, companionable, but how unmaternal.

I look forward to getting to know your children—and you too.

Gordon

That flippancy about the psychoanalyst sounds worse than I meant it to sound. I never really went to one; he was just a friend of Diana's. There's nothing more the matter with me than there is with anyone else. It's New York. A dreadful atmosphere.

The letter arrived on a Monday morning, ten days before the eleventh. Aylmer fetched the mail to his mother, who was in the midst of washing clothes. At her prolonged wail Bryan came running out of his writing room to see what had happened, and Roxana sang out from her sand pile, "What's the matter, Mommy?"

"I won't be able to write a word while he's here," Bryan groaned.

"He's your father," said Martha darkly.

"Grampa Gordon?" asked Aylmer.

"Yes dear," his mother answered, "Grampa Gordon. Go out and play with Zan."

"And stay out," said Bryan.

"Oh why couldn't this letter have come at any other time?" said Martha belligerently, but not exactly to Bryan.

"Because there was no other time."

"I suppose so."

"Of course," Bryan continued, "it might have arrived the afternoon of the eleventh. Then I could at least have written for the next ten days."

"Oh come on, you sensitive plant. You haven't lived in the same city with your father since you were ten."

"Twelve. But it's the childhood experiences that leave their deepest impress on the soul."

"Carry out this basket of wet clothes, and then go back to your room and do something about it. He's *your* father."

"Laundering seems to dull your razorlike wit, my love."

"Daddy," said Roxana at the back door, "is Grampa going to sleep in the cellar?"

At which there was another wail from Martha. "Where is he going to sleep?"

And Bryan ducked back to his room, where he tried to pick up the thread of his thought—he was translating Racine—but failed. He sighed, but to maintain his honor he stayed in his room till lunchtime reading a novel.

For lunch there were peanut butter sandwiches and raw carrots. Bryan did not object in words but he created a ruckus by putting jam on his peanut butter. The children were not allowed jam except on state occasions—their teeth.

"I suppose," said Martha, "your father will wreck what little discipline you let me keep over the children. The old goat. He probably wouldn't give them a second glance if he didn't think I'd mind."

"The size of the pitcher, my love, has nothing to do with the size of the ear. Caution."

"Do you have to be so coy, Bryan? After all . . ."

"My maternal little wife," said Bryan patting her behind as she poured the milk, "I think Gordon will find you as maternal as he could wish."

"And that's another thing," said Martha whirling so vigorously that she kicked the table and knocked Roxana's milk over. "I never read such an insulting letter in my life. If you suppose," she continued, while mopping up Roxana and the floor, "that I'm going to coddle a white-haired, broken-down old roué, you're thicker than even I thought."

"Well," said Bryan, "where is he going to sleep?"

"He paid *me* to worry about it, darling. So go back to *Phèdre* and don't fret your poetic soul about such mundane matters."

"You're pretty snippy for a person who opens other people's letters."

"Bryan, really, it was from your father."

"All I have to say is—he does not sleep in my writing room."

He marched out, his pennon ragged but flying.

Racine could not hold his attention, and by two he had finished the novel. He was working on the composition of a literary crossword puzzle—he had had a number published under another name —when the door opened to Martha.

"I know you can't be working, darling," she began, but hesitated when she saw him hunched over his desk. "You could help me, couldn't you?"

He leaned back in his chair but did not turn to face her.

" '*Un dieu vengeur te suit, tu ne peux l'éviter.*

Je t'aimais; et je sens que malgré ton offense

Mes entrailles pour toi se troublent par avance.' "

"I'm sorry," she said. "I'll take the children down shopping."

His problem was to find a nine-letter name whose first two letters were sh and whose seventh was w. There was none so he made a name up, Shaddower in this case: "That the sun may not shine in broad day" or "Shamus."

When Justin Mott, the third son, returned from work his wife handed him the following letter and told him the peas were nearly cooked. He read it fast.

My dear Justin,

I have before me a ticket which says I am to arrive in Oakland on July 11 at 8:03 P.M. I bought this ticket because I am getting old and want to see my sons. The truth is no one needs me in New York. Oakland is home.

I know from Charlene's most daughterly letters that you have an extra room for me. I shan't be more trouble than Charlene can bear, I hope, and I can't tell you how much I want to make the acquaintance of all three of you. Imagine, I have never seen my most beautiful grandson! How fortunate you are in your wife, Justin. Do with her better than I did with your mother. I hope Diana's well. Give Charlene a kiss for me. I haven't seen her since your wedding. Or you either, **my** dear son.

Your father

"What did he have to say, honey?" asked Charlene as she **was** taking off her apron.

"Here, baby, get into your high chair," said Justin picking **up** Michael.

Michael was well into his second year and not nearly so helpless as his parents supposed. As it was, picked up and stuffed into his high chair, he found it engaging to kick up the tray and poke one foot out through the side. There was more to put down in Michael than there was zeal in his parents for putting it down; they were young too.

"My, smoked pork chops and peas. What could be better? What do you get, baby? Scraped liver and spinach as usual?"

"And he loves it. What did your father say in his letter?"

"Let's not talk about disagreeable subjects while we eat."

"He said he was coming out here to visit."

"Yes."

"Glube blg wawa ffrts cheese," said Michael.

"You see, he wants cheese," said Justin.

"It just means he's feeling good."

"You won't even give my son cheese when he wants it."

"Yackety yackety. Get the cheese yourself if you want to."

He went to the icebox and got a piece of cheddar. Michael dunked the cheddar in his spinach and threw it onto the floor. Justin ungraciously mopped up.

"He's getting old and wants to see his sons," said Charlene as she picked a bone.

"So he says," answered Justin with a malevolent glance.

"Oakland is his real home now. No one needs him in New York."

"Look, you've read the letter. Let's not talk about it."

"I did not. When did I have a chance?"

"How do I know? While I was fussing with Mickey."

"But the letter's in your pocket."

"Well, maybe you steamed it open and resealed it."

But Charlene had burst into tears, and Michael was starting up slowly but ominously, like a fire siren.

Charlene was thought by some of her friends to be psychic; how else could she win at bridge so often? But Justin was a businessman.

"You don't believe me," she sobbed.

"I'm sorry, honey," he said with irritation as he bent over her, hugging her shoulders with one hand and tickling Michael's stomach with the other. "So you didn't read the letter. I still don't see . . ."

"I wouldn't dream of steaming open a letter."

"Well, I guess it's just a woman's intuition," he said.

"Thassawrai, thassawrai. Mama, mama."

His parents turned on him like heliotropes.

"Did you hear that?"

"He said 'That's all right.' "

"Cheese, cheese, cheese, cheese."

Michael crowed. His parents embraced.

"I'm sorry, baby," said Justin to his wife. "Here, read it, I'm sorry."

"It's just that you were so rough," she said. She disclaimed any pride in being psychic, but only did what she was prompted to do in these matters. "Well, I think it's sweet of your father to just come like this. Real familylike. Do you suppose he'll mind if *I* call him Gordon?"

"I don't suppose he'll mind if you call him Gordon."

"Are you being sarcastic, Justin?"

"Only irritated. Why should he mind?"

"I don't know. I just remember him as a very courtly old man. Sort of like a nobleman. An earl say."

Justin did not respond; he was mustering his miscellaneous knowledge of his father so that he might demolish in an orderly and accurate fashion this picture of him as an earl.

"We ought to get an innerspring mattress for the guest bed and a new rug for the guest room. I saw a bargain in rugs just yesterday."

"We ought not. It's a good bed and a good enough rug. Your

mother didn't complain of them when she stayed with us when Michael was born."

"Oh, mother. But we don't know how long your father is going to be with us. He didn't say. Maybe he even wants to settle down with us for the rest of his life."

"Oh no, oh no," said Justin, at first with the inflection of determination and then with that of horror. "Oh no, oh no, no, no."

"Why not? He has no one to take care of him."

"I don't know why not. Just not. He has three sons and two living wives. Why should he stay with us?"

"I like him."

"I don't."

"Justin!"

"He may stay here a couple of weeks, a month even. Then he goes to visit Roscoe or Bryan."

"I don't think Mickey will like firecrackers."

"And why not? He's a boy isn't he?"

"A baby boy. I was thinking, we ought to get Nancy to stay with him Thursday evening."

"Why Nancy? Is she sound absorbent?"

"We're going to Roscoe's on Thursday, to watch the fireworks over Lake Merritt. Can't you even remember your own family?"

"Oh yes . . . Mickey is my son. He can stand a little noise."

"I don't think so," she said lightly. Scowl darkened Justin's face. Seeing this little victory she added, "You frightened him, honey."

With the slightest readjustment of muscles his scowl became an anxious frown.

"I don't know how it is, but I manage a factory with a hundred and fifty men in it with less trouble than I manage you. In fact, I don't manage you at all. You always make me feel in the wrong."

She suppressed a very quiet smile and patted him on the arm.

"Tell me what happened today, dear," she said. "It's harder to manage a hundred and fifty than one."

Justin, not perceiving the fallacy in this proposition, brightened and gave her an account of his day as he always did. He did not yet know that she was not interested in his factory life; indeed she did not yet know it herself. She would respond to his statements with an occasional polite yes and is that so and really, but her eyes were not in harmony with her voice. He thought it was her way, and talked on.

Roscoe Mott, the eldest son, received no such letter from his father. Roscoe was forty, spare, and slightly dandyish. He was in the habit of watching an interlocutor with the air of one who seeks confirmation of his opinion of himself. This opinion fluctuated on the scale of pride rather extremely, and did not always receive confirmation. His wife, for example, did not give it him promiscuously.

"Roscoe," she said somewhat thickly for she had toothpicks between her lips, "do we have enough seltzer?"

"Hrmph," he answered from the dining room. He was ranging through the house with hostly eye alert that he might rectify error.

"You know you should see to it," she said as she rolled another delicacy in a strip of bacon.

"I am sure we have enough, Edwa."

"The last three Fourths we ran out of seltzer," she said as she speared the bacon. "And we ran out when the Tollertons dropped by. You always say you'll take care of the drinks but just look . . ."

"All right, I'll get it, all right."

"You might as well get John to go."

"All right. John!" There was no response. "I suppose he's around, Edwa? John!"

"There's no use shouting. He went down to the lake to watch them set up the stage for the fireworks."

"You might have told me. I suppose Henry has a date as usual?"

"Oh Roscoe, how can you talk so harshly about him? This may be the last summer he'll be with us. Who knows when he will love us so much again?"

"Hrmph."

"Well as long as you're going, dear, you might just as well get another package of cocktail napkins. There are so many of us."

"Yes, yes, yes. That's all?" He put on his hat, an exact, gray homburg.

"Don't forget, everybody takes seltzer but Martha."

Yet it had been the napkins she had wanted, and that had suggested sending him out in the first place.

As he left, he met Bryan and his family arriving, and by the time he had returned, Justin and Charlene had installed Michael in the baby bed upstairs. There was scarcely time for a highball before dinner was ready.

"We must hurry with dinner," he said serving. "It'll soon be time for the fireworks."

"The children won't want to miss them," said Edwa.

"If the children are the ones who won't want to miss them," said Martha, "then why must we bolt our food?"

"Honey," said Charlene to Justin before Edwa could have responded had she wished to, "do you suppose we ought to go home and get baby's cod liver oil?"

"Can't you give it to him tomorrow morning?"

"Yes."

"Then don't worry."

"And powder his bottom and button his sleepers," said Bryan in a crooning voice to Charlene beside him, "tuck him in tight and kiss him and tell him you love him, leave the door open just a crack and sing him good night."

She looked at him sentimentally, put her hand on his arm, and said, "You and Martha ought to have another baby."

"Ah, but it's not as simple as all that."

"It should be, for you. Really."

Bryan watched her a moment.

And Martha and Edwa were both watching him watch her, though he didn't notice it. Bryan had so many internal eyes, some like Edwa's and more like Martha's, scrutinizing him day and night that he paid very little attention to watchful eyes outside himself. Which accounted, among other things, for his attire as of a workingman at a ball game, in contrast to Roscoe's gray flannels and Justin's soft, expensive, sporty clothes.

"You know," said Bryan remembering Roscoe's injunction to hurry, "here we are, the assembled sons of Gordon." He held forth his glass of wine and drained it as though drinking a toast. "Sons of the famous Mott. True, Roscoe is known in the best real estate circles of the Bay Area, and I am known to critics and editors of literary magazines, and Justin is making his mark in the realm of tubes and condensers and frequency modulation. But essentially we are the three who are identified at a party, should someone want to know, as the sons of Gordon Mott. That at least we have in common, the shuddering loin."

He paused to pour himself another glass of wine and drink it. During the interval Martha said, "Pass the beets please," and Edwa urged Justin to have some more cold tongue. Bryan went on.

"He has set us an example which we have not followed, encumbered as we are by charming and devoted wives." He saluted each; only Charlene liked it. "Yet I propose that each of us, since we are not apt to act on our impulses as splendidly as he has done, tell a love story on occasions of our forgathering like this."

"Really Bryan," said his wife.

"I hardly think we have time now," said Roscoe.

"You are the senior brother," said Bryan. "Why don't you start off?"

"No," said Charlene before Roscoe could object, "you must start. You thought of it and anyway you have one to tell or you wouldn't have brought the subject up."

"That's true," Bryan said, "that's perfectly true. I am seen through." Martha snorted and Edwa stirred in her chair. "Very well, my story. I was down in the book section of the Good Will store one day. You know, down on Broadway and 5th or 6th."

"We know," said Martha.

"I was just looking around rather aimlessly, at Winston Churchill and F. Marion Crawford and Somebody Canfield. I noticed, only because she was in my way, a young woman also looking at books. She was perfectly unnoteworthy, perfectly. Hair-colored hair and eye-colored eyes and clothes that were a perfection of the ordinary. I doubt if I would recognize her again. She had good wrists though, very delicate and supple, only with listless, chapped hands."

"It takes a queen," said Charlene, "to look like anything in the Good Will."

"Yes, yes, that's it. That's what I was trying to get at," he said turning to her and addressing the rest of his story to her. "Nothing was happening when presently a young man, her gray counterpart, walked in and came up to her. She started a little when he touched her shoulder. 'Peter!' she said. 'How did you know I was here?' He smiled at her with a tenderness I cannot describe. His ordinary face suddenly shone with a love so little ordinary, so pure and true, that I held my breath to hear what he would reply. Her face reflected some of his radiance, very quietly. They had halos. —You understand, they were not touching each other at all. He stooped a little, and she still held a copy of some novel or other. They just looked into each other's eyes, smiling a little, aware of me and indifferent to my presence as though I had been another book. There was only a moment of this before he replied: 'How do I know my foot is in my shoe?' That was all the answer she needed. They walked out with little fingers linked, not talking, as ordinary as ever, and I have never forgotten them."

Bryan looked about the table commandingly; there was to be a moment of respectful, not to say reverent, contemplation following this apologue.

Charlene seemed sunk deepest of all, chin in hand, eyes in nether space, when dreamily she said, "How did you remember his name was Peter?"

"What difference does it make?" he snapped.

The sound of jaws in motion returned to the room.

"Well how?"

"Who cares what his real name was?"

"If you don't even know his real name how do we know it was a real story?"

"Reality is of the essence, not the detail," he said intending to silence her and nearly succeeding.

"I don't see," Martha put in, "anything so wonderful about what he said. Anybody knows where his foot is."

"How stupid can you get?" said Bryan wrathfully to Martha.

"It was really a very sweet story," said Charlene to him sweetly, making amends.

"Thank you, my dear, for those few kind words. —Come on, Justin, you must have one to tell."

"I don't want to."

"Honey," said Charlene.

"Well, all right. I'm no good at it, but the PBX operator down at the plant fell in love with the stationary engineer. He used to flirt with her, and he flirted too much. Well, he took her out a couple of times and when she found out he was married she ran off to Reno with the truck driver in the company pickup. He'd been in love with her for months but he had a birthmark on his neck."

"Not a bad situation," said Bryan.

"I think it's too bad for the truck driver," said Edwa.

"Justin," said Charlene gazing at him intently, "you never told me this story. When did it happen?"

"Last month, and I told you." His eyes opened wider. "At dinner once."

"There should be at least one more complication," said Bryan. "Pregnancy, relationship, threat, misunderstanding, something."

"I like it," said Martha, "just as it is."

"I forgot to say," said Justin wrenching his eyes from Charlene, "the truck driver is the brother of the engineer's wife."

"Ah, now we're getting some place" said Bryan.

"Really, honey," said Charlene, her eyes on the table, "I don't remember."

"You said at the time what a terrible way to get married it was."

"I must have been thinking of baby at the time you told it."

But she didn't believe herself, and no one else, who was paying any real attention, believed her either. Martha perceived that Justin and Charlene were making some unhappy discovery about themselves; therefore, having a profound trust in decorum as the lubricant of life, she began clearing table, to create stir and bustle that would restore the young couple to their social selves.

"No story, Roscoe?" said Bryan.

"Well, you know," said Roscoe with a condescending smile, "there's hardly time."

"Roscoe," said Bryan not without malice, "you looked remarkably like Gordon just then—the way you took out your watch and peered down your nose at it."

"Hrmph," said Roscoe, who viewed his character as being essentially an inversion of his father's.

"Gordon, Gordon, Gordon," said Edwa as she poured cream over her pudding. "Why all this talk about Gordon, Bryan? If you've mentioned him once you've mentioned him a dozen times."

"Bryan wants to see him," said Charlene in her automatic way.

"Come, my little oracle," he said as though she were dear to him but weak in the head, "wants to or expects to?"

"Wants to," she said defiantly.

"Maybe she's right," said Bryan to himself, only aloud, "maybe that's what I really want. She's an odd one.—My sweet, my pure, my apple-cheeked Cassandra, can you tell me why . . ."

"Justin!" she cried out. "You can't just sit there and let him insult me, even if he is your brother."

"Oh Charlene," said Justin.

"What in the world!" said Bryan.

Martha was gagging her laughter with her napkin.

"I won't sit by him another minute." Charlene got up, pudding in hand, and made a place for herself beside Justin. Once there she pressed his foot with hers, and whispered to him how horrible Bryan was, and paid no attention to Bryan's rather stiff-necked explanation of himself.

So love filled up the gap that Justin had found, and after that Charlene would not ask him much about his day at the plant and he would volunteer her very little; and there would be less to talk about when he came home from work, so they would talk even more about Michael.

Roscoe, who had gathered from Charlene's shift that some sort of realignment was going on, turned to Bryan with a rather stately motion and said, "What have you heard from Father recently?"

"He's coming to visit us next week."

"What!" said Charlene, Edwa, Roscoe, Justin.

"I got a letter a few days ago saying he was coming for a visit the eleventh. Is there anything so remarkable about that?"

"Who was he going to stay with?" asked Justin.

"I said I got the letter."

"He's going to stay with you?"

"For pity's sake, yes. What is there . . ."

"I got the same letter," said Justin, "only he said he was going to stay with us."

"What!" said Martha, Edwa, Roscoe, Bryan.

"Why," said Edwa in slow astonishment, "he did not write us a letter."

"It's a doubtful honor either way," said Bryan.

"But I write to him at least twice a year," said Edwa, who was not much interested in honor.

Two letters a year were as many as were written to Gordon by all the others in the room combined; they were silent.

"How very thoughtless of him," she said, and meant at least that.

There was a great *crack* outdoors, and the dark sky flashed bluish-white.

"The fireworks!" said Edwa.

"The children won't want to miss them," said Roscoe.

But the kitchen was empty.

"They must be up on the roof of the apartment house down the street," said Edwa. "Let's go down."

"I'd better stay with baby, hadn't I, honey?" said Charlene to Justin, her hands on his shoulders.

It rose to his lips to say he was going with the others, but he hugged her instead and said, "Sure, honey, I'll wait with you. We can watch from here."

The fireworks were a great success with the children. It was eleven before the families had reassembled themselves at Roscoe's. Bryan had been unable to interest anyone in talking about Gordon's letters; he felt even a little snubbed. He had decided to go over to see Charlene the next afternoon, ostensibly to talk about the letters, really to make friends with her again. But he changed his mind; as everyone was saying their good nights she ducked into her car before he could kiss her on both cheeks as he always had done before. He kissed Edwa instead, as he seldom did; she patted him as if he were a child, and sent him home.

The children were all in bed, and Roscoe was lying in bed watching Edwa work on her hair.

"On days like this," he said, "I'm thankful that all our family live in Oakland."

"Your head doesn't ache?" she said through her hairpins. It usually ached after family gatherings.

"No, not a bit. Fine young woman, Charlene."

"Mommy!" Mary called out.

"Not asleep!" said Edwa to Roscoe. "What, dear?" she said to Mary at the door of the girls' room; she was still fixing her hair.

"Roxana said that's how it would be at the end of the world, Mommy."

"Well, we'll never see it, honey. Go to sleep."

"She said it might happen any old day now."

"Oh no, it won't. She's wrong."

"She said so. She said she read it in a book."

"She was teasing, honey. Go to sleep."

"How do you know it won't?"

"God wouldn't let it happen."

"Oh."

"Sometimes," said Roscoe when she had returned, "I wish we didn't have to tell the children so many lies."

"What lies? I never tell them lies."

"Oh well, whatever you want to call it. The world may end any day you know. Stars do explode."

"Nonsense," said Edwa turning out the light, "that's a Mottish idea."

She got into bed and told him good-nght, and she was sound asleep before he had finally adjusted his pillow.

II

"Well my boy," said Gordon, "you seem to lead a very agreeable life."

Martha was just joining them, having put the children to bed. They were sitting about the fireplace, in which there was a small fire that was warming the darkness more than any chill in the air. Bryan disliked the thought of building a fire, but when it was actually burning he could stupefy himself gazing into the flames and afterward the embers dying down.

"We like it," he answered noncommitally.

"The children like it," said Martha positively.

"Indeed, indeed. Well they should. Tell me, Bryan, what are you working on these days? I've only seen that one book of poems you published some years back."

"Four years ago. Only individual verses since then, in magazines, a few in anthologies. I'm working on a translation of Racine at the moment."

"Racine!"

"I've done most of *Phèdre* and half of *Andromaque*. It goes rather slowly."

"I've always gathered somehow that Racine was untranslatable."

"Have you? That's a rather old-fashioned notion, like the one that *Lear* won't go on stage."

"It's a very strong impression all the same."

"Have you ever read Racine in French?"

"Yes."

"Oh. Well, do you see any reason why he can't be translated like any other great poet?"

"Yes. It sounds like prose in English."

"You're a scientist," said Bryan with a levity that was yet not far from surliness.

"The thing is," said Martha, who was darning socks, "that Bryan likes challenges. Racine is supposed to be untranslatable; Bryan sets about translating him. He tries his hand at a novel; it turns out to be too short for a book and too long for a magazine. He starts a poetic play full of fine speeches, but he's never been backstage and he won't go because he can't stand little-theater characters; the play is unactable. His stories almost always have some shocking passage or idea in them; therefore they're published, if at all, only in magazines no one ever heard of, with names like *Stormy Petrel* or *K* or *Tangent* or *South Dakota Quarterly Review*."

"It sounds," said Gordon, "as though he were ducking out from under."

"That's our Bryan," said Martha. She got up and kissed him on the back of the neck, but he was staring into the fire.

"Yet his poetry suffers from none of these complaints that I can see."

"Yes, but being a poet is rather like being a bird watcher; what competition there is comes from other bird watchers, and they are really doing it for its own sake, and no one else takes it seriously at all. Still it's respectable and everyone knows about it, and most people have even looked at poems a few times."

"Usually in zoos."

"He can be more serious about writing poetry since it's a less serious occupation."

"I understand that perfectly," said Gordon. "I work much better on something that has no apparent utility than on, say, a problem in electronics."

"You do," said Bryan heavily, "you do, eh?—You," he said at Martha, "have said too much too soon and too fast. Even if what you said were true, as it is not, even so you should not have said it. At least, not like that."

"Why, darling . . ." she began.

"What was wrong with what she said?" said Gordon.

"What she left out."

"Which was?"

"The world. Would you rather have sherry or port, Gordon? The sherry is better."

"Sherry."

"Sherry for you," he said to her. He stood up with a bitter expression on his mouth, glanced at each of them a moment, and went for the sherry.

"Well," said Gordon, "I hope he doesn't put poison in the wine."

"Come."

"Come what?"

"We don't keep poison in the kitchen."

"Good. Perhaps we oughtn't to be so harsh on him."

"It was very wrong of me to have said all that."

There was a little stillness between them.

"I must make it up to him," said Martha.

"How?"

"How? What a question. I haven't thought about it."

"I ask because my wives were always threatening to make it up to me for something atrocious they'd done."

"Didn't they ever do it?"

"Sometimes they would get me all involved in a project I had no interest in, such as a family picnic with some brothers and sisters of theirs. That's as close as they ever got to it, as I remember."

"You were poor at picking wives I should say."

"I must exempt Thelma from this condemnation." Bryan entered. "You remember Thelma, Bryan?"

"We met her only once. What about her?"

"I was just extolling one of her many virtues to Martha. She could choose with consummate tact precisely what would please me."

"It's a pity she died. No one else can."

The conversation came to a brief pause, which was filled with the whicker of blades.

"That was unnecessary of me," said Bryan.

"Worse than that," said Martha.

"Well, well," said Gordon. "Perhaps the air is clearer now."

"Tell me," said Bryan, "what sort of person was Thelma? I'd the impression she flowed with kindness rather than love."

"True. If we bore each other any love it was of a very pacific variety. She combined all the virtues of a nurse and a mistress, and I, I flatter myself, the best qualities of a patient and lover."

"But you are never sick," Martha exclaimed.

"Exactly. I was never sick. What better attribute can a patient have? And I was usually not around, which is a primary virtue in any lover."

"You talk of her so coolly," she said, "and here she's been dead only a few months. You really didn't love her, did you?"

"Pacifically. But the dead are so dead."

"I'm sleepy," said Bryan.

"Perhaps," said Martha, "we ought to clear up this misunderstanding about Justin and Charlene before Gordon goes to bed."

"There is no misunderstanding," said Bryan to her. "He knew what he was doing."

"I envy you two the openness of your warfare," said Gordon.

"Surely, Father, we could learn from you some of the subtleties of marital discord."

"Not at all, not at all. I was always, nearly always, courteous to my wives, but I used to murder them on an average of three times a month. That is not subtle."

"No," said Bryan.

"You mean," said Martha sharply, "in fancy."

"Well, there is a distinction," said Gordon, "though not, I am told, in the eyes of God."

"Bryan, you never had such an impulse, did you?" his wife asked.

"My dear, only the laws of the land have kept you from being an angel lo these many years."

"Motts," she said to her darning.

"You make it sound like an ugly little epithet," said Bryan.

"It was so intended."

"Your mother, Bryan, used to say Motts somewhat like that, only with heavier scorn. Maureen was cruder than you," he said addressing himself to Martha, "but a fine, high-spirited creature of the purest blood."

"I am not unacquainted with her," said Martha coolly.

"Ah, so you are, so you are. I find it difficult to remember that what is so totally past to me may have a living present of its own."

"Try it all the same."

"I will, I will indeed. And how is she now?"

"Mother seems contented enough with the man she lives with. Her second husband died a few years ago, you know."

"No, I didn't. Where is she living, Bryan?"

"Up in the Mother Lode country, in a little town named Poulterville."

"Tell me, does she still have, well, a physical life?"

"It was not ectoplasm that threw its arms about me last fall and called me her sweetest mistake."

"That last," said Martha, "was gratuitous of you."

"Oh," said Gordon, "that is exactly what he is. But what I meant by physical was, sexual."

"I am sure, Father . . ."

"No," said Martha, "she does not."

"It was perhaps indelicate of me to ask," said Gordon with a sigh.

"To ask me, yes," said Bryan.

"Well, well, no harm done."

"What's the matter?" asked Martha. "Past not past enough?"

"Oh it's dead now, but it kicked so when it was alive. She's not poor?"

"Not particularly. Tell me, what did you mean, I am a mistake?"

"Not what your low leer implies, son."

"Crude for a Mott," said Martha to Bryan, who was chagrined.

"Well, what did she mean and what do you mean?"

"I meant Maureen is, or was then, one of those who believe that the beautiful sentiment precedes the beautiful itch. With me her passion was handsome indeed, and by reverse logic she deduced that she must have loved me too. You were born before she discovered she didn't. The troubles we had while she was finding it out."

"So. I am the fruit of lust and hate."

"No!" cried Martha.

"Indeed not," said Gordon lightly. "Our desire was very great and very satisfied, and we were fond of each other. But the fondness she felt for me, when she came actually to look at it, seemed a pea beside the melon she had expected. A rather dry, yellowish pea at that."

"She does not speak of you bitterly," said Martha.

"I'm glad of that. A little regret perhaps?"

"Perhaps."

"I wish, Gordon, that you had not told me this in front of Martha."

"Husband and wife should have no secret one from the other," said his father.

"Huh," said Bryan, and left the room without saying good night.

"You must promise me, Martha, not to use this against him."

"I will not."

"Use it?"

"Promise. I view Bryan in the only way a wife can view a husband tainted with genius—simple and dangerous and not quite explainable. A slightly divine fool."

"That's a very inaccurate description of him. He may be foolish sometimes, but a fool he is not."

"No, no, I mean fool in the old sense."

"A fool in the old sense he is not. From the way you said that I would guess that you read that about a slightly divine fool in some essay. Somebody like Chesterton, flashy and wrong most of the time."

"I did not!" she cried with great vigor because what he had said was true.

"If I were to use any such word for Bryan, I would say he was artless. And I wouldn't trust his artlessness very far either."

"Artless." She was still rallying.

"Yes. He assumes that everyone is going to like him, which is artless enough. Of course you know him better than I."

"Well, whatever you call it I don't know what I would do if I couldn't laugh at him once in a while."

"Yet you seem fond of him."

"Yet!" She stopped putting her darning away to glare at him a moment.

"Well, well, my dear. It seems you will stay married a while yet."

"Of which I am thankful and proud."

"But the time will come, my dear—I hope unfaithfulness is not one of your bugbears."

"We move faster nowadays," she said. "But then, I am not so indiscreet as you." And she left him these shards of meaning to piece together if he would. At most, he discovered, they would not construct a whole sense.

By the time Martha had seen that the children were tucked in and had turned out the hall light Bryan was in bed with his face to the wall.

"Darling," she said affectionately as she took off her stockings.

He rolled over and looked at her.

"I'm terribly sorry I hurt your feelings."

"Echch," he said, like a cat whose tail has been stepped on, and rolled back.

"Oh dear, now I've done it again."

She undressed in silence. As she began her nightly toilet she said in a musing tone, "Gordon seems to have an effect on both of us."

At which Bryan began a grunt that became a roar, and she said no more.

She got into bed and patted his arm and kissed the back of his neck; he did not respond. When she turned over to sleep she pressed her bottom to his; she wriggled it once in a friendly way and then again. The third time she did it he rolled over and hugged her and bit her ear rather hard; she said nothing, but turned her face to him. He kissed her, and very soon went to sleep, with his arm over her body and her scent in his nostrils most comfortably.

"My dear," said Gordon as Charlene brought tea in to the three men, "marriage and maternity are turning you into a beautiful woman."

"Thank you," she said not blushing. "How do you take your tea, Father?"

"Medium strong and, I hope, straight. What kind is it?"

"Oolong with a little Darjeeling."

"Perfect. You could not have pleased me more."

This time she did blush a little.

"Why do you wear that frock?" Gordon continued. "It's false-naïve for you, my dear."

"Why it's sort of gay and young. Justin thought it set my figure off well. Didn't you, honey?"

"I like it," Justin said.

Charlene, without asking him, put two spoonfuls of sugar in Bryan's cup of tea and passed it to him with a knowing smile. He did not reach out for it.

"Charlene," he said mournfully, "it's Roscoe that likes sugar. I take lemon."

"Oh!" she said with dismay, but not much of it. "Really, Bryan, it's the only way I ever get you mixed up with Roscoe."

"It means something," said Bryan shaking his head. "I don't know what, but it must mean something. A dove was seen to fall lifeless before the statue of Mars yesterday. Signs of an evil age."

"Oh Bryan baby," she said hugging his head and winking at Gordon over it, "I'll never do it again, I promise. Forgive me?"

"This once," he said with more lightness in his voice than in his eyes.

"You are too beautiful," said Gordon, "to hug your male relative."

"That for you," she said snapping her fingers under his nose. "Cream and sugar, honey?"

"Please," said Justin. "I'm going to bring Michael in."

"Oh, honey, not while we're having tea—please not."

"In his playpen, Sharly?"

"Oh that's all right." She turned to Gordon. "The other day he looked so wise and solemn for a minute, Father, just like you. I'm so glad you're getting to know him now when he's still nothing but pure candy."

"Wise," said Gordon reflectively. "Wise. That's it, Charlene. In another five or six years your figure will be mature and your face will be wiser. What a pity that all the bloom will be rubbed off by then. It's impossible to be pretty and wise at once, and wise is better."

"I would say," said Bryan, "that your present loveliness, Charlene, is its own reward. I do not need to wait five years to love you dearly."

"I would say," said Justin bearing Michael—he was cut off by a biff on the nose with a pan. "I would say," he recommenced a little truculently, "that she's mine to love now and she'll be mine to love five years from now and I hope she'll be mine to love fifty years from now when she's wrinkled and cranky."

Charlene beamed at his sentiment and smiled at the crudeness of its expression and ran over to hug Michael, who biffed her too. It was a good noisy pan.

"Pure candy, eh, Charlene?" said Bryan as diversionary. Being a poet he could not easily separate a sentiment from its expression, indeed it went against his grain even to try; besides, this particular sentiment at this particular time annoyed him.

"Well," she said nursing her bruise, "after all you expect little boys to be rough."

"Certainly," said Justin as he swung Michael by the feet in a great arc. "If they're not rough enough you make them rough. Rough and tough."

He hurled Michael through the air onto the davenport; for a moment the baby's eyes were huge and scared, but then they crinkled and he squealed with pleasure, demanding more.

"Very well, Justin," said Gordon, "you have now displayed yourself as a he-man with mate and male young. That, however . . ."

"And," said Justin loudly—he was irked at the ringing din of these pellets on his armor—"more coming."

"Really, my dear?" said Gordon to Charlene.

"Oh Justin," she said reddening.

"How soon, Sharly?" said Bryan, though that name for her was Justin's special right.

"It may just be a false alarm," she said. "Seven months."

"No false alarm," said Justin. "Three boys and a girl, that's what we're going to have."

He was putting Michael through some more calisthenics of an inuring sort. His face was stern, his motions were bold, and his hands on the baby were firm and gentle as any healer's—though he would not have agreed to this had he been asked.

"All that," said Gordon, "has nothing to do with Charlene's beauty. Which, as I said, is the sort that improves with age, acquaintance, and experience."

"Is that so?" said Justin where "Oh?" would have been enough.

"I think it is."

"I mean, you're only talking about the sort of beauty that hasn't got anything to do with love, just admiration. What really counts is the beauty seen with loving eyes. That hasn't got anything to do with wrinkles and bloom and all that."

"But I see her," said Bryan, "with the eyes of love. And though I love her dearly, I love her none the less for being young and beautiful."

"As long as you put that 'dearly' on," said Justin as he turned to Michael, finished with this conversation.

"I am fortunate in my daughter-in-law. I wonder if my son deserves her."

"Of course he does," said Charlene, who was pouring tea where none was wanted.

"Do you not find this conversation flattering?" asked Gordon.

"Yes. Flattering."

"*Touché,*" said Bryan to his father.

"*Touché.*"

"You are going to stay a week apiece with all three of us?" said Charlene.

"Why," said Gordon taken aback a little, "that was my intention."

"You're going to settle down for the rest of your life among your sons."

"Yes," he said, "I had planned to."

"Do you know where you're going to stay?" she asked, and everyone was silent in the pause before Gordon answered.

"No, not yet," he said, and went over to Michael, showing for the first time his age in his gait and posture. "I have not decided yet, nor have any of you." He advanced a great tickling finger at Michael, who bit it. He settled down to winning Michael over. "My dear," he said to Charlene, though in a soft voice for Michael's benefit, "you have done what I had not intended to have done. How could you state so surely what my intentions were?"

"It's just a knack," she said. "It hasn't got anything to do with anything. I knew it when you wrote those letters to Bryan and us."

"Really. I had not expected that result."

"Yes. I knew that was what you were saying. You're really very shy."

At which there was braying laughter from his two sons.

"He is too," said Charlene sharply to Bryan, in whom she combatted, as she often did, the Mottishness that she could least abide.

"He's usually thought of as something of a wolf with women, you know," said Bryan.

"Oh that," she said. "Anybody can be a wolf that wants to be."

"A shy wolf," said Bryan.

"If you don't know what that means you're not much of a poet."

"Oh I know what it means," said Bryan, who wanted her to think of him as indeed much of a poet. "I'm just wondering if it applies."

"Certainly it does. Take my word for it."

At eight o'clock Michael fell over the side of his crib onto the floor and howled about it. All three adults came flapping and clucking in, and the day was begun.

By the time Justin had shaved, breakfasted, and left for work Michael had forgotten about his mishap, and Charlene was beginning to agree that he was probably not maimed for life.

As they were sitting over coffee she said to Gordon, "But he never did it before."

"I gather as much, my dear," said Gordon. "He begins to cease to be a baby, to become a kid. But then, it's a gradual process and he's been a baby long enough."

"Not for me, he hasn't."

"He thinks so."

"How do you know what he thinks?"

"Cuddle him and find out for yourself."

She tried to cuddle him, but he stiffened and yelled. Finally she released him onto the floor. He immediately ran to the sinkboard and grabbed a paring knife, which Charlene took from him, and then into the front room where he began banging on the piano.

"Well," she said to Gordon, "even if you're right you oughtn't to be so happy about it."

"Don't you want him to grow up?"

"Of course!"

"How?"

"Oh heavens Father, you push me so."

"How?"

"Just the way everybody does I guess. Not really." She glared at him.

"As he needs you less you love him less."

"No!"

He paid no attention to her cry. "That's the ideal form of a nasty necessity."

"Oh Father, nasty?"

"Its nastiness is clear enough when the roles are inverted, as they are with me."

"How could you say such a thing?" she said. On her way around the table to hug him it occurred to her how he might say such a thing, and she added, "to me."

"Well," he said into her right clavicle, "I do not deny that there are saints. Let St. Charlene increase the mundane calendar."

"Don't say such things," she said as she returned to her place. "It isn't safe. You don't know what might be listening."

"No, you don't," he replied, repressing a rejoinder concerning hubris on Redwood Road.

There was a demolishing interruption from Michael; then dishes to wash and beds to make and lunch to prepare; and after lunch while Michael napped, conversation in the patio sun-bathing.

"Would you mind, Father," Charlene said in that tone with which one customarily approaches a tender subject, "telling me something that I have never been able to make out from what Justin has said?"

"I would not, though I do not know what it is."

"It's about Justin's mother," she said looking at his sunglasses through her sunglasses.

"Ah, Diana," he said smiling. "You know her?"

"Hardly at all. She's lived in Omaha ever since I knew Justin. I just went back to visit her with him one summer."

"What did you think of her?"

"Oh, she's a splendid person. So handsome and dignified and very intelligent. I think she thought I was too flighty for Justin."

"Very likely she did."

"I can't say how much I admire her. Still, I'm just as glad it's you that's here and not her. She is, maybe, just a little cool."

"Oh, just a little."

"I don't want to be unfair to her, and I'm sure she is splendid in her position—it's a fine orphanage you know, one of the very best in the country, they say, it's all her doing—still . . . you know."

"Oh, I know indeed."

"I don't mean it that way."

He did not respond.

"What I wondered is . . . You see, Justin sort of resents you, what you and his mother did. He blames you sort of, though he won't say why and she never mentioned it, and I wondered if you'd tell me what went wrong."

"She didn't die soon enough."

"Father!"

She sat up and took off her glasses.

"That is not true and it is not funny. Never say such a thing again."

"You asked me. I told you."

"Why do you make it so hard for people to love you? What do you mean by such a thing?"

The expression of hurt appeared on his face, but she ignored it.

"Explain yourself."

"I meant that she did not die in my heart soon enough."

"Go on."

"She was the only woman whom I ever both loved and hated at the same time. If I had just hated her I could have left her decently, as I did for another reason Bryan's mother. But I could not leave her. Her coldness and air of superiority infuriated me. She seemed to condescend to me. She made love as a favor. So I hurt her as badly as I could, though I thought at the time I was moved by passion; I was unfaithful to her with her sister. I believe I have never done anything more reprehensible. Does that satisfy you?"

"Oh, that last was not kind. But why did you ever love her?"

"She was handsome and very intelligent and not always so cold. The coldness grew with time. And I had just been having more sensuality than was good for me in Bryan's mother."

"How you must have hurt her."

"We need not talk about it," he said lightly.

"Oh, but we must. Why did you have to do it?"

"We really need not," he repeated, so that she lay back down again.

Presently she said, "Then you married Thelma?"

"Then I married Thelma. She was a saint of sorts too. I had hoped we might reside in Oakland as we were dying. You would have liked her."

"I am sure I would."

"And it is not nothing to administer an orphanage well."

"Of course not. It's a wonderful thing to do."

"Well," he said arising, "a not entirely unhappy ending. I am too hot."

He looked down at her smooth, round, golden body for a moment. Partly he was sorry that his own was so pale and gnarled, for in earlier years he would not have restrained his desire for her because she was Justin's wife; but partly at this moment he was glad that it was so old, for he was kept by its age from making her unhappy, as he was sure he would once have done. He took himself into the house and set himself to thinking about electrons and their ways.

"Henry!" Edwa called up the stairs. "Come on down, Henry. Father Mott is here."

Gordon, in the living room, winced.

"Must she refer to me so? I am neither a priest nor a jolly old fellow with goodies in my bulging pockets."

"It's a custom," said Bryan, "like many another brought to us from the teeming middle plains of the nation."

"Let it teem in Nebrasky," said Gordon. "Here English is spoken. Roscoe, this is within your jurisdiction. See to it."

Roscoe, who was of the same height as his father, looked at him as though he were a good half-head taller; he managed this by holding himself very erect, tilting his face back a little, and looking down his bill like an ostrich.

"What would you prefer she call you to the children? Their other grandfather, you know, is often here."

"I don't know. Gordon, Grampa Gordon. Mott is not a name to be rolled on the tongue."

"Henry!" she called again. There was a trampling upstairs. "Come down now."

She joined the men.

"He's always going out in the evenings," she said apologetically. "There doesn't seem to be enough to hold the young people at home these days. But I made him promise," she said patting Gordon on the arm, "to spend a lot of time with his Father Mott before he leaves. He'll be with you all this evening, I know."

Gordon gave her a look (which was the only point of appearance that Justin shared with him) of pure, direct, calculating distaste. This he achieved by making his face blank as a sheep's and looking square-on at the object of his distaste.

"I'm sure we will both benefit by it," he said.

She saw that he was displeased with something, but being conscious of no malice or error in her behavior she thought he was bilious and was sorry for him.

Henry entered, being large, dark of mane, and marked by acne. He was eighteen. He had had a date.

"Hello," he said to no one in particular.

"Well Henry," said Gordon, "it is planned that you sit at my feet in a sort of diffused discipleship and become wiser by a week."

Henry looked up from under his eyebrows at his grandfather, suspicious and buffalolike. An extraordinary distance separated his eyes, and they glowed with hostility.

"Huh," he said. "It is, is it?"

"He plans to be in law," said Edwa putting her arm about him. "Harvard Law School."

"What sort of law, Henry?" asked Gordon.

"I don't know," said Henry. "Any kind, I guess."

"Patent attorneys make a lot of money."

"I guess so."

"Oh I know it."

Henry had nothing more to say.

"Edwa," said Bryan, "may I get the stuff that Martha phoned about? She wanted to give it to the kids before suppertime."

"Are they sick?" asked Roscoe down to Bryan.

"Same thing that Clyde and Mary had." He turned to Henry. "And don't forget, nephew, there's always real estate."

"Well, well," said Roscoe. "Let the boy make up his own mind."

"Yes, let him," said Gordon as though agreeing to some other proposition.

Bryan and Edwa left for the medicine chest. When he presently returned to the room where Roscoe, Gordon, and Henry were still stiffly standing, Bryan heard a phrase that stopped him for a moment: "Law's at the very bottom of what we have, of course." A sort of film, like a chicken's second eyelid, only not physical, covered his eyes. This happened when he was thinking in a special way or when he was hurt or when he was very despondent; it let him know what was happening in the world without having to feel about it.

"Well," said Roscoe to him, "we'll see you a week from Saturday at the latest."

And for a considerable moment (the sheep, the ostrich, and the buffalo staring at the chicken eyes) Bryan considered what it was that law could be at the bottom of. But then they all four shook themselves, and he said, "A week from Saturday?"

"Yes, Henry's farewell dinner."

"You're leaving so soon?" asked Bryan.

"August tenth," said Henry, to whom it seemed none too soon. "I'm going to spend two or three weeks with some aunts in New York before I go on to Harvard."

"Two of Edwa's sisters. They are in import," said Roscoe.

"Well," said Bryan, "fine."

"Fine," said Gordon.

"Hrmph," said Roscoe down his beak.

"Yeh," said Henry.

"Well, good-bye," said Bryan. "I'll see you before long."

Gordon followed him, to get a briefcase he had left in Bryan's car. Bryan had transported him over from Justin's this afternoon for his week with Roscoe.

"My God," he said to Bryan, "a whole evening unarmed amongst them."

"A whole week," said Bryan. "There's always *Time*. They take it."

"You abandon me, then?"

"Ah, my dear father, hope is deciduous."

"I see you for the first time."

"And me without a tie on. Farewell, Father Henry-at-the-feet Mott. May quiring angels guard thee."

"Unnatural child."

When Gordon went back into the house he was greeted by Edwa and the four smaller children. They were all scrubbed and lined up and awkward for the occasion. Everyone, including Gordon, knew what to say and said it.

"Grampa Gordon," said Clyde sturdily after this midwestern ceremony was over. "I know how to tie a bowline."

"Oh Clyde," said Ann, who was impressed less by Gordon than the other children were, "don't bother him with little-kid stuff."

"Well," said Clyde, who was the most impressed, "I can."

Gordon, who shared Ann's views on bowlines but after all was a grandfather, said in a kindly voice that he would like to see Clyde tie one; as he walked out with Clyde and John he winked and shrugged at Ann in a knowing way, as though she were an adult.

"Ann," said Mary when they were alone, "why did he wink at you?"

"Well," said Ann, who was not quite sure, "that's something you'll understand when you grow up."

"You're so grown up."

"Pretty much," said Ann. "Sometimes I feel a lot more grown up than you'd even understand."

"Huh," said Mary. "I suppose that's why you played seesaw with us today?"

Ann thumbed her nose at Mary and ran out of the room. Nose-thumbing was something for which Mary could tattle on Ann, but seeing nothing to be gained by it she decided to go watch the bow-line-tying instead.

Dinner was roast beef, broccoli, and mashed potatoes, cole slaw, bread and jam, and a choice of berry or custard pie. It was all very good, and Gordon ate far beyond his capacity; indeed, he was not allowed not to.

"Now, Father Mott," said Edwa as she served the pie, "we have a plan for every day this week. Sunday we're going to take a ride over to Marin County to the redwood grove."

"Can we all go?" said Clyde, who knew they all could not.

"Count me out," said Henry. "I've got a date."

"Perhaps," said Edwa to Clyde. "Don't worry, dear. Drink your milk. Monday we're going to have a picnic in Tilden Park. A real picnic."

"Can we ride the merry-go-round?" said Ann.

"Of course. We hope Daddy will be able to go with us."

"Grampa Gordon, " said John, who was already bored by the calendar of coming events, "are you going to live with us?"

Gordon expected a dead silence after this question or a sharp reprimand. Instead Edwa spoke in her usual tone.

"I don't think Father Mott knows yet where he's going to settle down, John. He knows that he's welcome to stay with us as long as he wishes, but I think we should let him make up his own mind before we ask him."

She was the first one in Oakland, indeed the first one anywhere, to say these words to Gordon; he found he could tolerate even "Father Mott" from her in such a speech.

She finished the seven days.

"And there's one thing more important than all the rest: Henry's good-bye dinner. You can't disappoint us, Father. You will be here for it won't you?"

"If it is at all possible," said Gordon. He knew, he resolved that it would be quite impossible, but he could not find it in his heart to tell her so now.

Roscoe asked him if he wanted some more coffee, and Gordon looked at him in amazement. He had been more conscious of silent, watching Mary than of Roscoe. He was going to say something elaborate to Roscoe about being an absentee host, but the thought of translating it into Roscoe's language oppressed him. Instead he went into the living room and sat in a very comfortable chair which Edwa said was now sacred to him.

To him there the smaller children came for jokes and advice and to say good night. Roscoe had a headache and went to his room early. Edwa stayed with Gordon and Henry for a while listening to their logy conversation. She was spurred by it to relate much more entertaining experiences of her own; by ten she too went off to bed. The moment she was gone Henry excused himself and went rushing off into the adolescent night somewhere. Gordon found a copy of *Time* he hadn't read before and looked at it, but it wasn't annoying enough to keep him awake. By eleven o'clock, against the habit of years, he was in bed and asleep.

III

"Henry," said Bryan, "this is the last time you will think of us as your uncles and aunts, your dad and mom. When the Harvard tenants have moved into your head we will have acquired first names in your mind and we will seem annoying heirlooms you can't decently chuck out. Is it not sad, Rosalee?"

The pink and blue at Henry's side giggled.

"Bryan," said Roscoe, who liked Rosalee, "will you pass the yams? . . . My dear, this is the best ham I have ever eaten."

"Thank you," said Edwa. "Henry went clear to the city to get the ham and up to Berkeley to get the cake. My little boy," she said squeezing his forearm beside her to his annoyance.

"Henry," said Justin, who was feeling more than seven years older than his nephew, "I never went to college."

"My goodness," said Charlene, "he knows you never went to college. Why say it?"

"What I meant was, Henry, I envy you this opportunity I never took."

"Why?" said Martha, who was suddenly seized with the urge to bring him down.

"Why?" said Justin. "Everybody should have a college education."

"Can't you manage your factory without one?" she asked.

"Yes, but think of everything I'm missing."

"I doubt," she said, "whether a Ph.D. itself would enable you to see what you don't already see, Justin."

He did not know what she had done to him, but he knew that she had done something.

"It's just an advantage," he said, "and I'm glad you're getting it, Henry. Michael is going to Harvard if I have to do his homework myself to get him good grades in high school."

"Justin," said Charlene, "reads great books, like Aristotle."

"Is there anything wrong with that?" he demanded in a belligerent if cracked voice.

No one answered; he shrank into silence, so sitting a bird that not even Martha had the heart to shoot again.

"I did hope Father Mott could be here tonight," said Edwa. "Henry had so little chance to benefit from being with him. Such a rare opportunity," she said, beaming at Henry.

"Oh Mother," he said in a sort of pastel agony.

"Henry," whispered Rosalee leaning against him, "be nice to her. She loves you so much."

He growled.

"You were able to be with Father Mott a good deal these past days weren't you, dear?"

"Yes Mother," said Henry, who viewed it as being hobbled in barren pastures.

"I'm sure you benefited greatly from knowing him."

"Yes Mother," said Henry for Rosalee's sake, for he had not.

"We should all be thankful to have known him," said Charlene.

"Oh we are still going to know him," said Martha. "For years and years, I have no doubt."

"Father Mott does have the best of health."

"Well, I know," said Justin in a voice so loud that everyone looked at him, "where he's *not* going to live from now on."

There was a short silence, which each of the three women felt she must smooth over for Rosalee's sake.

"Honey," said Charlene, "you mustn't be so aggressive about it. We don't know."

"That's something for another time," said Edwa.

"Sometimes," said Justin, "I don't even feel like he was my father."

This was Roscoe's province.

"Justin," he said, "we will not talk about that at the table."

"How could *he* be *my* father?"

"That will be enough, Justin," said Roscoe in a very loud voice.

Henry held his breath. It seemed to Henry that he could not possibly be a true member of this family but that God had put him among these exquisite clowns to test him. The day was coming when his true rank should be revealed.

As soon as the silence had relaxed a little he spoke.

"Mom, when are we going to have dessert? Rosalee and I have to get going."

"Time to clear the table for dessert," said Edwa. "Everybody's ready?"

"I'll go lie down in the living room," said Bryan, "while you all gorge."

It was lonesome in the living room, but he stayed till they were through.

As Rosalee and Henry were in the hallway preparing to go she said to him in one of those whispers that are like the sound of a bugle at dawn, "You sure have the craziest family. How do you *stand* them?"

Edwa, who heard it, was cut to the quick; but Roscoe, to whose ears also the sound reached, heard it not. The others thought less of Rosalee than they had, and all the adults went into the living room logily.

"The children will be all right, dear?" said Roscoe.

"Ann and John are very good with them today," said Edwa.

"Can we hear Michael if he wakes up?" said Justin.

"I just took a peek at him, honey. He's sound asleep."

"Well," said Bryan, who was sprawled on the couch, "here we

are. The last time we were assembled we had Gordon hanging over our heads."

"And now," said Martha, "we have him hanging around our necks."

"Martha!" said Charlene, "that's no way to talk."

"Why Martha," said Edwa, "you told me you didn't find him such a terrible burden."

"Not for a week, maybe, but what about for the rest of his life?"

"He's mighty damned healthy," said Justin.

"Honey!" said Charlene. "He's your father."

"How do I know? Only my mother knows whether that's true and she never said."

"Justin! That's unforgivable of you."

"He'll never live in my house," said Justin.

"Oh no?"

"No."

"The point is," said Bryan languidly, "he'll live with whomever he wants to live with. We have nothing to say about it."

And for putting that unpleasant doubt into words he was rewarded by having everyone turn against him.

"That," said Roscoe, "is scarcely true."

"He certainly can't live with us if we don't want him to," said Charlene.

"Say," said Justin, "whose side are you on anyway?"

"I'm not on your side," she said furiously. "I'm just against Bryan. And furthermore . . ."

"And furthermore," said Bryan, "your slip shows. Quit talking so much."

"You can't insult me!" she cried. "Justin!"

"Bah," said Justin.

"Are you trying to see," said Martha to Bryan, "just how mad you can get everybody?"

"I am sure," said Edwa, "that Father Mott will decide for himself where he is going to live. I know that he's welcome to live with any of us ('Oh yeh,' said Justin), but perhaps he might be encouraged to go live with Bryan as he ought."

"What!" cried Martha.

"Oh I see," said Bryan sitting up.

"Great," said Justin. "He lives off the old man anyhow."

"I see, I see," said Bryan.

"You do have plenty of room," said Edwa. "Bryan doesn't work. He could help Martha."

"If you think writing isn't work . . ."

"Shut up," said Martha. "Now, look here, Edwa, we're not taking him in just like that. I can't stand the old goat any more than anyone else can."

"Whose side are you on?" said Bryan.

"I'm on my own side," she said, "don't bother me."

Justin roared with laughter and Charlene scowled at him.

"I'm the only one who loves him," she said.

"That's all right," shouted Justin. "I hate him enough for two. Bryan gets Gordon."

Bryan strode over to him. "For two bits I'd knock your block off."

Justin fished a quarter out of his pocket. "Here you are, Blowhard. Let's see whose block gets knocked off."

Edwa and Roscoe separated them.

"Come now," said Roscoe. "When Gordon comes back from his vacation we'll talk to him about it. We won't make any decisions now."

"Oh the decision is made," said Justin. "Bryan gets him."

"Oh I do, do I? That for you, brother."

"You live off the old man. You can earn your keep for a change."

"Damn you. Who gave you a factory to manage? Who gave Roscoe a house and a fistful of shares in American Lite? What do you fatheads do with it?"

"Come on," said Martha, "Gordon will make up his own mind. You know that. Calm down."

"Justin," said Charlene, "if you don't quit insulting everybody I'll take Michael and go off to Mother's."

"Edwa," said Roscoe, "it was very ill-chosen of you to say that just then."

"Well, please, let's not disturb the children," said Edwa, who fancied she had heard scufflings on the stairs. She had.

"What did I ever do to get mixed up with a family like this?" said Justin. "Why don't you go to Greenwich Village with the other longhairs?" he said to Bryan.

"By God," said Bryan, "come outside and I'll show you who's the man around here. If you're not chicken that is."

"Chicken!" said Justin. "Against you? I'd be afraid of hurting you."

Charlene ran out in tears, and presently Michael began wailing. Justin left to follow her.

Martha walked, stiff-legged with fury, up to get Roxana and Aylmer. She found all six children sitting in the girls' room completely silent.

"Come on," she said with as much naturalness as she could summon. "We're going home now."

"Is anything the matter, Mommy?" said Roxana.

"You know there is," said Martha. "Don't ask foolish questions."

Edwa came in and quietly told her children to get ready for bed. With no objections, even ritualistic ones, they did as she bade.

"Aunt Edwa," said Aylmer, "we had a very good time."

"The ham was delicious," said Roxana.

"I'm glad you liked it," said Edwa.

"Come on," said Martha crossly and dragged them out.

"What's the matter?" said Roxana. "Don't you want us to be polite?"

"It's the wrong time," said Martha.

Justin and Charlene, with Michael in her arms, came out of the guest room and went straight out to their car without a word for anyone, even to Aylmer who said good night.

"They weren't kind," said Aylmer.

"It's never the right time to be unkind," said Roxana. "Is it Mommy?"

"No, no," said Martha, her voice full of both remorse and vexation. "Never."

The children bade Roscoe a long and very polite good night, with Bryan snapping at them to hurry up, and they went home.

Roscoe found Edwa preparing for bed.

"Edwa," he called from the bathroom, "where are the aspirin?"

"They might be on your night-stand."

"Yes. There are only two left."

"Isn't that enough?"

"I doubt it tonight."

"Well, they'll have to be."

"Are the children in bed?"

"Yes," she replied.

"I hope they didn't hear any of that disgraceful ruckus."

"I'm sure they did not. I don't think I'll bring the subject up with them. What do you think?"

"Of course not," he said. "Bryan was unforgivable."

"Well, you can hardly blame him." She was in bed settling herself.

"Well, he had to know sooner or later," he said.

"Roscoe," she said with a last flurry of feeling, "we're losing our first baby. Do you realize that?"

"Hrmph," he said; he did not think of Henry as his first baby and felt vaguely deficient as a father that he did not.

Bryan dropped his book and looked attentively at Martha.

"That's Gordon coming up the front steps," he said.

She dropped her darning. "Are you sure?"

"I can tell by his tread."

"Now darling," she said with alarm in her voice, "you must be firm. But do be polite."

"Oh yes," said Gordon, who had opened the door without having knocked, "oh gracious yes, do be polite."

"Gordon!" exclaimed Martha, standing up.

"Who else?"

"Why I thought it might have been Justin."

"Justin? Come, my dear Martha, since when has Justin taken to dropping in on you in the evenings?"

"I hoped he had come to apologize for something he said to Bryan."

"Well Gordon," said Bryan, taking his coat.

"Mommy," came Roxana's voice from upstairs. "Who is it, Mommy?"

"Not asleep yet," said Martha.

"I have a couple of bags that the taxi driver left down at the foot of the stairs, Bryan." Bryan went for them. "Let me go kiss the children good night, Martha."

"Very well. I did not realize you liked them that well."

"Nor did I, my dear, until I spent a week at Tahoe in a guest hotel with none but elderly, respectable people."

"Can we come see him, Mommy?" called Aylmer.

"I'm coming right up, children," he said. "I have discovered that

I am more attached to my grandchildren than I thought possible. One is so conscious of the irritations at the time one is with them, but afterwards that heaven of grandfathers, love without responsibility, is all that is left."

He bade them good night. Bryan put the suitcases in the guest room, Martha discovered that he had had his dinner at a restaurant, and they settled down in front of the empty fireplace.

"And what," said Gordon, bending forward and rubbing his hands as though there had been a blazing fire to warm them before, "what did Justin do that you should imagine he would come to apologize for it?"

"Well," said Bryan, "at Henry's farewell dinner we had a pretty terrific argument. He insulted me."

"Why?"

Martha looked distressed. Bryan gazed at her without expression for a moment before he answered.

"Well," said Bryan, "jealousy, I think. I had made rather a pass at Charlene before dinner."

"Oh," said Martha, looking greatly relieved, "he never knew about it."

"Maybe not with the top of his head," said Bryan, "but I think he knew it some place else."

"I hope that will teach you to lay off Charlene after this."

"Oh Martha," he said, "what's the good of a family dinner if I can't even kiss my pretty sister-in-law? Do you want me to read *Time* till dinner is served?"

"What frivolity," said Gordon. "Indeed, I might go so far as to say how jejune."

"He sounds worse than he is," said Martha. "At least worse than he is most of the time."

"The scoundrel's fallacy, that charm forgives all."

"Tell me, Gordon," said Bryan, "did you have a pleasant time at Tahoe?"

"What a paltry hypocrite. If you want me to believe such a question you've got to put a little conviction in it."

"Did you?"

"The weather and the scenery are, as you know, superb. This dispute with Justin the night of the dinner—was my name not brought up during the argument?"

"Yes."

"And with no excess of love, I dare say."

"No excess."

"Did you come to blows or stop at words?"

"Everyone conspired to keep us from actually fighting. I wish we had though, even if he'd beat me up a little. The satisfaction of landing one in the middle of that soul-less face is something I cannot forego forever."

"And Roscoe, what role did he play?"

"Oh my heavens," said Martha, "quit beating about the bush. They were arguing about where you are going to live."

Her face was very strained as she said this.

"Well," said Gordon, "you did prick my little balloon of circumlocution very neatly."

"No circumlocution," she said, "but an elaborate system for making us uneasy."

"That was not my intention."

"Perhaps. It was your accomplishment."

"I don't think," said Gordon, "that I'll go to live with Justin."

"No," said Bryan, "neither does he. He, in fact, sometimes doubts that you are his father."

"A convenient doubt for one in his frame of mind, but not a probable one."

"He does seem to have more mother than father in him," said Bryan.

"Yes, to his hurt. Well, but Charlene is a most attractive woman. You, I take it, agree."

"I do. The spontaneity of her emotions is rare and winning."

"I had not thought of her that way," said Gordon. "How do you mean it?"

"I'm afraid," said Bryan, "that this is not a propitious time for me to elaborate upon that theme."

"Martha," said Gordon, "what do you think of her charms?"

"Not being the woman under discussion, but being a woman, I do not think my opinion would be unbiased."

"The power of her charm," said Gordon, "does not lessen your much subtler attraction, my dear."

"I have often been told that. I have never believed it."

"Martha," said Bryan, "believes that there is just so much admiration to go around. The more someone else gets, the less for her."

"Well," said Martha, "if there weren't so many Charlenes around maybe more men would make passes at my subtle attractions."

"Yours," said Gordon, "are not the charms that ripen and then fade, but rather the intellectual powers that only mature with time and endure into the impotence of old age. They partake of eternity."

"Lovely," she said. "But who kisses my enduring intellect?"

"I," said Bryan.

"When I'm old and withered," she said as though he had not spoken, "I suppose I'm to sit around hoarding my few drops of eternity and look down on other women, since all they have is a thousand pleasant memories?"

"Memories," said Gordon, "are the easiest substitute for satisfaction, but they are no satisfaction. I think I can speak with more authority than you about this."

"Well, use it on someone who's more impressed with it than I am. Let's drop me as a subject."

"Sorry," said Gordon. "When I said, Bryan, that I was not going to live with Justin, I was thinking of another reason than his distaste for the idea. I fancy I could have dealt with that."

"The boredom then?"

"Oh no, boredom can be dealt with too. I am going to continue my work wherever I settle down. There are books and concerts and pictures. No, I was thinking that wherever I settle I want to settle for good, and I distrust the permanence of Justin's household."

"Oh come, Gordon," said Martha, "not everyone divorces as readily as you."

"So it would appear," he replied. "However, it seems to me that if the time ever comes when Justin opposes or escapes from Charlene's rule, she will leave him."

Neither of the others said anything—Bryan because he agreed and Martha because she did not want another argument.

"And I do not want to be left high and dry."

"That leaves you three choices," said Bryan.

"Three?"

"Yes. Roscoe, myself, or living alone."

"Ah, living alone. I thought of that once or twice, but I rapidly put it out of my mind. I even thought of marrying again, but no. I have decided to be old."

"Do you mean that?" asked Martha. "Or are you being ironical as usual?"

"I mean it. The irony is a protection from the pain of admitting it. It is not pleasant to run down, but it is even less pleasant to have to watch yourself doing it."

"Well, even wives get old," she said.

"Yes, but a grandfather is a great deal closer to heaven than a husband. I exist only in relation to others, so that in solitude I would blow up like a balloon and pop. I am what the resistance of others makes me. And grandchildren are like the arms of the acclaiming populace bearing the victor home."

"Stirring," said Bryan. "Well, Roscoe has four acclaimers around the house to our two."

"True, but yours are so superior in quality."

And just before Martha could say what she was going to say he forestalled her.

"I believe you know very little about Roscoe's mother."

"Very little," said Bryan. "My mother said once she thought you still loved Roscoe's mother when you married her. That was three or four years after she'd died, wasn't it?"

"Over three years. Her name was Hannah. I have never loved anyone else so much as I loved her. I often wonder whether her memory did not influence my later relations with women. She remained perfect in my mind—she was yielding yet firm, like healthy young flesh, beautiful, not quite predictable, and she thought I was a god."

"She died just in time," said Martha, but when she saw the blind pain in his eyes she apologized almost tearfully for her cruelty, and left the room to make tea.

"She is very good at deflating the male ego," said Bryan.

"At least that," said Gordon, and seemed to be going to relapse into silence.

"What were you going to say about Roscoe's mother?"

"Just that the memory of her somehow is made stronger by Roscoe. Something of her lives in him; what, I could not say, nor how."

They were silent until Martha had brought the tea in.

"And furthermore," said Gordon looking steadily at Martha, "Edwa is a great deal pleasanter to live with than you are."

The confusion of wounded feelings, and gratitude that it was not they whom he was going to live with, and shame which kept her from responding to this thrust reduced Martha to tears. Bryan looked very uncomfortable.

"Well, we're quits," said Gordon. "I shall go to bed if you don't mind. You may take me to Roscoe's tomorrow."

"I'll make up the bed," said Martha going out again.

"You are very unkind to those you love," said Bryan to Gordon.

"Always, when I have trouble dominating them. That's the great thing about Roscoe—I have so little trouble keeping him under. Besides he has respect for me, and respect is fear and love combined in proportions that suit my taste excellently."

"Why do you always make the better cause appear the worse?"

"It is usually the correct explanation of motive, I have found, and when it is incorrect it is incorrect in such a gratifying way."

"Well," said Bryan standing up, "whenever you want a good conversation you must call on us."

"That's why I came to you this evening," said Gordon. "One of the reasons. And when I want to recall my prime I will call on Charlene. You may tell Martha that she is not the least of the reasons I decided against settling down with you, nor the least of the reasons I almost did."

They went to the spare bedroom, where Martha was putting the finishing touches on the bed.

"May you both sleep well," said Gordon, meaning you ought to sleep badly.

"Of course," said Bryan, meaning I doubt if we will.

"It takes a lot to keep Bryan awake," said Martha, trying to mean by a brittle double-irony that a lot had happened.

"Oh?" said Gordon, and suddenly nobody knew what anybody meant any more.

Nobody knew what Martha meant by squeezing Gordon's hand hard and running from the room, or Gordon by turning his back to Bryan, or Bryan by approaching his father, flapping his right arm twice like a broken wing, and then going after Martha.

In bed Martha said to Bryan, "Oh darling, why was I so mean to him?"

"Well, don't worry about it. Now I can get back to work. I've lost the better part of six weeks."

"He made me be mean to him."

"No one is harder to forgive than the one who makes you behave badly."

"Is Edwa really easier to live with than I am?"

"No, of course not, my dear."

"Why does he try to be so sentimental with us? I didn't believe a word of that about Roscoe's mother, did you?"

"No, no, of course not."

"The old goat. He's so mean."

"Come, come. I love you dearly."

"You must forgive me for behaving like that," said Martha. "I'm sure he won't."

"I forgive you."

"I forgive you too. Well, I'll try to make it up to him."

Turning over, Bryan said, "Let's go to sleep now."

"I've got to do the wash in the morning," she said, and bottom to bottom they pretended to go to sleep.

Brother Quintillian and Dick the Chemist

I

Brother Quintillian Josephus at the age of thirty-five had achieved the station in life which he had desired from his earliest youth. In the days of his sad, timid, solitary boyhood in the streets of East Oakland, surrounded by dinginess and brutal fellows, the College of the Most Blessed St. Anselm had gleamed in his imagination as the green tranquility which only could requite his suffering years. St. Anselm's was a small college at the northeastern edge of the city, small and quiet and secluded among lawns and tall trees; he had seen it only three or four times when he was a boy with a very common name, Bob Johnson, for his family had had no car and he had not adventured about much on the streetcars by himself. But the green image of it glowed steadily in his mind like a vision of paradise. When he grew older he realized that he could find a place in St. Anselm's, but only if he became a professor there. So he had studied very hard, and he had found that he liked studying hard; he had joined the Congregation and had put in his years of teaching at dingy, brutal parochial schools in Stockton and Chico and South San Francisco. And now he was securely set, an Assistant Professor of Logic and Medieval History at St. Anselm's. But after two years of living in these most blessed grounds, teaching and disputing as he had long desired, he discovered that he would have to face after all a trouble long deferred; there was nowhere in this life for him to go to avoid it any longer.

A mile or so above St. Anselm's, in the hills but still in Oakland, lived an atheist named Dick Carson. Every weekday morning Dick drove his old Dodge down to Emeryville where he worked as the chief research chemist for the Universal Metals Corporation. The final purpose of his researches was to increase the profits of Universal Metals. However, it's a stinking world as anyone can see, and Dick considered himself luckier than most to find only this one thing to hate about his job. He lived in a new, modern house for which he had undertaken to pay $125 a month for fifteen years; it was so placed in a recess of a wooded mountainside that not another house, at least as yet, was visible from any of its windows. The house was designed to receive maximum benefit from the afternoon sun—Oakland is frequently overcast or foggy in the morning— and despite the surrounding trees it was both warm and bright on a good day. Dick had always wanted to be a scientist, and while he would have preferred it if he had been great he had settled down without much struggle to being good—"a sound man." He was an atheist because he saw no need for the hypothesis of a God at the basis of things in order to explain them; if he had seen the need he would have been perfectly willing to hypothesize the God, and he held no grudge against those who did. He could never have prayed to Him, however, and his acquaintance did not include many people who could. Dick was thirty-five too, and he too had a trouble; as he saw it, it had been pushed upon him by chance and there was nothing to be done but bear it. His wife of eleven years whom he had loved, had been mashed to death in an automobile accident.

The doubt of Brother Quintillian could turn words into sounds and faces into vacant masks. For a long time he had not recognized what it was that was attacking him so, for it had not been subtle and intellectual as he had thought doubt would be. No, his doubt knew that he could syllogize it away if it came at him roundabout, so it jumped on him with bared teeth and tore at him through his senses. He would be standing in front of a classroomful of fresh and sullen faces, in the midst, say, of the Albigensian heresy in Languedoc or of a tight demonstration that some men are not all non-dogs, when suddenly he would be left standing there with not a notion in his head about what the next word was to be. "Dante's hatred for Boniface VIII was a result of many factors, chief among which was—" Chief among which was what? What was the next word to be and which of these tilted-up faces cared? He was not even tempted to be facetious and say something like "—the horns of dilemma on the papal bulls" as he had done once successfully in a seminar. He simply, for a few seconds, had no idea what any of his words stood for any longer and no idea what these faces were doing in front of him. Then he would catch himself and go on. His attacks had not been frequent, and he had attributed them to dizziness or nerves or eyestrain. They would upset him for a few hours, and then he would forget about them. But one day his doubt, weary of these impermanent sallies, assaulted him in his very fortress, where he was kneeling at Mass.

Dick was not sentimental, but he had loved his wife, loved her and needed her. She had fitted out their house with a taste that had become his own; she had persuaded him to go to parties and concerts and plays, where he had usually enjoyed himself; she had filled the house with a color and cheer which his rather saturnine turn of character had at once groused at and loved. The rugs and curtains were left, the bright chairs and the concerts and the wide acquaintance, but there was no cheer in any of it now that she was dead. He stayed at home most of the time after her death, among the gay objects which with her absence became things only. Sometimes his friends, worried about him, would suggest that he ought to move out of this house which was full of associations for him, but he told them to shut up. He was not sentimental, and he knew that these objects of his were the things he liked best; to his taste they were functional and beautiful. To be sure he did not like them now, but he thought that he would again once he got out of his slump.

She's dead and gone and that's an end to it; things are things and it's morbid to go on talking about the whole mess; for Christ's sake can't a man be left to get over his own unhappiness by himself? He took many vitamin pills and lost sleep.

It was a six o'clock Mass in late September, a cool morning after a mild night. Brother Quintillian found himself in the pew behind old Brother Alphonsus, who spluttered and mumbled at his rosary. During the first part of the ritual he paid little attention to what was going on. It had happened so often before; his mood was sodden, the Eucharist exalted; like the seventy-seventh Hail Mary in a penance it seemed one more salaam to boredom. The acolyte who was swinging the censer was taken with a fit of annoying sneezes from the incense, and by the time he had lifted his eyes to glance at the sneezing boy the dreadful voiding had taken place. Father McElroy had become an old man in a silly costume, walking about, kneeling, bowing and bending, and bringing his hands together before him in a way that could not have been more inscrutable. As Brother Quintillian looked, he saw the celebrant like a chef turn over some pages of a book, repeat as it were the recipe aloud in his silly cook's language, look into the tabernacle as it were into a little oven, then step aside to wait till the crackers should be ready to eat. He was so astonished that anyone should do these things that he did not even find it ludicrous, he even forgot to rise and sit and kneel and rise with the others about him. Not until the bell tinkled did he come to himself, and then he was so horrified at what he had done that he sat back in the pew in a cold tremble. He felt that he could not have desecrated the Eucharist more profoundly had he blasphemed aloud at the moment of transubstantiation, and at the same time that it would be silly even in a ballet to dance around pretending to cook that flavorless, packaged fragment of God. When the rest of the community left he stayed behind as if in prayer; he was too weak to rise. He was wondering what he should do. Surely he was falling into a state of damnation.

For the psychosomatic theory of illness Dick had a physical chemist's scorn. When a high correlation between isolable personality traits and specific pathological symptoms could be demonstrated on a statistically sound basis he was quite willing to admit that there was some connection between the two; what connection he refused to say. Himself, he leaned towards the endocrine view: that both symptoms and traits derived from some malfunction of the ductless glands. This unhappiness of his could hardly be called a character trait, yet he had plenty of symptoms beyond those called for by his grief: bad sleep and bad dreams, sour stomach, irascibility, constipation, lethargy. Vitamin-complex tablets didn't do it, his doctor could discover no infection in him, and four days in bed resting didn't do it. He was driven back upon his endocrines, and in particular he suspected his pituitary gland, the controller. But what it was secreting, which of its many chemicals (sixteen, was it?) was doing the damage science could not yet tell him; there was nothing to be done. He could not bear to do nothing, so he fell back upon the remedy his mother had thought appropriate to any ill: diet. Sometimes he thought he benefited from cutting out all alcohol and fats, sometimes from eating only vegetables and milk, sometimes from a very high protein diet; but the only permanent benefit he got from the dieting was the discovery that he was mildly allergic to okra. Meanwhile, his sleeping was troubled by the memory of the newspaper photograph of his wife's body half-sprawled out of the car in which she had been killed, and his waking was troubled by the irrational thought that if only he had gone with her on that ride instead of going to a movie he might have saved her.

The day on which Brother Quintillian was praying in the chapel despite classes and meals, Dick was putting in his eight hours analyzing an aluminum alloy made by a competitor of Universal Metals. At five o'clock when Brother Quintillian emerged, half-staggering, Dick was buying yoghurt, wheat germ and canned glutenburger at a health food store.

Both of them were five feet ten inches tall, weighed about a hundred and fifty pounds, had ordinary brown hair, flecked blue eyes and rather fair complexion, and both of them were wondering how to get through the night.

II

Some of the brothers would be in the common room listening to the radio, reading the paper or talking; some would be out strolling, or pottering in some favorite part of the garden; some younger ones would be playing handball or working out in the gym. Brother Quintillian was afraid that if he went directly to his room from the chapel he would be thought aloof and proud. He would have preferred to take a walk in the mellow air, nodding to whomever he met and meditating on the flowers, but his knees would not support him on such a venture. He went to the common room. It took all his strength for him to open the heavy door in a natural way and to step inside the room confidently, unhesitantly. There were four other brothers in the room. When he entered, they glanced at him. The two who were talking fell silent, and the one next to the radio turned it down. He was sure that they were ashamed of him, embarrassed for him, even revolted by him; by some little gesture, some mumbled word he must have let them glimpse this morning at Mass his full impiety.

"Good afternoon, Brother," said Brother John. "Would you like to see the sporting page?"

Brother John's voice seemed altered a little, somewhat subdued, somewhat strained; he normally called Brother Quintillian by his nickname, Quin; he doted on baseball. Why then, Brother Quintillian wondered, did he behave like this? Surely he was being ironic in his offer? Surely he was being charitable to this leper?

"No thank you," said Brother Quintillian. He sank into a chair. "I think I will just rest here awhile."

He unbuttoned his collar in back and pulled his cassock up so that he could cross his legs.

"You look tired," said Brother Alphonsus, a strong old man.

"It's nothing, nothing. I'll rest awhile."

He was sorry he had not gone to his room to rest. He was making them very uncomfortable.

"It's Friday," said Brother Alphonsus.

"Yes, we're having fresh fish," said Brother Adrian.

"Do you know what kind?" asked Brother John.

"Halibut," said Brother Adrian. "I saw them unloading it."

"Do you like halibut?" asked Brother John.

None of the others answered, so Brother Quintillian knew that the question had been addressed to him. But he kept his eyes closed. His knees ached from the hours and hours of kneeling, and though he had not eaten or drunk all day he did not feel hungry. He was very tired, and he was sorry for the others, who were having to be nice to him. He would try to meet their charity by lightening them of the burden of courtesy, by pretending to doze.

"No," said Brother Gilbert from across the room, "he is not at all fond of halibut."

"What does he like?" said Brother John eagerly.

"How does he like it prepared?" asked Brother Adrian.

"Well," said Brother Gilbert, who was the epicure of the community, "he prefers a bouillabaisse, as I remember."

"Oh Gilbert, we'll never be able to get that for him by dinnertime," said Brother John. "What can we do for him?"

"No, I suppose not," said Brother Gilbert. "He likes finnan haddie."

"Can you prepare it?" asked Brother John.

"He has fasted since last night," said Brother Adrian. "We must be careful."

"If I had some," said Brother Gilbert, "I could prepare a mild sauce for it. And toast."

"Alphonse, you drive," said Brother John. "Go down right away to Spenger's and get a pound of finnan haddie. Anything else, Gilbert?"

"A jar of capers. But are you sure he wants to eat?"

"I'll go," said Brother Alphonsus, and left.

"He has not eaten for nearly twenty-four hours," said Brother Adrian. "He has been praying all day."

"A great humiliation," said Brother John.

They fell silent.

Brother Quintillian felt no hunger, least of all for finnan haddie. He wished only to be left alone. But he did not want to reject their kindness, so he said nothing.

"We should leave him to sleep a little," said Brother John.

"Yes," said Brother Adrian. "Gil, turn off the radio and come along."

"I must phone my sister before dinner," said Brother Gilbert.

"How is she getting along?" asked Brother Adrian.

"Very well. She's out of the cast now and her ribs are quite mended."

"I'm glad to hear that. Wasn't there a woman killed in that accident?"

"Yes, in the same car. A friend of hers."

"What was her name?"

"Sylvia Carson."

"Pity."

"A great humiliation," said Brother John mostly to himself as they went out the door.

Like a sea anemone after the tidepool falls still he slowly began to unfold. Sylvia Carson, Sylvia Carson. The name had been floating around during the past month, since the accident. He had some other association to it. He spent several minutes uncovering his recollection—that good-looking fellow he'd seen at so many concerts and recitals, a chemist to whose house he had gone a few months before with a mutual friend. He had never met the wife, Sylvia. She had not been a lover of music. Duane? Dan? Duke? Dick, that was is, Dick Carson. Poor fellow, to have his wife killed like that. He was probably not a believer; he would need friends now. Poor man.

Brother Quintillian made his way circuitously to the refrigerator, where he drank a glass of milk and put an apple in his pocket; went to his room to change into his black suit and select an album of records; and slipped out the side door. He did not feel weak any longer, and though he was sorry to disappoint the brothers who were getting and preparing the finnan haddie for him he could not have eaten it. He felt he should go immediately.

III

It took Brother Quintillian an hour to find Dick's place. The road was all uphill, and he got lost. His sore legs hardly obeyed him.

As he turned a corner among pines he saw the little house there below him. He sat on the bank to rest a bit and eat the apple—he did not want to be trembling with fatigue when he came to the door —and looked curiously at the house. There was a built-in ladder by the carport for the use of anyone who wanted to sun-bathe on the flat roof. The windows went from floor to ceiling; the wall that he could see was nearly solid with window. He was looking at the northern, back side of the house; he could see directly into the two bedrooms, one of which was tidy and perfect, the other rumpled and used. The only chair was a piece of yellow canvas artfully slung upon an iron frame, an angel-wing chair. The floor of the house was a slab of concrete only a few inches higher than the ground. The aim of all this, Brother Quintillian had read, was to be functional and to promote indoor-outdoor living. Brother Quintillian was an indoors man himself. He enjoyed the outdoors once in a while, on a beautiful day like this or in the well-ordered gardens of St. Anselm's, but the notion of mixing the two, of making little of the distinction between them, astonished him. He had no theory about this indoor-outdoor business except that it was very sophisticated; savages, he was sure, would never think of doing it (nature is man's enemy and only a sophisticate would doubt it). He saw Dick come into the white, mechanized kitchen, take pans off the wall and spoons from a drawer, and open a can. He threw away his apple core, picked up the album he had laid beside him on the bank, and went down the road to this solitary house.

He saw Dick glance up at him and scowl; his heart sank within him. But Brother Quintillian made a great point of maintaining an outward appearance of confidence and good manners. He went directly to the kitchen door, smiling, and nodded to Dick. With elaborate reluctance Dick wiped his hands and opened the door.

"I am Brother Quintillian. You may not remember me."

"I remember you."

Brother Quintillian had intended to say something consoling to Dick, but this tone of his clearly made it impossible.

"I brought some records which I hoped you would find interesting."

"Okay. Go in front and sit down. I'll be along when I'm through eating."

Manners required Brother Quintillian to say something about how he hoped he wasn't intruding. But it was clear that he was intruding and that Dick, if asked, would say that he was; he felt it more important to stay than to be polite. "Thank you, I will," he said, and went into the living room.

Not living room—living area. Dick was cooking in the kitchen area of the same room, on the other side of a partial wall. Behind a

full-length green hanging, as Brother Quintillian saw through an
opening in it, was one of the sleeping areas. The other sleeping area,
he remembered having seen, had four walls and a door, and the
bathroom of course did too, though the outer wall of the bathroom
was a pane of frosted glass. Brother Quintillian took his seat on an
odd but comfortable wooden chair, glad for a few minutes of freedom in which to look about him. There was not even an atavistic
fireplace in the room, just areas of white wall. There were three low
bookshelves and a narrow one that reached to the ceiling. On the
walls hung three abstract paintings and a primitive mask with corn
husks for hair. In the center of the room stood a glass table on iron
legs, low, large, free-form (that is to say, kidney-shaped); to his distress, on the wall in the darkest corner just above the telephone, he
saw an exquisite icon.

"Will you have something to eat?" Dick said around the corner,
still in a churly voice.

"No, no thanks."

"It's not much of a dinner, but you're welcome."

"No, no, you just go ahead. I'll be happy to wait."

And he was happy to wait, for in trying to understand what view
of things could produce this amazing house and what effect living
in it would have on a man's soul he quite forgot his own concern. It
was not that his doubt had been trivial or his experience that morning superficial; quite the contrary. But he had exhausted for the time
his capacity for spontaneous remorse; wonder at this house quite
made him feel happy, allowing him to forget what he could hardly
bear to remember—his own great sin.

He heard Dick serving himself up his meal, the spoon angry in
the saucepan. "How dreadful," thought Brother Quintillian, "to
have no God to submit to. How angry he must be with nothing to
do but blame chance, idiot chance. How afraid." Then Brother
Quintillian did something that a man of his delicacy, his scruples
could not have done in his situation without the strongest prompt-
ing, and he felt almost scandalized at himself for doing it: he tip-
toed to the record player, adjusted it without Dick's permission or
knowledge, and started playing the records he had brought. The
records contained an ordinary of the Ambrosian Mass chanted by
monks in a twelfth-century monastery. Technically the records were

excellent, and the machine was superb. The thin voices, sepulchral and echoing and very pure, seemed to Brother Quintillian in some way not entirely foreign to this angular, stark house.

When the first side was played, Dick appeared at the end of the dividing wall, plate in hand, and stood listening attentively. He tossed his forelock back with a sweeping motion of the head and his body was not so slouched over as it had been. His fair eyes, dulled when Brother Quintillian had come in, were bright and quick.

"Hey," said Dick between bites, "that's terrific singing. That's an Ambrosian ordinary, isn't it?"

"Yes, yes, in what is believed to be its purest form." Brother Quintillian stuttered a little in his pleasure.

"You get that quaver?" said Dick. "Lord, what technique."

"Yes indeed. One has to write to Europe for the album."

"I think I'll get it. How much they stick you?"

"I'm ashamed to say. Three-and-a-half dollars a record. I can get the address for you if you like."

"Sure, do that. Let's cut it till I'm through eating. I want to really listen."

"Certainly, certainly." Brother Quintillian stopped the machine.

"Hey Brother," Dick called from back of his wall again, "tell me something about those records. That's the best singing I've heard in months."

Brother Quintillian went to the end of the cooking area. Dick was sitting at a leaf that dropped from the wall.

"Well, I've done a little work in the modes of the chants. I'm no expert, nothing like one, you understand, just an amateur.—Pardon me, what a convenient kitchen you have here. I've never seen one more compact. They're usually so crowded."

"It's all right. It doesn't make the glutenburger taste any better."

"Ah." There was a brief silence. "Would you tell me, what is glutenburger?"

"Ersatz meat. It's all right with enough ketchup. Have some."

"Just a bite."

"Here's a fork. Isn't it poor?"

"Not very good. Why do you eat it?"

"Some sort of nutritional trouble. The doctors haven't been able to isolate it. I thought I'd experiment around with diet."

"Any luck?" asked Brother Quintillian smiling.

"None. If a man hasn't got an appetite he might as well eat health food. Brother, you're sure you've had dinner?"

"No, thank you, no dinner. I fasted today."

"Is that so?" said Dick looking at him with interest. "Nothing to eat at all?"

"When I decided to come up to see you—it's quite a climb—I drank a glass of milk and ate an apple."

"Is that so? I haven't tried fasting yet. Just one day?"

"Usually. It depends."

"Do you find it does you good?"

"I think it does. I think so very sincerely. I believe I shall do it more often from now on."

"Is that so?" Dick was through with his meal. "I think I'll try it myself."

"Pardon me, but I am not sure you understand. It's not just doing without food."

"I know about fasting," said Dick rather heavily. "I think I'll try it all the same. Maybe it'll help me sleep. I sleep on something hard, you know."

"Indeed?"

But Dick was annoyed with himself for all these confidences he was making. "Let's go listen to those records."

In the passageway there was some confusion because neither of these fastidious men wanted to touch the other and neither wanted to go first. Finally Brother Quintillian, guestlike and mumbling apologetically, went ahead. He started to seat himself, but Dick told him to go put on the records.

They listened for forty-five minutes with complete attention. They did not speak, but looked at each other only once or twice, at some particularly impressive passage.

When it was over Brother Quintillian turned the machine off, and Dick leaned back in his chair shaking his head slowly.

"What musicianship," he said several times. "What musicianship."

"You liked it?" asked Brother Quintillian eagerly. "I am delighted."

"Perfection of technique. Is this the only recording they've made?"

"I'm afraid it is."

What a pity it's all locked up in there."

"Maybe someday . . . ," Brother Quintillian said spreading his hands. "The monks were directed by Burckhardt, of course."

"Never heard of him."

"Oscar Burckhardt. He had a theory of phrasing which he developed from an annotated manuscript he found in Yugoslavia. He instructed this monastery in his method; they found it very difficult because it was so different from their own tradition. This is the result."

"A sound scholar," said Dick. "A damned sound man. The greatest pre-Baroque music I ever heard."

"Doesn't it suggest the arches of some of the Lombardy Romanesque cathedrals? The same austere intensity?"

"No," said Dick brusquely. "I don't have anything to do with cathedrals."

"Just the lines," said Brother Quintillian fluttering his hands.

An uncomfortable silence settled upon them.

IV

"I'll keep him at arm's length," thought Dick to himself. "He's trying to creep up on me with these cathedrals and Masses. He's a pleasant enough guy, but he can take a hint. I wonder why he came up to see me. Well, maybe I can learn something from him."

"Pardon me," said Brother Quintillian, "perhaps I had better go now. I really came just to play the records for you."

"Stick around," said Dick. "You've only been here an hour or so."

"We must have another musical evening soon."

"Sure, I've got a honey of a recording of Monteverdi; setting of a sestina by Petrarch. What form! It makes those lieder-writers look sick, for getting the most out of the words."

"I believe you," said Brother Quintillian. "I look forward to hearing it. Tell me, that icon over there? . . ."

"Sylvia's. She got it in Kodiak on a trip she took before the war. Sentimental, nineteenth-century stuff. Let's play chess."

"Oh yes. Still, it has its own charm. Chess? Oh dear, I'm not very good at it."

They set up the board and began an earnest game, the awkwardness between them gradually dissipating. In the midst of contemplating which of three weak moves it would be best for him to make, Dick spoke in a musing voice, not raising his head. "What do you know about the history of fasting?"

"You mean in the Church?"

"No."

"It's mentioned frequently in the Old Testament."

"Anything else?"

"It is usually connected with purification."

"I guess I'll take your bishop," said Dick.

"You oblige me to take your knight," said Brother Quintillian.

"Now what?—There's often something to these old customs."

"Wisdom of the folk?"

"A sound physiochemical basis, like the use of bread-mold poultices generations before the discovery of penicillin. Of course, there's a lot of crap mixed up with it too. Superstition and that sort of stuff."

"As there is with science."

"For instance?" asked Dick still in a brooding voice.

"Some of the mental healers."

"All of them. There's no experimental basis for their theories. They're about as scientific as a Christian Science practitioner or a piece of the true Cross."

"Dianetics," said Brother Quintillian.

"It's a shame."

"Pardon me, if you take that pawn I'll be able to capture your queen in two moves."

"Thanks. I'll take it back if you don't mind."

"Not at all. It would be a pity to spoil a good game with a trivial error."

"A trivial error but I lose my queen," said Dick, and lapsed into silence.

After the game Brother Quintillian stood up energetically, thanked Dick for his hospitality, took up his records, and said goodbye.

"Wait a minute," said Dick, "I'll run you down the hill."

"I won't hear of it," said Brother Quintillian. "It's only a few minutes' walk."

"You haven't eaten today. Your blood sugar level is low. It wouldn't be good for you."

"No, please, I beg you. It's a lovely night out."

"All the more reason for me to go out into it. I'm a safe driver."

"I had no thought. . . . Thank you very much."

As they were winding slowly down the hill toward St. Anselm's, Dick spoke. "You know, I'm enjoying this drive more than any I've taken for a long time."

"Why how extraordinary. What do you mean?"

"I'm not in a hurry," said Dick with uncalled-for energy. "I'm under no pressure. Sometimes I've thought that if I could just sit at home and never have to go out I'd be all right."

"Have you ever tested your theory, just stayed home for awhile?"

"Yes."

"Were you all right?"

"No. I could hardly wait to get back in my car again."

"I understand," said Brother Quintillian. "I understand very well."

At St. Anselm's, Dick parked and turned off the motor and the lights.

"Remember that three-voice Kyrie towards the end?"

"Like this?" said Brother Quintillian and hummed a few notes. "In unison?"

"Yes. I never heard anything so pure in my life."

"True, true."

For a few moments in the dark car side by side each was freed from his trouble, silently joined with the other in the memory of those thin and disciplined voices which celebrated by the very renunciation of overtone and separateness, by a perfect weakness, their fearful mortality.

"Good night," they said to each other in the dark, "good-bye."

V

He drove back to his house feeling more nearly at peace with himself than he had for some time. As he walked from the carport toward the front door a sighing of wind in the trees drew his attention upward. It was a cloudless night, rare for Oakland; the stars were shining brightly. He could remember the names of only a few of them, of only, he discovered by counting, fifteen of them. He sighed as he thought of the great pleasure it had given him to study astronomy in college. What's the point of all that studying if you forget most of it? What use is it? Just a game. Still, learning had been a great pleasure and always would be. Not the keenest pleasure he had known, but the most enduring. He turned off the lights in the main room and prepared for bed. On the stand beside the bed lay the current issue of a scientific journal; it contained a symposium on Einstein's unified field theory. He had read all the articles once and some he intended to read again, but though he picked it up he decided against reading it now. He turned off the light and lay on his back thinking.

The library lights were still burning, and from the student dormitories drifted radio music. He wanted to preserve intact the equanimity he had gained so recently and so tenuously; he would have to avoid any stray student or some Brother tardily walking in the garden at his offices. He got to his room safely enough, locked the door, and did not turn on the light. There were duties he knew he should be attending to, community duties, the daily duties of every Brother, the duties of a sinner. But he could not have performed any routine task well or profitably to himself, and he did not feel full of sin at this moment but rather full of wonder and joy. A holy wonder at the mysterious ways of God that had brought him thus to a deeper love for God by means of doubt and humiliation; joy in the thought of God's mercy and God's perfection. He undressed and lay on his bed naked to God. His heart beat fast, his breath labored, and tears filled his eyes. There was pressed from his deepest feeling a prayer of thanksgiving.

The theory that would reconcile the great contradiction in physics, that would include in itself all the known data, that would harmonize in a few utter symbols all inferior theories—that he must try to understand. He knew it would be the crown of years of hard work, and he knew he might never achieve his high goal. But he remembered the labor he had performed to grasp the quantum theory in a seminar he had taken and the final reward of it, and he knew, lying on his bed, that for him there could be no other full satisfaction in his life but to set out on that vague and perhaps unattainable and perhaps illusory quest for an understanding and an explanation of the limit of things. To be sure, he knew that even if he should attain this comprehension he would not be able to hold it long—that the arduous studies by which he would approach his goal would be too much for him to hold all at once in his mind, that the conclusion based on these studies would slip from him quickly. Quickly, but not completely, for though he would be able to reproduce the theory no better than he could now reproduce the quantum theory still he knew that once he had grasped it he would feel a security and solidity that nothing could take from him, and that even if he failed finally to grasp it he yet would feel that he had been engaged in the highest enterprise of all.

The prayer that issued in a tumultuous whisper from his mouth was extravagant and ungrammatical at times, but true; it was his own and it meant his thanksgiving. The words were not, like the Hail Mary, accurately placed and polished by centuries of use; but neither were they, like the beads he had told in the chapel that day, words strung on a cord of fear. In half an hour he was empty, empty and weary. He was ready to sleep, but the bed was too soft. How could gratitude to God survive such luxury as a warm, soft bed?

Even with a board between the mattress and the springs the bed was not hard enough. He did not quite see how lying on a hard surface could promote sound sleep; there was some physiochemical basis to it, no doubt, possibly connected with the tonus of the striated muscles. But he was not interested in speculating on it now; he was sleepy, and content that he had made up his mind at last about his life, about his high and private quest. He spread out a blanket on the floor, on the side of the bed away from the window, stretched himself out on it without a pillow, and covered himself with another blanket. His feet stuck out, but he didn't care.

In his high and narrow cell, with the window blind pulled tight, on the concrete floor, he rolled himself up in a single blanket and lay on his side, glad of the cold and hardness, as happy as he would be.

Faq'

During the war my geographer was a lieutenant in the Air Corps. On one of his trips to North Africa his plane flew over the lower edge of the Atlas Mountains, where they meet the Sahara. For long stretches the range was a desolation, as he had expected, relieved only by a few ribbons of green. No doubt rivers from melting snows came down these valleys and squandered themselves in the desert, supplying just enough water to keep a strip of trees and grasses alive on their banks. All this was what he had learned in his studies. But he had also been taught that no one lived on the south side of the mountains, and yet he was quite certain that in one of the valleys he had seen a cluster of huts and some smoke weaving up through the trees. The smoke could have been mist—though it was a hot clear day—but the huts were certainly human dwellings. His curiosity was aroused. He resolved to satisfy it as soon as he was able.

After the war, when he was able to investigate, he discovered only two references to anything that could possibly be identified as his special valley. The first was in a book written in 1837 by one Benjamin Huntley, *Exploring the Atlas Mountains*. Huntley mentions hearing of the existence of a village somewhere south of Mount Tizi, but he says he doubts if his informants were reliable. The other reference was in a twelfth-century Arabic manuscript now in the Royal Library in Madrid, a report on revenues from slave trading in Spain and Northwest Africa. On a map in this manuscript a spot considerably south and west of Mount Tizi is identified as Faq'. There is nothing in the text to explain Faq'; there was nothing but the word itself on the old parchment map. There was nothing else at all anywhere. What was he to do?

If he sought the assistance of one of the learned societies, he would certainly lose much or all of the credit for the discovery—if discovery there was to be. But the expenses would probably come to more than his purse could bear, unless he risked making the explorations quite alone and with no further reconnaissance by air. And it was a risk—the region was a true wilderness, mountainous, arid, huge, and inhospitable even to plants. But he was young and a good mountaineer and he could speak Arabic, and for years he had been risking his life for a lesser cause—to him—than this. His is the sort that wants every place to be given its right name; for him the words terra incognita signify an admission of defeat or a region of impenetrable cold; error is his evil. It was clear what he must do: discover Faq'.

I will not tell you much about the adventures he had before he reached his goal, the delays caused by the suspicion and incredulity of small officials, the hostility of the hill people, the grandeur of that wilderness in which he wandered for weeks not even sure of the existence of his goal, the privation and fatigue and load of bad doubt which only his pride could support, the great good fortune by which he was saved from starvation by a wounded eagle dropping from the skies near to him—too weak to kill it outright, he had to suck its blood. But finally he stood at the brink of a fertile valley, a valley flat and broad for these mountains, but inaccessible from above because of the sheer rise of the range and from the sides because of the steep cliffs and, as he found, uninviting from below because it narrowed to a gorge that emptied the river out precipitously;

but people lived here—it was Faq'. It took him three days to discover the tortuous route of access into the valley, and one whole day to get to the floor. Among rushes at the edge of the river he collapsed, one hand trailing in the water, flat on his belly, sunk at last into that weariness which his pride no longer needed to deny. He lay there for at least one day and perhaps two, he had no way of knowing. When he awoke he could scarcely roll over, and the hand which had fallen into the water was wrinkled white and seemed to be paralyzed. It was lucky for him that he was not discovered, for the women of Faq' would have killed him if they had found him asleep.

He finally rolled onto his back, and lay wondering whether he would ever be able to get up. But as he lay there in the soft rushes in the warmth of afternoon he began to notice, as though for the first time, that vast clean sky under which he had so long labored; and in his fatigue he could not resist the sudden fancy that the sky was not *over* him—he was not *below* its perfection, but rather he was a part of it. "For is not the blueness of the sky," he said to himself, "achieved only by the refraction of light on innumerable particles, which are about me here as well as out there, and maybe in me for all I know?" The longer he lay, looking not up but out, into, among, the more it seemed to him that the sky was not so absolute a blue as it had been on the days before. Yet there could be no mist, not here on this side of these mountains. He lay wondering whether so much blandness had deceived his senses, but he was swimming in that perfection all the same; and then suddenly an explanation for the seeming mistiness occurred to him. It was a light smoke haze. He remembered the curls of smoke he had seen from the airplane, and he observed that there was no wind. No doubt a nearly imperceptible film of smoke obscured his perfect vision. This saddened him for a moment, but then he thought, "Why is it not as absolute a perfection, the sky with this faint and even haze in it, as a clean sky? These smoke particles have been added, but thinly like the blue particles, perfectly distributed. They are not an adulteration, but a version of that other perfection, a part of it, distributed differently now than before; if it hadn't been for that tiny difference I would never have noticed the whole, huge sublimity, and who can say that one of these versions is truer than the other?" Full of these reflections he arose and went down the riverside in search of friends.

He had not gone far when he heard children's laughter in the woods across the river. The stream was neither very wide nor fast-flowing, and at its deepest it did not come over his chest; yet he thought he would never get across it alive. When he was ten yards from the opposite shore he fell in exhaustion into the stream, and floated on the current more dead than alive. But he was caught in an eddy where he lay with his nose and eyes just sticking above water, slowly revolving under the green shade of an hospitable tree like a log in the pool. All he had to do to save himself was to crawl up under the tree onto a pleasant bank. But it didn't seem worth the trouble. It was too lovely there to move, looking up into the twining imperfections of this tree, cool and still and spread out and wet, slowly going about in the eddy, finally without will, only a thing that once had been able to think and now was at peace in the enveloping water, in one complete embrace happy. He does not yet understand why he ever climbed out of the water. He was not conscious of making a decision. All of a sudden it came to him that the sun had gone down and it was time to come home; before he could reflect on this odd notion (where was home?) he found himself climbing out on the bank, a live man again. Never since then has he felt anything out of the ordinary about floating in a river or looking at the sky, and he doesn't know exactly how to explain the experiences of that day—his fatigue perhaps, or the special air and water there, or his relief at finding his goal. What he is sure of is this: while he didn't know what to expect from the people of Faq', he was prepared for it when it came.

It was dusk when he approached the huts. They were long and thin, and all of them pointed up the valley toward the mountains. There were no windows in them. They were interspersed among trees. At some distance he could see a large hut in which there were fire, cooking, noise, children. He crept up to the closest hut, and crouched on the dark side of it listening to the mutter coming from within. The muttering was fast and monotonous, in a man's voice. It seemed to be a praying in some Arabic dialect. He could make out some of the words, or thought he could; they seemed to be numerals. As he listened to that unflagging drone it occurred to him that this must be a machine, no man could do it; but then he heard a clearing of the throat and a slight pause, and he realized it was a man all right, but a man imitating a machine. A praying machine. He thought of hermits.

Footsteps approached. He glued himself to the wall. He heard a woman murmuring, a slight altercation, a moment of laughter, stirring sounds, and then footsteps going away. He looked carefully around the edge of the building and saw a well-built young man, not an old one as he had expected, and a young woman. Side by side they were approaching the building of light and noise. Others were coming to it also. There were no dogs around; at least none had smelled him out, none were barking. He crept nearer the communal house. The odor of cooking food nearly made him faint it was so pleasant. Nevertheless, he lay low a while, trying to understand what was going on. Everything about the scene appeared to be unexceptional and happy. There were several men and many more women and a good many children. Three old women came out into the darkness and on the way to their hut began singing quietly a song the like of which he had never heard. He saw a young man catch and embrace a struggling young woman at the door to the hut, to the general merriment, all with an openness which he had never so much as heard of among Mohammedans. He had no idea what would be best for him to do.

What he finally did was to walk straight toward the doorway crying as loud as he could, which was not very loud, "Food in the name of Allah!"

Well, they took care of him, fed him, and nursed him back to strength again. He learned later that he was the only outsider who had ever been allowed to live in Faq'—to stay alive, I mean, not just abide there. I think it was more than a matter of whim that he was allowed to stay. He was completely at their mercy and they could understand something of what he said, so much was in his favor; but mostly he helped himself with his own honest pride.

After he had eaten some of the vegetable stew which is their chief food, watched intently by a hundred dark, silent faces, the chief, Alfaleen, asked him in their dialect who he was. Now my geographer had noticed that no one had mentioned Allah and that the chief's style was very plain for Arabic, with none of those honorific courtesies universal among Mohammedans. He had noticed this, but hadn't known what to make of it. He answered, "Destroyer of boundaries." There was no response. Either they had not understood his accent or else they were not at all impressed. "Foe of all ignorance," he said. No response. "Seeker of truth."

Then Alfaleen said to him, "What must be?"

"What has always been will always be."

Alfaleen repeated, "What must be?"

"So long as there are hills the rain will flow down them in streams."

Alfaleen repeated, "What must be?"

"Each number will always have two neighbors."

But Alfaleen asked again, "What must be?"

And this time he gave the answer he would never before in his life have given: "Nothing." It saved him.

He has wondered a thousand times why he gave that unlikely answer. He had of course heard of the indeterminacy principle; he had heard, with fascination, that law is a matter of statistical probability and that truth is finally a matter of whichever of the many geometries best suits your needs. But since he had never been able to imagine such things he had not believed in them, and he certainly had never asked himself whether or not a stone *must* fall, two plus two *must* equal four. Yet he had said to Alfaleen, that black, cool, impersonal man, that nothing must be. He attributes this answer of his to the power of Alfaleen's mind. He was concentrating hard on understanding what was being said to him and on choosing the correct Arabic words for his answers, he was weak with fatigue, he sensed that much depended upon his answer, and he was alerted by the very strangeness of the question. Even so, he thinks it was the power of that other mind which put the answer into his mouth. He learned to respect that power.

For a week he convalesced. The women and children, among whom he stayed, treated him with all the friendliness in the world. Alfaleen had commanded him to tell them nothing about the place from which he had come, and had also commanded them not to ask him about it. He had nothing to do but to lie about listening to them, learning what their customs were and how they thought and what they were afraid of—not learning it so much as taking it in like the food and water and bright air. He observed that none of the mature men did any of the ordinary tasks, like gathering fuel, fishing, repairing the huts, irrigating the fields; they seemed to have some other work. The women did not resent this state of affairs; it had not occurred to them, apparently, that things could be otherwise arranged. The children were amazingly unrestricted and happy. There were at least twice as many girls as boys for some reason, but the women did not seem to treat the boys with any great reverence. The children were not allowed to go near the huts at the other end of the village (where he had heard the man praying like a machine). Every morning Alfaleen would take the boys over five off to school. The girls learned from the women. Boys were punished for being too rough, too "manly"; girls were punished for using a number over one hundred. The children had a game which they loved to play, with innumerable variations: a boy would sit in a special position and begin to count in a low regular voice, and a girl or perhaps two or three of them would try to distract him. They would use every means imaginable except hurting: shout in his ear, caress him, throw cold water on him, count backwards in his same rhythm, put food in his mouth. Some of the boys had developed amazing powers of concentration, but the wiles of the girls were irresistible. No boy could hold out for more than a quarter of an hour—but no ordinary boy would have held out against those girls for two minutes, whatever he was doing. One little girl, about eight or nine, who was particularly attached to him—a quiet thing with a clumsy, strong body, rather deliberate, rather grave—told him one morning that she had had a nightmare about the end of the world. She had dreamed, she said, that "they came to the end of the counting and I was one of the ones left over." A little boy who got angry with him once called him a "slow counter." From the awed silence and snickers with which the other children greeted this, he concluded that it was a serious insult. The women and children were the happiest he had ever seen; yet there was nothing intense about what they did. They seemed never to have suffered. He was too feeble, too contented to feel any strangeness about all this; while it lasted it seemed exactly the way things should be. But when he was strong again at the end of a week and Alfaleen removed him from his idyl he was glad it was over.

At first Alfaleen asked him questions about the world from which he had come. "Which men are most revered? Which have the greatest power? For what is a man put to death? What is God nowadays?" But the questioning did not go on for long. Alfaleen was feeling him out, determining just how to introduce him to the life which he was entering. To one who lives with beauty hourly, as to a man in love, the various semblances of beauty to which he may be exposed are all imperfect and not in the least interesting; he wants to be with the true beauty. Alfaleen's was the beauty of truth, and he wanted to share it. He tried tricks and deceptions in his questionings, but he was hopelessly honest; it was clear that no one had lied in Faq' for a long time.

Well, the upshot of it all was that he was deemed worthy to become a bearer of the mystery of the truth, a participant in it. He was taken to a hut of his own in the men's section of the village—a bare, dark, quiet hut—and there taught to count. One sat in a certain manner—the way the boys had sat in their game—weaved in a certain rhythm, closed one's senses to the outside world, thought only of the perfection of one's technique, and counted in a steady voice. He was given a block of numbers very high in the series, told certain permissible abbreviations and short cuts, and left each morning to his counting. Alfaleen instructed him each afternoon in the history and aims of Faq'. He understood it all in a way. He was quite good at counting. But then he had to be; anyone who fell below a certain monthly quota was put to death. So was any cheater. Alfaleen would prowl about outside the huts listening to the voices of the counters—two or three times a day he came by, so keen and trained that he could tell by the very cadences of the murmuring count whether the counter was in danger of falling behind. There were no cheaters.

In the tenth century, when the Arabs were conquerors of North Africa and Spain and were also developing advanced mathematical theories, a nobleman-mathematician named Alfaleen stopped in the province of Maraq' while en route to Spain to enter the faculty of the new college of mathematics. But he fell out with the theologians of Maraq' and was condemned for his heresy. Alfaleen had maintained that pure reason, and only pure reason, could ever achieve the truth, and that since thought was the greatest power in the universe then Allah must be thought. According to the theologians this was as much as to say that the Koran wasn't worth a couple of quadratic equations and that if God is idea then idea is God. To rescue the youth of Spain from such notions they recommended to the governor of Maraq' that he execute Alfaleen. But the governor was an old friend of Alfaleen's father; instead of executing him, he had him and all his party driven off into the granite wilderness to perish for heresy. And that would have been that; but by some hook or crook they fell in with a band of native blacks, founded Faq', and established a colony. Their descendants have lived there in peace ever since. They had no animals or tools, but none were needed. The outside world forgot they were there, and any stranger who happened to come to Faq' was put to death.

So far as their traditions tell, the constitution of Faq' has remained unaltered since its founding—the laws of reason are ageless. There is Alfaleen, the chief, the philosopher, the king; there are the men, who count; and there are the women, who do the work and tend to the men. The original Alfaleen, to whose genius Faq' owes its peace and its purpose, had by the exercise of pure reason seen the folly of racial distinctions; blacks and Arabs had intermingled as they desired, the third Alfaleen was himself pure black, and by now the blend of races is complete. He had seen the problem of keeping down the population; defectives, women who can no longer work, innovators, are all put to death. The ratio of women to men had been kept fairly constant at three to one. Though the women, having no souls, cannot be entrusted with the high mission of Faq', yet the actual survival of the colony has come more and more to rest upon them—they weed out the unfit, they maintain everyone physically, and they keep watch on the men. Indeed, though Alfaleen is the governor, it is the women who actually make and execute all the rules and customs—except, of course, those having to do with the only thing that matters, the exercise of pure reason, the counting.

For Alfaleen had set his people reason's purest problem: number. And each Alfaleen, chosen solely for his ability, spends his life in the contemplation of number and the attributes of number in the confidence that the penetration of this mystery, the final conquering of it, will lay bare the secret to all power. But not many men are capable of such true and ultimate endeavor; hence, as soon as the colony had stabilized itself, Alfaleen, like a good philosopher-king, had set his subjects to the accomplishment of a communal task, one which in its very nature surpasses any other that men have set themselves: counting. By hypothesis the highest nameable number is as far from the end as one is, and there is no end to counting. It is the function of Faq' to test this hypothesis in the only statistically verifiable fashion, actually by counting forever.

The women may not use a number greater than one hundred; the life of Faq' does not make larger numbers necessary and woman's reason would sully truth. Originally there was much defection from the strict regime, and at one time had the insurrectionists banded together they could have overthrown the rule of this godless theocracy, but Alfaleen won out. They have reached a very high number; they expect in our lifetime to reach the number beyond which numbers have no name. Into that darkness Alfaleen will shed the light of reason.

More and more in the past few centuries Alfaleen has come to believe that the core of the problem of number lies in its oneness-endlessness and that the original impulse which set the men of Faq' to telling the rosary of reason's mystery was by no means an expedient but rather an attempt to mechanize the mystery itself. For this, says Alfaleen, is not only the activity of reason, it is reason pure, this counting, because only incidentally does it correspond to anything outside man's mind. It becomes clearer and clearer that without this endless and exact demonstration of reason's truth all reason would be subverted and mankind go back to what it had been before.

Alfaleen said, and certainly he believes it, that there is a sense in which man's destiny hangs upon those counters in Faq', for that they do not reach the end of counting is the demonstration of all hypothesis. If they should reach the end, reason would have done what is impossible to it and the rest would be chess, for then they would have proved that reason too has its law—absolute positive correlation. But if they should quit counting—weary, exhausted, rebellious, defeated—then would you and I have succumbed at last to our weariness and rebellion and defeat, and the women would take over.

At first he was exhilarated by the novelty of the life and what seemed to be the importance of the counting. At the outset boredom was the dread at the back of his mind, but in fact he was never bored. The counting seemed to hypnotize him into a state of strange tranquility. He was tranced, as it were, into reason's realm. So much so, indeed, that it was not many weeks before he quite lost interest in exercise and food and the evening conviviality. Then girls taunted and seduced him, with an innocent artfulness and a voluptuous naïveté which he found (as had the boys in the game) irresistible. One night he counted in his sleep, and all the next day he was required to play with children and make love to young women and lie in the sun. Everything was communal in Faq', property and love as well as the great task. It was a world of reason and sense and trance, and he found it far happier than the world of mystery and strong feeling from which he had come. But eventually he began to think.

Or perhaps not to think so much as to remember. He remembered the anxiety and injustice and despair and the huge splendors of this world—the poverty, the right and wrong, the power, the pain. Especially the pain. He told himself again and again that ten thousand sink that one may rise, that whole cities stink in ugliness that fifty men may make and enjoy only a little beauty. But not all the reasonableness he could muster, nor horror at his memories, nor the truth and high pleasantness of Faq' could drive the thought of pain from his mind. For it was pain, suffering, moral agony, that his memories revolved about. It became clearer and clearer to him that he could not live without pain, not even thus happily, not even thus participating in the great task of man's noblest faculty. He tried hurting himself physically; he had a large rock balanced precariously once, ready to roll onto his arm and smash it. But the absurdity of such an act here in this equable valley stopped him from doing it. And afterwards the indignity he felt at not having been able to prepare a greater pain for himself than this which any accident might provide, not having been able to go through with even this little thing made him resolve to leave Faq' as soon as he could. For a long time he had been dissembling at his counting, with great anxiety and guiltiness. Now that he had resolved to leave, all this counting suddenly seemed silly to him, and he dissembled without a qualm.

He sat day after day in his hut making the sounds of counting, and often actually tranced into it—it had its own power. But most of the time he was planning his escape. It was necessarily an escape too, for anyone guilty of any defection, from bad health to rebelliousness, was without mercy or remorse killed. He collected food and water and made himself a substitute for shoes. He walked on rocky ground till his feet were horny. He played and swam very hard till he was strong and supple. He had no human ties to break; four of the women were pregnant at the time, one perhaps with his child, perhaps all four, perhaps none, he did not care. He would miss Alfaleen's cold, pure speculations, but never, he knew, so much as he now missed the pain of this world of ours. He lay in the sun till he was nearly as black as they, and in the middle of one stormy night he left. He was not pursued.

He returned to us after much difficulty. He is suffering with us now, and looking back at the bland perfection of Faq' with a sometimes acute nostalgia. But my geographer is determined never to go there again, for he is sure that though he does not know what is right for men ordered perfection is wrong, and that though suffering is bad the lack of suffering is much worse.

Miss Cudahy of Stowes Landing

I

Bingham could not knock at a strange door without a sense of adventure; to greet and win if he could whatever smiling or screw-eyed or blank stranger the door opened on made his heart beat a little faster, his breath come shorter. In the course of his duties with the Superior Court, he met very few new people, aside from lawyers or their secretaries; he liked the fact that in the manner of their official dealings lawyers still wear wigs, but he made no friends among them. He had a few acquaintances and family friends, and another friend, a woman, whom he might have married several years before but did not. Nearly every door he knocked at he had knocked at a hundred times before, except for the doors of old houses, which held his happiness.

So when one Saturday in early summer he knocked at Miss Cudahy's house in Stowes Landing and no one answered, he gratefully set about inspecting the exterior of the house with the attention it deserved. The telephone operator—in one of these small towns the central intelligence—had given him Miss Cudahy's name and had volunteered the information that she was old, suffered from rheumatism, and was very much the lady. He could see from the outside of the house that the operator had been right—only a lady would befit this grandest house in town; only a lady would have maintained it so handsomely against the sea weather of Northern California; only a lady would have kept a marble birdbath in the garden, a Latin sundial under that usually overcast sky, a bronze, stark-naked, well-patinaed faun in a Concord arbor.

For although he was not sure of the rose window over the door, yet the dormer windows, the overhang, the complication of the roof, and the five gables meant to him New England on a hostile coast. Stowes Landing had been built seventy years ago on the flats back from a three-hundred-foot cliff, north above a logging stream; the meadows stretched freely back for a mile to the line of forest and descending hills; nothing protected the houses from the sea breeze but a hedge for those that planted one. Yet Miss Cudahy's house stood two-and-a-half stories tall and massive, like some determined New Englanders bunched together, suspicious and prepared, resisting whatever the Indians, Spaniards, Mexicans, Russians, Southerners, Middle-Westerners, Chinese, Filipinos, Japanese, Africans, Italians, Armenians, of this dangerous land might have settled among themselves heathenishly to do. That was all right, what one expected, for 1880; but to find it so purely preserved, still yellow with green shutters, in these provinces of light stucco or stained wood, to be able to walk up to it behind its hedge in a legitimate—because pure—curiosity, this affected Bingham as strongly as some people are affected by shaking the hand that shook the hand of Lincoln. He was more excited, as he began his tour, than was altogether reasonable.

On the southern side of the house, the side where the hedge was only twenty feet tall, he found a grizzled little man leaning on the handle of a shovel. His stance and dull stare bespoke one who has worked hard and learned how to rest like a horse standing up; but there was no new-turned bed, no deep hole, only a small cleared space where he was probably going to plant a fuchsia, there being already sixty or seventy of them about the garden.

"Hello," said Bingham. The man did not respond, people frequently didn't. "The lady of the house is not home?"

"Happen Phoebe's out buying," he said in a British dialect so heavy Bingham could hardly understand him.

"I see. I hope you don't mind my looking around till she returns."

He had always made it a point not to start small talk in a situation like this; but that unresponsive gaze said to him, birth, marriage, death may be sizable enough to talk about mister but they are none too large. The man rubbed his chin on the end of the handle.

"I'm only interested in the house," Bingham went on, embarrassed to be introducing a subject so fugitive. "Miss Cudahy—could you tell me . . ."

But he heard, for the second time he realized, a sharp sound behind and above him, a sound as of a gem rapped against glass; when he felt the hairs stand up on the back of his hand he knew that he was being watched from behind the curtains by the eyes of one who had heard but had not answered his knock at the door. He left his sentence to dangle as it would and went on with his inspection; the man began to dig.

In the rear there was a pile of wood far more orderly than most of the garden, a vegetable patch, and a clothesline. And in the corner beyond the clothesline, half-hidden by an arc of delphiniums, there was a garden to itself, earth scratched and leveled, scarcely a dead petal on the blossoms, no rows but a wandering intermixed variety of plants and shrubs, stepping stones for paths; there were single roses and single geraniums, three tulips, Indian paintbrush, and succulents from the sea cliffs (most of them with small bright flowers, for June is spring in Mendocino) and a rolling fringe of yellow oxalis. He stood in a sort of wonder at the sweetness of that garden, at how dainty and feminine and itself it seemed down between the still-too-vigorous huge old house and the hedge which here was more than thirty feet in height. He wondered who Phoebe was.

That hedge—there were a number of such hedges along that part of the coast, but Miss Cudahy's was as dense and perfectly trimmed as any he had seen and much the highest. These hedges were dark green and thick and not very noisy even in the wind; very dark green, they were kept trimmed smooth as moss, with rounded edges, and this one which had ascents and dips in it for no reason that he could make out, at one point rose taller than the house; dark, impermeable cypress green, for though it kept out the wind it kept out everything else as well. He could not imagine how Chin-on-Shovel did the job of trimming, and he did not even want to imagine what it was like to live out a life with a prospect of gray skies, unkept fuchsias, and the dark of the green.

One at the front and the other at the rear, two arches ran through the hedge like the mouse runs that pierced the vast walls of Muscovite palaces. Through the rear gate as he was standing there a young woman entered, with a basket of groceries in one hand, a bonnet on her head—more a bonnet than a hat—and a spring to her step. "Hello," he said, but she did not look at him. He stepped forward between two delphiniums and called again. She stopped, her lips a little open with surprise, and looked at him with a directness, a lack of demure withdrawal, which rather surprised him. "Could you tell me, please," he began, but she turned from him and ran up the stairs and into the house. He could think of no better course than to wait for a few discreet minutes and go knock at the front door. This he did, though not without trepidation.

She answered, with lowered eyes. He apologized for having startled her and handed her his card. Without a word she walked back into the house. She appeared, at closer sight, a plain young woman, her hair drawn severely back to a bun, her face devoid of make-up yet not sallow, her clothes undistinguished for their color or grace; yet there was a certain tone to her body that set her off from an ordinary maid or housekeeper, a vigor to her step and a flirt, a fillip perhaps, to her skirts when she turned that charmed him. She returned and opened the door wide to him; he thanked her and stepped into the hall; she smiled, not just politely but as though she were suppressing some private amusement, and ushered him into the parlor.

There, swathed in pastel chiffons, lay a huge old woman on a chaise-longue.

"Mr. Bingham!" she called forth like the captain of one brig to the captain of another. "Come in, sir. Sit down." And she made what seemed to be some sort of complicated hailing motions with her hands.

"Thank you, Miss Cudahy," he said, and sat in a pale oak horse-hair chair near her. When he looked around the girl had disappeared. "I'm afraid I rather startled Phoebe out in the garden a few minutes ago."

"Did you?" she cried. "She did not inform me of that. And how do you know her name?"

"Your gardener, I gathered it from him."

"Ah yes, of course." And he saw how, with a loll of her great head and a flick of her left hand, heavy with rings, she peered out between the curtains invisibly. Then she, with a suddenness that surprised him, turned back and said to him sharply, "You're from the FBI."

He had seen witnesses caught off-balance, and had pitied them for their slowness and dullness; now here he was thrown by an old woman's judo.

"Who, me?" he said. "Oh no, gracious no. I'm only . . ."

"Very well," she waved his stuttering aside. "One of the other investigators. Which?"

"No, I assure you, I am interested in old houses. I enjoy them very much, and I . . ."

"I see." She paused, the sort of pause that did not permit him to speak. He sat watching her fill a curved pipe with tobacco, tamp it, and light up. "You may smoke," she said, and docilely he lit a cigarette. "You traced me through the California Historical Society."

"No," he said, "I am merely traveling, alone, along the Mendocino coast, looking for houses of the New England captains that settled here. And I found yours simply by driving down the street looking for it."

"How did you discover me behind this hedge?"

"By getting out of my automobile and looking through the gate."

"I see." She stared with a concentration as great as Phoebe's; it had an altogether different effect on him. "Well, you've seen the outside and you're in the parlor. What do you think?"

He began to exclaim over it, and rising asked her permission to investigate the parlor more closely.

"In good time," she said. "Sit down, Mr. Bingham. We will have tea."

She pulled a tasseled cord behind her head, and Phoebe appeared. She waved her hands at Phoebe with a mixture of fluttering and grace and indolence, and threw her head back onto the pillows.

"Pardon me," she murmured; her mouth fell a little ajar. "One has to rest a good deal. More than one would have chosen."

He could look at her closely now. It was a heavy, pale, sensual face with dark pouches under the deep eyes; she was not so old as he had originally thought, not over sixty. Her arms were bare and fleshy; day was, he imagined, when those white arms had excited at least the admiration of men. He could see that one of her legs, extended on the chaise longue, was bound in some sort of rubber legging reaching halfway down the calf; the other, foot on the floor, would have served well on a duke in the days of knee breeches. She breathed heavily, nearly wheezing. "Asthma," she muttered, "damned nuisance." He sat straight in his slick, hard chair.

At the sound of Phoebe with the tea tray at the door, he turned in pleased expectation. "Don't bother to speak to her," said Miss Cudahy scarcely moving her gray lips; he realized that she must have been watching him from under her lids. "Phoebe is deaf and dumb."

He blushed and did not know where to look.

II

He did not see them again for a month and would not have gone back at all, even to see the rest of the house, had it not been for the newel, which he had only glanced at as he had been leaving the house; there was not another in California to compare to it. The month was workaday and legal, marked only by his failure to persuade an owner in North Oakland not to redecorate a Victorian specimen with mourning veil eaves, and by a rather curious invitation to speak. He received a telephone call and then a visit from a cultivated, charming, shrewd little woman named Pickman-Ellsworth, who wanted him to speak to the Alameda Fuchsia Society about the use of fuchsias in New England. He had to explain to her that he knew little about the subject and nothing at first hand. She received his refusal without protest, yet she continued talking, about one thing and another; she said that she had read some of his articles in the magazine *Golden West*; she kept throwing him subjects, visibly trying to "draw him out." He did not quite understand her purpose. She had black, quick eyes and sat very erect in her chair. She spoke to her chauffeur as she left with precisely that combination of dryness, condescension, and politeness with which she had addressed Bingham.

The newel at the foot of the stairs drew him back, that exquisitely carved, white newel with its promise of fine interiors on the second floor; the fluted newel, and, he had to confess it to himself, a curiosity about Miss Cudahy's household stronger than his repugnance for her herself.

He opened the gate, went through the hedge tunnel and walked up the stairs to the porch without seeing the English gardener. He knocked the grand knocker—Miss Cudahy had no doorbell, indeed he felt that the electric lights in the old gas fixtures had advanced progress enough for her—and he stood waiting for Phoebe to open to him. He had calculated to himself what expression and gesture would best let Phoebe know the friendliness and pity he felt for her, what smile would blend recognition and warmth and yet least intrude upon her intimacy; the deference of the superior to the afflicted seemed to Bingham one of the few courtesies surviving from that high and better-mannered world lost to us to our diminution. This he had calculated—or, rather, had hoped to achieve—but he reckoned without Phoebe. How could he have known her? A glimpse of her, brown-dressed in the garden, scurrying like a quail for cover; as maid in the hall, eyes downcast, smiling; a tea through which she had sat like a little girl, knees tightly pressed together, watching with a twinkle in her eye everything they did. How could he have known that the moment she opened the door now and saw him her eyes would light up, her cheeks would flush rosy red, her poor voice would crack a little, her hands would open out to him? Open so warmly and impetuously that he, smiling, would clasp them warmly in his, to the distress of all courtesy but to his most grateful pleasure. He did not touch people with casual affection, but rather shrank from it; he preferred words of congratulation to a slap on the back, the smile of privacy to a cocktail-party kiss. Fastidiousness entails its dangers; he accepted them knowingly. But Phoebe's hands, rough-skinned and strong with work yet smaller than his, feminine in his, did not presume any intimacy or force any warmth of response: they extended him her words of greeting, inflection of her pleasure, her affection even, yet with hand's immediacy, touch's conviction. He smiled at her, foolish with sudden pleasure; his condescension snapped in her hands like a twig. He did not even feel embarrassed. It was as though he had known her a long time.

She took his hat and coat—it was a windy afternoon—and when she returned from hanging them up and found him admiring the newel she pointed out to him something he had not yet noticed: the baseboard running along below the banisters, fretted beautifully and out of pure exuberance, uselessly, obscurely. She clasped her hands in pleasure at his pleasure.

He started to his feet at Miss Cudahy's large voice, "Mr. Bingham, is that you?"

He pointed, and Phoebe led him by the hand to the parlor door; as she opened the door she let go his hand; after he had gone in she withdrew from them like a maid.

"Mr. Bingham," said Miss Cudahy, frowning as he advanced, "what delayed you in the hall?"

"The newel," he said. "And Phoebe drew my attention to the fretted baseboard on the staircase."

"Did she?" said Miss Cudahy. "I hope you are well." And she took his hand.

"Very well," he answered, and it was all he could do to out-squeeze the gray-faced, lame old woman. "I hope in turn that your health has improved."

"How could it?" she said; she lolled back and pulled the rope. "At my age, in a climate like this, with no one to talk to?"

"It is hard," he said; he could scarcely have said less.

"Do you know how hard?" she replied scornfully. Phoebe appeared and Miss Cudahy waved some message at her. "Mr. Bingham, are you intending to buy my house? What do you want of me?"

"Believe me, I am interested only in the beauty of your house. I study old houses as an avocation."

"Beauty comes high on the market these days," she said fixing him with her eye. "Some kinds of beauty. Does this kind?"

"No," he answered flatly. "It does not."

"Are you just here for the day again, Mr. Bingham?"

"No, I am spending part of my vacation exploring these parts."

"How much of it, do you think?"

"That depends upon many considerations."

"One of which is me, I take it?"

"Indeed," he said in the manner of a gallant, "how could it be otherwise?"

"The *Golden West* said you were a lawyer."

"Not exactly a lawyer. I am in legal work."

"Not a lawyer but in legal work," she repeated. "Slippery."

"Miss Cudahy," he said, arising, with all the dignity he could muster, "I would very much appreciate your permission to explore the rest of this house. I will take no photographs of it and write nothing about it for publication without your signed permission." This was more than she had let him get out during his entire first visit; only his anger had broken him through her complex defense so that he could now confront her simply with what he wanted.

"Ho," she shouted, "I've offended you, have I? I offend people. It usually takes longer with others. You are different. Sit down, young man, you've seen only this room and the hall, and there's more here worth the seeing you may be sure."

He sat down, gritting his teeth behind his smile. "The newel, Miss Cudahy, is worthy of McIntyre himself."

"Yes," she said quizzically, "worthy of him. In the master bedroom"—she knew how to play her mouse—"on the second floor, Mr. Bingham, where I have not been for three years—my damned joints," she said banging the knee of her left leg—"in the master bedroom, when you get to it, you will notice the mantel. McIntyre, is it? I must tell you about that someday."

"Why not tell me now?" he said with the last of his anger.

Phoebe came in bearing the tea things; neither of them turned toward her.

"Because, Mr. Bingham, it is not my pleasure."

They had tea.

III

For the twentieth time he looked at the note she had slipped into his hand: "Meet me outside the rear gate at 4:30." Already he had waited a quarter of an hour; a cold wind was blowing in from the sea; every fantasy of waiting afflicted him, wrong time, wrong place, accident, change of heart; he shivered back into his car. He did not happen to be looking when she came through the hedge and ran around the back of his car. Suddenly there she was, opening the door and slipping in beside him smiling. The ruefulness, the trace of anxiety vanished from her face when she saw how gladly he forgave her, her forehead smoothed, she squeezed his arm. What could he do but take her hands in his? The good humor and affection of her smile became a sort of radiance which warmed him, as he would not have believed possible three hours before.

What did she want? He started to draw out a pencil and paper, but she gently restrained his hands. With perfect good humor and seriousness, in a few quick gestures, she suggested driving somewhere, getting out, and walking. He started the car; she directed. On the cliff above a turbulent, rocky surf she stopped them and led him down a path. He heard a bell buoy offshore busy in its melancholy; he had never stood close to rough weather on the sea before. Phoebe sprang up onto a rock beside him and leaned her hand on his shoulder; her hair glistened with blown spray, there were tiny drops on her eyelashes; she kept looking from the surf back at his face expectantly; he did not disappoint her. She clapped her hands and occasionally her voice emitted some of its pathetic, ugly symptoms of excitement. She led him to a sort of overhang where they could squat protected from the wind; he noticed that Phoebe's free hand pressed feelingly against the rock, and he imagined her delicate excitement from the waves' crashing on the outside of the rocks of their cave. He knew that later he would worry about the propriety of his behavior with Phoebe, wonder what he should have done instead, speculate on what she was thinking, what his actions meant to her; but for the time that they huddled together there his affection for her, pure and unamorous as though she were a child, dissolved all questions of motive, propriety, consequence, and left only a residue of unalloyed content. Squatting in a cold cave with a view of lashing breakers under a heavy sky, damp, feet cold, holding hands with a deaf-mute girl he had met only once before, truly he thought himself seven sorts of fool, but he grinned at the thought.

She peered out of the cave at the sky, looked at him ruefully, and made some sign gestures; then, remembering he could not understand them, she put hands gently on his arm with a look of apology. Phoebe's gestures and the movements of her features expressed, with the economy and delicacy of a trout swimming in a clear pool, a range of ideas and emotions. Yet physically she was not delicate, but rather blunt and unsymmetrical; not pretty but, Bingham thought, one of the beautiful opposites of pretty. Then and there in the cave she taught him a dozen ordinary words in sign language: I, you, car, home, day, like, go, sea, be together, mama, not, must. They laughed a great deal as his fingers blundered some sentences together: I you together like go sea. When he asked her how to say happy she showed him, and house, and door, but when he wrote love on the sand with a twig she shook her head. She made the gestures of liking and being together, but pointed at love and looked at him reprovingly. He saw that she had more tact than he—and very likely more honesty. She told him then she had to go home to Mama. Mama? he asked her, and she nodded. Who? he said with his lips. Miss Cudahy, she wrote on the sand, sprang up, and ran off toward the path. For a few moments he watched her, incredulous and frustrated; he felt very fond of her. He watched her climb the path, not thinking, but only looking at the slight figure quick and graceful in its brown, practical, shapeless clothes; not feeling even, only wishing he knew her well. Just before he got up to follow her he remembered Miss Cudahy's hard look when Phoebe had spilled some tea on the table, and he shuddered to feel cold little feet creeping about his back as they would when, lying in bed on the way to sleep, he chanced to think about the latest advances in bombmaking.

Next morning, arriving just after the postman, he carried Miss Cudahy's mail up to the front door with him. He saw an envelope from Mrs. Pickman-Ellsworth. He was feeling grim when Phoebe let him into the parlor.

"Oh ho," cried Miss Cudahy after the civilities; she waved an envelope at him. "Let's see what Nell has to say about you. Just step into the dining room till I call you, Mr. Bingham, if you don't mind. You'll find Phoebe polishing the silver."

He fumbled among his unsorted emotions, unable to find the one that would suit his response; what he did was simply to thank her and do what she said. After all, he reflected, he had not yet seen the dining room.

Phoebe did not stop polishing, but whenever, in his inspection of the room, he passed near her she would rub against him a little like a cat. Miss Cudahy shouted him back.

"She says you're respectable," she said, and puffed on her pipe a few times gazing at him. "Good reputation, good family. I want you to stay with me, Mr. Bingham, for as long as you're going to be in this vicinity. I like you. You may have the master bedroom; someday I'll tell you who it was made for. Phoebe needs the society of a cultivated man. Poor creature. Do you like her?"

"Very much." But he did not want to talk about her to Miss Cudahy. "Thank you for the invitation. I do not want to intrude. . . ."

"Nonsense, that's my concern, not yours. There are not many literate people hereabouts—Mrs. Townson in Mendocino City, the Chiverses in Fort Bragg, who else? You ask me why I continue to live in Stowes Landing. My answer to you is, I don't. I live in this house."

"You have good taste in houses."

"Because it is your taste? Well, I like to be flattered, Mr. Bingham, but don't try to flatter me about my knowledge of New England houses. Between us we could write a good book on the old houses of this county." She puffed reflectively, gazing at him. "Mine's the best of course. Think it over. You could live here while we were at it. I want to look at my mail now. Would you be so good as to step into the garden and tell Japheth to spray the roses?"

He looked at the appointments of the parlor and hall with a new eye as he walked out; they were his to use, and she would tell him all she knew. On the front steps he imagined a roseate fantasy: a month, even six weeks of solid research and photographing, then one of the major contributions to the history of California architecture would be his. He even looked with a benevolent eye at Japheth, whom he found standing with some cuttings in one hand and clippers in the other, staring at a rose. He delivered his message with positive friendliness; Japheth winked at him, touched his cap with the clippers, and then, leering, pulled off a rose branch so that it half-split the cane. "It wasn't so in the old country," he whispered. Bingham left hurriedly. Walking away, he rummaged about in his mind for his fantasy, but he could not find it again.

Half from plan and half because it was the nearest entrance he ran up the back stairs and into the kitchen. Glistening copper pots and pans hung on the walls; the old wood stove took up far more room than it needed to by the standards of modern efficiency; there was a hatchet in the box with the kindling; three comfortable, mended kitchen chairs, envy of snobs, sat about the stove; the worn linoleum, black-and-white checkered, was as clean with scrubbing as a boy's ears; the kitchen smelled of apples and coffee. Some sort of odd combination of flag-arms, as in a railroad signal, was attached to the wall over the pantry door; even as he was wondering what it was for one of the flags, the white one, fell out at right angles—obviously a signal for Phoebe. It jiggled up and down; he stepped through the pantry into the dining room and went with Phoebe into the parlor again.

"Do you approve of my kitchen, Mr. Bingham?"

"I do. Phoebe keeps it in admirable order."

"It's a pleasant place to spend the supper hours in the winter, let me tell you. You must visit us in the winter."

"I should be delighted." He felt constrained to say something more. "Your garden must have been a prize at one time."

"It was."

"A great pity it has fallen into neglect."

"Do you have ideas for it, Mr. Bingham?" She was full of animation.

"Only the obvious ideas for the circumstances."

"The very thing!" she cried. "It would give you some exercise as we worked on our book. I can see by your figure you don't get enough exercise. Splendid, sir, a splendid addition."

He smiled painfully. "I don't enjoy gardening."

"Nonsense. You need it." She saw that she had gone too far. "Of course, of course," she went on heavily, "there would be no necessity. Japheth keeps the fuchsias from dying out. Phoebe would work with you in the garden. She likes it. She likes being with you."

Phoebe, having lip read the gist of the conversation, smiled up at Bingham so sweetly that he, in relief from the old woman, half reached out his hand to her in response; propriety halted him. Phoebe, seeing his broken gesture, stepped beside him and took his hand; all three laughed at his blush.

"Well," said Miss Cudahy, shifting her bulk about, "everything is working out handsomely. Phoebe must show you your room. You must fetch your things and install yourself. We shall take an outing one day soon, Mr. Bingham. Zenobia Dobbs has a house in Greenwood you should see the inside of before you leave here, and I doubt if you went alone that she would be so hospitable to you as I have been."

He did not thank her for her hospitality, as she apparently wanted him to do, because he did not think she had been moved by hospitality to do what she was doing. He said he should like to see the house in Greenwood.

"But where is this town?" he asked. "I don't recognize the name."

"They took to calling it Elk a few years ago. There are not many like you, Mr. Bingham, who cherish the old things. The world rots and we rot with it." She tossed some keys to Phoebe, fluttered her hand, and shifted herself back on her chair. Among her pale violet clothes, in that light that cast no shadow, her face seemed nearly ethereal. Yet her body was huge.

Upstairs Phoebe showed him the master bedroom; she kept looking from his face to the mantel or the bedstead or the molding, pleased yet puzzled by the great impression the room was making on him, trying to see it with his eyes. She showed him the bathroom, Japheth's room, a dark cupboard, and her own room facing west, austere this side of barrenness, feminine only in the lace curtains. Then, with sparkling eyes, dancing a little in excitement, taking both his hands in one of hers, she opened the door to the last bedroom. His impression was one of darkness, scent, frills, musty old letters. She threw open the shutters; they were in a boudoir, among a luxury which had made feminine and intimate the stern woodwork, the right-angled room. There was a satin quilt on the low bed; at the sight of it he made a mock gesture of indolence, and in an instant Phoebe was lying there. She took some pins out of her hair and shook it free, brown, fine hair. She laid her head at a certain angle on the pillows, curved one arm up over her head and the other onto her stomach, and turned her body in the fashion of all experience and luxuriation. It was only a moment until she bounced up smiling and clasping his hand, simple and young again.

He heard a clicking in the hall, and Miss Cudahy shouting that she wanted Phoebe. He told her; she put up her hair in a second. On their way down she flipped the hall flag back up into place. On the landing of the stairs, yielding to what impulse he did not know, he stopped Phoebe just to look at her intently. Her face was cheery and flushed; when she saw his expression she pressed herself against him, her head bowed onto his shoulder; he held her tightly a moment and kissed the top of her head. Miss Cudahy called again and they went on down.

She looked thunderous. "Mr. Bingham," she said. "I heard the springs squeak."

He was very angry. "I dare say you did. I pressed the mattress to see what it was like, and Phoebe sat on the bed in the south room."

"Sat on it!" cried Miss Cudahy and motioned to Phoebe to go stand beside her. "Sat on it indeed! She jumped on it."

"Yes and lay on it," he said, thin-lipped. "It is more luxury than she is used to."

"That was my room and my mother's before me. I have restored it. I intended that you should look at the architecture and not the décor. I am displeased."

"Indeed. As though the one were not a part of the other."

"Well," she said, and suddenly she smiled and put her arm around Phoebe's legs, stroking her thigh. "One cannot be too careful. What is your opinion of what you saw upstairs?"

"It all but equals the newel in excellence."

"Quite so. Now then, Mr. Bingham," she said affably, "I think we can manage a way of working together. There are problems, of course, not insuperable ones I trust. How soon will you be able to come?"

"Why . . . I am not sure. I would have to arrange for a leave of absence beyond my usual vacation allowance."

"Rather. It will take us months at least, by my plan."

"Oh, I don't . . ."

"You have no sentimental ties in Oakland? No, and Phoebe will be with us. You will be kind to Phoebe, Mr. Bingham? She has suffered from the lack of suitable male acquaintance."

"Why," he stammered, not knowing how to avoid indelicacy, "to be sure, I am fond of Phoebe, I will be kind, there is no problem."

"She means much to me, sir. Perhaps I try, as they say, to relive my youth through her. What does it matter? I mean her to be happy." She pressed her cheek against Phoebe's hip. "Did you ever see finer legs, sir?" Phoebe smoothed indulgently the iron-gray hair, smiling at Bingham. "We must handle Phoebe with care, must we not?"

IV

On his fourth morning at Miss Cudahy's he left at dawn to drive up the coast as far as Fort Bragg. The ragged coastline, the somber landscape illuminated by spring flowers, the old barns patched with moss, the sheep, the small towns all pleased him greatly, but he found no architectural points of interest to him, nothing he had not seen the like of before. He was not concentrating well, to be sure. He rubbered along, the amateur tourist; he said to himself that he had exhausted the district, but in truth he had left his thoughts disassembled behind. He returned to Stowes Landing not long after lunch, having intended to stay away until dark.

He knocked at the door, which was kept always locked; he had not been entrusted with a key. Finally the old woman herself answered.

"Ho," she said and pounded her cane on the floor in her pleasure. "I was wanting you. It's too fine a day to waste in old houses. We're going for an outing down to Greenwood. Good. Good. Give me ten minutes in my room and I'll be ready."

"Fifteen," he said. "I want to clean up before going out again."

"Very well," she answered and stalked down the hall toward her room. "That's a fine sun they've got out there. Damn the hedge on a day like this."

There was not a sound upstairs as he washed and changed. There seldom was. He wished he knew whether Phoebe was in her room.

Miss Cudahy clumped back into the hall again and called him down. She was in front of the hall mirror arranging on her head a wide-brimmed, violet hat with a fringe of tiny tassels.

"We're off!" she cried. "Zenobia Dobbs, you must see her house. I haven't been in it for years. So you like my newel, Mr. Bingham." He exclaimed again that he did. "It's never been photographed." He said what she wanted him to say. "Well, help me down the stairs."

"I did not realize you could go down steps, Miss Cudahy."

"Down I can make it. It's up that breaks my back. You'll have to get Japheth to help you get me up."

She leaned heavily on his shoulder, taking the steps one at a time, and at the bottom she paused to snort like a horse.

"Where is Phoebe?" he asked.

"In the kitchen, I suppose. Where she belongs at any rate."

"She is coming with us?" he asked, just barely polite.

"I had not planned that she should."

"She would enjoy it," he said. "I will fetch her."

"Zenobia and she do not hit it off."

"Then I shall take Phoebe for a walk while you have tea with Mrs. Dobbs."

She did not answer him but started off toward the south side of the house.

Phoebe was not in the kitchen, not anywhere downstairs. He had to open the door to her room to see if she was in it. She was lying crosswise on her bed, like a child, her head and bare arms bright in the sunshine that poured through her window. She had taken off her shoes and stockings; her legs were stretched up the side of the wall, one foot rubbing the other. He shook his head to clear it, and told her—he had learned more of her sign language—to put on her bathing suit and come for a trip. She clapped her hands with joy, leaped up, and pushed him out of her room playfully.

They found Miss Cudahy waving her cane at glowering Japheth and threatening to beat him. Bingham led her to the car.

"Hmph," she snorted as the three of them drove away. "They said he was hopeless but I knew I could handle him. The fools, they decided he needed love and kindness, but he took it for weakness. I've had him for years, and I give him unbuttered bread and a whip. And liquor on Saturday night."

"Miss Cudahy," he said, "have you ever considered having Phoebe taught to speak? I believe there are people who . . ."

"I have considered it, Mr. Bingham, but I shall not have it done. She is happy. At Mrs. Dobbs' you will return for me at five o'clock, and she will show you the house. You might leave Phoebe in the car."

"I would hate to leave Phoebe in the car," he said, and he told himself that only if the house were very attractive would he do it.

Phoebe, seeing their angry heads, leaned forward from the back seat and laid a restraining hand on each of them.

"In the eyes of God, Mr. Bingham, she may be worth ten of us. Meanwhile she does what I tell her to do and I'd thank you to remember it." He just managed to swallow his anger. As it were in payment she said, "My grandfather, of whom I was telling you yesterday, brought the newel and the two mantels around the Horn on his own ship. They cost him a fortune."

He touched Phoebe's hand with his and so did Miss Cudahy. They smiled at her and fell silent. There was brilliant sunlight all the way to Elk.

They spent two hours on the beach alone. There was a tunnel through a tall rock island a few yards offshore through which the ocean drove, frothing and soughing; once, the tide coming in, a great wave made a whistling noise in the tunnel. A northbound ship near the horizon spent the two hours going out of sight. They found some crabs in a pool and scared them back into their ledge and laughed at their anger and clicking. The water was too cold for swimming but they waded in it a little; most of the time they lay on the sand. Bingham thought her legs to be in the lovely hinterland between trim and heavy, and from the way she took off her skirt, from the way she displayed them and drew his head once down into her lap, he knew she wanted him to admire them, to touch them with his fingers. There was scarcely a moment when they were not touching.

He asked her if she wanted to learn to speak. She smiled rather wistfully and nodded, but told him she was happy anyway. He told her it was a shame that Miss Cudahy would not do it. She shook her head and put a finger on his lips. He told her there was a school in Oakland where she could learn to speak. She closed her eyes, smiling, till he promised not to continue with the subject, and she kissed the tip of his nose. They were half an hour late for Miss Cudahy. He did not think the Dobbs house worth enough to abandon Phoebe in the car just to see it.

Miss Cudahy did not seem to mind their being late; she seemed mellow. Several times on the way home she motioned for Phoebe's hand, pressed it against her cheek, nipped at her finger with her lips. "You are keeping our bargain, Mr. Bingham," she said. "I have never known Phoebe to be happier. Tomorrow may be a good day for you to commence your photography."

Japheth and he together got her up the front steps; the problem was to transport her in such a way as to let her think they were only helping her. Japheth did not even try, and she was furious with him. Once she beat Bingham on the neck. "I'm so sorry," she trumpeted. "Mistake, mistake." And she beat Japheth the harder for her error. He spat on the steps as he went back to work in the garden.

At dinner Bingham found it just possible to be civil. Miss Cudahy was wheezing a good deal and did not make much demand upon him; he was able to brood inward upon his own thoughts. They were not even thoughts, just two strong sensations about which his mind prowled and peered with no result: Miss Cudahy's mistaken blow on his neck and, quite as vivid though smaller and softer, the warm light kiss Phoebe had put there as soon as she could to make up for the blow. He had not been struck in anger since he was a child, nor kissed so tenderly. He did not know what to make of such strong experience. He felt neither anger nor gratitude, felt nothing that deserved so differentiated a name as resentment, say, or affection; indeed, so far as he knew he felt nothing except, on the skin and down into the muscles of his neck, the two touches of the two women. Yet, when at the end of the meal, staring at a crumb like a yogi, he did not hear Miss Cudahy ask him a question and she rapped on her tumbler with her ring, barking out, "Mr. Bingham," he started from his chair and glared at her wildly a moment, leaned on the edge of the table, and whispered intently, "No! No!"

"No coffee?" she said, a little taken aback.

He subsided under Phoebe's restraining hand. "Sorry," he mumbled, "I was thinking of something else. Yes, coffee please." He had been feeling more than touches on the neck, and with that feudal rap on the glass some of it began turmoiling up and out.

He did not even assist Miss Cudahy from her chair, but bolted into the kitchen where he wiped dishes for Phoebe as she washed. She kept her eyes downcast on her business, even when he patted her arm for attention or physically turned her head about she did not look at his eyes, but only at his lips or at his hands stumbling and tripping in their rush like lips stuttering from anger; once she caught the frustrated things and kissed each palm gently, then turned back to her suds. He stood beside her, the kisses warm in his hands, just staring at her; feeling his chin begin to quiver he bustled back to his job. But his anger was gone, and all he felt now was that Phoebe was altogether delicate and alive and pitiable and needing to be saved. He understood now, without hatred, how Miss Cudahy would want to hold her; but Phoebe must be saved, more, she must want to be saved.

As she was hanging up the dishcloth, finished, he held her waist with a gentleness she immediately recognized, for she looked back over her shoulder up into his eyes; he kissed her; scarcely moving, she yielded against him. There were tears in their eyes when they drew apart, and at that instant Bingham felt that he might have fetched her coat and hat and driven her off to Oakland without an objection from her. But she must freely desire to leave Miss Cudahy, she must not be swayed from that old woman's will only to become subject to his, though better, will. He sat her by the oven, poured a cup of coffee for each of them, sat in front of her so that their knees touched, and asked her, "Will you come to Oakland with me?" It would have been coy of her, gazing against his earnest gaze, to treat his question playfully, to pretend she didn't take him seriously—the leap of eagerness that brightened her eyes and pressed her hands together meant to him only that she wanted to come to Oakland, yet she did not sign the answer in return. "I can take you with me when I go. I have friends you can stay with till we find a permanent arrangement for you. Don't worry, I will make it a point to see you often." It would have been weak of her, under his insistence, to have begun crying in order to avoid meeting his challenge, yet he saw tears come to her eyes after his last pressing. He would have relented—must she not choose freely—but that she answered him then: I owe Miss Cudahy so much.

"Of course," he answered, "and you can return to her if you want, but you owe it to yourself to go to the school."

She needs me, Phoebe pleaded, what would she do without me?

And with that he pounded the table, but not too loud, for fear Miss Cudahy would hear him.

It would be like a betrayal, Phoebe told him.

"You must leave her sooner or later," he responded—No, her

head shook—"you owe it to yourself to go now." She buried her face in her hands, but in a heat of compelling he pulled them away and clutching her wrists hard said with his lips, "You must come with me."

She wilted then, as though he had uttered a magic formula, composed of common words perhaps but nonetheless magic. She would come if he would get Miss Cudahy's permission.

"But no, but no! You must come of your own free will."

Shaking her head, miserable, she sat on his lap and hid her face against his neck, so that all he could do, imagining how the old woman would greet such a proposal, was to hold Phoebe as though she were crying, in need of comforting; yet he was conscious of her warm breathing, of her lips half-kissing the soft joining of his shoulder and neck, of her woman's body which his hands were embarrassed now to hold.

Old Japheth came in for coffee and at the sight of them muttered, "Bitch! Bitch!"

In a desperation of confusion, Bingham pushed Phoebe off his lap and, flapping his hands, went up to his room.

But there was no peace for him there. To rescue her became, as he writhed on the bed in that handsome, alien room, his obsession and immediate need. His pain was purer and stronger than it could have been had he suspected for a second that there was more causing it than the desire to liberate an oppressed, afflicted person he knew. But as it was that pain was so great that he had to creep back downstairs again hoping to find Phoebe in the kitchen alone where he could bring matters to a head, for he did not know what he would do if she did not assert herself tonight. The afterwards would work itself out, and if Miss Cudahy should suffer then she should suffer.

As he reached, silently, the bottom step he saw through the half-open door to the parlor Phoebe sitting beside Miss Cudahy, who was lolling back in the chaise longue looking at her from under her eyelids and fondling her arm. For a long time he froze on that step; all he felt for that painful time was the gracefully curving, worn, smooth old wood of the rail in his hand. Quivering with emotions he did not understand and no longer cared about controlling he went into the room. As he spoke, but not until then, he realized from the suspicion of quaver in his voice that he would not be able to stand up to the old woman.

"Miss Cudahy," he said as evenly as he could manage, "I thank you for your hospitality, but I am leaving."

"What?" she cried, altogether surprised. "You are just becoming one of us."

"I am not. I am leaving immediately."

"You have not taken your photograph yet."

"No," he said; he had thought he would be adamant. "I am obliged to leave suddenly." He would make no excuse, only get out. But his eye was drawn by the exquisite proportions of the frame around the window behind the two women. "Perhaps when I come back up later this summer I shall be able to complete my study."

"*Our* book, Mr. Bingham?"

"Of course, of course, complete our study."

"Perhaps. We shall see." She thrust unhappy Phoebe from the chair. "I shall get to the bottom of this."

He packed in five minutes. Phoebe was waiting for him in the hall, tears in her eyes. He wrote down the name of the motel where he was going to stay the night and told her to come there first thing in the morning. She nodded, and looked at him in bewilderment, longingly.

At the front door he was touching her hands good-bye and telling her she must come as soon as she could, when Miss Cudahy shouted, "Send Phoebe to me at once!" He kissed her quickly on the cheek and left.

V

Waking in that alien, ugly motel, he could not remain alone but neither did he want to go near the surge of the sea. He walked toward the hills through a pleasant pasture, and as he was walking he heard bleating sheep on the other side of a fence—he watched them in the light of the high moon. They stared at him for a moment like citizens in a bus, and when he rattled the top rail of the fence they stared at him again and shied away. He played with them off and on for an hour or more, an hour of relief; their stares were simple and sufficient, they left him alone.

He lay in bed feeling as though he were floating. He put his hands under his head and gazed at the moon, not thinking so much as watching thoughts dance through his mind. The moon had wheeled into the western sky by the time he had fallen asleep.

A rattle at the door awakened him. The moon had set. He sat up and called, "Who is it?" There was another rattle and a low, amorphous cry. He opened the door to Phoebe. She grasped both his hands in hers, hard, and threw herself face down on the bed, crying, turned away from him. He closed the windows and built a fire in the stove, and then for fifteen minutes or so sat on the bed beside her, stroking her hair and arms, shuddering a little with alarm, ready to weep himself that he could say nothing to her.

At last she turned her face toward him, and gradually her crying subsided. Her mouth, now that he came to watch her face so closely, lost the contours of grief and reassumed its usual expression; hers was somehow softer than most mouths, less revealing of character, more innocent. She ceased to make those hard, inchoate cries that disturbed him. She became Phoebe again. He was astonished in a new way at how tenderly he felt toward her, thinking of what she must be suffering now partly for his sake.

"Did she scold you?" he asked, and her answer was only the most rueful smile in the world. "What is this?" He bent down to look at three fresh bruises on the back of Phoebe's leg, just above the knee. "Did she hurt you?" he said to her. She shrugged; what difference did it make? "Pinch?" She shrugged: yes, but it was the least of my pain. "Vicious," he muttered to himself, pounding the fist of one hand into the palm of the other, "damned, cruel, vicious old bitch."

Phoebe made him sit beside her and asked him if he would ever come back to the house. He told her no. Her lip quivered, she threw her arms around him as though to hold him forever and pulled him down beside her. When he could he freed himself and told her she must go with him. When are you leaving? Tomorrow, he answered, and she turned from him again to cry. He was trembling with anger so hard that Phoebe finally turned over and smiled as best she could. He gave her his handkerchief to use for her tears.

He lay down facing her and put his arm over her waist; their legs were touching. They lay looking at each other peacefully, touching gently. But it seemed to him after a time that something was required of him; the simplest, easiest thing to do would be to kiss her, but just because it was so easy he distrusted it, and besides it would be taking advantage of her as he had sworn to himself not to do; perhaps he should renew his offer to take her to the school in Oakland, assuring her again that he had meant it.

But when she saw what he was starting to tell her she stopped him, tenderly but certainly. Her hand, still and yet alive, lay curled against his throat, warm and other and loving, and seemed to him to reproach him for some lack. It was all he could do to support her unflinching gaze; in no way did she actually reproach him yet he could not respond to that gaze with a smile or in fact with any expression at all. It was not a response her gaze sought, but somehow him himself; an unpitying, devouring, utterly unmalicious gaze, it did not demand, it took. As the uneasy night wore on, lying half-embraced on his left side awkwardly, he gradually suffocated with the knowledge that Phoebe had the unopposable rights of one who, in a way he was appalled to imagine, loved.

At the first evidences of dawn he leaped up and dressed, telling her that for the sake of her reputation she must leave the motel immediately. She lay, watching his bustle with her steady, innocent, direct gaze. He stood before her, urging her to rise. Is this the last time I shall ever see you? He could not bear her directness.

"No, no, of course not, it's all settled. How could you say such a thing? You are going with me to Oakland, today, now, as soon as you've packed your bags. We're going to Miss Cudahy's now." He was frenetic and pressed too hard. "I'll be waiting for you in the car outside the hedge at nine o'clock. It's all settled?"

She smiled into tears, into the tears, he thought, of joy, and nodded. She pulled him down on top of her and held him so hard and kissed him so ardently that he was alarmed. They left the motel. For a moment, parking outside the hedge, kissing her again, he had the wild notion of driving off with Phoebe then and there, however it might look. But before he had time either to act on the impulse or to reject it, with a cry that startled him she had opened the door of the car and run in.

At nine o'clock she had not emerged from that tunnel in the hedge, nor at quarter past. At nine-thirty he got out of the car and went in the front gate. At the window of her room on the second floor Phoebe was standing, wearing her bathrobe, evidently crying. She kept shaking her head. She made a gesture, from her heart to her lips to him, that could have meant only one thing. His heart throbbing in his throat with the pity and the loss, he made the signs "Together, we must go together." If there had been any way for him to get her free from that house he would have used it at that moment; he blamed himself for having let her come back at all; he could scarcely bear to think of her life locked in as it would be and had been. She buried her face in her hands and turned slowly from the window.

He ran to the front door and pounded the knocker; there was no response. He knocked till the great door reverberated; he would have shouted had he not been afraid of alarming the neighbors. Finally there was the sound of a cane and of coughing at the end of the hallway. He trembled; his lips were tense with the recriminations with which he would greet Miss Cudahy.

She opened the door, wide, and stood staring at him. "Yes?"

Instantly he became aware of his dishevelled appearance. "As you know, my work, it is. . . ."

"Go get your Kodak, Mr. Bingham," she said, guttural with scorn. She pointed with her cane, holding her arm out full length, the garments trailing. "You may photograph my newel if you're quick about it." His mouth opened, but he did not say anything. "Mind you don't go upstairs," said Miss Cudahy, and went back down the hall.

He turned, went down the steps, and ran to his car. On his way back in, burdened with his camera and lighting equipment, he glanced furtively up, and was grateful to see that Phoebe had drawn the curtains to her room. He had to run out again for his tripod because he could not hold the camera steady. There was not another sound in the house as he worked. In fifteen minutes he had finished and left.

The NRACP

THE NATIONAL RELOCATION AUTHORITY: COLORED PERSONS

Office of Public Relations   *Colored Persons Reserve*
                                                Nevada

Dear Herb,

Pardon the letterhead. I seem to have brought no stationery of my own, it's a dull walk to the commissary, and I found this paper already in the desk drawer.

Your first letter meant more to me than I can say, and the one I received yesterday has at last aroused me from my depression. I will try to answer both of them at once. You sensed my state of mind, I could tell it from little phrases in your letter—"open your heart, though it be only to a sunset;" "try reading *Finnegans Wake*; if you ever get *into* it you won't be able to fight your way out again for months." I cherish your drolleries. They are little oases of half-light and quiet in this rasping, blinding landscape.

How I hate it! Nothing but the salary keeps me here—nothing. I have been driven into myself in a very unhealthy way. Long hours, communal eating, the choice between a badly lighted reading room full of people and my own cell with one cot and two chairs and a table, a swim in a chlorinated pool, walks in this violent, seasonless, arid land—what is there? There seem to be only two varieties of people here: those who "have culture," talk about the latest *New Yorker* cartoons, listen to imitation folk songs and subscribe to one of the less popular book clubs; and those who play poker, talk sports and sex, and drink too much. I prefer the latter type as people, but unfortunately I do not enjoy any of their activities except drinking. Since I know the language and mores of the former type, and have more inclination toward them, I am thrown with people whom I dislike intensely. In this muddle I find myself wishing, selfishly, that you were here; your companionship would mean so much to me now. But you knew better than I what the Colored Persons Reserve would mean—you were most wise to stay in Washington, most wise. You will be missing something by staying there, but I assure you it is something well worth missing.

I must mention the two universal topics of conversation. From the filing clerks to my division chief I know of no one, including myself, who does not talk absorbedly about mystery stories. A few watered-down eclectics say they haven't much preference in mysteries, but the folk songers to a man prefer the tony, phony Dorothy Sayers-S.S. Van Dine type of pseudo-literary snobbish product, and the horsy folk prefer the Dashiell Hammett romantic cum violent realism. There is one fellow—a big domed Irishman named O'Doone who wears those heavy rimmed, owlish glasses that came into style a couple of years ago just after the war—who does nothing but read and reread Sherlock Holmes, and he has won everyone's respect in some strange fashion by this quaint loyalty. He's quite shy, in a talkative, brittle way, but I think I could grow fond of him.

Everyone finds a strong need to read the damnable things, so strong that we prefer the absolute nausea of reading three in one day—I did it once myself for three days on end—to not reading any. What is it actually that we prefer not to do? I can only think of Auden's lines, "The situation of our time Surrounds us like a baffling crime." Of our time and of this job.

What are we doing here? That is the other subject none of us can let alone. We are paid fantastic salaries (the secretary whom I share with another writer gets four hundred dollars a month, tell Mary *that* one), and for one whole month we have done nothing while on the job except to read all the provisions and addenda to the Relocation Act as interpreted by the Authority or to browse at will in the large library of literature by and about Negroes, from sociological studies to newspaper poetry in dialect. You know the Act generally of course, but I hope you are never for any reason subjected to this Ph.D.-candidate torture of reading to exhaustion about a subject in which you have only a general interest. But the *why* of this strange and expensive indoctrination is totally beyond me. I thought that I was going to do much the same sort of public relations work here on the spot as we had been doing in the State Department; I thought the salary differential was just a compensation for living in this hellhole. That's what everyone here had thought too. It appears, however, that there is something more important brewing. In the whole month I have been here I have turned out only a couple of articles describing the physical charms of this desiccated cesspool; they appeared in Negro publications which I hope you have not even heard of. Beyond that I have done nothing but bore myself to death by reading Negro novels and poetry.

They are a different tribe altogether; I would be the last to deny that their primeval culture is wonderful enough to merit study—but not by me. I have enough trouble trying to understand the rudiments of my own culture without having this one pushed off onto me.

I have been stifled and confused for so long that all my pent-up emotions have found their worthiest outlet in this letter to you, my dear friend. I have been vowing (as we used to vow to quit smoking, remember?) to stop reading mysteries, but my vows seldom survive the day. Now I do solemnly swear and proclaim that each time I have the urge to read a mystery I will instead write a letter to you. If these epistles become dull and repetitious just throw them away without reading them. I'll put a mark—say an M—on the envelope

of these counter-mystery letters, so you needn't even open them if
you wish. I'm sure there will be a lot of them.

Does this sound silly? I suppose it does. But I am in a strange
state of mind. There's too much sunlight and the countryside fright-
ens me and I don't understand anything.

Bless you,
Andy

March 14

Dear Herb,

It wasn't as bad as I had feared, being without mysteries. We get
up at seven and go to work at eight. Between five and six in the
afternoon there's time for a couple of highballs. From seven or so,
when dinner is over, till ten or eleven—that's the time to watch out
for. After you have seen the movie of the week and read *Time* and
The New Yorker you discover yourself, with that autonomic gesture
with which one reaches for a cigarette, wandering toward the mystery shelf and trying to choose between Carter Dickson and John
Dickson Carr (two names for the same writer, as I hope you don't
know). On Sundays there's tennis in the early morning and bowling in the afternoon. But those gaping rents in each tightly woven,
just tolerable day remain, no matter what you do. At first I thought
I should have to tell myself bedtime stories. One evening I got half-
drunk in the club rooms and absolutely potted alone in my own
room afterward. First time in my life. Another time O'Doone and I
sat up till midnight composing an "Epitaph for a Mongoose." I
can't tell you how dreary some of our endeavors were; O'Doone still
quotes one of mine occasionally. He's a strange fellow. I can't exactly figure him out but I like him in an oblique sort of way. Neither
of us fits into any of three or four possible schemes of things here,
and we share a good deal in general outlook. But he can amuse
himself with a cerebral horseplay which only makes me uneasy.
O'Doone has a French book—God knows where he got it—on
Senegalese dialects; he goes around slapping stuffy people on the
back and mumbling, "Your grandmother on your father's side was a
pig-faced gorilla" or else a phrase which in Senegalese has something
to do with transplanting date trees but which in English sounds ob-

scene, and then he laughs uproariously. In any event, he's better off than I, who am amused by almost nothing.

Now that you have been spared the threatened dejection of my counter-mystery letters I must confess to the secret vice which I have taken up in the past week. It grows upon me too; it promises to become a habit which only age and infirmity will break. I had thought it a vice of middle age (and perhaps it is—are we not thirty-eight, Herb? When does middle age commence?). I *take walks.* I take long walks alone. If I cannot say that I enjoy them I do look forward to them with the eagerness with which an adolescent will sometimes go to bed in order to continue the dream which waking has interrupted.

Not that my walks are in any way dreamlike. They are perfectly real. But they take place in a context so different from any of the social or intellectual contexts of the CPR day and they afford such a strong emotional relief to it that I think they may be justly compared to a continued dream. My walks, however, have a worth of their own such as dreams can never have. Instead of taking me from an ugly world to a realm of unexplained symbols they have driven me toward two realities, about which I must confess I have had a certain ignorance: myself and the natural world. And standing, as I feel I do, at the starting point of high adventure I feel the explorer's excitement and awe, and no self-pity at all.

I have recaptured—and I am not embarrassed to say it—the childhood delight in stars. That's a great thing to happen to a man, Herb: to be able to leave the smoke-and-spite-laden atmosphere of bureaucracy, walk a few miles out into the huge, silent desert, and look at the stars with a delight whose purity needs no apology and whose expansiveness need find no words for description. I am astonished by the sight of a Joshua tree against the light blue twilight sky, I am entranced by the vicious innocence of one of the kinds of cactus that abound hereabouts. I enjoy these garish sunsets with a fervor that I once considered indecent. I cannot say that I like this desert —certainly not enough to live in it permanently—but it has affected me very deeply. I think that much of my trouble during my first month here was resisting the force of the desert. Now I no longer resist it, yet I have not submitted to it; rather I have developed a largeness of spirit, a feeling of calm and magnificence. Which I am sure is in part lightheadedness at having such a weight of nasty care removed all at once, but which is wonderful while it lasts.

But it's not *just* lightheadedness. Some obstruction of spirit, an obstruction of whose existence I was not even aware, has been removed within me, so that now I can and dare observe the complexities of that catalogued, indifferent, unaccountable natural world which I had always shrugged at. One saw it from train windows, one dealt with it on picnics, one admired the nasturtiums and peonies of one's more domesticated friends, one approved of lawns and shade trees. What then? What did one know of the rigidity of nature's order or of the prodigality with which she wastes and destroys and errs? I came here furnished only with the ordinary generic names of things—snake, lizard, toad, rabbit, bug, cactus, sagebrush, flower, weed—but already I have watched a road runner kill a rattlesnake and I am proud that I know how rabbits drink. Do you know how rabbits drink? If you ask what difference it makes to know this I can happily reply, "None at all, but it gives me pleasure." A pleasure which does not attempt to deny mortality, but accepts it and doesn't care—a true pleasure and one worth cherishing.

11 P.M.

I owe it to you, I know, to give a somewhat less personal, less inward account of this place. But a calculated, itemized description of anything, much less of so monstrous a thing as a desert, is beyond me. Instead I'll try to give you an idea of what effect such physical bigness can have upon the people in it.

Our buildings are situated at the head of a very long valley—the Tehuala River Valley—which is partially arable and which is good for grazing purposes in both the upper and lower regions. The highway into the valley (that is, the highway that leads to the east, as well as the railroad) runs not far from our settlement. Being public relations, we are located just within the fence, a huge, barbarous fence with guards. We have had a rather surprising number of visitors already, and hundreds more are expected during the summer. Our eight buildings are flat-roofed, gray, of a horizontal design, and air-conditioned. But our view of the valley is cut off by a sharp bend about four or five miles below us. The tourists, in other words, can see almost nothing of the valley or of the Reserve stretching for eight hundred miles to the southwest, for this is the only public entrance to the Reserve and no airplanes are permitted over any part of it. Around the turn in the upper valley is yet another even more barbarous, even better guarded fence, past which no one goes except certain Congressmen, the top officials (four, I believe) in the NRACP, and SSE (Special Service Employees, who, once they have gone past that gate, do not return and do not communicate with the outside world even by letter). All this secrecy—you can fill in details to suit yourself—is probably unnecessary, but it does succeed in arousing an acute sense of mystery and speculation about the Reserve.

Well, being no more than human I walked the five miles to the bend the other day, climbed a considerable hill nearby, and looked out over the main sweep of the valley for the first time. I was hot and tired when I reached the foot of the hill so I sat down—it was around 5:30—and ate the snack I had brought. When I reached the top of the hill the sun was about to set; the long shadows of the western hills lay over the floor of the valley and in some places extended halfway up the hills to the east. Far, far to the west, just to the north of the setting sun, was a snow-capped mountain, and immediately in front of me, a mile and a half or so away, stretched the longest building I have ever seen in my life. It had a shed roof rising away from me and there were no windows on my side of the building. Nothing whatsoever broke the line of its continuous gray back. It was at least a mile long, probably longer. Beyond it lay dozens of buildings exactly like this one except for their length; some of them ran, as the long one did, east and west, some ran north and south, some aslant. I could not estimate to my satisfaction how large most of them were; they seemed to be roughly the size of small factories. The effect which their planner had deliberately calculated and achieved was that of a rigidly patterned, unsymmetrical (useless?) articulation of a restricted flat area. Nothing broke the effect, and for a reason which I cannot define these buildings in the foreground gave such a focus and order to the widening scene that lay before me that I stood for the better part of an hour experiencing a pure joy—a joy only heightened by my grateful knowledge that these Intake buildings were designed to introduce an entire people to the new and better world beyond. The fine farms and ranches

and industries and communities which would arise from these un-
developed regions took shape in the twilight scene before me, shim-
mering in the heat waves rising from the earth.

But presently it was quite dark—the twilights are very brief here—
and I was awakened from my reverie by the lights going on in one
of the buildings before me. I returned to the PR settlement and to
my solitary room in a state of exaltation which has not yet deserted
me.

For an hour, the Universe and History co-extended before me and
they did not exclude me. For while I am but a grain on the shore of
event only within my consciousness did this co-extending take place
and have any meaning. For that long moment mine was the power.

I will write again soon.

Andy

March 20

Dear Herb,

You complain that I didn't say anything directly about my voyage
of discovery into myself as I had promised in my last letter. And that
the internal high pressures of urban life are blowing me up like a
balloon in this rarefied atmosphere.

Maybe so. I'll try to explain what has been going on. But I forgot to take a cartographer on my voyage, so that my account may
resemble, in crudeness, that of an Elizabethan freebooter in Carib-
bean waters. (If I had the energy I'd try to synthesize these balloon
voyage metaphors, but I haven't.)

It all began when I asked myself on one of my walks why I was
here, why I had taken this job. $8,000 a year—yes. The social impor-
tance of the project—maybe (but not my personal importance to the
project). Excitement at being in on the beginning of a great experiment in planning—yes. The hope of escaping from the pressures of
Washington life—yes. These are valid reasons all of them, but on the
other side—why I should want *not* to come here—are better reasons
altogether. An utter absence of urban life. No friends. No chance of
seeing Betty. The loss of permanent position (this one you pointed
out most forcefully) in State for a better paid but temporary job here.
Too inadequate a knowledge of my duties, or of the whole NRACP

for that matter, to permit me to have made a decision wisely. And an overpowering hatred of restrictions. (Never once, Herb, for three years to be allowed to leave this Reserve! I've been sweating here for seven weeks, but 156 weeks! Christ!) Now I had known, more or less, all these factors before I came here, all these nice rational, statistical factors. But when I asked myself the other night in the false clarity of the desert moonlight why I had chosen to come, why really, I still could not answer myself satisfactorily. For I was still certain of one thing: that none of the logical reasons, none of my recognized impulses would have brought me here singly or combined.

Being in the mood I also asked myself why I had continued to live with Clarice for five years after I had known quite consciously that I did not love her but felt a positive contempt for her. Betty accounted for part of it, and the usual fear of casting out again on one's own. But I would not have been on my own in any obvious sense; I am sure you know of my love affairs during those five years; I could have married any of three or four worthy women. I asked myself why it was that from the moment Clarice decided once and for all to divorce me (she did the deciding, not me; I don't think you knew that) I lost my taste for my current inamorata and have not had a real affair since.

These questions I was unable to answer, but at least I was seriously asking them of myself. I was willing and able to face the answers. The key to the answer came from my long-limbed, mildly pretty, efficient, but (I had originally thought) frivolous and banal secretary, Ruth. She is one of those women who because they do not have an "intellectual" idea in their noodles are too frequently dismissed as conveniently decorative but not very valuable. Perhaps Ruth really is that, but she has made two or three remarks recently which seem to me to display an intuitive intelligence of a considerable order. Yet they may be merely aptly chosen, conventional observations; it is hard to tell. She interests me. She has a maxim which I resent but cannot refute: "There are those who get it and those who dish it out; I intend to be on the side of the dishers." (Is this the post-Christian golden rule? It has its own power, you know.) In any case, the other day I was sitting in my cubicle of an office, in front of which Ruth's desk is placed—she services two of us. I had my feet up on the desk in a rather indecorous fashion, and I had laid the book I was reading on my lap while I smoked a cigarette. I suppose I was daydreaming a little. Suddenly Ruth opened the door and entered. I started, picked up the book, and took my feet off the table top.

Ruth cocked an eye at me and said, "You like to feel guilty, don't you? All I wanted to know was whether you could spare time for a cup of coffee."

So we went to the café and had coffee and didn't even mention her statement or its cause.

But it set me thinking; the longer I thought about it the better I liked it. I had always discounted wild, Dostoevskian notions like that as being too perverse to be true, but now I am not at all sure that frivolous, red-nailed Ruth wasn't right. So long as Clarice had been there to reprove me for my infidelities I had indulged in them. When her censorship was removed, the infidelities or any love affairs at all lost their spice, the spice being the guilt that she made me feel about them. Then, having divorced Clarice, I took this job. The job is a sop to my sense of guilt at being white and middle-class (that is to say, one of Ruth's "dishers"), a sop because I am participating in an enterprise whose purpose is social justice. At the same time it is a punishment because of the deprivations I am undergoing; yet the actual luxury of my life and my actual status in the bureaucracy, high but not orthodox, privileged yet not normally restricted, nourishes the guilt which supports it. I suppose Freud could tell me what it is that causes the sense of guilt in the first place, but I am not going to bother to find out. There are certain indecencies about which one ought not to inquire unless one has to. Social guilt—that is to say a sense of responsibility toward society—is a good thing to have, and I intend to exploit it in myself. I intend to satisfy it by doing as fine a job as I possibly can; furthermore I intend to find a worthy European family, Italian perhaps, who are impoverished and to support them out of my salary. I must confess that the CARE packages we sent to Europe immediately after the war made me feel better than all the fine sentiments I ever gave words to.

I am grateful that I came here. I have been thrown back upon myself in a way that has only benefited me.

We begin work soon. The first trainload of Negroes arrived today, five hundred of them. They are going through Intake (the buildings I described in my last letter) and our work, we are told, will commence within a few days. Exactly what we are to do we will be briefed on tomorrow. I look forward to it eagerly.

Andy

I read this letter over before putting it in the envelope. That was a mistake. All the excitement about myself which I had felt so keenly sounds rather flat as I have put it. There must be a great deal for me yet to discover. As you know, I have never spent much of my energy in intimacies, either with myself or with other people. One gets a facismile of it when talking about the universal stereotypes of love with a woman. But this desert has thrown me back upon myself, and from your letter I take it you find my explorations of interest. However, you must not expect many more letters in so tiresome a vein. I will seal and mail this one tonight lest I repent in the morning.

April 10

Dear Herb,

I have not known how to write this letter, though I've tried two or three times in the past week to do it. I'm going to put it in the form of a homily with illustrations. The text: "There are those who get it and those who dish it out; I intend to be on the side of the dishers."

First, in what context did it occur? It is the motto of a charming young woman (any doubts I may have expressed about her are withdrawn as of now; she is all one could ask for) who is not malicious and who does not in the least want to impose her beliefs or herself upon other people. She sends one hundred dollars a month to her mother, who is dying of cancer in a county hospital in Pennsylvania. When she told me she was sending the money I asked her why.

"Why?" said Ruth. "I'm disappointed in you to ask me such a thing."

"All right be disappointed, but tell me why."

She shrugged in a humorous way. "She's my mother. And anyway," she added, "we're all dying, aren't we?"

The important thing to note about Ruth is that she means it but she doesn't care. Just as she doesn't really care whether you like her clothes or her lovely hair; she does and you should—the loss is yours if you don't. She was reared in a perfectly usual American city, and she has chosen from its unconscious culture the best in custom and attitude.

But she said it here in the public relations division of the Colored Persons Reserve, here where there is as much getting and dishing out as anywhere in the world, where the most important Negro in the Reserve, its president, may be in a very real sense considered inferior to a white window washer. The first time O'Doone heard her say it (he had dropped by to talk awhile and Ruth had joined us) he made the sign of the cross in the air between himself and Ruth and backed clear out of the room. He didn't return either. I'm sure he's not religious. I don't know why he did that.

What does the statement imply? Primarily it makes no judgment and does not urge to action. It is unmoral. "There is a condition such that some people must inflict pain and others must receive it; since it is impossible to be neutral in this regard and since I like neither to give nor to take injury I shall choose the path of least resistance. I shall ally myself with the inflictors not because I like their side and certainly not because I dislike the other side but only because in that way I myself am least interfered with." No regret, no self-deception (*it is impossible to be neutral*), only true resignation. This circumstance is as it is, and it will not and should not be otherwise. There is a certain intensity of joy possible after resignation of this order greater than we frustrated hopers know. (Where do I fit into this scheme? I think I have discovered one thing about myself from contemplating Ruth's maxim: I want profoundly to be a disher, but my training has been such, or perhaps I am only so weak, that I am incapable of being one with a clear conscience. Consequently I find myself in a halfway position: dishing it out, yes, but at the behest of people I have never seen, and to people I will never know.) Ruth took a job with the NRACP for the only right reason: not for any of my complicated ones nor for the general greed but because she saw quite clearly that here was one of the very pure instances of getting it and of dishing it out. She left a job as secretary to an executive in General Electric for this. I think she gets a certain pleasure from seeing her philosophy so exquisitely borne out by event. Ruth is twenty-seven. I think I am in love with her. I am sure she is not in love with me.

Tell me, Herb, does not this maxim ring a bell in you? This girl has had the courage to put into deliberate words her sense of the inevitable. Do you not admire her for it? And is she not right? She is right enough. If you doubt it let me tell you what our job here is.

The authorities consider the situation potentially explosive enough to warrant the most elaborate system of censorship I have ever heard of. To begin with there is a rule that during his first week in the Reserve every Negro may write three letters to persons on the outside. After that period is over only one letter a month is permitted. Now all letters leaving here during the first week are sent to PR where they are censored and typed in the correct form (on NRACP letterhead); the typed copies are sent on and the originals are filed. The reason for this elaborate system is interesting enough and probably sound; every endeavor is to be made to discourage any leaking out of adverse reports on conditions in the CPR. There are some fourteen million Negroes in the nation not all of whom are entirely pleased with the prospect of being relocated, and there are an indeterminate number of Caucasian sympathizers—civil liberties fanatics for the most part—who could cause trouble if any confirmation of their suspicions about the CPR should leak out. We have put out a staggering amount of data on the climatic, agricultural, power production, and mining conditions of the region, and we have propagandized with every device in the book. Yet we know well enough how long it takes for propaganda to counteract prejudice, and sometimes how deceptive an apparent propaganda success can be. We are more than grateful that almost the entire news outlet system of the nation is on our side.

Well, after the three letters of the first week have been typed and sent the writer's job begins. Every effort is made to discourage the interned Negroes from writing to the outside. For one thing we keep in our files all personal letters incoming during the first month. Anyone who continues to write to an internee after this month needs to be answered. The filing clerks keep track of the dates, and forward all personal letters to us. (The clerks think we send the letters on to the internees.) We then write appropriate responses to the letters in the style of the internee as we estimate it from his three letters. We try to be as impersonal as possible, conveying the idea that everything is fine. Why do we not forward the letters to the internees to answer? First of all we do, if the internees request it. They are told that they will receive letters only from those persons whose letters they request to see, and such a request involves yards of red tape. Very few are expected to use the cumbersome mechanism at all. Secondly we write the letters for them simply to save ourselves time and trouble. We would have a lot of rewriting to do anyway; this method assures us of complete control and an efficient modus operandi. Any Negro outside who writes too many insistent letters will be, at our request, relocated within a month; we do not want any unnecessary unhappiness to result from the necessarily painful program. Friends and relatives are to be reunited as fast as possible. Whole communities are to be relocated together to avoid whatever wrenches in personal relationships we can avoid.

Is not this getting it and dishing it out on a fine scale? All for very good reasons I know, but then is it not conceivable that there are always good reasons for the old crapperoo? Sometimes I feel absolutistic enough to say, *if it's this bad for any ultimate reason whatsoever then to hell with it.* After which sentiment comes the gun at the head. But then reason reinstates my sense of the relativity of values, and on I go writing a letter to Hector Jackson of South Carolina explaining that I've been so busy putting up a chicken house and plowing that I haven't had a chance to write but I hope to see you soon. (I doubt if I will.)

Andy

I forgot to mention—I have a special job, which is to censor the letters of all the clerical personnel in PR. One of my duties is to censor any reference to the censorship! A strange state of affairs. None of them know that this job is mine; most think the censor must be some Mail Department employee. I must say one looks at some people with new eyes after reading their correspondence.

I need hardly say—but in case there is any doubt I will say—that this letter is absolutely confidential. How much of our system will become publicly known I cannot guess but naturally I don't want to jump the official gun in this regard.

April 12

Dear Herb,

Let me tell you about the strange adventure I had last evening. I am still not quite sure what to make of it.

Immediately after work I picked up a few sandwiches and a pint of whiskey and walked out into the desert on one of my hikes. One more meal with the jabber of the café and one more of those good but always good in the same way dinners and I felt I should come apart at the seams. (Another thing I have learned about myself: I am ill-adapted to prison life.) I had no goal in view; I intended to stroll.

But I found myself heading generally in the direction of the hill from which I had looked over the Tehuala Valley and the city of CPR Intake buildings. I came across nothing particularly interesting in a natural history way so that by early dusk I was near to the hill. I decided to climb it again and see what I could see.

The first thing I saw, in the difficult light of dusk, was a soldier with a gun standing at the foot of the hill. I came around a large clump of cactus and there he was, leaning on his rifle. He immediately pointed it at me and told me to go back where I belonged. I objected that I had climbed this hill before and that I could see no reason why I shouldn't do it again. He replied that he didn't see any reason either, but I couldn't just the same; they were going to put up another fence to keep people like me away. I cursed at the whole situation; if I had dared I would have cursed him too, for he had been rude as only a guard with a gun can be. But before I left I pulled out my pint and took a slug of it. The guard was a changed man.

"Christ," he said, "give me a pull."

"I should give you a pull."

"Come on," he said, "I ain't had a drop since I came to this hole. They won't even give us beer."

"All right, if you'll tell me what the hell's going on around here."

He made me crouch behind a Joshua tree, and he himself would not look at me while he talked. I asked him the reason for all the precautions.

"They got a searchlight up top the hill with machine guns. They sweep the whole hill all the time. They can see plain as day in the dark. They keep an eye on us fellows down here. I know. I used to run the light."

"I haven't seen any light," I said.

He glanced at me with scorn.

"It's black," he said. "They cut down all the bushes all around the top part of that hill. Anybody comes up in the bare place—pttt! *Any*body. Even a guard."

"I still don't see any light."

"Man, it's black light. You wear glasses and shine this thing and you can see better than you can with a regular light searchlight. It's the stuff. We used to shoot rabbits with it. The little bastards never knew what hit them!"

I didn't want to appear simple so I didn't ask any more questions about the black light. He was an irascible fellow, with a gun and a knife, and he had drunk most of the bottle already.

"Why do you let me stay at all?" I asked.

"Can't see good in the dusk. Not even them can't."

I couldn't think of anything more to say.

"I used to be guard on the railroad they got inside. Say, have they got a system! Trains from the outside go through an automatic gate. All the trainmen get on the engine and drive out. Then we come up through another automatic gate and hook on and drag it in. Always in the daytime. Anybody tried to hop train, inside or out—pttt! Air-conditioned box cars made out of steel. Two deep they come. Never come in at night."

"Are you married?"

"Ain't nobody married up front, huh?"

I didn't answer.

"Well, is there?"

"No, but there could be if anybody felt like it."

"Well, there ain't even a woman inside. Not a damn one. They let us have all the nigger women we want. Some ain't so bad. Most of them fight a lot."

He smashed the pint bottle on a rock nearby. "Why didn't you bring some real liquor, God damn you?" he said in a low voice full of violence. "Get the hell back home where you belong. Get out of here. It's getting dark. I'll shoot the guts out of you too. Bring me something I can use next time, huh? Get going.

"Stay under cover," he shouted after me. "They're likely to get you if they spot you. They can't miss if it's dark enough."

The last I heard of him he was coughing and spitting and swearing. I was as disgusted as scared, and I must confess I was scared stiff.

I walked homeward, slowly recovering my emotional balance, trying to understand what had happened to me with that guard, the meaning of what he had told me. For some absurd reason the tune

In the Gloaming kept running through my head in the idiotic way tunes will; I was unable to concentrate intelligently upon the situation.

I heard a sound at some distance to my left. I stopped, suddenly and inexplicably alarmed to the point of throbbing temples and clenched fists. A slim figure in brown came through the cactus; as it approached I could see that it was a young woman. She did not see me, but her path brought her directly to where I was standing. I did not know whether to accost her at a distance or to let her come upon me where I stood. By the time I had decided not to accost her I could see that it was Ruth.

"Why Ruth!" I cried with all the emotion of relief and gratified surprise in my voice and perhaps something more. "What are you doing here?"

She started badly, then seeing who it was she hurried up to me and to my surprise took my arms and put them around her body. "Andy, I am so glad to see you. Some good angel must have put you here for me."

I squeezed her, we kissed, a friendly kiss, then she drew away and shook herself. She had almost always called me Mr. Dixon before; there was a real affection in her "Andy."

"What's the matter?" I asked her. "Where have you been?"

"I didn't know you took walks too."

"Oh yes. It's one way to keep from going nuts."

She laughed a little and squeezed my arm. I could not refrain from kissing her again, and this time it was not just a friendly kiss.

"Where did you go?" I asked again.

"To that hill. I went up there a couple of times before. There was a guard there who wanted to lay me."

We didn't speak for a few moments.

"I think he almost shot me for giving him the brushoff. I didn't look back when I left, but I heard him click his gun. You don't know how glad I was to see you."

So we kissed again and this time it was serious.

"Wait a minute," she said, "wait a minute."

She unlocked her arm from mine, and we continued on our way not touching.

"I had some trouble with a guard too," I said. "I wonder why they're so damned careful to keep us away."

"Mine told me they didn't want us to get any funny ideas. He said things aren't what they seem to be in there."

"Didn't you ask him what he meant?"

"Sure. That's when he said I'd better shut up and let him lay me or else he'd shoot me. So I walked off. I'm not going to call on *him* again."

I put my arm around her. I can't tell you how fond I was of her at that moment, of her trim, poised body, her courage, her good humor, her delightful rich voice and laughter. But she only kissed me gently and withdrew.

"I want to keep my head for a while, darling," she said.

I knew what she meant. We walked on in silence, hand in hand. It was moonlight. If I was lightheaded now I knew why.

When we were about half a mile from our buildings we came across O'Doone also returning from a walk.

"Well," he said brightly, "it *is* a nice moon, isn't it?"

It wouldn't do to say that we had met by accident; I was embarrassed, but Ruth's fine laugh cleared the air for me.

"Nicest I ever saw," she said.

"Did you ever walk up that hill," I asked him, "where you can see out over the valley?"

"Once," he said in a surprisingly harsh voice. "I'd rather play chess."

We went into one of the recreation rooms and O'Doone beat me at three games of chess. Ruth sat by, knitting—a sweater for a cousin's baby. We talked little, but comfortably. It would have been a domestic scene if it had not been for the fifty or sixty other people in the room.

Herb, what does it all mean?

Andy

April 20

Dear Herb,

[If all goes well you will receive the following letter from Ruth's cousin, who will be informed by O'Doone's sister to forward it to you. O'Doone's sister will also send you instructions on how to make the invisible ink visible. I first wrote the letter in visible ink, intending to mail it in the usual way, I was prepared to take all the certainly drastic consequences that would come from its being read by someone of authority. But O'Doone's invisible ink (what a strange fellow to have brought a quart of it here! He said he had brought it only to play mysterious letter games with his nephew. I wonder.) and Ruth's baby sweater, upon the wrapping of which I write this, combined to save me. If the authorities catch *this* I don't care what happens. It takes so long to write lightly enough in invisible ink for no pen mark to show on the paper that I doubt if I will have the patience to use it often. Most of my letters will be innocuous in regular ink. I may add an invisible note or two, between the lines, in the margin, or at the end. O'Doone says it's not any of the ordinary kinds and if we're careful the authorities are not likely to catch us. O'Doone is strange. He refused to take this whole ink matter for anything more than a big joke, as though we were digging a tunnel under a house, O'Doone pretending we are just tunneling in a strawstack to hide our marbles, myself trying to protest (but being laughed at for my lapse in taste) that we are really undermining a house in order to blow it up. Which perhaps we are. In any event I don't have the energy left to rewrite this letter, I'll merely copy it off invisibly.]

I cannot tell you how shocked I was to discover the familiar, black censor's ink over five lines in your last letter. The censor censored! I had not thought of that. In my innocence I had thought that we writers in the higher brackets could be trusted to be discreet. One would think I was still a loyal subscriber to the *Nation* I was so naïve. But no—I am trusted to censor the letters of inferiors (I suspect my censorship is sample-checked by someone), but my own letters are themselves inspected and their dangerous sentiments excised. And, irony of ironies, your own references to the fact that my letters were censored were themselves blacked out.

Who is it that does this? The head of PR here? That's a strange way to make him waste his time. One of his assistants? Then the head must censor the assistant's letters. And the chief board of the NRACP censors the head's letters? And the President theirs? And God his? And . . . ?

Which is the more imprisoned: the jailer who thinks he is free and is not, or the prisoner who knows the precise boundaries of his liberty and accepting them explores and uses all the world he has?

I am a jailer who knows he is not free. I am a prisoner who does not know the limits of his freedom. All this I voluntarily submitted to in the name of a higher freedom. Ever since my adolescence, when the New Deal was a faith, liberty has been one of the always repeated, never examined articles of my creed. Well, I have been examining liberty recently, and she's a pure fraud.

One thing I have learned: you don't just quietly put yourself on the side of Ruth's dishers, you become one of them yourself. A disher *has* to dish it out, he cannot help it at all, and he pays for it. Or maybe I am only paying for my guilt-making desire to be a more important disher than I am.

Ruth was surprised at my distress upon receiving your censored letter. She only shrugged. What had I expected, after all? It was inevitable, it was a necessity. That's the key word, Herb, *necessity*. Not liberty, *necessity*. True liberty is what the prisoner has, because he accepts *necessity*. That's the great thing, to recognize and accept *necessity*.

I've been working slowly toward a realization of this. I think my decision to work in the NRACP came from recognizing the social necessity of it. The Negro problem in America was acute and it was insoluble by any liberal formula. This solution gives dignity and independence to the Negroes. It staves off the depression by the huge demand for manufactured products, for transportation, for the operations of the NRACP itself; but perhaps most important of all, it establishes irrevocably in the American people's mind the wisdom and rightness of the government, for if capitalism must go (as it must) it should be replaced peaceably by a strong and wise-planned state. Such a state we are proving ourselves to be. Very well. I accepted this. But what I forgot was that I, I the individual, I Andrew Dixon, must personally submit to the stringencies of necessity. The relics of the New Deal faith remained to clutter up my new attitude. This experience, coming when and as it did, particularly coming when Ruth's courageous wisdom was nearby to support me, has liberated me (I hope) into the greater freedom of the prisoner of necessity.

At least such are my pious prayers. I cannot say I am sure I fully understand all the strictures of necessity. I *can* say I do not enjoy those I understand. But pious I will remain.

Remember the days when we thought we could *change* necessity? Democracy and all that? How much older I feel!

Andy

May 1

Mary my dear,

Please let me apologize—sincerely too, Mary—for having neglected you so cruelly for the past months. Herb tells me you are quite put out, and well you might be. I can find no excuses for it, but I will stoutly maintain that it was not a question of hostility or indifference to you, my dear. Actually I have been going through something of a crisis, as Herb may have been telling you. It has something to do with the desert, and something to do with the NRACP, and a lot to do with the charming young woman whose picture I enclose. She is Ruth Cone. We are getting married in a couple of Sundays—Mother's Day. Why Mother's Day I really don't know, but she wants it so there's no help. The details of our plighting troth might amuse you.

A couple of evenings ago I was playing chess in the recreation room with a man named O'Doone, my only friend here. Ruth was sitting beside us knitting some rompers for a cousin's baby. From time to time we would chat a little; it was all very comfortable and unromantic. O'Doone, between games, went to the toilet. When he had left Ruth said to me with a twinkle in her eye, "Andy darling, don't you see what I am doing?" I replied, "Why yes, my sweet, knitting tiny garments. Is it . . . ?" And we both laughed heartily. It was a joke, you see, a mild comfortable little joke, and no one would have thought of it a second time except that when we had finished laughing it was no longer a joke. Her face became very sober and I am sure mine did too. I said, "Do you want children, Ruth?" "Yes," she replied. "Do you want to have my children?" "Yes," she said again, without looking at me. Then with the most charming conquest of modesty that you can imagine she turned her serious little face to me, and we very lightly kissed. O'Doone had returned by then. "Well," he said in a bright way, "do I interrupt?" "Not at all," I answered, "we have just decided to get married." He burbled a little, in caricature of the overwhelmed, congratulating friend, pumped our hands, and asked us when we were marrying. "I

don't know," I said. "Why not tomorrow?" "Oh no," said Ruth
severely, "how can I assemble my trousseau?" At which O'Doone
went off into a braying laugh, and we set up the chess pieces. "Bet
you five to one," he said, "I win this game in less than sixty moves."
I wouldn't take his bet. It took him about forty moves to beat me.
Thus did Dixon and Cone solemnly vow to share their fortunes.

It's the first marriage in PR. Everybody will attend. The chief
promised me Monday off and temporary quarters in one of the
guest suites. We are to get a two-room apartment in the new dormitory that is nearly completed. Such privacy and spaciousness will
make us the envy of the whole community. I'm sure there will be a
spate of marriages as soon as the dormitory is completed. We will
not be married by a holy man, partly because neither of us believes
in it and partly because there isn't one of any kind on the premises.
(I wonder why there were those detailed questions about religious
beliefs on our application forms.) There was a little trouble at first
about who was authorized to marry people here. The PR chief, as
the only person permitted to leave the place, went out and got
himself authorized to do it legally. I think he rather fancies himself
in the capacity of marrier. He runs to paternalism.

Ruth urges me—she assumes quite rightly that I have not done it
already—to tell you some of the homely details of life here. Of our
sleeping rooms the less said the better. The beds are comfortable,
period. We live quite communally, but very well. There's a fine
gymnasium with swimming pool and play fields attached—tennis,
baseball, squash, fencing, everything but golf. There's the best library (surely the best!) in the world on American Negro affairs, and
a reasonably good one of modern literature. We have comfortable
working quarters and a long working day. There is a fine desert for
us to walk around in, and I have come to need an occasional stroll
in the desert for spiritual refreshment. And we eat handsomely, except for vegetables. In fact, the only complaint that I have of the
cooking is the monotony of its excellence: roast, steak, chop, stew.
Almost never liver and kidneys and omelettes and casseroles, and
always frozen vegetables. Well, probably the Negroes will be produc-
ing plenty of vegetables within a few weeks. There's lots of liquor of
every kind. There is a sort of department store where one can buy
everything one needs and most of the luxuries one could want in
this restricted life. There's a movie a week—a double-feature with

news and cartoon—and bridge or poker every day. A microcosmic plenitude.

As for the rest of our routine life here I can think of nothing interesting enough to mention. We work and avoid work, backbite, confide, suspect. It's a bureaucratic existence, no doubt of that.

Will this epistle persuade you to forgive me?

Now you must write to me—soon.

Devotedly yours,
Andy

(*In invisible ink, between the lines of the preceding letter*)

O'Doone, who sometimes gives his opinions very obliquely, came to me today with some disturbing figures. He wasn't in the least jaunty about them and I must confess that I am not either.

According to *Time*, which seems to know more about the CPR than we do, there have been about 50,000 Negroes interned already, and these 50,000 comprise nearly all the wealthy and politically powerful Negroes in the nation (including an objectionable white-supremacy Senator one of whose great-great-grandmothers turns out to have been black). The leaders were interned first, reasonably enough, to provide the skeleton of government and system in the new state which they are to erect. *But*, O'Doone points out, we have yet to receive from them a request for letters from an outsider, and if any Negroes at all are going to make such requests it must surely be these, the most important, the least afraid of red tape. (He also pointed out that not one of the entertainers or athletes of prominence has been interned. That, I'm afraid, is all too easily explained.) You see, says O'Doone, you see? But he didn't say, Why? to me, and I'm glad he didn't, for I can't even guess why.

Another statistic he had, concerned the CPR itself. We all know that the figures on natural resources in the CPR are exaggerated. Grossly. Fourteen million people cannot possibly live well in this area, and O'Doone demonstrated that fact to me most convincingly. Economically, the Negro problem in the U.S. has been that they provided a larger cheap-labor market than consumer market. Now the false stimulus of capitalizing their beginnings here will keep American industry on an even keel for years and years, but after that what? O'Doone bowed out at that point, but I think I can press the point a little further. They will provide a market for surplus com-

modities great enough to keep the pressures of capitalism from blowing us sky high, meanwhile permitting the transition to a planned
state to take place. Very astute, I think, very astute indeed.

June 12

Dear Herb,

Why I have not written, you ought to be able to guess. I will
not pretend to any false ardors about Ruth. She is wise and winning
as a woman, and everything one could ask for as a wife. I love her
dearly. She has not read very widely or profoundly, but I think she is
going to do something about that soon. We are happy together and
I think we shall continue to be happy during the difficult years to
come. What more can I say?

Why are happiness and contentment and the sense of fulfillment
so hard to write about? I can think of nothing to say, and besides
Ruth is just coming in from tennis (it's 9:30 Sunday morning).

10 P.M.

Ruth has gone to bed so I will continue in another vein.

I have been discovering that the wells of pity, which have lain so
long locked and frozen in my eyes, are thawed in me now. I am
enclosing a letter which came in from a Negress in Chicago to her
lover in the CPR, and his response. It is the first letter from inside
except for the usual three during the first week that I have read.
Apparently a few have been coming out now and then, but this is
my first one. I cannot tell you how I pitied both these unhappy
people. When Ruth read them she said, "My, what a mean man! I
hope he has to collect garbage all his life." I cannot agree with her.
I think his little note betrays an unhappiness as great as the
woman's, and even more pitiable for being unrecognized, unap-
preciated. Judge for yourself. I can think of nothing to add.

Andy

Honey, dear child, why don't you write to me? Don't you even remember all those things you told me you'd do no matter what? And you're
not even in jail, you just in that place where we all going to go to sooner
or later. O I sure hope they take me there with you. I can't live without
you. But I don't even know who to ask to go there with you. I went to
the policeman and they said they didn't know nothing about it. I don't

know what to do. You don't know how I ache for you honey. It's just like I got a tooth pulled out but it ain't no tooth it's worse, and there is no dentist for it neither. There's a fellow at the store keeps bothering me now and again, but I assure him I don't want him, I got a man. I thought I had a man, you, but I don't hear nothing from you. Maybe you got something there, I don't see how you could do it not after those things you said, but if you have tell me so I can go off in some hole and die. I don't want this Lee Lawson, he's no good, it's you I want, sweetheart, you tell me it's all right. I *got* to hear from you or I'll just die.

Dear ————,

I've been so busy baby, you wouldn't believe how busy I've been. You'll be coming here pretty soon and then you'll feel better too. It's nice here. We'll get along fine then. You tell that guy to leave you be. You're my gal. Tell him I said so.

Yours truly,

————

(*In invisible ink*)

I didn't include these letters because I thought they were in the Héloïse-Abélard class, but because I wanted to say something about them and also because they gave me more invisible space.

The man's response came to us already typed. That very much astonished me, and O'Doone, when I told him, let fly a nasty one. "I suppose," he said, "they have a couple of writers in there writing a few letters in place of the Negroes, which we then relay. Complicated, isn't it?" Not complicated, upsetting. Devastating. What if it were true? (And I must say this letter has an air more like the PR rewrite formula than like a real letter. Then *none* of the Negroes would have even filtered connection with the outside world.) Why? Why fool even us? Is there no end to the deception and doubt of this place?

O'Doone posed another of his puzzles yesterday. He read in the current PR weekly bulletin that the CPR has been shipping whole trainloads of leather goods and canned meats to China and Europe for relief purposes, under the government's supervision, of course. O'Doone came into my office at once, waving the bulletin and

chortling. "How do you like it?" he cried. "Before we get a carrot
out of them the Chinese get tons of meat." Then a sudden light
seemed to dawn on his face. "Where did all the cattle come from?"

A strange thing happened: O'Doone's intelligent, sensitive face collapsed. The great domed forehead remained almost unwrinkled, but
his features looked somehow like one of those children's rubber faces
which collapse when you squeeze them. No anguish, no anxiety,
only collapse. He left without a word. I wish he had never come
here with that news.

Last night I lay awake till three or four o'clock. I could hear
trucks and trains rumbling occasionally throughout the night, entering and leaving the Reserve. But that guard I met at the foot of the
hill told me that they only bring internees in the daytime. Are those
shipments? How can it be? Sometimes I am sick at heart with doubt
and uncertainty.

I dreamt last night that I was a Gulliver, lying unbound and
unresisting on the ground while a thousand Lilliputians, all of them
black, ate at me. I would not write the details of that dream even in
invisible ink. Not even in plain water.

July 4

Dear Herb,

Hail Independence Day! Some of the overgrown kids around here
are shooting off firecrackers. No one is working. It is all very pleasant. I suppose March 20th will be the Independence Day of the
new Negro nation—the day when the first trainload arrived. How
long ago that seems already. I do not think I have ever been
through so much in so short a time.

Now for the real news. Ruth is pregnant! Amazing woman, she
remains outwardly as humorous and self-contained as ever. No one
else knows her condition because she wants to avoid as much as
possible of the female chatter that goes with pregnancy. She insists
upon playing tennis still. Yet she is not all calmness and coolness;
when we are lying in bed together before going to sleep she croons
little nonsense hymns to pregnancy in my ear, and yesterday afternoon at the office she walked into my cubicle and placed my hand
over her womb. Then she kissed me with an unviolent passion that

I have never known before in my life. I tell you, she's a wonderful woman.

How miraculous is conception and growth! I no more understand such things than I really understand about the stars and their rushings. One event follows another, but I'm sure I don't know why. If you permit yourself to, you get back to an archaic awe realizing that you have started off a chain of miracles. I never had a sense of littleness when observing the naked heavens, of man's puniness, of my own nothingness. Perhaps it was a fear of that feeling which for so long prevented me from looking upward at all. I mentioned my reaction to O'Doone on one of the first occasions of our meeting. He nodded and said, "But is not a man more complex than a star, and in every way but one that we know of more valuable?" What he said remains with me yet, and when I am presented with the vastness of the stars and the forces which operate within them I am impressed and excited but not depressed by the imagined spectacle. Their bigness does not make me little. My own complexity does not make them simple. Perhaps man is no longer the center of the universe, but neither is anything else. That I have learned.

But when I am presented with the proof of the powers that men (and myself) possess, I still feel a little off balance. When Clarice was pregnant with Betty I had no such feeling. I felt annoyed chiefly. But now, in this desert, in the CPR, I have been sent back at last to fundamentals, to the sources of things; I realize fully how unaccountable is birth of life. Ruth, who never departed far from the sources, is less embarrassed in admitting her sense of mystery.

One thing I am going to teach this child if it can be taught anything: that the humane tradition has been tried and found wanting. It's over, finished, kaput. A new era of civilization commences. Once kindness and freedom were good for something, but no more. *Put yourself in his place*—never. Rather, fight to stay where you are. I think we are entering upon an age of reason and mystery. Reason which accepts and understands the uttermost heights and depths of human power, man's depravity, and his nobility—and, understanding these, dares use them toward a great and future goal, the goal of that stern order which is indispensable to the fullest development of man. Mystery toward all that is not explainable, which is a very great deal. Rationalism failed, for it asserted that everything was

ultimately explainable. We know better. We know that to destroy a
man's sense of mystery is to cut him off from one of the sources of
life. Awe, acceptance, and faith are wonderful sources of power and
fulfillment. I have discovered them. My child shall never forget
them.

Andy

(*In invisible ink*)

I have put the gun to my temple, Herb, I have pointed the knife
at my heart. But my nerve failed me. There were a few days when I
was nearly distracted. My division chief told me to stay home till I
looked better, but I dared not. I think it was only Ruth's pregnancy
that saved me. My newly awakened sense of mystery plus my powers
of reason have saved me. This is the third letter I have written you
in a week, but I threw the others away. I knew they were wild and
broken, and I was not sure at all that I was physically able to write
in such a manner as to avoid detection.

It came to a head two weeks ago. O'Doone entered my office, his
face looking bright and blasted. He dropped a booklet on my desk
and left after a few comments of no importance. The booklet was
an anthropologist's preliminary report on certain taboos among
American Negroes; the fellow had been interviewing them in Intake. There was nothing of special interest about it that I could see
except that it was written in the past tense.

I expected O'Doone to reclaim the booklet any day. For some
reason he had always done the visiting to me, not I to him. He was
very restless and I am slothful. But a week passed and no O'Doone.
I did not meet him in the café nor in the recreation room. I went to
his own room, but he did not answer. The next day I went to his
office and his secretary told me he had not shown up for two days.
I returned to his room. It was locked. The janitor unlocked it for me.
When I entered I saw him lying dead on his bed. "Well, old boy,"
I said to drive the janitor away, I don't know why, "feeling poorly?"
He had drunk something. There was a glass on the table by his bed.
There was no note. His face was repulsive. (That is a mystery I have
learned to respect, how hideous death is.) He was cold and somehow
a little sticky to the touch. I covered his face with a towel and sat
down. I knew I should call someone, but I did not want to. I knew

the janitor would remember letting me in and my staying too long. Yet I felt that was something I must do. What it was I could not remember, something important. It took me an eternity to remember: the invisible ink. I knew where he had kept it; it was not there. I looked throughout his room and it was simply gone. I left.

I still did not notify anyone of his suicide. I was not asking myself why he had done it. Or perhaps I was only shouting, Where's the ink? in a loud voice to cover up the little question, Why? I went to our rooms and straight to the liquor shelf, took down the Scotch, poured myself a stiff one, and drank. It was horrible; I spat it out, cursing. Then I recognized the odor; O'Doone had come over, poured out the Scotch (I hope he enjoyed it himself), and filled the bottle with the invisible ink. At that I broke down in the most womanish way and cried on the bed (never ask, Why? Why? Why?).

Ruth found me there some time later. I told her everything that had happened, and she immediately pulled me together. She had the sense to know I had been acting more oddly than was wise. She notified the right people and O'Doone was disposed of. No one asked me any embarrassing questions, and no official mention of O'Doone's end was made anywhere.

I must continue this on a birthday card.

(In invisible ink on a large, plain Happy Birthday card to Mary)
I had still not allowed myself to ask why he had done it, but Ruth put the thing in a short sentence. "He was too soft-hearted to stand it here." She was right; he was a Christian relic. He knew more than he could bear. I resolved to go that very evening again to the hill where the black searchlight threatened the night.

Some sandwiches. Four half-pints of whiskey. A hunting knife (a foolish gesture, I know). Plain drab clothes. The long walk in the still hot, late-afternoon sun. Sunset. The huge, sudden twilight. Then I was within sight of a guard (not the same one I had seen before) standing by the new fence at the foot of the hill.

I crept up toward him under cover of brush and cactus till I was close enough to toss a half-pint of whiskey in his direction. His bored, stupid face immediately became animated by the most savage emotions. He leveled his gun and pointed it in my general direction.

He could not see me, however, and rather than look for me he crouched, eyes still searching the underbrush, to reach for the bottle. He drained it in five minutes.

"Throw me some more," he whispered loudly.

"Put the gun down."

I aimed my voice away from him, hoping that he would not spot me. I was lying flat beneath a large clump of sagebrush. There was a Joshua tree nearby and several cactus plants. He pointed the gun at one of the stalks of cactus and crept up toward it. Then he suddenly stopped, I don't know why, and walked back to his post.

"What yer want?" he asked.

I tossed out another bottle. He jumped again, then got it and drank it.

"What's going on in there?"

"They're fixing up the niggers," he said. "You know as much about it as I do."

He began to sing *Oh! Susannah* in a sentimental voice. It was beginning to get too dark for my safety. I was desperate.

I tossed out another bottle, only not so far this time. When he leaned for it I said very clearly, "You look like a butcher."

He deliberately opened the bottle and drank off half of it. "Butcher, huh? Butcher?" He laid down his gun and took his villainous knife out. "I'm no butcher. I won't have nothing to do with the whole slimy mess. I won't eat them, no sir, you can do that for me. But I can do a little carving, I think. No butcher, you son of a bitch. You dirty, prying, nigger-eating son of a bitch. I'll learn you to call me a butcher."

He was stalking the cactus again. He lunged forward at it and with much monotonous cursing and grunting dealt with it murderously. Meanwhile I crawled out on the other side of the sagebrush and ran for it. He never shot at me. Nothing happened except that I too ran full tilt into a cactus and had to walk hours in agony of flesh as well as of spirit. I vomited and retched till I thought I would be unable to walk further.

I must continue this letter some other way.

Andy

(*In invisible ink on the papers wrapping another sweater for Ruth's cousin's baby*)

I told Ruth nothing of what I had learned; not even *her* great sense of the inevitable could survive such a shock, I think. Yet sometimes it seems to me that she must surely know it all. I do not want to know whether she knows. Could I support it if she did?

It was more painful pulling the cactus needles out than it had been acquiring them. But she removed them all, bathed the little wounds with alcohol, and put me to bed. The next morning I awoke at seven and insisted upon going to work. I sat all day in my office, eating crackers and drinking milk. I didn't accomplish a thing. It was then that my chief told me to take it easy for a while. I was in a sort of stupor for a couple of days; yet to everyone's consternation I insisted on going to work. I accomplished nothing and I intended to accomplish nothing, it was just that I could not tolerate being alone. In fact today was the first day I have been alone for more than five minutes since I returned from the walk. But today I have regained a kind of composure, or a semblance of composure, which for a time I despaired of ever possessing again. And I know that by the time I have given shape enough to my thoughts to put them on this paper for you to read I shall have gained again a peace of mind. To have you to write to, Herb, that is the great thing at this point. Without you I do not know what I would have done.

So much for my emotions. My thinking, my personal philosophy, has gone through at least as profound an upheaval as they. In the chaos of my mind, in which huge invisible chunks of horror hit me unexpectedly from unexpected angles again and again, my first coherent and sensible idea came in the form of a question. "Why did they make it possible for me to find out what has been going on?" (For I finally realized that it was no fluke that I had discovered it, or O'Doone either, or anyone with the suspicions and the courage for it. When the atom bombs were being produced, the whole vast undertaking was carried off without a single leak to the outside. So if I had been able in so simple a way to find out what had been going on in the CPR it was only because they didn't care. They could have stopped me.)

Then I thought, invisible ink is scarcely new in the history of things. Perhaps they have been reading my correspondence with you all along and will smile at this letter as they have smiled at others. Or perhaps they haven't taken the trouble to read it because they simply don't care.

Perhaps the authorities not only did not care if we gradually found out, but wanted us to. Why should they want us to? Why, if that were true, should they have put up so formidable a system—double fences, censorship, lies, etc., etc.—of apparent preventatives?

The only answer that makes sense is that they want the news to sift out gradually and surreptitiously to the general population—illegally, in the form of hideous rumors to which people can begin to accustom themselves. After all, many knew generally that something like the atom bomb was being manufactured. Hiroshima was not the profound and absolute shock in 1945 that it would have been in 1935, and a good deal of the preparation for its general acceptance was rumor. It is in the people's interest that the CPR function as it does function, and especially so that they can pretend that they have nothing to do with it. The experience of the Germans in the Jew-extermination camps demonstrated that clearly enough. It would do no good for me to go around crying out the truth about NRACP, because few would believe me in the first place and my suppression would only give strength to the rumors—which are required and planned for anyhow.

But I still had to set myself the task of answering, Why? What drove them (whoever *they* are) to the decision to embark upon a course which was not only revolutionary but dangerous? I accepted the NRACP as inevitable, as *necessity*; there remained only the task of trying to understand wherein lay the mystery of the *necessity* and of adjusting myself to the situation. The individual, even the leader, has no significant choice to make in the current of event. That current is part of natural law; it is unmoral, cruel, wasteful, useless, and mysterious. The leader is he who sees and points out the course of history so that we may pursue that course with least pain. It is odd that we Americans have no such leader; what we have is committees and boards and bureau heads who collectively possess leadership and who direct our way almost impersonally. There is nothing whatsoever that I myself would like so much as to be one of those wise, courageous, anonymous planners. I think I possess the wisdom. But in place of courage I have a set of moral scruples dating from an era when man was supposed to have a soul and when disease took care of overpopulation. The old vestigial values of Christianity must be excised in the people as they are being excised in me. The good and the lucky are assisting at the birth of a new age; the weak and unfit are perishing in the death of an old. Which shall it be for us?

For my own part I think I am in a state of transition from being one of the unfit to being one of the fit. I feel it. I will it. There are certain external evidences of it. For example, I was face to face with the truth at the end of April, but instead of acknowledging what I saw I turned to my love for Ruth. Yet that refusal to recognize the truth did not long survive the urgings of my sense of necessity. And I remember when being confronted with piecemeal evidences of truth that I was unable to explain a number of them. You know, Herb, how accomplished a rationalizer I can be, yet this time I did not even *try* to rationalize many of the facts.

It is dawn outside. I cannot read this letter over, so I am not entirely sure how incoherent it is. I feel that I have said most of what I wanted to say. I am not very happy. I think I shall sleep the better for having written this. I eat nothing but bread and fruit and milk. A bird is singing outside; he is making the only sound in the world. I can see the hill which separates us from the Intake buildings. It's a pleasant hill, rather like an arm extending out from the valley sides, and I am glad it is there. I am cold now, but in three hours it will be warm and in five hours hot. I am rambling I know. But suddenly all my energy has leaked out. I walk to the door to see Ruth so happily sleeping, mysteriously replenishing life from this nightly portion of death, and I think of that baby that she is bearing and will give birth to. If it were not for her and the baby I am sure I should have gone mad. Is not that a mystery, Herb? Our child shall be fortunate; it is the first conscious generation of each new order in whom the greatest energy is released. There are splendid things ahead for our child.

It is not my fault. I did not know what I was doing. How could I have known? What can I do now?

I stare at the lightening sky. Exhausted, I do not know why I do not say farewell and go to bed. Perhaps it is because I do not want to hear that little lullaby that sings in my ears whenever I stop: I have eaten human flesh, my wife is going to have a baby; I have eaten human flesh, my wife is going to have a baby.

Remember back in the simple days of the Spanish Civil War

when Guernica was bombed how we speculated all one evening what the worst thing in the world could be? This is the worst thing in the world, Herb. I tell you, the worst. After this, nothing.

Perhaps if I lay my head against Ruth's breast and put her hands over my ears I can go to sleep. Last night I recited Housman's "Loveliest of trees, the cherry now" over and over till I went to sleep, not because I like it particularly but because I could think of nothing else to recite.

My wife is going to have a baby, my wife is going to have a baby, my wife is going to have a baby.

Bless you,
Andy

Children of Ruth

Ruth Adams, a vigorous woman of fifty-five, had lived all her life in the same house and intended to be living in it when she died. The house suited her tastes and needs to perfection; it was spacious and well-proportioned, it had no needless decorations, yet it served the requirements of comfort, it was entirely respectable, yet admired by persons of every taste. It was, in fact, a part of herself. When she tried to imagine herself without her house she did not know who she would be; it was her scholar's books and her painter's brush and her farmer's soil. Her attachment to it was so strong that she refused to go as delegate to out-of-town conventions, no matter how worthy the cause at hand. In defense of her refusal, strange in one who took so many good causes to her heart, she argued that in order to effect one's ends at a convention one must use every device of unscrupulous politics—compromising, if only in that corrupt practice, one's most cherished beliefs. This may be true, but it is doubtful if she would have objected so strenuously if she had not been reluctant to leave her house. Certainly whenever a convention of the sort that interested her was held in San Francisco or Oakland she made her influence felt in ways that can only be called political. Chief among these ways of hers, though she was not conscious of duplicity or of putting on pressure when she did it, was her inviting key delegates to visit her or even to stay at her house during the convention. The commodious grace of the house and her assurance in it exercised an influence which only the most insensitive or hostile delegates could resist.

Twice in her life Ruth had been tempted to leave her house, each time because of the love of a man. The first occasion had been when she had barely emerged from girlishness and had not yet emerged from her girlish love of a college companion, Luke Adams. It was during the first world war. They felt hurried; they married; Ruth had produced a daughter and was pregnant with a son when Luke enlisted and was shipped overseas. Luke contracted tuberculosis in the trenches; at the war's end he was dying in a hospital in France, and it was then that Ruth was tempted to leave her home for a long voyage overseas. But the doctors assured her the trip could not save him, and since both the babies were sick with flu at the time she stayed home where she belonged and let Luke die by himself. She grieved over his loss and reproached herself for not having gone to him, but the reproaches had so little substance that she eventually forgot them, and the loss while great enough at the time gradually came to seem less and less devastating to her. Luke by inclination and temperament had been destined to a prominent position in the YMCA; while the YMCA was a virtuous organization in Ruth's view, yet as the years went by her taste inclined more and more toward a headier sort of man than it was likely to produce.

The other temptation had been in 1930 when she had fallen in love for the second time. The man was a large, indocile, irresponsible, domineering major named Frederick Kotowski. She disapproved of his profession, his philosophy, and his effect upon herself; yet when he demanded that she marry him and go off to China where he was being stationed she almost went. In fact she put her house up for sale and began packing her dishes. She was with child at the time and her friends kept telling her how right she was to marry Kotowski. But when at the last she decided not to go with him but to stay in her home and bear a child out of wedlock those friends who did not fall off began applying the epithet courageous to her.

The epithet stuck. When a few years later, alone and unaided, she dug up the evidence to convict three city officials of embezzlement, the local newspapers too applied it to her. Her defense of Japanese-Americans at the beginning of the second world war won for her the final laurel of fugitive fame: favorable epithets in *Time* magazine ("gray-haired, brave Ruth Adams . . .").

So she had preferred her snug house to the danger and mystery which loving Kotowski meant; she wrote him after the child was born and never heard from him again. In 1942 the child, Erasmus Oliver Adams, received notice that his father had been killed in the Philippines and that he was the beneficiary of a ten thousand dollar life insurance policy. Ruth put the money aside for the time when he would need it, spent half a day wondering why she had ever loved a man like Kotowski, and then turned back to helping the Japanese-Americans. For their sake she thought of flying to Washington, where she might put pressure on some senators and bureaucrats, but she did not trust herself so far afield and sighed with relief when she was told she could not get priority to travel on the planes.

Now she was as active as ever, except that she had to rest for a couple of hours every afternoon; as active but not quite as self-assured, for the Japanese-American battle—which she had of course lost—had made her realize for the first time that the collective fate of the people of Oakland was scarcely at all in their own hands.

The house Ruth lived in had been built by her father shortly before she was born. Orestes Stull had been an advanced architect of his time and had made a great deal of money from the designing of private houses for the well-to-do of Berkeley and Oakland. He refused to design public buildings in a style acceptable to city officials of those gingerbread decades, and despite his vogue among the expanding class to which he catered, he was never left completely free in his designing of houses. Always the husband insisted upon a bay window or the wife declared she would die without a rear staircase or they both agreed that the fireplace should be in a wasted corner. Throughout the '80's his fame and fortune grew, and by the early '90's he had the money to build for himself the house at 17 Denver Place, the home which he had been perfecting piecemeal in the houses of others.

It was built of redwood—an ancient, dark, straight-grained wood —and there was no part of it which was not useful, functional. Still, though every beam had its use, some of them might have been larger than necessary because to him they looked better large; some of them might have been placed at a graceful angle and not at the angle of greatest efficiency; they had an architect's rather than an engineer's usefulness. The living room was spacious and low of ceiling for those times. To keep it from being gloomy Stull had put casement windows along two walls; one side yielded a view of lawn and trees and the other a small prospect of the Bay. It was neither a formal nor an intimate room, but either as one willed, and it was always beautiful. One ate in the kitchen, which was huge and airy. The kitchen was redwood too, unpainted; as coolers and gas ranges and refrigerators and Mixmasters kept being invented, Stull and Ruth after him had them incorporated into the paneled walls. One had the impression of cupboard doors clean yet darkened by the years of cooking in that comfortable room, and of bright pottery on open shelves and large workboards. There was none of that surgery feeling, glistening and well-arranged, which is a kind of ideal nowadays: shining implements and white purring machines and housewife in white smock and clocks and a deadline for a dinner of lamb chops and peas. In the Stull kitchen guests frequently sat till midnight talking over coffee; the chairs were kitchen chairs and a great deal better for thinking in than right-angle, dining room chairs or an overstuffed davenport. In every bedroom there was a copy of a painting on the wall: a Turner countryside, a Cézanne still life, some Audubon birds. The study was lined with books; the cellar was stocked with home-canned fruit, a barrel of apples, and a few cases of wine; the attic was full of odds and ends of furniture and boxes full of old curtains or, later, of Stull's manuscripts and drawings. Ruth had a great many photographs on the walls of her room, of each member of her family, of her friends, of the Parthenon and ruins of Rome and Mont-Saint-Michel; she kept them all and added to them as the years went by; she seldom looked at them but she would have been diminished by their absence. From the outside the house was dignified but unostentatious; indeed it appeared plain to the owners of the mongrel imitations which surrounded it. To them its comfort without their antiseptic luxuries was a sort of perversity, its flagrant honesty a temptation and a threat. Neither Stull nor Ruth nor Ruth's three children ever made friends with their neighbors.

Ruth's friends were scattered throughout the Bay Area; and, while she had no secret requirement that they should live in houses like her own, decent and dignified, yet it turned out that most of them did. Some lived in apartment houses and some in stucco co-ops, one in a tenement and a few in shacks, but most lived in houses solid and separate and her oldest friend lived in a house only slightly less beautiful than her own. Though Ruth was no snob and though she had never in her life said so to anyone, she could not imagine a better way to live than this. She had decided long ago that she had a right to it. Whenever someone who had not yet made a treaty with his sense of injustice asked her how she could bear to live thus when so many must exist in the hovels and caves of poverty she would answer that all should be able to live as she did, that the sacrifice of her happiness would not ease their misery, that progress was a leveling upward. She was her father's only child—her mother had died in childbirth—and when he had died he had left her this house and a fine income from the rent of several apartment buildings. Some of these apartments had declined into tenements and most were hideous, but they were better managed and cheaper than any others in town. When she was challenged for living off these rentals she answered, justly, that it was a deplorable injustice which, having inherited, she did with as best one could do; under another landlord her tenants would be worse off. When her older son, Eugene Gracchus, suggested once that she donate the apartments to their tenants she was not even ruffled; it was logical in a way, as most of his ideas were, but like much logic it went counter to all her experience.

Her public life was a matter of committees and civic agencies and the expression of upright opinion. Hers was a philosophy full of sympathy and eschewing scandal, of hope and good works. She was in excellent health, she was an example of virtue and good fortune, yet such an example as to baffle envy. She was respected more than most of us are and was hated less, yet she was not a happy woman because of her children.

It is a Sunday afternoon in September, somewhat misty, as hot as it is likely to get in Oakland; there is a little breeze in from the sea— climate is not one of the enemies here. Even so, Gene is wearing the blue wool turtleneck shirt he usually wears around the house. He has never been a seaman; he likes this shirt because he is seldom too warm, because his neck is long and thin and easily chilled, and because he is used to it. Gene is well over six feet but he is so thin and pale that he gives the impression not of being tall but of being too long. Ruth is still lying down on a cot in the back garden, waiting for the family to gather for dinner as is their custom on the Sabbath. This dinner is about all that remains for them of that Fourth Commandment which their Puritan ancestors made so much of once long ago.

"Mother." His voice, which is not low, rises to its treble when he is excited in any uneasy way. It is high now.

"Hello dear." With a quick gesture Ruth lifts her arm from across her eyes, and quickly turns her head to look at him. She is ready to relax again if he has nothing important to say.

"Does anything need to be fixed for dinner?"

His huge, smooth bluff of a forehead is wrinkled. She can tell that he has something to say which it will take him many indirections to get at. She lays her arm by her side and stares up through the branches of the cherry tree spreading above her.

"No dear. Miriam will help me get things ready."

"Well, Dorie will be here before long."

Dorie is his fiancée.

"I suppose."

It is Dorie's habit three Sundays running to arrive too late to help in the kitchen; on the fourth Sunday she will come so early as to do more than her share. Gene has not noticed this habit of Dorie's. Ruth has; her "I suppose" is rather dry.

"Is E.O. going to be here for dinner?"

E.O. is Erasmus Oliver, who has exacted from everyone but his mother the obligation of calling him by his initials. He has told his friends that his father was a Texan who named him, in Texas fashion, by initials only.

"He said at breakfast that he would be."

The puckered lines about her mouth, the combined result of determination and false teeth, become more puckered yet with the determination of hiding the pain which thinking of Oliver gives her.

"Is he going to get a new motorcycle?" asked Gene, though he knew the answer. His intention with these questions—at least what he accomplished with them—was to make his mother as little at peace as he himself was.

Ruth, however, did not understand about such tactics and would not have believed them of Gene if she had been told; she answered therefore truthfully and painfully.

"I will not give him the money. That is not quite correct. I will do everything I can to prevent his owning a motorcycle. It is not the money. He says he will work for the money." She turned more directly toward Gene. "What can he do? He has no training."

"He knows all about cars. Maybe he'll get a job in a garage."

"If that's what he wants," she answered. But the sadness was all in her eyes; her voice and mouth were controlled and allowed Oliver freely the right to work as he wished.

"There's nothing wrong with being a mechanic," Gene said.

"Nothing at all. It's the motorcycle that's so wrong. Everything it means."

She closed her eyes. Gene took a last puff on the cigarette he was holding and flipped it into the shrubbery. He walked restlessly to the other side of the cot and looked down at her.

"Mother," he began, his voice pitched a little higher than before. "Yes Eugene?"

"You know that I've been having good results in my chess lately."

"Yes dear."

"The next international tournament is to be held in Tokyo."

She could not see how this information affected her. She did not answer.

"I have been invited to attend with the American team."

"Really?" She half sat up with excitement. "You would be with the masters then?"

"Yes. I think it may have some importance for my future."

Ruth saw little point in chess except as a way of relaxing, but if Gene was going to take chess seriously it was obviously desirable for him to be very good at it. Her congratulations were sincere, but as always when she spoke of chess there was a note of bewilderment in her voice.

"I am so glad for you. I hope with all my heart you do well. Do you know anything about the others?"

"Oh yes. There will be some excellent Russian players there. The great Polish master is dead."

"Well," she said reclining again, "it makes me happy to think of you being there."

Gene's brow wrinkled again in irritation; he thought she was deliberately not helping him, whereas in truth she did not know he wanted her help.

"The point is, Mother, I haven't the money to go."

Now for something as important to him as this Ruth would never have denied him the money, and Gene knew it. But Ruth herself did not know it, though he thought she did. He thought not only that she knew it but that the long process of reasoning herself into it, which she always went through, was a method of reproaching him. She had nothing like reproach in her mind; though she did not know it she was providing her conscience with good reasons for giving this money to him.

"How much more do you need, dear?" She put her arm back across her eyes. All he could see of her face was the rather stern-looking mouth; it irritated him too.

"Five hundred dollars. I've looked into the cost by boat. I'd rather not fly."

"When is it to be held?"

"Next May."

"You would have to leave in March."

"I'd rather go in February. As long as I'm there I'd like to see something of Japan."

She was silent. It was in her silences that he felt the reproach most keenly, the reproach of being thirty-three and good for nothing. A chess player. Lives in his mother's house. Doesn't even earn his own living but lives off the rents of houses which his grandfather paid for. A professional amateur. Couldn't get a good job if he wanted one.

"Then you would get married next summer."

"Yes."

In Ruth's mind conscience was still tipping the scales. She had promised her sons to double their incomes when they were married.

She thought that what she allowed them was sufficient, and for simple tastes it would have been, but neither of them had simple tastes. Also, she had promised a heavy contribution to the American Civil Liberties Union for the prosecution of some white farmers who were combining to ruin the Japanese farmers in their county. She felt she ought not spare the money from that lawsuit for Gene's happiness.

"Of course," he said, "I could borrow it. But I'd rather not be in debt when I marry."

His features seemed to crumple when he said this. Overtopped by his huge forehead they looked squeezed down by it, pushed together by too much intellect and anxiety and reproach. She could hear all this in the quaver in his voice, as of one who holds back tears or rage, and she could not bear it.

"No, son, no. You may have the money. I hope it gives you great satisfaction."

Her voice was steady and ungrudging, not very warm, but then it was never a very warm voice.

Gene walked off, not very happy. He stood looking at flowers for a time. On a lovely afternoon when there is nothing to do one is supposed to enjoy natural life whether in a garden, a park, or the countryside. Gene had often done so or thought he had. He was especially fond of going with Dorie to the Golden Gate Park and of walking about or sitting on the lawns for an afternoon, and when he had been a child his mother could give him no greater treat than to take him to the country for a day. Now he stood looking at a bank of wisteria and felt nothing; he was too honest to pretend he was liking the flowers, but he was mystified, as he had been before, at his own emptiness and its cause. What he lacked was eyes of another to see through, warmth of another to feel the beauty through, another's openness to open him. He stood staring dejectedly, and at the sound of his sister's maternal yoo-hoo and her children's yelps he ran upstairs to his room. He liked Miriam, but she showed him nothing; he was fond of George and Penny, but children's candor alarmed him a little; he thought her husband Bill, an actuary and a ski enthusiast, to be a thumping bore.

He found Dorie writing at his desk.

"Dorothea! When did you come?"

"Hello Gene." She looked at him a little abstractedly. "I had to finish a letter to Pris and all the dogs in town were barking under my window. Do you mind?"

"Of course not. Go ahead."

He walked over and patted her shoulder; she squeezed his hand with a rather mechanical affectionateness and turned back to her letter. Gene lay on his bed looking at his room, which though he had lived in it for twenty-nine years pleased him as the wisteria was supposed to have done.

He liked the roof beams above him and the redwood paneling; he found the irregularities in its shape, caused by two closets, to be a convenience as well as a guard against the boxlike effect a room can give. He liked the Klee painting he had on the wall over the desk and the Braque over the bookcase; the books, which were not numerous but very well used; the piano, which he had learned to play on as a child and still did not neglect; the confusion of equipment in the corner where he was himself assembling the best possible record player; the low chair and ottoman; the plywood chessboard stuck behind the bookcase and the cheap chess men, chipped and dirty, scattered on the desk; the rugless floor; the hard mattress; Dorie at his desk. Liked everything in the room—which almost contained his life—except himself. As he lay on the bed, pleased with what he had done and what he was going to do but not with himself for doing it, he realized that it would take more than an absent-minded squeeze of the hand from Dorie to make him feel good again.

She had stopped writing for a moment and sat gazing out the window.

"What are you saying to Pris? Give her my best."

"What?" said Dorie turning toward him and focusing her eyes on him.

"I said, what are you writing to Pris about?"

"Oh nothing much."

"Well come over and give me a kiss. I'm a little low."

"I'm busy darling."

"What are you writing about? Your bridal plans?"

He thought he was being ironic, but as often happened to him his irony was neither strong enough nor delivered in such a way as to make its intent clear. People would take his ironies straight or think he was being facetious or ignore them altogether. Dorie took this one straight.

"In a way."

"What do you mean?"

"Well I was telling her the possibilities in this house, when we ever get a chance to fix it over."

He reared up in dismay. "What do you mean? What's wrong with it as it is?"

This house had sheltered him all his life, it had been kept in good repair, and he liked it. He could just conceive of living in another house, but this one he could not imagine improved by anyone— certainly not by Dorie, whose taste, though he loved her, he deplored.

"I was telling her what a distinguished-looking room the living room would be if the walls were white plaster and maybe, though I'm not sure, if the ceiling were white too, in between the beams."

She stole a look at him; she knew she was trespassing and wanted to see how he accepted it. His forehead was wrinkled, his eyebrows were raised, he was stroking his jaw with one finger; it was an expression and gesture characteristic of him when he was observing or trying to understand something. She went on.

"The kitchen, of course, would have to be redone from one end to the other. It's hopelessly out-of-date." He did not even blink. "I think those brown shingles on the outside walls are very drab. Wouldn't it be more striking to put gray composition shingles over them?"

"No," he said whinnying with annoyance.

"They're fireproof too."

"My mother would never consent to modernizing this house, and besides she has three children. Why should we have it to ourselves? You're wasting your time."

"It's terribly dark and gloomy. The only thing it has is a good floor plan and lots of windows, but it's terribly inefficient. It's *slow*, if you know what I mean."

"I don't and I don't want to." His voice was at the top of its register but not loud. "And even if we inherit it I wouldn't agree to a single one of your ideas. I like it and I feel an obligation not to change it."

She saw that it would be a long campaign. She chose to be feminine at the moment and went over to kiss him.

"You're too late for that," he said pushing her off. "Besides, you ought to go down and help Mother and Miriam."

"All right, darling. Just one kiss to show you love me."

They kissed. She coquetted with him a minute, shaking her hair in his face and biting his nose with her lips; he smiled. She went back to finish her letter and he watched her.

Gene was a great watcher. His favorite way of dealing with his fellows was to watch them: people at concerts, at ball games, at church, skid-row bums, a class of deaf and dumb children being herded through the zoo, pregnant women standing in streetcars, children playing paper dolls or chasing each other, himself in a mirror, his mother, Dorie now. He prowled the city like a photographer, looking, and he saw as well as a good camera. Not as a good photographer, but as a good camera, for there were too many things which he was afraid of for him to be able, as a good photographer must, to love or pity or censure what he saw so very clearly. Mostly he saw curiosities and matter for jest. He would follow a woman with a cleft palate and a Louisiana drawl as she bought food from counter to counter in the Tenth Street Market, watching her anger and timidity with clerks and listening to her cloudlike words form and amalgamate and seem to mean something and dissolve—she became a joke to tell. He liked to get a glimpse of people who had not pulled their blinds down undressing for bed—not for pruriency's sake but because they looked so ludicrous scratching, yawning, half-naked, so much like each other. Of course, he was not always just the camera; a mother with her baby, a Negro in a streetcar full of whites, or always a blind man, these he saw with more than his physical eyes. But now as he lay watching his fiancée, it was a joke for himself that he was after.

"Dorie," he said, "can you move around this way a little. I like to look at your leg like that."

Flattered, she obliged him, but it was not her legs he wanted to see. They were plump and not well tapered at the knee and ankle; crossed as they were now the fleshy calf was pushed out of shape and the crossed leg stuck out at an angle of pure vulgarity. It was not her legs he wanted but for her to think that it was; also he could get a better profile of her whole person thus. It was a pleasant, rotund little profile; after a child or two it would be dumpy. The babyishness of her face was accentuated by her soft, fluffy hair and her ready smile; as Gene knew, the babyishness was flatly contradicted by the coolness and judging in her pale blue eyes. She was concentrating on her letter or seeming to; however, he could see her glance rest on her leg from time to time. She adjusted her skirt so that it came down a little further over her untrim knee. As though tired of her shoes she slipped them off; her arched feet were her prettiest point, her feet and the coloring of her skin like a fresh strawberry peach. When she nonchalantly dropped the shoe off Gene felt that his joke had worked; content, he went to the window to watch the family in the garden.

His tall and slightly stooped sister and his dumpy little mother were just turning from a flower bed to go into the house. They were talking; he could tell by the way his mother was patting the back of one hand in the palm of the other that something had put her out of patience. Bill was on the cot reading the Sunday paper, and the children were climbing the apple tree. A sprinkler was revolving sedately in one corner of the lawn. It wasn't much of a scene, no cleft palates or goiters in it, but Gene was feeling a sentimental glow over it as he watched—sentimental because if he had been down there it would have seemed quite different to him, full of little dangers to be guarded against. Dorie, ignored, left her letter and came to stand beside him.

"How can Miram look so sleek, a mother of two kids?" she said in her unbabyish voice, with a lingering on certain vowels that some women learn at sorority houses and neglect to unlearn afterward.

Miriam was sleek after a lean fashion, if you were in the mood to see her that way. Gene was not. He was thinking Miriam looked well groomed or chic.

"No," he said contemplatively, "she isn't a bit frowsy, is she?"

He went over to the confusion of wires about the record player and began doing something. Dorie looked to see if her slip was showing and returned to the letter, but she could not concentrate on it any longer. She put on her shoes, and before going downstairs went over to kiss Gene. He was still annoyed at her; he responded to her kiss with some amorous horseplay of a kind she disliked. But their parting sounded amiable enough, Dorie because she was still making amends for her earlier trespass, Gene because he thought he was being ironic in his amiability and because it is so risky not to be amiable.

"And the American Medical Association?" Ruth was saying, tapping one hand nervously in the other.

"I'm afraid they'll be against it, but one can never be sure."

"On the contrary one can be quite sure. I'm grateful for organizations like the AMA and the American Legion. You always know precisely where they'll be and what they'll want and how they'll go about getting it, and you always know that in a pitched battle they'll win."

"Mother, I never heard you sound so cynical."

"It's called realistic," said Ruth very dryly.

"Mother!"

"Go ahead, my dear, take your own path. If I were thirty-five I would do it as you are doing it. By the time you've learned all the tricks for yourself, you'll be taking naps every afternoon too."

"You think," said Miriam a little timidly, "that I've just been wasting my time? I hoped—"

"Nothing of the kind. You will have awakened a few more people to their responsibilities."

Miriam groaned.

"You might even succeed," said Ruth.

"My God! I want to get something done! Awaken people to their responsibilities."

"Think of it this way if it makes you feel better. I do sometimes. In every good deed you do, by just so much do you retard the progress of corruption."

Ruth was very fond of this sentence and Miriam had heard her say it a score of times before, yet never had it penetrated so far as it did now. She groaned again; there was not a trace of humor in this groan as there had been in the first one.

"Pay no attention to what I've said, dear," said Ruth. In a rare demonstration of affection she kissed Miriam on the cheek. "I'm out-of-sorts today." Then, with an association of ideas she herself did not recognize, her voice changing with the change of subject, she added, "Did you know that Gene is going to Tokyo next spring to attend the chess tournament?"

"No!" Miriam exclaimed, relieved to have something cheerful to exclaim at. "The world championship tournament?"

"I believe so. He'll marry Dorie when he comes back."

"Mother!" yelled George. "Look!"

He was straddling two limbs high up in the apple tree. He achieved the effect he desired: the women came squawking in alarm to get him down and in an affectation of being disgruntled he lowered himself to a safer limb. Bill had fallen asleep with the paper over his face, and Penny was sitting in the lowest crotch of the tree eating an apple. Surveying their work with approval and possessive pride mother and daughter turned to the kitchen.

Dorie entered one door as they the other. There was an involuntary change in Miriam the moment she saw Dorie. Miriam too had belonged to a sorority in college, though only for a year; although she had hated the sorority and although she was not proud of the accomplishment she could be as shellacked, as hard, as stamped by the great machine as the next woman. In Dorie's presence she assumed that smiling and vacant-hearted type she deplored. All during the preparation of dinner the two kept up a chatter about food and clothes which meant nothing but that they did not like each other.

It distressed neither of them, only Ruth. Ruth did not chatter, and she would never have permitted herself to dislike her daughter or her future daughter-in-law, except perhaps when she first woke up in the morning when all things seemed worse to her and at the same less hopeless. Yet there was something in Ruth which was not unlike their machined perfection. Her undemonstrativeness might have become their empty assertions of affection: there were too many darlings in their acquaintance, they so loved to do this or that, things were too frequently charming. Her reserve, which was a respect for the privacy of others, might have become their dreadful intimacy—which permitted them at a bridge table to describe their husbands' potency—and their yet more dreadful aloneness when trouble marked them and left them only the hard and hollow sympathy of their friends. Her house might not have meant to her grace and a decent life but have been a cause of pride, as it would have been for them, a thing of which others should be made envious.

Sometimes as she was lying in bed the first thing in the morning it seemed to Ruth that those who, like Dorie and Miriam, would arrogate to themselves this air of cold superiority must surely be mean spirits, but later in the day she would reprove herself for her unkind thoughts and remember their excellences. What she found very hard to forgive in them was the pride they took in their meanness; snobbery is a small but nasty version of that most cardinal sin.

"Mother," said Miriam as she was preparing the salad, "I do hope E.O. gets here for dinner." Her tone of voice was warm and genuine, for she was fond of her younger brother, and furthermore it was a tactful thing for her to say. She had noticed his absence, she had observed her mother prick up her ears when a car seemed to be stopping in front of the house, and she knew how much her mother counted on these family dinners; more, she knew with what pain her mother would account to them for his absence at table. But lest it seem tact and only tact she added what was perfectly true but did not have to be added, "He's so nice with the children." In it all there was nothing but affection and honest feeling, yet she could be so catty and unkind as to make Ruth sick at heart.

Though the cattiness seemed more natural to her, Dorie had far too much strength of character actually to become the role she played. Her baby face, her smooth manner, and her naïve opinions on public matters were devices she used to get what she wanted. In her first husband she had married a man who fitted the type she seemed to be: a handsome, country club, fun-loving dealer of a man, a successful broker, a baffled husband, venal to his marrow. She had divorced him, and now what she wanted was Gene; no one knew why, not even Gene, no one but herself, and she could not have explained it with her impure, machined vocabulary which had no words for motive as complex as this. Without the words for an idea it is very difficult to have the idea at all; she called it love (though she knew that love was only a part of it) and everybody was satisfied but Ruth.

The family sat down to dinner half an hour late without Oliver.

Oliver was in another part of town, one where he felt more at home than in his mother's house. He was at Iggy's Igloo down on East Fourteenth Street. The hot-rod gang usually hung out at Sleepy's on 92nd Avenue below East Twelfth Street, but because Oliver and his best friend Jack felt they had got beyond the hot-rod stage they went to Iggy's, a motorcyclists' hangout. They were not contemptuous of hot rods by any means, a hot rod can kill you as dead as a motorcycle, but it was their opinion that it would not kill you quite so soon. The way they put it to themselves was: A rod's okay, but there's more kick in a bike. After Oliver had wrecked his third rod he had not built up another but was saving himself for a motorcycle; Jack had traded his rod in before he had wrecked it and now had an old but still lethal English bike.

A little after noon they had roared up, Oliver sitting behind Jack, to Iggy's, revved her up and turned off the ignition so she would backfire, and gone in for some beer. Iggy did not care whether they were under age as long as they sat in the back room to drink the beer.

Iggy was alone at a table in the main room, half asleep over the Sunday paper.

"Hey Iggy!" shouted Jack.

"What's the matter, man?" said Oliver. "Stay up too late last night?"

"Well boys," said Iggy pushing himself to a standing position, "is it beer already you want today?"

"You got it, man," said Oliver snapping his hat at Iggy, "you got it. Two of the brew."

Oliver had been wearing for the past couple of days a very small black bowler cocked over one eye. It was held in place by an elastic that went around his head; upon the slightest provocation he would pull it away from his forehead and let it snap back. His intention was to set a new fad, but the fad wasn't taking on much. The hat was decidedly silly; most people, even most motorcyclists, do not like to look silly in their own eyes at least. Oliver, however, rather liked to make himself look silly; he had a pervasive sense of his own unimportance which he could make good use of only by seeming to ridicule himself. Yet he was not a buffoon; he could not obtrude himself upon other people as much as a buffoon must. His attitude was: I'll go along with everything and have a good time and be one of the boys, but if somehow or other I happen to become the center of attention I'll be all prepared to be laughed at. Consequently he wore a small, tight smile on his lips nearly all the time—embarrassed, deprecatory, supercilious, ironic, friendly, depending on how you looked at it. Consequently too he was a leader of his friends only in the matter of fads; there he was ahead of them all.

They went into the back room and sat at a small round table with a red-check cloth on it. On one wall there was a shelf with two large and handsome steins on it, and on the other walls were rather soft photographs of Bavaria.

"Hey Iggy," said Oliver when the beer arrived, "anybody been around yet?"

"No, today you are the first."

"What's the matter, Iggy?" said Jack jovially. "You're droopy. Best friend die?"

Iggy smiled and shrugged his shoulders, but his watery blue eyes behind their glasses said, though not to them exactly: To an old exile all friends are dead. He went back to his paper.

"Hey," said Jack to Oliver, "you get the money for a bike?"

"Naw, I can't get my hands on it till I'm twenty-one."

"Your old lady won't give it to you?"

"Naw. I'm going to get me a job."

And Jack laughed, with a sort of bellowing formality recognized by them as expressing incredulity.

"Oh, E.O., what you going to be this time, a garbage collector?"

Oliver's tight little smile, which had nothing to do with mirth, tried to be supercilious, tried to suggest that he knew something that Jack couldn't guess. But Jack wasn't fooled; since he had known him, Oliver had kept none of his jobs for more than a few weeks. Oliver had picked fruit, driven a delivery truck, been a surveyor's helper, washed dishes, worked in a cannery, worked in a warehouse, and held a dozen more jobs like these. Either he had simply not showed up for work one day, or had been fired for loafing, or else had earned as much money as he'd wanted at the time and then had formally quit.

"I got me an in at the plumbers' union. They make good dough."

"Yeh?" said Jack, full of doubt. "How you going to get in?"

"I know somebody who knows somebody."

Jack shrugged with apparent indifference. "How good of a bike you going to get?"

"I figure I'll borrow me seven hundred dollars and pay it back in a year. That'll get me a pretty fair motor."

"Nobody'll lend you seven hundred dollars."

Oliver just smiled.

Jack shrugged again; it was his favorite gesture. "You got one lined up?"

"No," said Oliver leaning forward, "but I know what I'm going to get when I lay my hands on that ten thousand. I'm going to get me a chrome job, with a straight pipe and a butterfly cutout. . . ."

He'd been through the catalogue of his motorcycle's charms so often that both he and Jack knew it by heart, but the more elaborate and set his imaginings of it the keener was his anticipation. He had hardly got started on his recital when someone came in the front door—a melodious, feminine voice spoke to Iggy. Oliver continued, unconsciously raising his voice a little. When he had quite finished, Jack suggested his favorite variation, harder but puncture-proof tires. Oliver was giving his usual response, "Aaah, I'll get me a new set of tires every month," when the curtain to the back room parted to a young woman in motorcycle clothes. She was brown-skinned and had short black hair; she was strong and carried herself like a man, though her figure was amply female; her eyes were dark and bold, her face was impassive, and her thin, lubricious lips scarcely moved when she spoke.

"Hi Jack," she said; she seemed to be trying to make her beautiful voice harsh but succeeded only in making it sound flat and strained.

"Hello Jo Ann."

"Who's your friend?" she said pointing at Oliver with the glass of beer in her hand.

"E.O. Adams. Come on and sit down."

"E.O. Adams? I've heard about you."

"This is Jo Ann Rakoczi," said Jack.

Oliver's little smile tried to express indifference but he only looked pleased. "Glad to meet you," he said. "You have a nice motor."

She nodded and looked at him without expression. Oliver was excited; he had seen her at the head of her gang a dozen times, fearless and confident it seemed to him; he had seen her perform a perfect figure eight in the middle of East Twelfth Street, stopping the traffic with complete nonchalance. He thought she was beautiful, and she would have been beautiful if it had not been for the hardness with which she shellacked herself and which Oliver admired in her.

Under her gaze he did not know what to say; he knew that boasting would not succeed with her and he felt that the exaggerated cowardice with which he sometimes talked about his hot-rod exploits would not amuse her. So he said nothing and only stared at the ring on her hand. Saying nothing became Oliver; he was well-built and handsome, and though he sat in a sort of slouch and though his face was marred by a scar on the cheek he looked like a strong man affecting indifference to his strength. His embarrassment, which was really a kind of modesty, disguised as it was by his smile and his slouch, seemed to Jo Ann a kind of indifference to herself. To overcome this indifference without seeming to became her immediate object.

"You're all alone?" asked Jack.

"Yes. We had a party last night. Everybody else is still laid up from it."

"Sit down," said Oliver dragging a chair into place with his foot.

"Thanks. Say, it sounds like you're after a pretty sharp motor."

"Yeh. I'm coming into some dough in a few months."

"What you got now?"

"Nothing. I wrecked my last rod, but I'm tired of rods. Kid stuff."

"Oh I don't know," she said looking at the scar on his cheek. "I got up to 135 out in Richmond one time in a rod. Brakes wasn't worth a damn either."

"Oh yeh," said Oliver hastily, "*high-grade* kid stuff, but a bike's got more kick to it."

"Oh yeh," said Jo Ann, "a lot more kick."

"A lot more," said Jack.

"I know a guy," said Jo Ann, "that's got a damn good motor he'd probably sell. Want to go see it?"

"How much he want for it?"

"Four hundred dollars. It's a good machine. Not as good as mine except on turns. It's a little heavier. But it's got as much soup as I've got."

"I got no money."

"Borrow some. Get a job."

"Of course, this one would just fill in. I'm coming into some real money in a few months." And suddenly, with a boldness that astonished himself, Oliver looked down straight into her eyes and then at her lips. "Sure," he said as though he was meaning something else. "I'll come with you. Give me a ride?"

"Sure."

Oliver turned to Jack. "You got anything to do?"

"No," said Jack getting up expectantly, "I got nothing to do."

"Well find something, man," said Oliver winking at him in such a way that Jo Ann could not see it. They left Jack crestfallen.

Oliver had never intentionally been so rude to anyone before in his life. He judged that any man whom Jo Ann admired would do things like this, and he winked to soften the unkindness to his friend. But as they roared away toward Alameda his conscience was uneasy.

He yelled in Jo Ann's ear, intending to say, "How long have you known Jack?" but saying instead, "What's Jack to you?"

"When we used to be kids we were neighbors. What's it to you?"

"I don't know. He's my buddy."

"Yeh, but he hasn't got much nerve."

They didn't speak again because of the noise, but Oliver felt impelled to tell her one of his what-a-coward-I-was stories, impelled by an obscure sort of loyalty to Jack whom he had betrayed and who was cowardly too and by a sense of flying under false colors now with Jo Ann. So when they stopped in front of Jo Ann's house in Alameda he told her, with grotesque exaggeration, how he had been so frightened in a time run on the Richmond streets once—the hot rod before him had blown a tire and rolled over—that he had cut his rod out at eighty-five with the excuse that his supercharger had gone on the fritz. The story was true, but he told it so quietly and with such great exaggeration that Jo Ann thought he was making it up to defend his friend; she thought he was saying, "Even a brave man can lose his nerve sometimes," and she admired him for his loyalty, his honesty, and his courage.

The motorcycle for sale belonged to Jo Ann's brother, who was at sea. Oliver climbed on it and followed Jo Ann up the steepest streets to Skyline Boulevard, and there he performed feats which froze his guts with fear and at the same time flushed his face with pride. But the only tribute that he won from her was when he performed a power spin that nearly pulled his left leg off.

"Say," she said, "that's good. You ought to get a steel shoe."

"I will, when I get me a real bike."

And he roared down the winding road so fast he had to clench his teeth to keep them from chattering, but always with the tight little smile and always ready to wave nonchalantly at his friend who was not afraid. She was not afraid in truth; she had discovered exactly how good she was on a motorcycle and she would do anything up to her limit and nothing beyond it. She was as afraid as Oliver of seeming afraid but she was wiser than he, less reckless, for he was afraid not only of fear itself but of the danger as well; that was an emotion she had not felt, purely and simply, for years. A rock in the road was something to avoid for her; for him it meant five painfully broken ribs or a broken neck.

At 3:30, feeling hungry, they roared down the hills to 17 Denver Place and roared up the driveway to the garage just as the rest of the family were starting to eat dessert.

"That's where my room is," he said to Jo Ann, pointing to the room over the garage, then led her into the dining room.

"Hi Mom," he said snapping the black bowler at her; she had begged him the day before not to wear it in the house. "This is Jo Ann; Jo Ann, my mother. Those are the rest of my family."

Ruth concealed the hurt she felt and said how do you do in an even voice. Gene looked at Jo Ann in her jeans and kidney belt and tight man's shirt, at Oliver, at his mother; he said nothing but watched the three of them closely, holding his eyebrows very high. Miriam was furious, said nothing, and glared at Oliver. Oliver missed none of their reactions.

"You got to the pie already," he said. "We'll go out in the kitchen and get some of the stuff that's left over."

"I'll fix it for you here," said Ruth. "I can easily lay another place."

"Don't bother," said Oliver. "Jo Ann can dish it up. Anyway, we aren't dressed for the occasion." He leered at Miriam, who was well turned out as always. "I'm thinking of buying her brother's bike."

"What?" said Ruth in a sharp constrained voice.

"Sure," said Oliver; it was easier for him to say these painful words to his mother in front of everyone and casually, for he knew that she could not reproach him openly here and now. "He's at sea and it's a good job."

"Please, Oliver," she said, "for my sake—"

And no one knew what was threatening Ruth at that moment—Oliver because he dared not see it, Dorie because she did not wish to, Gene because it was so risky—no one but Miriam. Only she saw on Ruth's face the dark shadow pass, heard in Ruth's voice the cracked will, felt in her own sympathetic heart the stark and nameless fear. Stark—she put her hand on her mother's arm and held it tightly; nameless—when she saw Ruth's self-composure return she did not seek to name that fear but to forget it.

All this took but a few seconds. Oliver snapped the bowler again and pushed Jo Ann before him into the kitchen. He had accomplished a great deal in this minute of boorishness—and it was boorishness. He knew the amenities and had violated them for his own purposes. For one thing he infuriated his sister, and that was always worth the trouble. For another, he put his mother in her place for not giving him the money for a motorcycle; of course, she did not know that the pain he was giving her was for that reason, but he knew it and felt that it justified him in what he did. But only barely justified him, for he had another reason for his behavior of which he was not aware: his family was certain to disapprove of Jo Ann; by hitting first he protected himself against their disapproval, especially against his mother's, which he could hardly bear. He need not, of course, have brought Jo Ann home at all, but he wanted to impress her with his mother's house and the style in which they lived. Though he kept his room over the garage littered with bolts and dime magazines he was proud of his mother, her house, and her life. It all seemed useless to him, but pretty; to Oliver part of the prettiness of a thing was always its inutility.

Also he wanted to seem strong and dominating and indifferent in the eyes of Gene and Jo Ann. With Jo Ann he succeeded, with Gene he failed completely. Oliver held Gene in a peculiar respect. Though he was contemptuous of Gene's physical frailty and what seemed to him his unmanliness he was in awe of Gene's intellect. "He's a brain," Oliver would tell his friends, who all felt about a brain as he did—after all scientists are brains and everybody knows about scientists. But even about his unmanliness Oliver was not sure; after all Gene always managed to get women to go around with, and here he was engaged to quite a good-looking one. More, Gene had been in the war and Oliver hadn't. To be sure, Gene had been conscripted against his will and had spent his time in an office decoding messages and not out shooting or bombing the enemy; still, decoding messages is sort of like the FBI and everybody knows about the FBI. Perhaps most important of all was that Oliver knew of no way by which he could hurt Gene short of knocking him down, whereas Gene could make Oliver very uneasy simply by raising his eyebrows high and staring right at him as though he were decoding him. For these reasons Oliver was trying to appear tough in Gene's eyes now; he would have winced if he had realized that Gene was pitying his shaky bravado.

With Jo Ann he succeeded, however. Jo Ann would never have been allowed to speak so rudely to her mother, who was old-fashioned about teaching children their manners. Jo Ann thought that Oliver kept his family in their place; she took Ruth's silence for submission to his domination, and admired him for it. Therefore when a little later Oliver slapped her on her ample bottom as she was leaning over to pick up a spoon Jo Ann did not hit him fiercely as she would normally have done but said menacingly and close to him, "What'd you do that for?" And when he grabbed her and kissed her, she kissed him back. It was hard to make her submit, but once down she was fierce in demanding that she be held down hard.

Jo Ann was not alone in thinking that Ruth had submitted to Oliver. "Mother," said Miriam indignantly when Oliver and Jo Ann had disappeared into the kitchen, "why do you let him get away with stuff like that? It's terrible."

"He's a man now," said Ruth gravely. Her lips were pursed with pain but her eyes and voice were steady. "He's free to do as he wishes, as you are, my dear."

But Miriam fumed, outraged and inconsistent. As a mother she gave Penny and George even more freedom and indulgence than she herself had been allowed when a child. She put up with their rages and insults with great equanimity, acceded to many of their wishes, and let them have very bad manners. But she could not bear to think that at the age of twenty they would still be capable of such behavior as this of Oliver's; according to her scheme will should automatically assert itself at some point in a child's career, bringing with it good manners, respect for convention, and a sense of adult responsibility. It all seemed so simple to Miriam because she had been contented with herself most of her life. Contented, she could afford when she wished to seem considerate of others, which makes up for any amount of technical flaw in manners. She might have bethought herself, had she not been so satisfied with her lot, that one who is truly guided by a code of behavior (as she thought herself to be) need not and can not employ that code of bitchery she used so readily with Dorie; that Oliver, who was far from content with himself and had like herself been allowed much freedom as a child, was behaving perhaps more crudely than she behaved with Dorie but no worse. Instead of so reflecting she indulged herself in that sort of indignation which comes not from seeing injustice done, but from seeing someone else betray one of your placid beliefs as you might have done it yourself.

"Mother, I think this knuckling under to Oliver is a shocking dereliction of duty on your part."

"Do you? To my mind love for my children is more important than any duty, and love forgives." But she spoke with a voice in which there was more censure of Miriam than forgiveness of her; furthermore her practice as a mother had been the reverse of this statement.

"One of your duties was, as you saw it, to love us," said Gene blandly. "Always. And don't forget—Miriam is your child too."

Ruth felt that if she stayed at this table any longer she would break down. Without excusing herself she went to her room and lay on the bed. When Miriam had accused her of neglecting her duty Ruth had felt unfairly blamed. She had done something wrong so she deserved blame, but it had been an error in judgment and not in intent so she deserved commiseration as well. And when Gene had said that she should forgive her child Miriam too, she knew that he had said it not because it was true—though it seemed to be true—but because it would hurt. So as she lay on her bed it seemed to her that Oliver's cruelty, so much more childlike, so much less willed than theirs, was the action of one to whom she had done some secret injury that neither she nor he understood and neither had wanted; love for him filled her heart, and dread of the damage she was yet to do.

Miriam, full of wrath—wrath the greater for the moment of dread she had felt on her mother's account and had then put out of her mind—went into the kitchen and asked Oliver in an affable voice if he had heard that Ruth had given Gene the money to go to Japan for the chess tournament. She did it not to wound Oliver but to cause her mother trouble. She succeeded.

At first, in his generosity of heart, Oliver rushed in and congratu-
lated Gene on his good fortune; there was general concord for a
time, with Jo Ann silent on the sidelines ignoring the children who
wanted to talk to her. But this amity did not suit Miriam at all. As
she stood at the front door with Bill—they were leaving the children
till evening while they went to a cocktail party—she said to Oliver
with a burst of machined enthusiasm, "Now you can get the money
for a new motorcycle, E.O. Maybe Jo Ann's brother's."

Oliver was happy, but Gene saw what she had done.

"Good-bye now," said Miriam sweetly. "Take good care of my
children."

She took Bill in tow and left.

Gene and Jo Ann were silent, for their separate reasons. Dorie
was in a friendly mood and tried to start a conversation; that Ruth
and Miriam had behaved badly elevated Dorie's spirits. No one took
her gambits, though Oliver might have had he not been moved by
desire; on pretext of showing Jo Ann around the place he took her
up to his room.

Under the supervision of Gene and Dorie, who were doing dishes,
the children seemed quite content to play by themselves in the back.
It was a mild evening, and there were very few ways they could hurt
themselves except on the motorcycles beside the garage, and those
were forbidden them. Dorie went to the back door once in a while
to glance at them; once they ran up the stairs to Oliver's room, but
he had locked the door as he always did whether at home or
abroad. Dorie ordered them to stay away from his room.

Her feeling of elevation had not left her, and with it was coming
a feeling of amorousness. The soft and pleasant air, the absence of
anything urgent to do and of anyone to impress herself upon,
Gene's rather attentive glances at Jo Ann before she had disappeared with Oliver, the not having made love for a long while, all
these combined to turn her mind to love-making. So as they were
finishing the dishes and Gene began some of his amorous horseplay
(which meant this time not that he was annoyed with her but that
he was ready if she was and if she wasn't she could tell him to quit,
no harm done) Dorie responded in the way that meant she was
ready too—that is, she began to talk in a serious manner about all
the arrangements, the ways and means, the possible obstacles, who

might interrupt, ought anything else to be done first. Dorie was not afraid to talk about love; on the contrary, with fearless frankness and in a special tone of voice she would scrutinize all the mechanics of love-making with that dispassionateness which, like a shamed but flagrant nakedness, can be so sure a safeguard for one afraid of love itself. It was a chilling beginning all in all, and Gene was as usual chilled.

Their arrangements were made. She was to go to his room and wait for him there till Ruth awoke. She would be safe there, for Gene allowed no one but Dorie to go into his room. When Ruth came down he told her that he didn't know where Oliver was and that Dorie had gone home; then he went up to his room and to Dorie.

While the small children were still in the house to be watched and read to and fed Ruth was in a happy frame of mind. But after Miriam and Bill had returned and taken them home, Ruth suddenly felt empty and nervous. She wandered through the house disconsolately; its familiar beauty did not please her at all. Hiding in it, holed up in it was her son Gene, who though a full-grown man did nothing but play chess. For all she knew, indeed she was sure of it, Dorie was in his room with him. Not even as an excuse to herself did she disapprove of their love-making, but she could not remain in the same house with them. More deeply than she knew, she—who had not had a man for twenty years—resented this woman of Gene's. She saw the gleaming handlebars of the motorcycles outdoors and knew that up in his room Frederick Kotowski's son had taken a woman, knew furthermore that if she asked him he would deny it. She did not know why her sons thought that they had to deceive her.

It was still a warm night and she lay down on the cot. She was conscious only of the bright stars and of the darkness in which they were lost. She felt not just in words but with her whole heart that it had been better for her if she had never been born.

As she lay there Ruth heard the door to Oliver's room open; she could see him descend the stairs and go to the dark house. The light went on in the kitchen; he was opening cupboards and clashing silverware. She arose and went in the back door.

He started when she came in. "Hi Mom. Where've you been?"

"Lying on my cot in the back yard. It's a beautiful night."

"It sure is."

"Do you want me to fix you a little snack?"

He could not refuse her without an explanation of why he wanted to take a double portion to his room to eat; rather ungraciously he thanked her and sat down.

"Where's Gene, Mom?"

"Up in his room, I think. Miriam and Bill came for the children a little while ago."

"They're mighty sweet kids. Penny's the cutest little girl I ever saw."

"She's awfully fond of you, Oliver."

"Yeh," he said with pleasure, "she is."

A little silence began, which both of them tried to think of a way to fill. Ruth began another subject for small talk, a movie she wanted him to see; it was a short-lived topic too.

Oliver thought that his mother was going to reprove him for coming to dinner late, for entering rudely, for the black bowler, and for bringing in Jo Ann so brusquely; as their mutual uneasiness increased and he gulped without pleasure the good food she prepared for him, he began to think that she wanted not to reprove him openly but to punish him by making him thus uncomfortable. He resented this deviousness. She had no such intention at all—quite the reverse. In the sadness that had overcome her as she was lying on the cot it seemed to her that everything that had gone wrong with her children must surely have been her own fault, though she did not understand what she had done and knew she had not done whatever it was intentionally. She too was thinking of his cruelty this afternoon, but she felt that somehow she had made him do it to her; her pain she could stand, every mother must, but the thought that she had driven him to it against his own nature she could not bear. She wanted him to forgive her for having made him do it, and she thought he understood her impulse and rejected it; she thought the sullenness of his mistaken resentment was unforgiveness, and her feeling of guilty failure deepened.

But though these complex misunderstandings made a barrier between the mother and son, they were not the chief danger; that was too great for either of them to face before they had to. It was this event which Oliver's resentment and Ruth's sense of failure were preparing them for; it was painful and wasteful, and neither of them wanted it and both felt it was coming. Nothing anyone could have done could have prevented it.

"Hey Mom," Oliver said forcing himself up from his sullenness; there had been a long, grave silence which he felt he should interrupt by a triviality, but the pressure that made him speak was so great that it was not a trivial thing he said. "Hey Mom, Sis says Gene's going to go to Japan."

"Yes," she said brightening. That both of them respected Gene's intellect was something to cling to in this strait.

"Will he ever be the world's champion, do you think?"

"I certainly hope so. But he seems to think he never will be."

"Well, it'd be swell if he could." He had finished eating. He should have left his mother before speaking again, before the danger had been exposed and run toward. But this would have happened only if he had known what he was about to do, and he did not.

"How much money will it take him to get there?"

"I don't know, dear. He had to have five hundred dollars from me." She ought not have said this, but it was true and she told the truth, and it took the last step in the dark, the step that both of them had been dreading in the way that one dreads a sure pain.

"Well gee, Mom, that bike of Jo Ann's brother's only costs four hundred dollars. Let me have it, will you? It's only fair. I'll pay you back when I get that ten thousand."

With all her heart she wanted to say yes, here it is; he would have loved her then and forgiven her. But she had decided long ago that it would have been wrong for her to encourage him in his destructive passion for fast cars and motorcycles; she felt it to be her duty to try to restrain him from his desperate courses until he had matured a little and straightened out. She had told him all this before, more than once, but he was nearly a man now, he would have his ten thousand dollars soon. She could have given in without any great sense of shame. She probably would have given in had it not been for one thing: it would have been a method of bribing his love— more, of bribing her own conscience, of cheating her sense of failure, and that her pride would not let her do. So once again she allowed her duty to thwart her impulse. While her understanding of her duty was sound and good her impulse was sounder and better yet, for her impulse was usually to do something for someone and her duty was usually to abstain.

"No," she said. "You know how I feel about your motorcycle, Oliver. Won't you please me just a little . . ."

"What the hell!" he shouted suddenly and stood up. "Gene gets this, Gene gets that, now he gets five hundred dollars and I don't get a dime. What kind of a deal is that?"

"Oliver! Do not speak to me in that tone of voice."

"Why not?" he shouted louder yet. There was a menacing expression on his face; he could be heard throughout the house. "Why not? Tell me that. I've always got the short end of the stick and I'm sick and tired of it. Okay, you can take your money and shove it. I'm getting out of here."

"Oliver, I'll put five hundred dollars in the bank against your name. It's not the money. I just don't want you to kill yourself with those machines."

"What I do is none of your business." There were tears, not only of rage, in his eyes. "I never asked to be made a bastard but you made me one, and the least you could have done about it was to be a mother to me. Okay, play your damn favorite. I won't bother you any more." He went to the back door.

Crying, Ruth held to his arm. "Forgive me," she said, "forgive me."

"I wouldn't forgive you," he said, "if you was dying. I couldn't. You made me. I won't be back either."

Gene and Dorie heard the shouting. Dorie was frightened and urged Gene to go down and make peace. He told her to be still. They lay in bed in the dark, listening. Not until the motorcycles had roared away did Gene arise.

"Get dressed." He whispered, though he was positive that his mother was still in the kitchen. "I'll keep her talking in the kitchen till you creep out the front door."

"Why can't I just stay here as I always do, till she goes to bed?"

"When she's upset she even comes into my room." This was not true. He only wanted Dorie to leave him alone.

In his turtleneck sweater and tennis shoes, holding a cigarette in fingers that were not entirely steady, his eyebrows very high on his high forehead, Gene entered the kitchen. Ruth did not take her face from her hands. She was still crying. At first he did not know what to do. He walked over to the sink to knock the ash from his cigarette. It occurred to him to pat his mother on the shoulder, but he decided against it; had he been in her place he would not have wanted to be patted. He could think of nothing to say. He felt chilly, though it was warm. He put out his cigarette and stood with his hands in his pockets, watching her. It occurred to him he ought to leave her alone. So he went out from the kitchen and walked through the house aimlessly. He found himself oppressed by the dark, inward, spacious house, but he could not go outside because there was nothing at all out there but dark. He turned on the lights in the living room. The dark redwood panels seemed to absorb the light. He wished for a moment that this room, that all the rooms in the house, were white and geometrical as Dorie wanted them to be. It was not ordered enough for him now; it allowed him to be whatever he chose to be within its own broad limits and he did not know who he was. He had to go back into the kitchen where his mother was, but he needed an excuse to return. He discovered that he was hungry, returned, and ate a ham sandwich.

At last Ruth raised her face to look at him; he was washing his long fingers under the tap. Her eyes were puffy and red, and the puckering about her mouth was replaced by ugly swellings and teeth marks in her lower lip. She looked at him, beseeching mercy. In his high-pitched, exact, merciless voice he answered the look.

"Well, you and Oliver seem to have had an argument."

No one else in the world but Gene would have thought then that he was being ironic and light; these bad ironies of his were sharp knives with notched blades.

"He has left home, Gene."

The pathetic are ugly if you close your heart to them.

"Well, he's nearly of age."

"He hates me. Why does he hate me?"

"Oh well, he's hot-tempered."

"No, he is not. What shall I do?" Like a man in a well she clutched at a rope to find it a snake falling back in with her.

Gene shrugged.

"Why?" she said. "I taught him what was right and wrong. Why does he choose this?"

"Why didn't you offer him the motorcycle he wants? He'll get one anyway. Do you think it is right to make him feel bad about what he loves so much, just because you don't approve of it? Why indeed?"

"If I had given him what he wanted, I would have been ordering him in a way. Surely it is better to let him be free." It was her last appeal.

"It is worse to subvert," he said.

She looked at him almost blankly. "Did I not leave you all free to choose?"

"You cut our anchors. That is different."

"Is it not the noblest thing for a man to be free?" she cried out over him.

"Yes," he said and drew in his neck like a turtle, "yes, oh God, yes."

"Gene," she said bitterly, "my son is full of hatred for me. He has left me. Why has he done this?"

She called Oliver "my son" as though Gene were her enemy, and indeed for that moment he was not her son but her conscious enemy.

"Do you understand what I'm saying? Does it mean anything more than words to you?"

In his highest pitch he answered, "Try to take some Nembutal, Mother. Sleep is the best restorative."

"Sleep," she said with such bitter scorn as he had never heard from her, "sleep." She put her face back into her hands and her shoulders shook.

Gene went to his room and the sixty-four squares and thirty-two men of chess. For the hundredth time he set himself to work on trying to find the weakness in his own variation of the Ruy Lopez opening, but the chess could not keep him from hearing his mother's movements. He heard her when she came up the stairs slowly, heavily. He heard her dial a number and talk in a low voice to someone; he could not tell who it was but from her voice he guessed it was some old trusted friend. He wanted to open his door and listen to her conversation but he did not have the nerve. Then she went up to the attic and moved something heavy; he was racked with curiosity to know what she was doing, what was happening in the long silences between the rustling and shifting noises. Perhaps she was looking at old pictures or reading old letters; he could not imagine what else she could be up to. But at last she came back down to her room and was silent. After an hour he opened his door and looked down the hall. There was still a crack of light under her door. He applied himself to the Ruy Lopez, knowing that he could not sleep until her light was off.

Nothing could keep him from listening with all his might for her movements. He knew that for Ruth this was a night like two others he could remember. One had been when the first Japanese-Americans had been taken off to the Relocation Camps. The other he remembered from his childhood, the night after Sacco and Vanzetti had been executed. All that night he had slept badly and full of dread, for whenever he had awakened he had heard his mother walking up and down in the house, and sometimes she had cried out in a terrible voice, "What is wrong? What is wrong? What should I have done?"

The Beatification of BobbySu Wilson

Four years ago when the miracle at BobbySu's tomb started up I was interested like everybody else to read about it, though I didn't believe in it. Then one day Mal Tobey came around and let me know there was the possibility the firm I'm with might want to get in on it. He was pretty vague about where I came in—my profession is fund-raising—but he said if anything came up he'd throw some business our way. Naturally I said I'd go along with him on the deal, and if there was anything I could do to let me know. Just at that moment I didn't have anything booked or anything coming up in the near future, so I got the green light from my boss to brush up on the details on the BobbySu deal, just in case. All I could remember was that she had been three years ahead of me at McClaskey High, and that I was a senior when she died in 1930 and caused all the stir. I swore I'd never go to church again I was so disgusted, and I didn't till just recently.

When she died, the people in her parish in East Sansom (which was my parish at the time, though I never saw her in the flesh that I know of) were so impressed with how holy she was that they took up a handsome collection and had her put away in a marble mausoleum, one of the best in Whispering Glades, and they really had it decorated with angels over the doorway and a long Latin inscription on the side. All this was paid for by working people too. Well, four years ago, at Easter, 1950, BobbySu's mother went down into the mausoleum to put flowers on the tomb the way she did every year, and she saw fluid coming out of the tomb. It was April and there hadn't been any rain since February. Besides, Whispering Glades is very well drained, and they *guarantee* no seepage in an all-metal casket. The mausoleum was dry enough everywhere else. She couldn't understand it. She went straight to Father O'Dwyer. He got the cemetery officials to go look at it. Nobody could understand it. Fortunately we have a Bishop in Sansom, and Father O'Dwyer got him that same afternoon. The Bishop made everyone concerned swear they would wait till the whole matter had been thoroughly investigated.

The next morning the fluid was still coming out. That afternoon they opened the tomb. There were six people present: Father O'Dwyer and Mrs. Wilson, who had both seen BobbySu when she was put away, Bishop Magoon, one official from the cemetery, and two county officials. They all swore that the body was in a remarkable state of preservation and that it was in exactly the same position it had been in when it was buried, which is important for a saint, with hands at the side palm up so the bruises of the stigmata could be seen. The fluid was coming from the palms of the hands, and it had made a small seepage hole in the bottom of the casket.

This isn't one of the superstitious backwashes of the world. Sansom is as up-to-the-minute a city as you could find anywhere for the size, and the Bishop told them that a story like this would cause a big sensation and maybe do the faith a lot of harm. The Church is very particular about the public relations angle, so he made them promise not to say a word about it to anyone.

But Mrs. Wilson had brought along an empty little bottle that some liver pills had come in and when nobody was looking she let some of BobbySu's fluid trickle into that bottle and took it home. The reason was that next door she had a pious neighbor whose left arm had been paralyzed for five or six years, and the doctors hadn't been able to do a thing for her. Mrs. Wilson took the fluid to her in the pill bottle, told her all about it, and rubbed a few drops on the woman's arm. They prayed together to BobbySu to intercede with Our Lord to cure the arm. And in the morning it was well. Now that was too much for Mrs. Wilson to hold back. She contacted Father O'Dwyer. Bishop or no bishop they had to spread the word. It was the hottest word-of-mouth campaign I ever saw, and I've been in on a couple, but it was two days getting to the papers. I heard that the Bishop tried to kill the story, but it was too big for him to handle.

As I said, I didn't believe in it, no more than anybody else; on the other hand I didn't exactly disbelieve in it either. The day of miracles is over I said to myself. When something like this happens they ought to get the scientists to work on it, and if the scientists can't explain it then they ought to play it down. With BobbySu the newspapers were hitting it up for all it was worth. It was good copy so nobody could blame them. But once the story got started, the Church just encouraged it; it turned out the reason Bishop Magoon sat on it at first was so he'd be in a better position to push it when it did break. All this struck me as being pretty poor, and even after Mal got me thinking about it from my own angle I didn't like it too much.

The weekend after Easter so many hundreds of pilgrims came to see the tomb that the Whispering Glades people had to fix regular roped-off walks around it, like a giant sequoia in a national park. This was really good copy, naturally, and they even got newsreel men to cover the story. They shot the pilgrims praying before the tomb, and BobbySu's home, and Father O'Dwyer, and even some clothes her mother had saved and some old schoolbooks. It wasn't the jazziest newsreel I ever saw, but it was a popular success all right. I don't want to give the idea that all the publicity was favorable to the miracle, but still, antagonistic or sensational or favorable, there was a *terrific* amount of it. It makes you think those thinkers are right when they say we are returning to an age of faith.

About the time Mal got me interested in the business the second miracle transpired. An old Italian laborer had been having a fever for two weeks, so his wife got his sons to drive him up to Whispering Glades and carry him with a fever of 102° on a windy day to the mausoleum. He kissed the mausoleum and prayed, and he scraped a little of the marble off with a jackknife. He took the marble dust home and drank it in a glass of wine that same day, and by the next day his fever had gone away. I went around to see the old man myself, and there was no doubt about it—he had been sick for a long time and now he was well again. The doctors couldn't explain it. Of course, it wasn't a miracle in the first degree, as Father Polycarp said later; nowadays, as he said, vaccination and antibiotics and such like are cutting down on bonafide first-degree miracles, though there are quite a few ailments left that respond to saints and relics. Still, this one was enough to get the ball rolling.

There was a big movement right away to get BobbySu canonized. Father O'Dwyer spark-plugged it but all good Catholics were behind it a hundred per-cent. The Bishop acted reluctant to get under way so soon, but so much pressure was put on him that he did it. The main thing in canonizing, at first, is to get a good investigation by authorities from outside the district. That's how I got to know Father Polycarp; he was the devil's advocate.

By June, when he was brought over from England, my firm had got in on the deal and I was put in charge of general good will among non-Catholics; what it amounted to was fund-raising on a commission basis. Mal Tobey took care of all the Catholic end of it, but there was so much non-Catholic interest that I had enough digging to keep a sweat up. Whispering Glades contributed, of course, and public-spirited groups with an eye on Sansom's fame, like the Boosters and Kiwanis and even some unions and lodges and business firms. Well Father Polycarp didn't want to be always around the promoters of the cause, and yet he didn't want to be too unfriendly to them either. Now I sort of took to him, so when I heard he was looking for a place to stay I thought of the guest room I'd fixed up in my basement. The main thing was he didn't want a lot of promoting around him, which suited me to a T. I insinuated to him where I stood in my own thinking; it seemed to suit him, so I offered my basement room to him at a nominal price and he moved in.

I remember the first real conversation we had, after dinner the third day he moved into our spare room. He was a thin-faced, dark-complected, high-strung kind of a man and he had that supercilious, chopped-off way of talking that keeps you on your toes. His whole

name was Father Polycarp Botts and his lay name had been Cecil.
You could tell there was plenty of that limey Cecil Botts in him,
Oxford and all that sort of thing, don't you know. My family really
didn't like him, but I thought he had a good sense of humor. Anyhow, he took a glass of port wine after his dinner, and this particular
evening he was drinking his port wine and I was drinking my highball. We were in the front room looking out over the city, a million
dollar vista, with the lights of East Sansom twinkling below us and
the river in the background and the evening star out. He was smoking a pipe.

"Tell me, Stanmer," he said aiming at me with his pipestem,
"what would you do if this whole affair turned out to be fraud-
dulent?"

"Do?" I said. "I wouldn't do anything."

"No, I suppose not. What would you think?"

"Well, I'd be pretty surprised. I don't think Father O'Dwyer or
Mrs. Wilson are frauds."

"It's happened."

"You mean they just set out to cheat everybody?"

"Mm," he said with his teeth clenched on his pipe. I gathered he
meant yes.

"Well, I don't believe it."

"Suppose they didn't know they were cheating, as you put it, but
they were all the same. Then what?"

"You'd have to do some fast talking to convince me of that."

"The devil is an expert at fraud," he said in a sort of a dry way,
"and so are hysterics. Suppose."

I thought about it for awhile, but the main thing I thought about
was what was he getting at? He knew I'd been brought up a Catholic. What was he trying to pull on me? The devil's in hell.

"Well, I think I would be relieved, honestly," I said. "I don't like
this stuff very much."

"Quite."

I waited for awhile, but he was off on cloud nine.

"You don't think it's possible," I asked him, "that this is a fake?"

"Mm," he said around his pipe.

There wasn't anything more I could think of to say, and before
long he went down to his room.

The first thing Father Polycarp cast doubt on was the stigmata.

Evidence seen on the corpse when the coffin was opened was not valid. The cause of death was listed in the county courthouse as heart failure. Only two people could be found who would swear they had seen the wounds on her hands before she died, Father O'Dwyer and Mrs. Wilson (BobbySu's sister Mary Jane didn't count because she was feeble-minded). Father O'Dwyer and Mrs. Wilson said that BobbySu had been sick all during Lent of 1930. She spent most of her days and nights praying, and she finally got to the point in fasting where she didn't eat anything but a little bread and water. On Good Friday she couldn't get out of bed and she said she had the worst kind of a headache, all around the crown of her head. That evening on the palms of her hands dark bruises showed up. The doctor said she needed rest, she was run-down. The priest saw what was what: she was in a state of ecstasy. She prayed off and on all Saturday night. She didn't even recognize her mother. She hadn't had a thing on her stomach since Thursday. On Easter morning at about sunrise, her mother said, she sat up in bed, stretched up her arms to Heaven, cried something in some other language—the same thing three times, her mother couldn't understand what—and then fell back dead. There was a real other-worldly smile on her face, and her hands fell at her sides palm up so the stigmata showed clearly, just the way they fixed her in the casket.

The testimony of two prejudiced witnesses, according to Father Polycarp, wasn't enough. That was a body blow to the promoters of the cause, particularly as Bishop Magoon agreed, and at this stage the Bishop had a lot of authority. Naturally Father Polycarp wasn't high on the list with the Catholics of Sansom, and in some ways I was put on the spot by having the devil's advocate in my home. However, the way I figured it was I ought to be objective about the whole matter and nobody was more objective than Father Polycarp. It was his job to be objective. This way I could be sure that nobody was being swindled. The truth was I got so I really enjoyed talking with him once in a while. Here was a professional Catholic whose duty was to test this thing, and I could see he was doing a good objective job of it.

"Stanmer," he said, "what would you say constituted heroicity of virtue?"

"I'm sorry," I said, "but I don't think I get you."

"The practice of heroic sanctity. A saintly life."

"Well," I said, "in my thinking somebody like Florence Nightingale had it."

"Quite. Unfortunately she was Anglican."

"Well, what about somebody that converted a lot of natives?"

"Possibly. But what is one to say for a girl who had such bad acne that she was afraid to meet people; who was incapable of comprehending simple algebra; who talked very little because her s's tended to sound like sh's, especially in front of t, p, or k. Some of the children in her high school called her Kraut because of it. One shouldn't expect intelligence and charm along with saintliness I suppose. All the same atrocious acne and an IQ of 80 . . ."

We sat without saying anything for awhile. It was August and hot, and the mosquitoes were bad. I was slapping one behind my right ear just as I was asking him this question.

"What about helping the deformed and crippled? She did that a lot you know."

"Yes I know," he said in as flat a voice as I've ever heard. "Tending monstrous infants. Nursing sick spastics. She was very good to her sister. No doubt about that."

"Well," I said, because he seemed to be feeling the same things I was feeling, "it's quite a problem."

"BobbySu," he said with a terrible edge to his voice. He got up.

That really puckered me. What, if you don't mind my asking, is wrong with BobbySu for a name? Just because the Britishers don't have it *yet*, they look down their nose at it. What difference does it make what a saint's name is? But he went away so fast that I didn't have time to collect my thoughts. That edge to his voice, his cool manner, and him being a priest made him mighty hard to get back at.

I was really upset that night. I don't think I got to sleep before three or four o'clock, which is pretty unusual for me on the whole. The next day I went around to Mrs. Wilson's and saw a relic of BobbySu's, a history test paper from the eleventh grade. She had got a D— on it. It was funny; you wouldn't have known there was anything in the least special about it except for the cross she had drawn in the upper left-hand corner of the first page. It was a pretty cross, and she had put the regular JMJ on it the way a lot of Catholic pupils do, only she had added a T, for St. Theresa of Avila her mother said. When you see a thing like that it makes you stop and think.

Father Polycarp left two days later. He had his report all filled out and his job was done, at least for the time being. So I more or less cooled down. Anyhow the first phase of the process was over now. They'd gotten the Holy Father himself to dispense with the time factor—they had to get him to do it because it hadn't been fifty years yet since BobbySu had died. Everything indicated that she'd at least be venerabilized even if she didn't get any further. Meanwhile, nothing could be done till some more miracles came off.

The thing is, getting anyone canonized a saint is harder than appealing a case to the Supreme Court. You've got to get the person declared a venerable, then you've got to get him (or her as the case may be) beatified, and then canonized. Canonization is just beatification all over again, only more expensive. And money! As Father Polycarp said, "It was provident that BobbySu was born in rich America. I don't think the Irish could have afforded her." Of course, with a *spectacular* saint details like money just take care of themselves, but BobbySu isn't spectacular—sort of run of the mill you might say.

Well, things were simmering along for about three years, no more miracles or anything, and it was getting to the point where all the BobbySu hullabaloo was just one of those things. Then four months ago, Ash Wednesday, 1954, some new evidence turned up about her life—good strong evidence too. On Easter day the fluid seeped out of her tomb again and two more miracles were worked. One of these new cures was a blind man whose sight was restored. The other was a woman who had been dumb for ten years and suddenly she could speak after she had put a few drops of the liquid from the tomb into her mouth. She wasn't even a Catholic, in fact a Christian Scientist, but it counted all the same. Well, the new evidence and the new miracles gave the cause a big boost here in Sansom and in Rome too, and Father Polycarp came back to investigate. It was now, or anyhow two months ago, that matters really came to a head for me.

The thing is, all this was forced on me, really forced. I was getting along all right, neither a believer nor an atheist, still not against the Church or anything like that. I was just about like everybody else, making a good living. I own my own home, I have a good solid wife and four lovely children. I can't brag I never cheated on the wife, but I haven't been too bad a family man. I don't vote the ticket, I vote the man. So when the miracles flared up again I was pretty up-set. My thinking on the matter wasn't at all clear or objective. I was as glad as could be to see that cool Father Polycarp again. Nobody around here had a sense of humor about it this time; they were either all for it or dead against it.

Which leads me up to *the* day. It was a Thursday. I came back from lunch and found a pamphlet on my desk, a reprint from some magazine I never heard of. Somebody had paid to have it distributed all over town. Usually I threw away stuff like this, but this one really hit me below the belt.

What would happen now, 1954, to a man who swore before a judge that some crazy old woman with five cats and no friends had been making little statues of him and sticking pins through them, so that he had been having fierce pains in the lower right-hand region of his abdomen? We would take out his infected appendix and test his sanity. But four hundred years ago what would have happened? The old woman would have been killed as a witch. Things have improved since then. We have advanced. *That's what you think.*

What is happening right now, 1954, to a group of people in San-som, who claim that some magic fluid is oozing out of a twenty-four-year-old tomb so wonderful that it makes the lame walk, the blind see, and the sick get well? Do we condemn their superstitiousness and pity their ignorance? Do we explain about hysterical blindness and lame-ness? Do we carefully check up on these so-called cures six months later? Do we ask why it is that a strong solution of ferrous tartrate in water (that's what the chemists say this ooze consists of) has no effect on the dumb unless it is applied with all the fanfare of high-pressure magic? Not a bit. What we actually do is say, "How wonderful," and kneel down in front of the grave of the poor, abnormal girl who is sup-posed to have caused all this. In fact, that very large section of human-ity called the Roman Catholic Church is deciding to give her the high-est honor it can bestow on anyone, dead or alive: make her a saint.

No healthy person is going to be happiest, or think anyone else is happiest, when they are suffering intensely. Yet we are told that this Saint of Sansom, this BobbySu Wilson, was happier than any of us can ever be—in fact, was *ecstatic*—when in her last illness she was lying on her sick bed with a hideous headache about to die of it. No healthy person is going to drink some fluid which is supposed to be coming from a decomposing corpse. Yet we encourage people to do it, against all the laws of reason and hygiene, and we are told that the magical cures that result from this vileness are proof of God's power and goodness. Some of us have a healthier, saner God than that.

When the Pope, who is the only man in the world who is never wrong, stands up in St. Peter's, as he probably will in a few years, surrounded by Cardinals in blazing costumes and watched by eighty thousand of the gullible faithful, and declares in a dead language over the public address system "in honor of the Holy and Indivisible Trinity" that the Blessed BobbySu Wilson is "inscribed in the catalogue of Saints," then there will be a mighty rejoicing arising from the hearts of millions of unhealthy, deluded people from Rome around to Sansom and from Sansom around to Rome again. *What will you do about it?*

What did we do about the sickness of fascism? What did we do about yellow fever? What are we doing about the sickness of communism? What are we doing about poliomyelitis?

What are we doing about this sickness that is one thousand nine hundred and fifty-four years old and will never heal of itself?

My first reaction when I finished reading it was I threw it away into the wastepaper basket. But I was so upset I couldn't work any longer that day. At the door of my office building there was a woman handing out these pamphlets. I took another one and put it into my pocket.

Nobody was home when I got there. I went into my bedroom to lie down. I kept thinking to myself, "He's right, that fellow's right. Mal gave me a bum steer when he put me on this job. I should never have taken it." Then as I was lying down I heard this rising and falling hum down in the basement. I felt jittery as all hell. It seemed to come from Father Polycarp's room but he'd never let out a peep before. I went down.

Right outside his door I could hear that it was his voice. I looked in the window. There he was on his knees, as prissified as ever, with a ramrod up his backbone, on the cement in front of a little crucifix he'd hung on the door to the furnace room. His hair was brushed neat, and I saw that he had put a towel down to protect the toes of his shoes. I knocked and went in.

He didn't turn around till he came to the end of his prayer, then he looked at me with a frown on his face. I've never seen anybody's eyes that looked the way his looked then.

"Did you see this, Father?" I asked him.

He got up and sat on the bed. He looked at the pamphlet a little while, rubbing his left knee with his hand. Then he gave it back to me. "It's too late for that," he said impatiently.

"What do you mean?" I said. I guess I was a little wild because he gave me a quick glance from the side of his eyes. "It's never too late for the truth, is it?"

"Ah truth!" he said, only too loud, like he couldn't control his voice right. "I tell you it's too late, simply too late."

He sort of sank back into himself. I make it a practice to leave a man be when I can, but today I had to know what was what.

"What do you mean?" I asked him again. "Do you have something new to go on? Look, Father, let me in on it. I'm in a bad way."

"Nothing new," he said, only he was depressed now and didn't even look up at me. "Not new, very old. Oh, very very old." He laughed, not a nice laugh.

"Come on, Father," I said, "give it to me. I can't wait."

"Why," he said standing up. He raised one arm as though he felt like taking a swing at me, and glared. "Why, she appeared to me, that's all. She appeared to me as plainly as you do right this minute. That's all. Nothing new about that, eh Stanmer?"

"Father," I said and sat down quick. "Father."

"Yes," he said and began walking up and down. "I had lunch with Bishop Magoon. Nothing happened. A glass of good wine, a traminer I think. Yes, one of the Napa Valley traminers. I left his house at one o'clock. I had nowhere in particular to go. I felt very sleepy suddenly. It's a thing I've never done, sleep after lunch. It doesn't even occur to me to do it. Yet I was so sleepy I could barely drag myself back here. I fell down on the bed like an ox that's been hit between the eyes with a sledge. Then she appeared to me." He looked at me, and from the expression on my face, whatever it was, he went on to say, "Oh it was no dream." The thing that struck me about his voice was its sincerity. It rang true. Nobody could lie in a voice like that. "She was there as plainly as you are. Right here in this room, over against that door to the furnace room. She held her hands out to me a bit and her head was a bit over to the left. She had on a long, light blue robe that came down over her feet. She was a few inches off the floor. Stanmer," he leaned at me all of a sudden, "you wouldn't believe how beautiful she was, as in her photograph, but utterly different, transfigured. All she said was 'Cecil, do you doubt me?' She didn't smile, yet she wasn't in the least melancholy. It was a quite different expression from any I've ever seen before. Beatific, Stanmer," he said sort of surprised, "why of course, beatific." He started thinking.

"Then she disappeared?" I asked him. I wanted to get the whole picture.

"I suppose. I really didn't notice. I snapped out of it." He shrugged. "I was a doubter, Stanmer. Worse, I was a scoffer. I really don't know now precisely what I did believe. Nothing. I have much to atone for. I'll not be the devil's advocate any longer. Leave me, Stanmer. You must wrestle with your own conscience. No one can help you. I have much to atone for."

I went back up to my room and I had to lie down. I was having a funny feeling in my stomach, as if a swarm of bees was looking for a place to roost. I wasn't exactly thinking of anything; I just felt terrible. Then all of a sudden it really hit me. I sat up in bed and I was trembling. I was more scared than I've ever been since I used to be afraid of going to hell. It really got me—to think of her appearing to him right here in my own house, right in my own guest room. With things like that going on around you, you can't tell what might happen, and I thought I didn't even believe in miracles.

I went back down to Father Polycarp's room. He had the curtain pulled over the window. I couldn't hear any noise from inside, and he didn't answer when I knocked and called to him.

"Father," I said, "Father, I'm really in trouble; you've got to help me, I've got to know."

Finally he opened the door again. He had taken off his shoes and his collar, but the worst thing was that he had taken out his false teeth. I didn't even know he had false teeth, and it was a real shock to see him all of a sudden with his cheeks caved in. It made his eyes fiercer than ever.

"I've got to know where she stood," I said to him, "what she looked like."

I guess I persuaded him, because he let me in. I could see he was making a big effort, but I didn't care what he did so long as he told me what I wanted to know.

"Here," he said and went over to the door of the furnace room, "about six or seven inches off the floor, framed in the doorway. She was in a simple blue robe, light blue, like a clear sky. No adornment or belt. Her hair was free about her shoulders. She was like this." He took the same posture as he had described before. "I honestly can't see that it matters much, all these details."

"Sort of like the statue of the Virgin in St. Joseph's," I said to myself, but he heard me and he didn't look like he appreciated it. It's as pretty a statue as I've ever seen. "She was really there?"

All he did was nod. I didn't know what to say. There was something to say but I couldn't think of it. I looked around the room. The first thing I saw was his false teeth in a glass of water grinning at me. All of a sudden I was as scared as I had just been in my room alone.

"Father," I said in a pressuring way, "Father, what does it mean?"

"You know as well as I."

"You're the one," I said, "not me. I put a lot of stock in you, Father. I'd like to go along with you all the way in this thing. It didn't happen to me, it happened to you."

"You must pray and meditate upon it."

"I don't know how to meditate," I began, but when he looked at me I said, "Okay. What should I pray?"

"Start with the rosary."

"All right. This is the real thing, isn't it?"

"Do you think I have any words for you?" he said, only in a kindly way.

"If it's true it's true for a long time, and if it's false we haven't missed so much. I believe," I said, and then I left him alone.

What I should have said was, "I want to believe," because by the time I'd got back upstairs I wasn't so sure. My stomach wouldn't take anything for dinner, and I went to bed early. I had a bad night. I prayed, and it bothered me how a dead person could appear like that to anybody, scientifically speaking, though I certainly believed that Father Polycarp meant what he said. That was the trouble; I couldn't get away from him, and his opinions meant so much to me I just couldn't ignore them. Besides she had appeared in *my own* basement. It's not so easy to get away from a thing when it's right in your own basement. All the same, how do you fit it in? It won't fit. I'm no priest or hermit or anything. I can't just say to the wife after dinner, "By the way, honey, BobbySu was in the basement yesterday." I can't tell some business associate in a cocktail lounge how the devil's advocate saw an apparition of a saint in my guest room. Yet a thing like this, the way I look at it, is so important it *ought* to fit in. I was as miserable as I've ever been in my life, and I prayed to God to let me alone. But I couldn't get away from Father Polycarp's eyes. By morning I knew that much. His eyes were sincere; they had seen her. I would never be able to get away from that and I wouldn't be able to get away from all the rest of it either —fit or no fit.

That morning I went to see Father O'Dwyer about myself. Mostly he just told me what you'd expect under the circumstances, penitence and so on. There's a lot to be said for it too, the old tried and true that people say; it's comfortable and at the right time it means a lot. But that wasn't all he did. He sized me up right; he knew I'd be the type that had to *do* something. Here he is, a dandruffy little old parish priest with no more on the ball than the next guy, but he did a really professional job of handling me. I knew it and I liked it. You just can't beat an organization like the Church that can make a grade-A product out of ordinary material like him. What he told me was that I should make a shrine in my basement where BobbySu appeared. And I'm going to.

I'm not telling just everybody about it, but what I'm going to do is to get it all fixed up so it'll be ready to open to the public when she gets to be a Blessed. There'll be plenty of time and I'm going to do it all myself. I've got the money for it if I just save what I've been dribbling away on nonessentials. Besides, it's not going to be elaborate, just a tastefully decorated room with a statue of her in front of the furnace room door where she appeared to Father Polycarp. I asked him to give me more details so I could get a beautiful likeness made on the order of the one in St. Joseph's, which was made in Italy by an internationally known artist in the outskirts of Rome. Father Polycarp would not help me, but he was decent about it. "Sorry, I'll have nothing more to do with it, Stanmer. They haven't used blue like that in saints' robes since Giotto, and no modern art pains me more than pious terra cotta. But it's the spirit that matters." He meant it too, so I couldn't get offended. It *is* the spirit that matters. I want it to be a statue of the real BobbySu, not the acne and such but her spirit. Acne is just there for people to stumble over if they want to, the way I did. What you've got to do is rise above it, forget about it. You can always find something to stumble over if you want to.

Well anyway, I'm working at it all now, starting the plans, cutting a new doorway into the furnace room, opening up the necessary channels to get the statue ordered and imported. There's plenty to think about, and I'll never be able to express my gratitude to Father O'Dwyer for giving me something to work on outside myself. Like they say, you've got to forget yourself, especially in a thing like this. I've got to see if the city will help me with the parking problem, what with the crowds that'll be coming to the shrine on Easters and our house being up here in the hills where the streets are narrow. There's plenty for me to keep my mind on, and it's given me peace of mind the like of which I never would have believed. Because I know it's all going to come true sooner or later. I like the feeling that it will be done whether or not I get a chance to finish it up. It's all just a matter of time.

Love among the Old Folk

It was Case's regular practice to call on Hattie every morning at eleven o'clock after she had finished listening to the *Luster-lene Variety Hour*. All the other radios in the house would be tuned to *The Saga of Wanda Ryan*; part of Case's motive in calling on Hattie was to seek sanctuary with someone who also disliked *Wanda Ryan*. Moreover it was a pleasure to talk to somebody who wanted to hear what he had to say and who did not talk back.

He announced his visit by a rap on the door before he entered.

"Well Hattie," he said as he closed the door behind him, "it's a nice clear day out. I think the green ought to be dry enough now for a game this afternoon."

She smiled and waved her left hand a little in greeting. She had had a stroke two months before, and she would never recover the use of her right side.

"Well, was it a good program this morning?" She nodded. "Those radio fellows," he said shaking his head. "Five days a week and always something new. *Ja*. Well, give me a good boxing match any time." He started to laugh, a laugh caked dry with age but still warm, still human. "Or a football game." He laughed harder, rocking his round little body back and forth on the straight chair. "Or the world series," and he laughed so hard that he broke down in phlegmy coughing.

Hattie looked worried and patted his knee with her left hand. She made certain sounds—low, howling, unsteady sounds—which were not quite English and which seemed badly combined with her frail features and melancholy eyes; she was trying to tell Case to read the paper to her. "*Ja, ja,*" he said after he had quit coughing, "I read now." He adjusted his spectacles on his nose and opened to the editorial page. He never understood what she said, but there was nothing else that she would have been likely to say and this was what he had been going to do anyway. She thought that he had understood her, and was pleased with this sign of improvement.

Hattie did not care a hoot for the daily opinions of the *Examiner* editorial writers; what she cared for was that Case wanted to read them to her. She had had a year-old competition with Melissa, the other roomer in the Hooks' house, for the attentions of Case, and it was clear now that Hattie had won.

Melissa was quite grand in a palsied way. She had been something of a singer fifty or sixty years before, a glory she had not forgotten. Melissa scorned the favors of a fat little old Dutch butcher like Case Hook, but she could not scorn the lack of these favors.

Today at 11:30, after the passions of *Wanda Ryan* had been harrowed again and quelled again, Melissa came to the door of Hattie's room. "Oh," she said standing in the doorway, "I hope I am not intruding."

Hattie howled a little and motioned with her hand. Case laid down his paper, settled his glasses back on his head as he always did when he had finished reading something, and told Melissa to come in.

"Quite a good program today," said Melissa. "Of course it is nothing beside what I was accustomed to in better days. Duse, Bernhardt. Ah." She flourished her handkerchief a little and gave her wobbling head a toss of pure panache. "Nothing. Still, one must make the best of what one has. Case, I find it very surprising that you do not enjoy the *Wanda Ryan* thing."

"Ney," he said, "I like better the paper."

"There are good things in it. Hattie, my dear, did you have a good night?"

Hattie signified by a smile and a nod that she had had a good night.

"My poor dear," said Melissa taking Hattie's slack right hand for a moment, "my poor dear. At least you are not in pain. It is a blessing for those who can be comfortable in their affliction."

Now Melissa herself was in no pain; her worst problem was getting food into her mouth without spilling it. Hattie, on the other hand, had a permanent sense of pressure and prickling in her paralyzed members, but she would have had more trouble explaining to the others what she felt than their sympathy was worth—the endless sympathizing, the daily questions to which there must always be the same, same answers. She preferred to fall in with their comfortable view: that since like a plant a paralyzed limb cannot move, then like a plant it also cannot feel. She nodded and smiled at Melissa again.

"How she needs," said Melissa to Case, "all the love and companionship she can get now."

"Ja," said Case uneasily.

"I spent last evening with Carrie Pellissière," said Melissa pronouncing the surname in a perfect—a very pluperfect—French manner.

"Ney," said Case, who had not understood her, "I don't know."

"Carrie," said Melissa dropping Hattie's hand, "Carrie Pellissière, Hattie's sister."

"Ney," said Case, "I seen her once or twice."

"She is a fine woman," said Melissa, "a woman of refinement and culture."

"Ja," said Case, "Hattie's sister."

"She would be a valuable addition to any community," said Melissa. "I think I could persuade her to join us."

"Ja," said Case beginning to laugh. "Trinka tell me Carrie save a theater program she see in Paris where you sing." He laughed himself into a cough again. "I remember she tell me. We laugh."

Josephine Melissa Froumier, contralto, in Beethoven's *Ninth*

Symphony, 1897, Paris École des Études Musicales—her big role. Carrie, the Michigan girl on a tour, had saved the program of that concert because that very evening Jean-Jacques Pellissière, a dashing young lawyer from Lyons, had asked her to marry him.

That same year Melissa had married a rich American lawyer, who had thereupon immured her in Sacramento, where he had begot three children upon her. It was clear enough to Melissa which of them had come off with the better husband.

"An amusing coincidence," said Melissa smiling at her memories, at the tricks of chance.

"*Ja,* well," said Case, "I think I go bowling pretty soon now."

"It seems a fine day," said Melissa. "Think over our opportunity."

"What?"

"Our opportunity to add Carrie Pellissière to our group."

"Ney," he said arising. "All the rooms are full."

"There is the guest room."

"Well, that's for guests, Trinka says. You see Trinka."

"But if you say she comes, Katrina will agree."

"I don't know," he said at the doorway. "I send her up now." He went downstairs.

"I am doing what I can for you, dearest," said Melissa taking up Hattie's spoiled hand again. "Your darling sister is such a cultured woman. Our only problem will be to persuade her to come live in a house with such people as this. Not that the Hooks are inferior in any real way, oh no, but they are certainly lacking in refinement." She smiled knowingly at Hattie. Her vision was not good; she did not see the distaste in Hattie's eyes behind the weak smile. "The refinements which a person of Carrie's cosmopolitan background is so accustomed to. She is handsomely situated now of course. The Lakecliff gives the best of service; there isn't a finer hotel in Oakland. And her room has a fine view of Lake Merritt; transportation is so accessible. But I know you have told her of our family. That's something not even money can buy. I am so sorry for those who live alone or with ungrateful children." Melissa reached into her bosom for a scented handkerchief with which she wiped her eyes under their glasses. "My eyes are watering so much these days. Excuse me. It's so fortunate for you, dearest, that your eyes are still good. You have a great deal to thank your lucky stars for. It's so terrible to have to impose yourself upon your children, inconveniencing them. Or a home—a home." She shuddered. "Really, Hattie, I think we are doing Carrie a service to bring her here with us. A hotel is so cold, so impersonal. I am sure my sons are very happy to have me come to live here. They insisted so much that I shouldn't go to a hotel, and I know it was not a question of money. They are both doing so well in their careers. Real successes. But they simply hadn't the room in their homes for me. Such active people, both of them. No, no, a family, Hattie, a family is the best solution. We must bring Carrie here with us."

Hattie acquiesced because it would have exhausted her to communicate her disagreement. But she did not rejoice in this plan, for Carrie looked down on her, and outshone her completely and always had, and had much more money than she. All Hattie had was her stroke; it was not enough. Besides, though Hattie had a son in Boston who paid her board and room, Carrie had a daughter right down in San Jose who invited her to dinner four or five times a year and who had produced two grandchildren for her to show pictures of and to brag about.

Downstairs Case put on his hat and his sweater and looked about for his wife. She was in the kitchen making bread.

"Trinka," he said, "they want to bring Hattie's sister to live too. I tell them you come up and talk about it. I don't care."

"Carrie Pellissière," she said punching the dough vigorously. "Oh ho, what airs she has. We got no room."

"Okay. You go talk."

"Unless, Kees Hoek"—she would not English his name any more than she had ever Englished her own—"you get that Hattie to go to a hospital. What you think, we're a hospital? Thelma a nurse?"

"Neen!" he cried. "She's okay. We take her in well, we keep her sick. *Ja.* You do with Carrie anything, okay. Hattie stay."

Katrina turned her back on him and muttered, "Dutchhead," mostly to herself.

"*Ja,*" he said angrily, "Dutchhead Hoek, okay. She has stroke? Too bad, we keep her. Thelma don't have to bathe her, her nurse does that. Twice a week. We get twenty dollars a month extra. Okay. Maybe she like to see her sister."

"You go bowling," said Katrina. "Leave me alone."

"I think we have Carrie live here."

"You think, you think! I don't think. Go on."

He went up the hall toward the front door, muttering to himself. Thelma came out of the parlor where she had been vacuuming the rug. Thelma was unmarried and very strong. She did most of the work in the house, which meant that she was busy a good sixty hours a week—more if one of the old folk was sick. But she was no servant, for she got no pay. She was the Hooks' daughter.

"Papa," she said smiling, "are you going out now?"

"Dutchhead," he muttered, not even looking at her.

"What Papa?"

He shook his head.

"Tonight I'm going to the show. You ought to come along too. You don't get much entertainment."

"Ney," he said at the door, "I go bowling."

She looked after him wondering what was wrong, whether she had done something to offend him. She was worried but she forgot to quit smiling. Adjusting her hair beneath her bandanna she went into the kitchen.

"Hello Mama. How's the bread coming?"

"You like anybody more come live here?" Katrina demanded.

"Oh it all depends," said Thelma smiling more than ever.

"Hattie's sister. You know that Carrie Pellissière."

From her mother's snappish tone of voice it was obvious that this had been the cause of some quarrel with her father. Thelma avoided quarrels.

"What do you think, Mama?"

"What do I think? Who cares what I think? That old Dutchhead, he don't care."

"It would be a lot of trouble. But it would be nice for Hattie."

"Nice for Hattie," said Katrina with scorn. "A nice hospital nice for Hattie, nicer too."

"Then there's the guest room."

"*Ja*, what we do for a guest room with that Carrie in it?"

"Of course, Mama. Still, we don't have any guests."

"You can never tell, Thelma, we might someday. It's a good thing to have a guest room."

"Sure, Mama, for emergencies."

"*Ja*. Besides you work enough already. Plenty to do without no fancy lady too."

"More money though, Mama."

"*Ja*, more money." She lapsed into silence while she shaped the loaves. "Well, we get along okay now. That Dutchhead, he don't care how many people die here. She'll die, you'll see. Bad stroke. He don't care. Well I care."

"Maybe it's a good idea to have Carrie here when Hattie dies, Mama. She'll pay good too. We need the money. Everything costs so much."

"Neen!" said Katrina. "In that family they die all the time. Neen, see?"

"All right, sure Mama. Maybe I'll win something tonight."

"Eh?"

"Sure, at the show they're having a big drawing. A hundred prizes with a mammoth first prize. A fully mechanized home."

"Eh?"

"Sure, fully mechanized home on a view lot. Brand new with two bedrooms and a garage. If I win that then we can rent this house, Mama, and live there in peace."

"*Ja*. Does it have a hot water heater?"

"Mama, fully mechanized. Automatic water heater and electric stove and refrigerator and washing machine and furnace. Everything the heart could desire."

"Well, you go win it, Thelma." She laughed. "What the old Dutchhead do then?" She laughed hard.

"Mama!"

"You clean the rug. I go up to see them upstairs. Those two old ones."

But by the time Katrina had got to the top of the stairs Hattie was dead of another stroke. Melissa gave a very piercing shriek and came banging out against the door of Hattie's room.

"Katrina! Katrina! My God, what has happened?"

Katrina mumbled a curse under her breath in Dutch. "Dead?" she said to Melissa at the door.

Melissa, her handkerchief at her trembling mouth, could only nod.

"Stroke," said Katrina flatly, and went in to look at the body.

Thelma came running up the stairs, not smiling.

"My dearest," said Melissa grabbing one of Thelma's hands, "I was holding her hand just like this, just so, talking to her. Suddenly she made a little sound. I can't explain. Not a strange sound. But my intuition told me look at her. Oh Thelma, we must trust our intuition." Melissa buried her face in her hands. "Too shocking, too much for me. Help me to my room."

Katrina came out into the hall.

"What should I do, Mama?" said Thelma on the point of tears herself.

"Put her to bed."

"You, Mama?" said Thelma over her shoulder as she was supporting Melissa into her room.

"I call the coroner."

"Thelma!" cried Melissa straightening up suddenly. "Thelma, we must call her next of kin."

"*Ja*," said Katrina on her way downstairs.

"Katrina," cried Melissa leaning over the banisters, "you must call Carrie immediately. She must come be with us. She needs us."

"*Ja*, I call her."

"Oh, poor Carrie, the poor delicate creature. My heart goes out to her."

"She can have Hattie's room," said Katrina. "Same price."

"You must come lie down," said Thelma.

"How close death is. We are surrounded by it."

"You never can tell," said Thelma.

"Cover her, Thelma. Cover her poor old face."

"Yes," said Thelma, and at the thought of it easy tears brimmed from her eyes.

Melissa took off her glasses and lay back on her satin chaise longue. "My spirits," she said with a large gesture, her left hand held to her eyes. "My spirits, then leave me."

Thelma put the bottle into her trembling hand, pulled the dress down over her knees, and went to cover Hattie.

Downstairs, Katrina sat by the telephone with a sour expression on her face.

"I'd better go get Papa," said Thelma trying to smile through her tears.

"Why?"

"Well, he ought to know. You know . . ."

"Ney. Let him play. He's just in the way here."

"I'll make you some soup, Mama. We need to keep up our strength."

"Why not?"

"Do you think I ought to take some up to Melissa?"

"She has words, don't she? Let her use them."

"I'll go now, Mama. You rest awhile."

"Let me alone," snapped Katrina. She went over to a couch and for a moment hesitated whether to lie on it. She decided it would be too much trouble to get up again for soup in ten minutes and sat leaning sidewise against a pillow. She was small and slack, and her hands were gnarled. "Old Dutchhead," she mumbled. "She could die just as good in a hospital. Too many people dying around here. Dying, dying, dying." She closed her eyes and napped.

At two o'clock the men came for Hattie. At three o'clock Case came home. At three-thirty Carrie arrived in a taxi.

Carrie was of medium height and held herself upright. She wore a fur coat; it was a squirrel coat and not new, but she wore it as though it were a fine chinchilla. Her hair was carefully and frequently dyed to match the fur. She had cancer of the liver, which is incurable, but she had never told anybody about it. She had had her last lover when she was sixty-five, before her face had quite disappeared behind a mask of wrinkles.

Thelma, as the maid, went to the door to answer Carrie's ring. Katrina, as the hostess of the house, leaned against the jamb of the door to the parlor. Melissa, as friend, bumped, blinking and tragic, right past Katrina to get to Carrie first. Case, as Case, sat drinking his coffee.

"My dear!" cried Carrie to Melissa when the door opened.

"Carrie!" cried Melissa opening her arms.

"Isn't it dreadful," said Carrie depositing her umbrella on Thelma as she went past her. It was one of Carrie's peculiarities always to take an umbrella when she went out in case the weather should turn against her.

"I must tell you about her last moments," said Melissa as they embraced. "She passed so quietly. I am so grateful that I could be with her."

"Hlo," said Katrina.

"It is so sad," said Thelma with fresh tears ready in her eyes.

"Dear Mrs. Hook," said Carrie disengaging herself from Melissa. "I am so happy that my sister was surrounded by such an atmosphere of friendliness in her last days."

"*Ja*," said Katrina, "friendly."

"Mrs. Pelissière," said Thelma tentatively.

"Yes Thelma?" Carrie said in a cool voice, half-turning.

Thelma had intended to say something comforting, as Carrie had guessed from the tone of her voice. But Carrie liked having at least one servant about her and she was testing to see whether, in case she wanted to move in here, Thelma was thrall enough. She was.

"Mrs. Pellissière, may I take your coat?"

"Thank you, Thelma. Will you help me? Please hang it up on a wide hanger. I'm careful with the shoulders."

"I'll try."

"And my dear Mr. Hook," said Carrie advancing upon him.

"*Ja,*" said Case grinning on his way up from his chair. He was stiff from bowling.

"How often," said Carrie taking one of his hands in both of hers, "how often Harriet had told me how much your companionship meant to her."

"Well, I read the paper to her."

"You know," she said rather intimately to him though the others were about them, "there is not a man in our family—my family now, I should say. My brother is dead, my daughter's husband has left her. My son is in New York. Harriet's son is far away. Mr. Hook, I am going to ask you to do me the greatest favor I could ask of any man. I am going to ask you to escort me at Hattie's funeral."

"*Ja,*" he said grinning more than ever, "well, I don't know."

"I had rather thought," said Melissa sniffing a bit, "that since I have a little difficulty sometimes Case would walk by my side."

"What's that?" cried Katrina catching on. "What's that? He walk by me. Sure. He's my man."

"Oh dear," said Thelma, "would you like some coffee, Mrs. Pellissière?"

"Thank you Thelma. With cream and two lumps of sugar."

"You will stay to dinner with us too, won't you," asked Thelma.

"I would like nothing so much as to be with you all today. Hattie's family!" Carrie opened her arms to them.

"I hope you like lamb stew," said Thelma.

"It doesn't matter at all. Anything."

Thelma left for the kitchen.

"Now,"said Carrie, "I must hear about Hattie's end."

"It was so peaceful," said Melissa fishing in her bosom for her handkerchief again. "I was sitting beside her, just chatting about the future and her good fortune in not suffering. How inspiring to think that she went with her thoughts on higher things. What a difference it makes to those left behind."

"She want you to come live here," said Case.

Melissa was very annoyed at his blurting it out so crassly. She had been going to lead up to it gradually when she had Carrie by herself.

"That was in her mind," said Melissa. "She was thinking of others."

"*Ja*," said Katrina. "Well, you can come if you want to."

"Thank you so much," said Carrie going over to her. "I am so moved by your generosity."

"Same price," said Katrina.

"I would need more room. I must think about it."

"Carrie my dearest," said Melissa taking her by the elbow, "you must come up with me and see her bed."

"You aren't in any hurry are you?" said Carrie to Katrina.

"Ney, any time before Sunday."

"Come dearest."

"I must," said Carrie.

Thelma entered with coffee. "Don't you want your coffee?"

"Just bring it up after us," said Carrie, and she did.

Carrie was not very interested in Melissa's story about Hattie's death. She kept looking shrewdly about the room. When Melissa had exhausted her subject, Carrie spoke. "The furniture is quite agreeable. I would have the mattress changed, of course."

"The mattress? Poor Hattie said it was very comfortable. Innerspring."

"A superstition. I'm superstitious, Melissa. I could never sleep on the same mattress someone died on."

"Especially not your own sister."

"That has nothing to do with it." She made an odd clicking sound in her mouth. "My damned upper plate is giving me trouble." She took it out and began wiping it with a handkerchief. "I've got to have more room than this! That's why I have to leave the Lakecliff. No room."

"We have a guest room too," said Melissa. "Right adjoining this. Perhaps you could have it too."

"Splendid. We must look at it."

She was putting her teeth back in as they opened the door. Thelma was standing in the hall waiting to see if they needed anything, but Carrie thought she was eavesdropping.

"Thelma," she said severely, "show me the guest room."

"Certainly, certainly, Mrs. Pelissière. It's not used very often. Would you like to stay here tonight? I can make it up for you." Thelma saw that Carrie was displeased with her, and tried to make up for it as best she could.

Carrie did not answer her but strode into the room and looked about. She approved of it. "That will be enough, Thelma. Our coffee cups are in the other room."

"Thank you," said Thelma, and went in for the cups.

"I hope you will join us dearest," said Melissa in a rather shaky voice. "They are a warmhearted family."

"These are airy rooms and very pleasantly done up. I would save a good deal of money over the Lakecliff. Still, what a view." The windows gave on 55th Street back yards. "I must think about it." But she had already made up her mind to come here, because it would be the pleasantest place she knew of in which to spend her months dying. "I am going to lie down."

"And think of poor dear Hattie," said Melissa. "I will leave till dinnertime."

"How long will that be?"

"About an hour."

"Tell me, how often is the guest room used?"

"I really can't say, dearest. I can't remember that it has ever been used since I have been here. Now you lie quietly if you can."

The house fell quiet for an hour. All those in it lay quiet, except for Thelma in the kitchen, who was busy preparing dinner. Out of respect for Hattie they did not even listen to the radio, as they usually did during this time.

At quarter to six Thelma rang the triangle in the front hall. The old folk bestirred themselves. At six all five sat down. The meal consisted of mustard greens, lamb stew, very soft white bread, honey, coffee, and for dessert a heavy turnip pudding with an orange sauce. Everything was put on the table at the beginning of the meal. As in a progressive school everybody went at his own speed without much regard for the speed of the others. Carrie took displeased note of all this and wondered how she could use her displeasure to strengthen her bargaining position.

"Papa," said Thelma to Case, who was already on the last lap, "how is the pudding?"

"All right Thelma. Not like it used to be in the old country."

"You always say that."

"Well," said Katrina, "he's right. I can't even make it the same myself." She was still eating stew.

"I think," said Melissa, who in her care to avoid dribbling on herself was lagging far behind, "that it is very commendable of you, Thelma, to try to make the old dishes for your parents."

Thelma turned rosy with gratitude.

Carrie, perceiving in what coin this servant was paid, took a few pennies out of her pocket. "You're a very good daughter, Thelma," she said. "I am sure it must give you a wonderful sense of satisfaction to think of how marvelously you have stood by your parents."

"She's a good girl," said Case.

"*Ja,*" said Katrina.

"There aren't many children as devoted as you," said Melissa.

"Your parents must be proud of themselves every time they look at you," said Carrie. "There are so few in this world who can, particularly nowadays. *Cette grosse-là, Melisse, elle n'a pas de mari, hein? Qu'en dites-vous?*"

"*Non, pas de mari.*"

"*Jamais?*"

"*Jamais,*" said Melissa. She was embarrassed to be talking about Thelma in front of her thus, though Thelma, suffused with happiness, had not noticed the shift into French, and neither Case nor Katrina was paying enough attention to care. "Tell me, my dear, what parlor is going to handle the services?"

"What?" said Carrie.

"I mean Hattie's services."

"Oh, the Cloister of Harmony."

"Eh?" said Katrina.

"She just said, Mama," said Thelma, "that she's going to have Hattie buried by the Cloister of Harmony."

"That's all right," said Katrina, "we'll go."

"Such a lovely columbarium too," said Melissa. "Are you having her interred, dearest, or preserved in a crypt?"

"I think cremation," said Carrie, having got to the turnip pudding and getting no further.

"It's cheaper," said Katrina.

"It's so distressing," said Melissa, "to think of these matters at this time, but we must." She smiled, but only Thelma smiled in return. "Who are you having to conduct the services?"

"The man the Cloister has, whoever he is. Hattie was no church-goer."

"If you would like, dearest, I could ask Dr. Peabody to officiate. He's very capable, so cultured."

"What's the difference," said Katrina.

"I'll just have the Cloister of Harmony," said Carrie impatiently. She pushed her pudding away as though it was food that revolted her, not the turnips, and spoke decisively. "I have thought about coming to live with you," she said to Case.

"*Ja.* Good."

"I would bring my own mattress and curtains, and I would have to have some special services."

"What's the difference," said Katrina.

"*Ja*, well," said Case, "you pay extra for special things."

"Certainly. And I need the guest room along with the other one."

"Neen!" cried Katrina.

"Trinka!" said Case. Then he turned to Carrie, "You pay extra for that too."

"Naturally."

"Thirty dollars a month for that."

"No, too much."

"She can't have!" cried Katrina. "We need a guest room."

"I'll tell you," said Carrie, "I'll take it for twenty dollars a month and let you have it for any guest you have."

"All right," said Case.

"Who does the work?" said Katrina to him. "Who wants things nice here?"

"Ney," said Case, "what guest we ever have?"

"I have not decided," said Carrie, "absolutely to take it. I just want to see if we could come to terms."

"A family is *so* nice," said Melissa. "So much nicer. And ours is a superior family. Case is so helpful with me when I go out. I some-times have trouble at the street corners." She smiled at Case.

"You will walk with me at the funeral?" said Carrie to Case. "I have no other man at all."

"Well," said Melissa tossing her head.

"Ney," said Katrina flatly.

"If you will excuse me," said Thelma and left the table precipitously for the front hall.

"Where are you going?" asked Carrie.

"Out," said Thelma. "Just out."

"To a movie," said Katrina.

"I hope you don't mind," said Thelma at the door to Carrie, smiling nervously. "On such a day as this."

"What movie is it that's so good?" said Carrie.

"Oh it's a drawing, a mammoth drawing. I have eighty-five tickets saved up for it."

"Yes," said Carrie, "yes, go."

She turned back to the others. Case was lighting a cigar, Katrina was pouring herself a third cup of coffee, Melissa was trying to pour orange sauce onto the pudding. Carrie had much more money than she had time left in which to spend it, and there were at least half-a-dozen men she could get to escort her at Hattie's funeral; nevertheless she drove her bargain.

"I would pay forty dollars a month extra, for the room and for breakfast in bed and a few other little extras."

"Okay?" said Case to Katrina.

"Forty dollars. Okay."

"Oh Carrie . . ." Melissa began.

"*If* I decide to come."

"You couldn't!" Melissa cried. "Not come?"

"About the funeral," Carrie began.

"Ney," said Katrina. "Nothing to say."

"Hattie was so fond of you," said Carrie to Case. "You meant so much to her in her last days. I would hate to think of anyone but you there."

"Well," he said, "I read the paper to her. Poor woman."

"It means so much to me and I am sure it would have meant so much to her."

"Kees, neen!" said Katrina.

As it did every once in a while Carrie's liver fluttered; she felt pressed for time.

"I would like so very much to come to live with you," said Carrie in a final tone of voice, "but I could not bear to if I didn't have complete faith in your loyalty."

"You must pardon me, dearest," said Melissa. "Katrina. Case." She went to the door. "So painful to hear." With a sniff she went upstairs.

"Well," said Case indecisively.

Katrina angrily stirred her coffee, muttering to herself in Dutch. "How old are you?" she said sharply to Carrie.

"Seventy-six," said Carrie, understanding perfectly the drift of her question and relishing the way she would take the answer.

"No noise after nine o'clock," said Katrina.

"Just the radio if I can't sleep?"

"No noise!" cried Katrina. "No radio."

"Oh all right."

Case coughed.

Katrina stirred her coffee some more, drank it down, and mumbling, "Forty dollars, *ja*," stood up. "Okay, Kees," she said and started out of the room.

Case grinned at Carrie. "Okay, she say."

"Dear Case," said Carrie moving toward him and taking one of his hands, "I can't tell you how much your support means to me at a time like this."

Case began to laugh, rocking back and forth in his chair and finally choking up. Carrie laughed too, merrily and youthfully.

"What's the difference," said Katrina, and went cackling with laughter into the parlor to lie down.

Hymn of the Angels

Sidney did not much like the old-fashioned façade of the Hilton-Sansom, but once inside he found the lobby had been brought as far up-to-date as wall-to-wall gray could bring it and he was satisfied. Two telephone messages were waiting for him: one, marked urgent, he stared at a moment then crumpled up and threw away—let the little fish catch him if they could, they'd appreciate him the more for their trouble—the other, from a Father Hilary at Mount Mary, he took with him to his room.

Even though this new room was so Hilton-familiar Sidney studiously set about clearing it of its hotel welcome and advice and warning, then spread out on the dresser a local paper and read as he wandered about undressing; he moved a chair, flipped on the TV set and saw that its three channels were reasonably clear, scanned the movie ads, brushed his teeth as though he had just got up,

scratched his back, glanced over a coast-to-coast columnist—it made
the room his own. His eyes were caught by an advertisement for
the Club Continentale, from nine to one Sharon Vee and the
Happy Hipsters. Sidney perked up immediately, made a grimace at
the message from Mount Mary, and put in a call for Sharon.

"Siddy!" She was putting on her little girl voice, which probably
meant she wasn't sure yet how glad she was to hear from him.

"How are you, baby?"

"What are you doing in a hamlet like this?"

"Business," he began.

"Naturally business!" she squawked. "You dope, I mean what're
you doing?"

"Right now I'm inviting you to dinner tomorrow night."

She purred. "Siddy, you're sweet. Only I can't tomorrow. There's
a reason. Couldn't you tonight? How long're you going to be in
town?"

"Tonight I'm supposed to go to a monastery for dinner."

She giggled.

"Business," he snapped, "business. Look, you can't make it tomorrow?"

She purred downward. "Let's just have an early dinner now. Can't
we, sweetie? I really have been missing you."

He liked to be missed. "Okay honey. Seven at your place?"

"Make it six at yours?"

It was already 4:30, and he'd eaten a large lunch on the plane.
He clicked his teeth in annoyance. "Where's the best restaurant?"

"The Hilton."

"Good, that's where I am already. Get here by six."

"Aw honey, come and get me? I'll have to wear my costume for
the show tonight. Please? I may have trouble getting in and out or
something. It's so tight."

His mouth twitched in irritation. He thought she was making him
jump just to show that she could still do it. Then he chuckled. "I
get it. You've got a wolf at your heels. Right?"

Her purr arched in acquiescence and gratitude, curled up in his
lap, and went to sleep.

He called Mount Mary and left a message for Father Hilary that
he would be unable to go out to dinner; showered, shaved, and
dressed with care. He hadn't felt better in months.

With his two hundred dollar, light gray suit cut to the minute, his onyx cuff links, his blue Sulka tie, Sidney felt up to her, even though she was two inches taller than he.

She squealed when she opened the door to him, hugged him, gave him five warm kisses all around his mouth, and told him he'd lost weight; she asked him which earrings he preferred. He chose the silver-wire mobiles with amethysts. She wore a floor-length, light blue sheath that ruffled out just above the knees; it came up to her throat, where it was held by a necklace, but it left her arms and back bare. Her bosom was more pin-up than Sidney had ever seen it before; he knew just how falsy this was, but she was right to fill it out, she had hips to go with it, and she knew how to carry herself. Her hair had a wild look, as though she'd just got out of bed; he appreciated how much it cost to produce that look and keep it in place. When they left her hotel and again when they entered the lobby of the Hilton they looked good. Sidney loved it. "We're the best in town, baby," he said, and she cuddled his arm and wrinkled her nose at him.

He half-turned with annoyance at a tap on his shoulder. At first glance he did not recognize the knobby, big, pale face looking down at him; the man wore a black suit, an ecclesiastical collar, and an odd sort of black beret that did not flop, and he had a gap-toothed smile.

"Mr. Goldfarb," he said and stuck out his hand, "I'm Brother Patrick."

Sidney clicked his fingernails in irritation. "Of course." He wanted to punish him for showing up like this. "Sorry. I phoned your place an hour ago. I can't come."

Brother Patrick's face fell. "Sure," he said. "A man like you, in New York and all, meets so many. It's nothing, sir, and of course I'd remember you." His bland forehead puckered. "You could come out to us tomorrow then for sure? The thing is, Mr. Goldfarb, we can't always be sure of Brother Dennis."

He did not look properly off-balance. Sidney introduced him to Sharon, but the only sign of confusion he saw in Brother Patrick was a slight wavering of the eyes when they shook hands. Sharon, however, who had been raised a Catholic, pulled her blue gauze scarf about her shoulders in embarrassment.

"Tomorrow at five," Sidney said. "Can you come for me?"

"Sure," said Brother Patrick. He obviously did not know it was time for him to go, or else he did not know how to; he had taken root like the Irish potato he resembled.

"We have an appointment," said Sidney; he took Sharon's arm and they walked off.

"What on earth!" she whispered.

"The monastery I was telling you about. A record in it maybe."

"You mean they got something *good* buried around here?"

"Look, baby," he said firmly, "anything I got anything to do with is first-class." Sidney gestured about the dining room, and looked Sharon up and down with approval. "First-class."

When they were seated, Sharon looked at him with a tinge of worry in her eyes. "And you're just here to make a record of monks?"

"Not just."

"What I mean is, what're we having dinner for—old-times sake?"

"As a matter of fact, yes."

As a matter of fact he wanted to see if she had some information he could use. But it was so clear she was feeling sentimental that he wanted to make her feel good. Besides, he liked an obstacle such as this for its own sake.

He began to reminisce. He said he had recently had lunch with Henry, Sharon's former husband, and she softened even more.

"What a sweet guy. How is he?"

"Say," Sidney went on, "what's his niece's name? You know, Lily's daughter."

"Linda. What about her?"

"Nothing. I just haven't heard about her for a long time. It's funny—you know how things keep tying together. Here I'm going to see some musical monks and Linda's father became one. What's his name?"

"Is he out here, Siddy?" she cried.

"Not so far as I know," said Sidney, who knew that he was the Brother Dennis in the monastery. "What was his name back when?"

"Fred Stauffer. Isn't it all funny?" She was looking at him suspiciously.

"He was a good clarinetist too," said Sidney. Having got what he wanted he set about sweetening her again. "It's really funny the way people drift in and out of each other's lives." He took one of her hands in both of his. "You know what, honey?"

"What, Siddy?"

"I liked smooching with you more than any other woman I can remember."

She blushed and lowered her eyes. "You shouldn't say things like that. You're sweet though. Now let's change the subject."

"I was soft on you, honey. You knew that."

"Aw sure," she said and patted his hand. "We were consoling each other on the rebound, and it was good too. Now," she declared and went back to her steak, "that's enough of that. It's a good thing you don't have anything to do with Fred Stauffer. He'd be impossible to handle."

"Eh," said Sidney flourishing his fork, "handling people is my business." He was pleased with himself. He had handled her without her even knowing it, and he was telling her so without her even getting it. His virtuosity was partly due to his having nothing much at stake with Sharon. He had not expected her to have any important information for him, but had just probed about in case something usable turned up.

The way jerked through industrial suburbs and dragged through acres of stucco shacks and finally eased out among fields of stubble the color of honey.

"How d'you like our car, Mr. Goldfarb?" said Brother Patrick settling down in his seat and taking off his beret.

Sidney said it was a fine car.

"Sure," said Brother Patrick, "all blue inside—dashboard, upholstery, steering wheel. Snappy, huh?"

"I wasn't going to say anything—not tactful—but I was thinking this is a pretty sporty car for monks. You know?"

Brother Patrick rocked with laughter and the car weaved on the road. "Tactful!" he snorted. "Jesus bless us, tactful!"

"What's the matter?" Sidney snapped. "Don't you think I got tact?"

"Sure, Mr. Goldfarb, sure you have," said Brother Patrick and flapped a hand at him. "It's the tact you'll need for Brother Dennis, that's all."

"Look," said Sidney, "what I am is a recording engineer, not an impresario. Is that clearly understood?" Brother Patrick looked at him slack-jawed. "We can do as good a job technically as any firm in the industry. But the prima donnas, even if they're monks—no. Okay?"

"Sure, Mr. Goldfarb," said Brother Patrick, "I had no idea otherwise." He did not talk again for a good while, and Sidney was pleasantly conscious of his occasional, worried glances.

The buildings of the Seminary of Mount Mary, in Spanish mission style with thick white walls and arched passageways and red-tile roofs, described a great horseshoe on the upper slopes of a mountain looking out over miles of hills and dim vineyards; up the slope two wings extended, and the main building where Sidney was shown into a room formed the base of the horseshoe. In the large enclosed area onto which his windows looked he saw graveled paths, trimmed hedges, rose bushes and beds of low flowers, an arbor, a statue, small lawns, and a trickling fountain. Despite his hurry to freshen up for cocktails Sidney first allowed himself a sip of this quiet. He liked it, it was alien, he was not sure how much of it he wanted.

Father Hilary, the director, was standing by the fireplace in the attitude of one a good six feet tall; in fact Sidney and he were much of a height, five feet five, though Sidney was fatter. From the hearty unction of his greeting and his way of offering the old-fashioneds and from his baby face and bland voice Sidney sized him up as one who thinks he knows how to handle city slickers. So what? He'd show him. The table was set for three, and it was obvious from Brother Patrick's big eyes for the table service that he was staying.

"No Brother Dennis?" said Sidney not concealing his annoyance.

"I hope," said Father Hilary dropping his eyes, "you may meet him after dinner."

"You *hope?*"

"Soup is served," said Father Hilary.

After they were seated and the Brother-waiter had withdrawn, Sidney persisted, "I don't get it. Doesn't he live here?"

"To be sure. But I have given him permission to reside in a building somewhat apart. You may have noticed the small dwelling up the hill above the grotto?"

"No," said Sidney, who was not entirely sure what a grotto was, "I didn't."

"After dinner, if you would like, we will stroll around the grounds."

He started to go into the history of Mount Mary, but Sidney, as soon as the *coq au vin* had been served, came back to Brother Dennis.

"Let me get something straight, Father. Pardon me, but I don't have all the time in the world. How come you can't just say to him, 'Come on down and meet a man on business?' I thought he had to take orders. What is he, a hermit?"

"I could, of course," said Father Hilary. "Brother, will you pour the wine please? This is our Cabernet Sauvignon, Mr. Goldfarb. We are proud of it."

"Great," said Sidney to whom it tasted like any other red wine, "it's really great." More was needed. "Fine bouquet." This seemed to have been the right thing to say.

"Of course Brother Dennis performs his religious duties with the rest of the community, Mr. Goldfarb, but he has set himself a severe discipline in which music, as you can imagine, plays a decisive role. For this reason he is permitted a seclusion greater than normal."

Brother Patrick leaned over, a conspirator again. "He's a genius."

"Well," said Father Hilary deprecatorily.

"That's what it boils down to," said Brother Patrick.

"Brother," said the director, "we don't want to overdo the matter." He turned, formally, bodily, from Brother Patrick and toward Sidney. "I feel as did my predecessor in this office, Father Albert . . ."

"May he rest in peace," said Brother Patrick, and Father Hilary flicked a frown at him.

". . . that Brother Dennis's devotion to his work is of such an order as to exempt him from many of the inessential aspects of our daily routine. For this reason and also for the reason that his performance of his duties has been examplary I hesitate to interfere with his music in any way."

"But you're the boss," said Sidney.

"Mr. Goldfarb, in your company you are the vice-president in charge of operations?" Sidney nodded. "You must have a number of employees under you, some highly trained?" Sidney nodded again. "Do you give them no latitude? Do you order them to do this or that without consulting their wishes and abilities and needs and temperament?"

"Am I a fool? you're asking. If *I* try to shove a good man around he'll quit on me."

"There's that," said Father Hilary. "Brother, more wine for our guest. Mr. Goldfarb, we approached you, of all the men in the field . . ."

"That reminds me, how did you ever get onto my trail?"

"Brother Patrick was visiting his mother in New York and he has a cousin on the Cardinal's staff." Father Hilary cocked an eyebrow and Sidney nodded. "I was saying, we approached you as the one most likely to handle this matter successfully."

"You mean on the technical end? You know, all I am is a glorified recording engineer. Don't let that vice-president jazz fool you."

"Ah?" said Father Hilary, "we were thinking of more than mere technicalities. We had been given to understand you were—well, tactful."

Brother Patrick caught Sidney's eye and they both laughed.

"I gather, gentlemen, that you have discussed the question?"

Sidney did not want to go into it. "As a matter of fact, Father, I do know something about the type of music from a job I had for a high-brow outfit right after the war. But there's another angle to it." He bared his teeth and watched for reactions. When he punched with a fact he liked the fact blunt. "You see, I'm personally acquainted with Brother Dennis's illegitimate daughter Linda." As a matter of fact he had met Linda only once.

Brother Patrick's mouth fell open, but Father Hilary only cocked his head. "Indeed?"

"A friend of mine over in CBS is her uncle—I'd just as soon not mention him by name if you don't mind—and I got to know Linda through him. He roomed with Brother Dennis when he was still Fred Stauffer, when they were in college."

The table was cleared and charlotte russe was served. Over coffee and brandy they sat sidewise to the table, carefully slipped the foil off cigars which Father Hilary passed out, and lighted them from the urn-shaped, silver-plated lighter on the table.

"I should judge, Mr. Goldfarb, it might be prudent not to bring up the subject of Brother Dennis's earlier life in your discussion with him."

"If it's all the same to you, Father, I think I'll just play this whole thing by ear." Through the French windows he watched a covey of cowled seminarians in dark brown robes twitter along the road. "You know, tact? Technique?"

Brother Patrick coughed and belched smoke. For a long time,

while watching the dusk condensing in the valley, Sidney enjoyed the feel of Father Hilary's speculative gaze resting on him.

Gardens to Sidney meant public parks or things that exterior decorators installed in the suburbs. Nor was he used to strolling. For half an hour or more the three of them strolled along the garden paths, inhaling the evening scents; passing the grotto in which he made out a statue of the Madonna; pausing to talk by a statue of Diana in flight, her head turned over her shoulder; circling the fountain, which he learned was fed by a spring—and he enjoyed it. He no longer particularly cared whether anything came of this visit; he was just enjoying it for its own sake in a way he was not used to.

A tall seminarian with folded hands came up to the director. "The practicing has begun, Father."

"In the minor chapel?"

"No, Father, in the choir loft. Father Bede is on the organ."

"We will be there shortly, Brother. You may go along." He turned. "We are fortunate. The acoustics may be better for your purposes, Mr. Goldfarb."

The main chapel, dimly lighted, struck Sidney as ordinary, and furthermore it had a bad echo. He prowled about in search of a spot suitable for placing a microphone and found none; he could not see the singers well. In ten minutes he left the building followed by the other two.

"I'm sorry, too much echo. The room's impossible."

"We've got other rooms," said Brother Patrick anxiously.

"Sure," said Sidney, "but you know they were just doing straight Gregorian chant. The market's saturated with it from the best European monasteries."

"Perhaps," said Father Hilary, "we do not have so much to offer."

"Oh, but," said Brother Patrick, "what about the manuscripts?"

They were still on the steps of the chapel; Father Hilary was standing below the other two, half-turned as though expecting them to be following. Sidney got a certain satisfaction in looking down at him in the faint light.

"They have yet to prove their full worth. I'm afraid, Mr. Goldfarb, we may have brought you on a wild goose chase. Won't you come back to the library with me? I should like you to meet some of the others of our community."

Sidney stepped down to go, but Brother Patrick caught his arm and leaned down at him beseechingly.

"You've got to hear our countertenor," he said. "You could stay overnight."

"Brother!" said the director sharply.

"But Father, he can't go without at least hearing Jerome. What an organ he's got, Mr. Goldfarb. Brother Dennis says it's one in millions. You can hear him in the morning."

"If you wish, Mr. Goldfarb? But no, Brother, I think our guest has had all he wants."

"Not yet." But Sidney's interruption was ignored.

"You may go to the brothers' common room, Brother Patrick."

Sidney, not wanting to interfere with discipline, watched till Brother Patrick, head low, was out of earshot. But Father Hilary spoke first.

"Shall we go, Mr. Goldfarb?"

"Is this countertenor, Jerome, in there now?"

"No, Brother Dennis is saving him."

"For what?"

"I thought," said Father Hilary, "you had been briefed on all this?"

Sidney had been. "Here's what I want, Father. I have to be in Sansom by 12:30 tomorrow and I want to hear this Jerome."

"I shall do what is possible. Shall we go now?"

Father Hilary's new tone of voice implied that he was not going to find it possible to do much. The slippery bastard, Sidney thought to himself.

A little after ten, pleading fatigue, he asked if he might take the local paper with him and retire. In truth he was irked by the priests, none of whom he liked any better than Father Hilary; they lounged in leather-upholstered chairs, legs crossed, cowls crumpled at the back of their necks, and pumped him for anecdotes about the famous.

He had not yet established himself in this monastery room but was still puzzling at a cuff link, glancing from it to the newspaper, when he heard a knock. As he was saying, "Come in," the door opened enough to admit Brother Patrick's flat, grinning face.

"Mr. Goldfarb," he said in a stage whisper, "you can see Brother Dennis right away if you'd like to. He's walking."

"Bring him in."

"Oh," said Brother Patrick, "I couldn't do that, sir. He's walking."

"Where?"

"Out in the garden of course, where we were before." Brother Patrick anxiously withdrew his head and looked back down the hall. "Are you coming?"

It was trouble and it was beneath him, but he liked Brother Patrick, who was now in his robe and who, Sidney was sure, was disobeying orders by being here at all.

"I'll come."

"Then I'll just step in here till you're ready."

Sidney pointed at the glamour-puss picture of Sharon Vee in the paper. "She was married for a while to that CBS guy I mentioned, Linda's uncle." Sidney had nothing to gain from punching Brother Patrick with this fact but the pleasure of seeing his eyes pop. He liked him. "Small world, huh Brother? I met Sharon in the Music and Art high school."

"I didn't know," said Brother Patrick seizing the new subject eagerly, "that you were a trained musician too."

Sidney made a wry gesture. "I got an ear, Brother. I got a grade-A performing ear."

The Madonna was illuminated from below by a small spot concealed in the ground cover surrounding her grotto; otherwise what light the garden received came from the windows of the buildings and by now there were only a handful still shining; the moon was new and faint. At the place where the path turned toward the grotto Brother Patrick caught his arm; when Sidney looked at him questioningly he put a finger to his lips and pointed. Peering, Sidney made out a very short figure on the path before the grotto, bare head inclined, motionless, stiff. They just stood there watching; as Sidney's eyes adjusted to the dark he could make out Brother Dennis's head more clearly; it seemed enormous for a man of such shortness. The Madonna in her artificial cave looked pretty. He heard the puddling sound of the fountain, he heard an owl. After several minutes Brother Dennis pulled his cowl over his head, abruptly grew by two feet, and Sidney, who had not realized Brother Dennis had been kneeling, fell back a pace in astonishment. Brother Patrick plucked at his sleeve and they hurried up to the shadowed figure. By reflected light from the Madonna Sidney could make out something of his features: his cheeks were sunken, his brows jutted like cliff weeds, his neck was scrawny. He stood at least six feet four inches tall.

"Who is it?" he said disagreeably. "Oh it's you, Pat." He lowered his brows at Sidney, and his large mouth fell into a sardonic contour, higher on one side than the other. "Who's this?"

After his initial astonishment, in which there had been a streak of fear, Sidney was inclined to dislike Brother Dennis, if only because of his voice; Sidney distrusted big men with small voices. But he believed in giving a man a chance.

Brother Patrick spoke. "This is Mr. Goldfarb of Imperial-Lighthouse Records, Brother Dennis."

"I don't want any records."

"No, Brother. You know, I told you already. The Cardinal's office?"

"He is not my Cardinal."

"What harm would it do if Mr. Goldfarb listened to the practice tomorrow morning?"

Brother Dennis shrugged. "What good would it do?"

"I might enjoy it," said Sidney with dignity.

Brother Patrick pleaded. "You ought to let him at least hear Jerome once."

"He is by no means well enough trained to appeal to Mr. Goldfarb's presumably expert ear." Brother Patrick slumped. "Excuse me," Brother Dennis added in his thin voice, and started to walk off.

"So," said Sidney, angry but controlled, "so working for the greater glory of God gives you the right to be unkind to a stranger."

Brother Dennis stopped dead in the path, and then with great labor turned around, and came back to them. "Why should I make a record, Mr. Goldfarb?"

"Look, Brother, there's nothing I can tell you about why anybody should or shouldn't make a record. In addition to which I want to be open and aboveboard with you—I'm not sold on the idea myself. I was more or less roped in on this. It's strictly a business feeler on my part, and from what I heard in the church there this evening I'm not enthusiastic. Countertenors, there's a market opening up for them. How big I don't know. It makes a difference what they sing, naturally. So you see, I'm flying blind as yet. All I can tell you about that you don't know already is money. Royalties. Depending on what we think of the item, what we price it at, how big a pressing, you should get fifty cents a record, somewhere in that neighborhood. So—money. Okay, Brother?"

"Money," said Brother Dennis with a scorn worthy of the heavy, dark lines of his face. "Half a dollar a record to titillate aesthetes."

"Who you titillate is your own business." Sidney saw the big hands clench. Having got even he felt generous; besides he was a little scared. "Excuse me. I didn't mean that the way it sounded."

There was a leaden silence.

"Well," said Brother Patrick tentatively.

"Incidentally," said Sidney, "as long as I'm here—your daughter Linda told me to say hello for her."

"Linda!" cried Brother Dennis and stuck his head forward on its long neck.

"Certainly. She's a very fine young lady."

"*You* know *Linda?*"

This time the silence was bronze and rang like a gong.

"Look," said Sidney, angry at the insult but satisfied at having got Brother Dennis so far off-balance, "as long as I've come this far I might as well listen to the rehearsal tomorrow morning. Probably nothing will come of it, but I'd just as soon. Where and when?"

Brother Dennis smacked his lips; when they closed again they made a sour and melancholy line. His large, shaggy head swung toward Brother Patrick. "Eight o'clock in the minor chapel," he said in a voice not only quiet but defeated. "We will go through the Palestrina for Mr. Goldfarb." He started to leave, then turned. "Good night," he said and they answered him.

"Good!" whispered Brother Patrick squeezing Sidney's arm.

"What's good about it?"

"Oh ho, as long as he's let you go this far maybe you'll get to the manuscript hymns. They are what we're after all along."

"*He* doesn't do any of the singing, I hope?"

"Brother Dennis? Oh no sir."

"With that voice of his he'd better not."

"So tell me, Shary, you're here in Sansom alone?"

She looked huffy. "What do you think I'd be stepping out with you for if I wasn't?"

"You know what Henry said about you?"

"What do you mean, he *said?*"

"I mean he told me once in the strictest confidence. He said he trusted you, the limit, up to the hilt. He said as long as you were his you weren't anybody else's and he knew it."

"Aw," she said, "did he say that?" She stared out over the other tables. "We just didn't make a go of it," she said mostly to herself.

Sidney took the opportunity to glance about; he was gratified to see two men leaning toward one another, whispering and side-longing at Sharon.

"Well," she said resuming her public smile, "tell me about the monks."

"I don't know. It was pretty dull as a matter of fact—routine. They've got a countertenor who may be terrific. They think so anyhow."

"A what?"

"A countertenor, a man with a voice like a contralto, only different. Very nice."

"You mean queer?"

"With a monk who asks? He don't act queer. Anyway it was probably a waste of time." He shrugged.

She stuck her tongue out a little at him, meaning for him not to worry about it. He was not sure what he wanted from her—he was not even sure she had anything more for him—but it was always worth-while exploring. First stir her up.

"So what happened to the guy with the patch over his eye?"

"Turk," she said.

"Yes," said Sidney, "the pusher."

"Pusher! Who ever said Turk was a pusher?"

"Never mind."

"I do mind. He was no pusher. He was on it maybe—anyway he was hooked for awhile—but anybody said he was a pusher lied."

"Okay baby, I believe you. I was just asking."

"You never met him?" He shook his head. "Well he caught me when I was in Las Vegas getting a divorce from Henry. See, we both had engagements at The Beachcombers."

He watched her tell him all about Turk, watched more than listened, listened more to the tones of her voice than to her words. He was careful not to look into her eyes any more than he could help; they appealed too much, he was not sure for what, but the appeal itself made him uneasy. There was some very soothing mood music being piped into the dining room; so long as she was talking about herself it wouldn't matter whether he paid much attention to what she said. He allowed himself to drift back into the emotions he had felt for her two years before.

"You know, Shary," he said when he could, "I was just waiting for you to come back from Nevada. I was and you never came back."

"Come on, Sid," she said rather harshly, "let's don't start down that route again. Okay?" He shrugged. She winked. "For my own information," she said, "I'm just curious, that's all, who'd you ever hear say Turk was a pusher?"

"Forget it. Maybe it was Tommy Gunn, how can I remember every little detail?"

She looked satisfied. "That creep."

"Shary," he said as she settled back in her seat, "I heard you were in New York this spring."

"As a matter of fact I spent Easter with Henry. I was in town and I just felt like seeing him. He's *too* sweet, that's the thing." She began to drift off again, but he wanted her and patted her hand a little more than sympathetically. She smiled. "Linda was there."

"I haven't seen her since she still had braces on her teeth."

"Well," said Sharon, "she's not going to turn the world upside down on her looks, you understand, but Henry says she's smart. She's an oddball if you ask me—no make-up, talks deep like a man, dirty fingernails."

"Maybe she should see an analyst."

"Analyst!" Sharon cried. "What do you think? At that college of hers they all have analysts, Henry says."

"So she's going to an analyst already?"

"Look," she said clutching his arm, "this is private. These are people's lives we're hashing over. You understand, Sid? She's a good girl and she adores Henry and she keeps her troubles to herself. That's something these days."

"Sure it is."

"And she likes it that way and so does Henry and I'm sorry I breathed a word of it."

"Okay," said Sidney with irritation, "what do you take me for, I write for *Confidential* or something? So what does she want to do with herself? Music?"

"No," said Sharon leaning forward, frowning, beseeching, "she wants to be a social worker."

"Sure," said Sidney. The monks had made him edgy and she was no better; besides it didn't look as though she had anything he could use. He glanced at his watch. "Who could blame her? Say, I hate to do this, but you said you had to get there early."

"She's got her heart set on it, Siddy, you know? A plain-Jane social worker? She wants it?"

"All right, all right," said Sidney, "so the analysis is taking hold. Good."

"What the hell," said Sharon slumping in her chair, "with a father and mother like she has it's a wonder she isn't any goofier than she is."

"What's the matter with Lily?" said Sidney perking up.

"You know." But he did not know. "She's in. She's been in for a couple of years. Henry doesn't talk about it."

"That's terrible, it really is. What's she in?"

"I don't remember the name of it. Up in Connecticut somewhere."

"But what *is* it? A bughouse?"

"Aw," she said, "a mental hospital. Not too much hope." Then she glared at him. "Here I am running off at the mouth to you again. Now forget it, see? Just forget the whole thing."

"That's really terrible about Lily," said Sidney and meant it. "You think I got no respect for her? You never said a word to me, okay?" He had what he wanted. He was feeling jumpy as a cat. "Damn it all, baby, it's tough. Now come on, we got work to do—you got yours and I got mine. It's been good seeing you. I mean it, it really has."

She was angry and there were tears in her eyes, but he was too edgy to smooth her down again.

At six in the morning the phone rang. He let it ring three times while he lay collecting his wits, wondering who it could be.

"Goldfarb speaking."

"Mr. Goldfarb, I'm sorry to bother you, sir, but there's a Brother Patrick here to see you and he says it's important."

"What the hell does *he* want?" Sidney roared, but when he heard the desk clerk's distant voice begin to repeat a polite version of the question he said with resignation, "Tell him to come on up."

He was there in a minute, the gaps between his teeth wider than ever. "I know it's early sir, but they're running through the hymns this morning. I have it from Brother Jerome himself. At eight-fifteen, and God knows when you'll get the chance again. I hope you haven't got any appointments you can't break today, Mr. Goldfarb. I cut Mass and drove all the way in on purpose to get you. This is it."

"Does Father Hilary know you're here?"

Brother Patrick's face fell. "Why shouldn't he?"

"And Brother Dennis?"

"No, but he's expecting you back sometime or other."

"You sure are going to a lot of trouble, Brother, and you don't even sing." Brother Patrick just gazed at him. "All right," Sidney said, "you win." Sighing, he lifted the phone from its cradle and ordered breakfast. "I have a luncheon appointment at twelve sharp."

Brother Patrick winced. "I'm pretty sure I could get you back in time."

The trouble was that the Cardinal's office had contacted the chairman of the Board of Directors, who was both Catholic and the biggest stockholder. Sidney had hoped to get out of Sansom without seeing Mount Mary again, and do the rest of the negotiating if there should be any by long-distance telephone. But no, from Brother Patrick to the boss was a direct pipe line.

Brother Patrick steered him toward the minor chapel and then rushed off to his work, reluctantly waving good-bye from the corner. Finding himself alone in the chapel Sidney inspected it with a care he had not had time for the day before. It was severely undecorated except for the marble-topped altar and the stained-glass windows; the proportions of the room, long and narrow with a high ceiling, added to the impression of severity. The windows confused him; saints and ribbons of Latin, as one would expect, but all in modern designs and in color combinations much too striking to seem religious.

"Mr. Goldfarb." It was Brother Dennis alone. "I had not expected to see you again." Or, his voice implied, wanted to see you either.

"Well you know, Brother, I was impressed in spite of myself. I really was. And the longer I thought about it the better I liked it. You know?" Brother Dennis just looked at him. "As for Brother Jerome," Sidney added, "I haven't made up my mind yet."

"The lad needs far more training. It would take an order from the Pope himself to make me expose the lad to the public as he is now."

"I didn't know you ever had voice training," said Sidney blandly. "I thought you were a clarinetist."

"I was," said Brother Dennis, in his voice a new quality that sounded to Sidney like defensiveness, "but for the music we are working on conventional voice training is inappropriate. I don't know what else I can do."

"Would you mind telling me about these hymns?"

Brother Dennis looked at him heavily, then sighed. "Father Bernard discovered the manuscripts in Rome four years ago. The notation has caused us trouble. They are believed to be pre-Gregorian."

"Really?" said Sidney with animation. "There could be a story in this, how he found them in a forgotten monastery maybe? Research?"

"You will find a full account of the manuscripts and their musical significance in a journal of liturgical music or perhaps of musicology, I have not decided which, within a year or two. It is being written now."

"Sure, but I meant the human story. There could be something good." He was thinking of the record slipcover: THE MONKS OF MOUNT MARY PRESENT LOST TREASURES.

"There will be no such story."

"No? Why not?"

"Because Father Bernard is dying of cancer and I will tell you nothing."

Five fresh-faced, smiling student Brothers came in, indiscriminately young.

Sidney retired to the back of the chapel, where he spent the next half-hour simmering down. The singers were facing the altar, and Brother Dennis, though he was facing the body of the church, did not glance at Sidney. They were working on a song the like of which he had never heard; he had to admit that Brother Dennis had got the right four singers to support Brother Jerome's strange and beautiful voice; there was a ruggedness to their timbres which kept each separate from the others, and yet his wholly different-sounding voice gave the four a unity by way of contrast. The hymn had neither harmony nor counterpoint, and its melodic line no tune; the phrasing was causing them trouble, all the more because Brother Dennis himself was not sure what he was after. Sidney could not withhold his respect for the man, who was giving himself to this creative interpretation totally, and when suddenly he caught the long, subtle rhythms already mastered by these five boys his respect became ungrudging.

At 9:45 they took a half-hour break. "Brother," said Sidney catching him on the way out, "I'm impressed. This is a different caliber of singing from the Palestrina."

"We have a long way to go yet," said Brother Dennis. "You might not believe it but I'm glad I know jazz, it helps me with this music."

"So the wild man is tamed," said Sidney. Brother Dennis surprised him with a smile. "Say, Brother, you might be interested to know it—Henry has settled down too, in a different way naturally. And he's crazy about Linda, he really is."

"I have renounced all claims to my past," said Brother Dennis.

Sidney knew this was a delicate situation because he had never heard Henry so much as mention Brother Dennis, and whenever he had referred to Fred Stauffer it had been briefly and with embarrassment. Even so, because of his own desire and because of a certain quaver in Brother Dennis's voice, Sidney decided to go on needling; all he had to lose was a prestige record.

"She's going to be a social worker, you know, that's what she wants to do. Well anyway, Henry's got himself a stable marriage this time, I'm confident. His present wife is an old friend of mine—that's how they met incidentally—and you can rest assured they're doing all right. Henry's grown up a lot in the last few years. He never told me too much about those wild years, just a word now and then. I gather he was heavy on the hooch and you favored the ladies?"

"Ladies!" said Brother Dennis. Sidney nodded watchfully. "That is absolutely not true."

"Oh? That's what people say. I've heard it elsewhere too, that you were keen on the girls."

"I was a voluptuary," said Brother Dennis with blazing eyes, "but

I was never promiscuous. Sometimes, God forgive me, we used to stay in bed from the time we woke up till dinnertime, making love, slowly, five and six times, and talking about our bodies. We could spend hours. . . . I was luxurious, yes. But Lily was the only one. There was no other. You know Lily?"

"I've met her," said Sidney in a voice diminished with shock.

Brother Dennis wet his lips; the cowl obscured all but the boldest of his features, the deep-set eyes, the heavy brows, the gaunt cheeks, the full and shiny lips. "How is she?"

"Sick. Seriously, so I heard. It's mental. She's in an institution."

"It has come to that," said Brother Dennis, and walked away from him.

If Sidney had come here in his own car he would have driven away at that moment and not returned. Brother Dennis disturbed him in a way and to an extent he could not handle. But having to ferret out Brother Patrick and make up excuses for leaving was more than he felt up to. He settled himself in the last row of pews. There was nothing to look at but the windows. He developed an acute dislike of one in which the colors were dominantly green and yellow—a yellow sheep, a green shepherd. What kind of Catholics were these? He was dreadfully offended by Brother Dennis's confession of sensuality; it had not been a confession even, just a declaration, an explanation, with perhaps a tinge of pleasure mixed in. Sidney could never have said such a thing to anyone of any woman, even if he had done it, which God forbid; a roll in the hay, yes, he had hinted at things like that plenty of times, a conquest, part of the game; but to dwell on it, to say he'd spent all day in bed with a woman who was *named* yet, and to say he'd relished it, five or six times . . . even to do it . . . and for a monk to say so, without so much as lowering his voice, in fact raising it, right in tne vestibule of his own church. . . .

The young men returned and clustered in the front of the chapel, chirping in quiet voices, glancing back at him from time to time, giggling. Brother Dennis came in ten minutes late, and said "angelorum" to the singers, who made gestures of surprise. Brother Jerome took a position at the east wall and the other four faced him at the west wall. As Brother Dennis gave his recorder an experimental toot his eye came to rest on Sidney; he frowned, then fumbled inside his robe and fetched out a piece of slate gray paper. As he walked down the aisle Sidney was surprised to see him smiling. He rested one knee on the seat in front of Sidney and leaned against the back of the pew, like a friend.

"This hymn is the only one I'm anything like satisfied with. Here's a photostat of the original manuscript to give you an idea of what we had to work with." He went back.

Sidney tried to study the photostat, but he could not make head or tail of it; he did not know what quantities the signs indicated, nor was he sure that he could make out the one melodic line accompanying the Latin text; there was nothing on the paper but words in a script whose first word, *angelorum*, he could decipher only because he had heard it and odd musical notations hit or miss above the words. The recorder began and after a bar the five voices joined it.

Brother Dennis had pushed back his cowl as the singers had done, and Sidney was amazed to see that his hair was nearly white and stood out on every side; it looked splendid above the dark brown cloth. He swayed his head as he played, but he beat his right foot to another rhythm entirely. The recorder, the quartet, Brother Jerome, all were following the same line, yet there were subtle variations of intensity and phrasing which gave the effect of a complexity far beyond anything Sidney could analyze. Suddenly the recorder stopped and the four rough voices fell to half-volume; Brother Jerome tilted his head back and opened his mouth like a bird, and the sweet tones soared out with a beauty that made Sidney catch his breath. On the last word, *fidelibus*, Brother Jerome was alone; yet he filled the room. His singing seemed to Sidney to be perfectly voluptuous, an essence of voluptuousness, only safe.

Sidney did not know what to do; a solitary audience could not clap and besides he was in a church. Brother Dennis walked back to him, eyes aglow. Sidney nodded at him and smiled as best he could; he regretted all his unkind thoughts about Brother Dennis.

"We're going through it again; the phrasing was off in a few places. Listen to the suspense in those last vowels, *i, e, i,* and the sense of completion in that last *u.*" He made the sound with his lips and half-sang it; he was no singer and his voice was weak, yet Sidney got a glimpse of what he meant.

"Brother, I never heard anything like it."

Brother Dennis went back to the singers and began talking to them.

Sidney heard a *psst* from the chapel door; Brother Patrick's face was peeking in. Sidney made a circle of his thumb and forefinger and closed his eyes as though in rapture; Brother Patrick grinned and grinned and blinked his eyes several times and disappeared.

They went through the hymn again. Brother Dennis ghost-sang every syllable with Brother Jerome, floated him with his gestures, leaned toward him, watched his mouth as though his life depended on every sound. To Sidney the gesture with which Brother Dennis rounded off the last note seemed that of a man caressing a woman's hip.

The five young men pulled their cowls up and came down the aisle; Sidney smiled and nodded at them, and they glanced at him several times and smiled as they passed. Brother Dennis came up to him.

"It's the best," said Sidney. "I don't care whether there's a market for it or not it's got to be heard."

"You understand, Mr. Goldfarb, we're a long way from mastering all of them. This is the only one I'm satisfied with."

"That's all right."

"It may be years."

"You're the doctor, we'll be waiting."

"As for the acoustics . . ."

"Don't worry," said Sidney, "we have a few tricks up our sleeve."

"I was in the wine caves recently."

"Where?"

"In the caves where the storage vats are kept, for the wine to age in. I heard one of the working men singing in a vat he was cleaning out. It made an interesting effect. I have hopes we may be able to work something out in the caves."

"Anything you say, Brother."

"There is a different kind of silence in the caves. And the sound of airplanes does not penetrate."

"Planes!" Sidney cried and held his nose. "Especially the jets!"

"And it is possible, not certain in any sense, just conjecture on my part, but it is possible that these hymns were sung in the catacombs."

"Oh?" said Sidney and shivered a little.

"In the catacombs," Brother Dennis said raising his arms, "when we were being persecuted by the Romans—to sing a hymn of the angels in God's heaven. . . ."

"It's really wonderful," said Sidney remembering that his mother's parents had been killed by the Cossacks. "It really is."

"The important thing," said Brother Dennis his arms descending, "is that I mustn't arrange too much, modernize in any way I can help. Everything about it has to be perfect."

"Sure, Brother, I'm prepared to go along with you on anything you say. I'll put every modern facility at your disposal."

"No!" said Brother Dennis. "At the disposal of the hymns!"

"That's it, that's what I meant to say. It's the hymns."

Back at his hotel by 2:30 Sidney felt at a loss; he had a half-hour appointment at five for business cocktails and a business dinner at seven and his plane left at ten; meanwhile he found he could neither rest nor read. He told the hotel operator to put in a call to New York, but as soon as he replaced the phone in its cradle he lifted it again and canceled the call; long-distance business would not ease his mind.

He wanted to think about the music and his experience of hearing it, which still glowed inside him. But both the music and his experience listening to it had been so different from any he knew that he had no words to talk about them with. He could not even talk to himself about them. Intensity, strangeness, and loss of words —he shook himself and set his attention on business.

From the way Brother Dennis had not reacted at the mention of a royalty of maybe fifty cents a record Sidney was reasonably sure he could bring it down ten or twenty cents. It was obvious that the order was prosperous but not greedy, and that Brother Dennis personally did not care about such things as royalties. Even as he was thinking this Sidney lost interest in the business part of it. Dealing was a habit which at the moment he was not pleased to have. He forced his attention back to the royalty; it occurred to him that Father Hilary might very well be shrewd enough to hire a lawyer who would be tough about money. All right, all right. Fifty cents was the top, he'd said it and that was the limit; a prestige record they'd be lucky to sell five thousand copies of—hymn of the angels yet.

At the thought of the song the tiny belligerence he had begun to work up dissolved. Instead he felt hurt. Here he loved the music like nothing he'd ever heard, he was ready to give them sixty, even sixty-five cents a record, and they go hire a watchdog to worry him. The thought of their not trusting him made him not angry but unhappy. Couldn't they tell how much that record meant to him?

On the chance he telephoned Sharon's hotel. Her line was busy. He left his number for her to call him back. Thinking of her, he remembered the afternoon two years before when he had nearly proposed to her. He'd taken her up to his apartment after a recording session and told her he enjoyed being with her more than with any other woman he'd ever known. She told him he was sweet, he really was. They'd necked on the sofa for awhile, but she said she couldn't do it with a man unless she was married to him. Then he'd said something—he was no longer sure exactly what—about loneliness and old friends and both parties living their own lives. If she'd wanted him to propose he would have done it, but somehow, though he was sure she liked him, he hadn't quite got the words said.

The telephone rang. "Hi, Siddy baby."

As soon as he heard her voice—its bold facsimile of affection, its vague suspicion, its publicness made harsher by the instrument—he changed his mind. "I just wanted to say good-bye."

She sounded sorry and wanted to see him, wanted to just enough, sounded just sorry enough.

He started to tell her about the hymn and the Brothers, but instead switched over to telling her about the record he was going to get from them and how he planned to exploit it. "I mean it, Shary, I really do." He did not know exactly what he meant, but he knew he meant something.

"It's been wonderful seeing you, Siddy. Thanks for everything."

He thought that he felt sympathy underneath the hardness of her voice. "Keep in touch," he said. In the comfortable, friendly seeming, old shoe of a phrase he felt like himself. She did her purr job on him and he liked it. "I got to hang up now. I got a crowded calendar for the rest of the day." Saying it, though it was not true, made him feel normal again. "Bye now, baby. Keep in touch."

Among the Dangs

I graduated from Sansom University in 1937 with honors in history, having intended to study law, but I had no money and nowhere to get any; by good fortune the anthropology department, which had just been given a grant for research, decided that I could do a job for them. In idle curiosity I had taken a course in anthro, to see what I would have been like had history not catapulted my people a couple of centuries ago up into civilization, but I had not been inclined to enlarge on the sketchy knowledge I got from that course; even yet, when I think about it, I feel like a fraud teaching anthropology. What chiefly recommended me to the department, aside from a friend, was a combination of three attributes: I was a good mimic, a long-distance runner, and black.

The Dangs live in a forested valley in the eastern foothills of the Andes. The only white man to report on them (and, it was loosely

gossiped, the only one to return from them alive), Sir Bewley Morehead, owed his escape in 1910 to the consternation caused by Halley's comet. Otherwise, he reported, they would certainly have sacrificed him as they were preparing to do; as it was they killed the
priest who was to have killed him and then burned the temple
down. However, Dr. Sorish, our most distinguished Sansom man, in
the early thirties developed an interest in the Dangs which led to my
research grant; he had introduced a tribe of Amazonian head-shrink-
ers to the idea of planting grain instead of just harvesting it, as a
result of which they had fattened, taken to drinking brew by the
tubful, and elevated Sorish to the rank of new god. The last time he
had descended among them—it is Sansom policy to follow through
on any primitives we "do"—he had found his worshipers holding a
couple of young Dang men captive and preparing them for ceremonies which would end only with the processing of their heads;
his godhood gave him sufficient power to defer these ceremonies
while he made half-a-dozen transcriptions of the men's conversations
and learned their language well enough to arouse the curiosity of his
colleagues. The Dangs were handy with blowpipes; no one knew
what pleased them; Halley's comet wasn't due till 1986. But among
the recordings Sorish brought back was a legend strangely chanted
by one of these young men, whose very head perhaps you can buy
today from a natural science company for $150 to $200, and the
same youth had given Sorish a sufficient demonstration of the Dang
prophetic trance, previously described by Morehead, to whet his
appetite.

I was black, true; but as Sorish pointed out, I looked as though I
had been rolled in granite dust and the Dangs as though they had
been rolled in brick dust; my hair was short and kinky, theirs long
and straight; my lips were thick, theirs thin. It's like dressing a Greek
up in reindeer skins, I said, and telling him to go pass himself off as
a Lapp in Lapland. Maybe, they countered, but wouldn't he be
more likely to get by than a naked Swahili with bones in his nose?
I was a long-distance runner, true, but as I pointed out with a good
deal of feeling I didn't know the principles of jungle escape and had
no desire to learn them in, as they put it, the field. They would
teach me to throw the javelin and wield a machete, they would
teach me the elements of judo, and as for poisoned darts and sacri-
fices they would insure my life—that is, my return within three years

—for five thousand dollars. I was a good mimic, true; I would be able to reproduce the Dang speech and especially the trance of the Dang prophets for the observation of science—"make a genuine contribution to learning." In the Sansom concept the researcher's experience is an inextricable part of anthropological study, and a good mimic provides the object for others' study as well as for his own. For doing this job I would be given round-trip transportation, an M.S. if I wrote a thesis on the material I gathered, the temporary insurance on my life, and one hundred dollars a month for the year I was expected to be gone. After I'd got them to throw in a fellow-ship of some sort for the following year I agreed. It would pay for filling the forty cavities in my brothers' and sisters' teeth.

Dr. Sorish and I had to wait at the nearest outstation for a thunderstorm; when it finally blew up I took off all my clothes, put on a breechcloth and leather apron, put a box of equipment on my head, and trotted after him; his people were holed in from the thunder and we were in their settlement before they saw us. They were taller than I, they no doubt found my white teeth as disagreeable as I found their stained, filed teeth, but when Sorish spoke to me in English (telling me to pretend indifference to them while they sniffed me over) and in the accents of American acquaintances rather than in the harsh tones of divinity their eyes filled with awe of me. Their taboo against touching Sorish extended itself to me; when a baby ran up to me and I lifted him up to play with him, his mother crawled, beating her head on the ground till I freed him.

The next day was devoted chiefly to selecting the man to fulfill Sorish's formidable command to guide me to the edge of the Dang country. As for running—if those characters could be got to the next Olympics, Ecuador would take every long-distance medal on the board. I knew I had reached the brow of my valley only because I discovered that my guide, whom I had been lagging behind by fifty feet, at a turn in the path had disappeared into the brush.

Exhaustion allayed my terror; as I lay in the meager shade recuperating I remembered to execute the advice I had given myself before coming: to act always as though I were not afraid. What would a brave man do next? Pay no attention to his aching feet, reconnoiter, and cautiously proceed. I climbed a jutting of rock and peered about. It was a wide, scrubby valley; on the banks of the river running down the valley I thought I saw a dozen mounds too regular for stones. I touched the handle of the hunting knife sheathed at my side, and trotted down the trackless hill.

The village was deserted, but the huts, though miserable, were clean and in good repair. This meant, according to the movies I had seen, that hostile eyes were watching my every gesture. I had to keep moving in order to avoid trembling. The river was clear and not deep. The corpse of a man floated by. I felt like going downstream, but my hypothesized courage drove me up.

In half a mile I came upon a toothless old woman squatting by the track. She did not stop munching when I appeared, nor did she scream, or even stand up. I greeted her in Dang according to the formula I had learned, whereupon she cackled and smiled and nodded as gleefully as though I had just passed a test. She reminded me of my grandmother, rolled in brick dust, minus a corncob pipe between her gums. Presently I heard voices ahead of me. I saw five women carrying branches and walking very slowly. I lurked behind them until they came to a small village, and watched from a bush while they set to work. They stripped the leaves off, carefully did something to them with their fingers, and then dropped them in small-throated pots. Children scrabbled around, and once a couple of them ran up and suckled at one of the women. There remained about an hour till sunset. I prowled, undetected. The women stood, like fashion models, with pelvis abnormally rocked forward; they were wiry, without fat even on their breasts; not even their thighs and hips afforded clean sweeping lines undisturbed by bunched muscles. I saw no men.

Before I began to get into a lather about the right tack to take I stepped into the clearing and uttered their word of salutation. If a strange man should walk in your wife's front door and say "How do you do" in an accent she did not recognize, simultaneously poking his middle finger at her, her consternation would be something like that of those Dang women, for unthinkingly I had nodded my head when speaking and turned my palm up as one does in the United States; to them this was a gesture of intimacy, signifying desire. They disappeared into huts, clutching children.

I went to the central clearing and sat with my back to a log, knowing they would scrutinize me. I wondered where the men were. I could think of no excuse for having my knife in my hand except to clean my toenails. So astonishing an act was unknown to the Dangs; the women and children gradually approached in silence, watching; I cleaned my fingernails. I said the word for food; no one reacted, but presently a little girl ran up to me holding a fruit in both hands. I took it, snibbed her nose between my fingers, and with a pat on the bottom sent her back to her mother. Upon this there were hostile glances, audible intakes of breath, and a huddling about the baby who did not understand any more than I did why she was being consoled. While I ate the fruit I determined to leave the next move up to them. I sheathed my knife and squatted on my hunkers, waiting. To disguise my nervousness I fixed my eyes on the ground between my feet, and grasped my ankles from behind in such a way—right ankle with right hand, left with left—as to expose the inner sides of my forearms. Now this was, as I later learned, pretty close to the initial posture taken for the prophetic trance; also I had a blue flower tattooed on my inner right arm and a blue serpent on my left (from the summer I'd gone to sea), the like of which had never been seen in this place.

At sundown I heard the men approach; they were anything but stealthy about it; I had the greatest difficulty in suppressing the shivers. In simple fear of showing my fear I did not look up when the men gathered around, I could understand just enough of what the women were telling the men to realize that they were afraid of me. Even though I was pelted with pebbles and twigs till I was angry I still did not respond, because I could not think what to do. Then something clammy was plopped onto my back from above and I leaped high, howling. Their spears were poised before I landed.

"Strangers!" I cried, my speech composed. "Far kinsmen! I come from the mountains!" I had intended to say *from the river lands,* but the excitement tangled my tongue. Their faces remained expressionless but no spears drove at me, and then to be doing something I shoved the guts under the log with my feet.

And saved my life by doing so. That I seemed to have taken, though awkwardly, the prophetic squat; that I bore visible marvels on my arm; that I was fearless and inwardly absorbed; that I came from the mountains (their enemies lived toward the river lands); that I wore their apron and spoke their language, albeit poorly, all these disposed them to wonder at this mysterious outlander. Even so they might very well have captured me, marvelous though I was, possibly useful to them, dangerous to antagonize, had I not been unblemished, which meant that I was supernaturally guarded. Finally, my scrutinizing the fish guts, daring to smile as I did so, could mean only that I was prophetic; my leap when they had been dropped onto my back was prodigious, "far higher than a man's head," and my howl had been vatic; and my deliberately kicking the guts aside, though an inscrutable act, demonstrated at least that I could touch the entrails of an eel and live.

So I was accepted to the Dangs. The trouble was they they had no ceremony for naturalizing me. For them every act had a significance, and here they were faced with a reverse problem for which nothing had prepared them. They could not possibly just assimilate me without marking the event with an act (that is, a ceremony) signifying my entrance. For them nothing *just happened*, certainly nothing that men did. Meanwhile, I was kept in a sort of quarantine while they deliberated. I did not, to be sure, understand why I was being isolated in a hut by myself, never spoken to except efficiently, watched but not restrained. I swam, slept, scratched, watched, swatted, ate; I was not really alarmed because they had not restrained me forcibly and they gave me food. I began making friends with some of the small children, especially while swimming, and there were two girls of fifteen or so who found me terribly funny. I wished I had some magic, but I knew only card tricks. The sixth day, swimming, I thought I was being enticed around a point in the river by the two girls, but when I began to chase them they threw good-sized stones at me, missing me only because they were such poor shots. A corpse floated by; when they saw it they immediately placed the sole of their right foot on the side of their left knee and stood thus on one leg till the corpse floated out of sight; I followed the girls' example, teetering. I gathered from what they said that some illness was devastating their people; I hoped it was one of the diseases I had been inoculated against. The girls' mothers found them talking with me and cuffed them away.

I did not see them for two days, but the night of my eighth day there the bolder of them hissed me awake at the door of my hut in a way that meant "no danger." I recognized her when she giggled. I was not sure what their customs were in these matters, but while I was deliberating what my course of wisdom should be she crawled into the hut and lay on the mat beside me. She liked me, she was utterly devoid of reticence, I was twenty-one and far from home; even a scabby little knotty-legged fashion model is hard to resist under such circumstances. I learned before falling asleep that there was a three-way debate among the men over what to do with me: initiate me according to the prophet-initiation rites, invent a new ceremony, or sacrifice me as propitiation to the disease among them as was usually done with captives. Each had its advantages and drawbacks; even the news that some of the Dangs wanted to sacrifice me did not excite me as it would have done a week before; now, I half-sympathized with their trouble. I was awakened at dawn by the outraged howl of a man at my door; he was the girl's father. The village men gathered and the girl cowered behind me. They talked for hours outside my hut, men arrived from other villages up and down the valley, and finally they agreed upon a solution to all the problems: they proposed that I should be made one of the tribe by marriage on the same night that I should be initiated into the rites of prophecy.

The new-rite men were satisfied by this arrangement because of the novelty of having a man married and initiated on the same day, but the sacrifice party was visibly unmollified. Noticing this and reflecting that the proposed arrangement would permit me to do all my trance research under optimum conditions and to accumulate a great deal of sexual data as well I agreed to it. I would of course only be going through the forms of marriage, not meaning them; as for the girl, I took this vow to myself (meaning without ceremony): "So long as I am a Dang I shall be formally a correct husband to her." More's a pity.

Fortunately a youth from down the valley already had been chosen as a novice (at least a third of the Dang men enter the novitiate at one time or another, though few make the grade), so that I had not only a companion during the four-month preparation for the vatic rites but also a control upon whom I might check my experience of the stages of the novitiate. My mimetic powers stood me in good stead; I was presumed to have a special prophetic gift and my readiness at assuming the proper stances and properly performing the ritual acts confirmed the Dangs' impressions of my gift; but also, since I was required to proceed no faster than the ritual pace in my learning, I had plenty of leisure in which to observe in the smallest detail what I did and how I, and to some extent my fellow novice, felt. If I had not had this self-observing to relieve the tedium I think I should have been unable to get through that mindless holding of the same position hour after hour, that mindless repeating of the same act day after day. The Dangs *appear* to be bored much of the time, and my early experience with them was certainly that of ennui, though never again ennui so acute as during this novitiate. Yet I doubt that it would be accurate to say they actually are bored, and I am sure that the other novice was not, as a fisherman waiting hours for a strike cannot be said to be bored. The Dangs do not sate themselves on food; the experience which they consider most worth seeking, vision, is one which cannot glut either the prophet or his auditors; they cannot imagine an alternative to living as they live or, more instantly, to preparing a novice as I was being prepared. The people endure; the prophets, as I have learned, wait for the time to come again, and though they are bitten and stung by ten thousand fears, about this they have no anxiety—the time will surely come again. Boredom implies either satiety, and they were poor and not interested in enriching themselves, or the frustration of impulse, and they were without alternatives and diversions. The intense boredom which is really a controlled anxiety, they are protected from by never doubting the worth of their vision or their power to achieve it.

I was assisted through these difficult months during which I was supposed to do nothing but train by Redadu, my betrothed. As a novice I was strictly to abstain from sexual intercourse, but as betrothed we were supposed to make sure before marriage that we satisfied one another, for adultery by either husband or wife was punishable by maiming. Naturally the theologians were much exercised by this impasse, but while they were arguing Redadu and I took the obvious course—we met more or less surreptitiously. Since my vatic training could not take place between sunrise and sundown I assumed that we could meet in the afternoon when I woke up, but when I began making plans to this effect I discovered that she did not know what I was talking about. It makes as much sense in Dang to say, "Let's blow poisoned darts at the loss of the moon," as to say, "Let's make love in broad daylight." Redadu dissolved in giggles at the absurdity. What to do? She found us a cave. Everyone must have known what I was up to, but we were respectable (the Dang term for it was harsher, *deed-liar*) so we were never disturbed. Redadu's friends would not believe her stories of my luxurious love ways, especially my biting with lips instead of teeth. At one time or another she sent four of them to the cave for me to demonstrate my prowess upon; I was glad that none of them pleased me as much as she did for I was beginning to be fond of her. My son has told me that lip-biting has become if not a customary at any rate a possible caress.

As the night of the double rite approached, a night of full moon, a new conflict became evident: the marriage must be consummated exactly at sundown, but the initiation must begin at moonrise, less than two hours later. For some reason that was not clear to me preparing for the initiation would incapacitate me for the consummation. I refrained from pointing out that it was only technically that this marriage needed consummating and even from asking why I would not be able to do it. The solution, which displeased everyone, was to defer the rites for three nights, when the moon, though no longer perfectly round, would rise sufficiently late so that I would, by hurrying, be able to perform both of my functions. Redadu's father, who had been of the sacrifice party, waived ahead of time his claim against me; legally he was entitled to annul the marriage if I should leave the marriage hut during the bridal night. And although I in turn could legally annul it if she left the hut I waived my claim as well so that she might attend my initiation.

The wedding consisted chiefly of our being bound back to back by the elbows and being sung to and danced about all day. At sunset we were bound face to face by the elbows (most awkward) and sent into our hut. Outside the two mothers waited—a high prophet's wife took the place of my mother (my Methodist mother!)— until our orgastic cries indicated that the marriage had been consummated, and then came in to sever our bonds and bring us the bridal foods of cold stewed eel and parched seeds. We fed each other bite for bite and gave the scraps to our mothers, who by the formula with which they thanked us pronounced themselves satisfied with us. Then a falsetto voice called to me to hurry to the altar. A man in the mask of a moon slave was standing outside my hut on his left leg with the right foot against his left knee, and he continued to shake his rattle so long as I was within earshot.

The men were masked. Their voices were all disguised. I wondered whether I was supposed to speak in an altered voice; I knew every stance and gesture I was to make, but nothing of what I was to say; yet surely a prophet must employ words. I had seen some of the masks before—being repaired, being carried from one place to another—but now, faced with them alive in the failing twilight, I was impressed by them in no scientific or aesthetic way—they terrified and exalted me. I wondered if I would be given a mask. I began trying to identify such men as I could by their scars and missing fingers and crooked arms, and noticed to my distress that they too were all standing one-legged in my presence. I had thought that was the stance to be assumed in the presence of the dead! We were at the entrance to The Cleft, a dead-end ravine in one of the cliffs along the valley; my fellow novice and I were each given a gourdful of some vile-tasting drink and were then taken up to the end of The Cleft, instructed to assume the first position, and left alone. We squatted as I had been squatting by the log on my first day, except that my head was cocked in a certain way and my hands clasped my ankles from the front. The excitements of the day seemed to have addled my wits, I could concentrate on nothing and lost my impulse to observe coolly what was going on; I kept humming *St. James Infirmary* to myself, and though at first I had been thinking the words, after awhile I realized that I had nothing but the tune left in my head. At moonrise we were brought another gourd of the liquor to drink, and were then taken to the mouth of The Cleft again. I did, easily, whatever I was told. The last thing I remember seeing before taking the second position was the semicircle of masked men facing us and chanting, and behind them the women and children—all standing on the left leg. I lay on my back with my left ankle on my right and my hands crossed over my navel, rolled my eyeballs up and held the lids open without blinking, and breathed in the necessary rhythm, each breath taking four heartbeats, with an interval of ten heartbeats between each exhalation and the next inspiration. Then the drug took over. At dawn when a called command awakened me, I found myself on an islet in the river dancing with my companion a leaping dance I had not known or even seen before, and brandishing over my head a magnificent red and blue, new-made mask of my own. The shores of the river were lined with the people chanting as we leaped, and all of them were either sitting or else standing on both feet. If we had been dead the night before we were alive now.

After I had slept and returned to myself, Redadu told me that my vision was splendid, but of course she was no more permitted to tell me what I had said than I was able to remember it. The Dangs' sense of rhythm is as subtle as their ear for melody is monotonous, and for weeks I kept hearing rhythmic snatches of *St. James Infirmary* scratched on calabash drums and tapped on blocks.

Sorish honored me by rewriting my master's thesis and adding my name as co-author of the resultant essay, which he published in *JAFA* (*The Journal of American Field Anthropology*): "Techniques of Vatic Hallucinosis among the Dangs." And the twenty-minute movie I made of a streamlined performance of the rites is still widely used as an audio-visual aid.

By 1939 when I had been cured of the skin disease I had brought back with me and had finished the work for my M.S. I still had no money. I had been working as the assistant curator of the University's Pre-Columbian Museum and had developed a powerful aversion to devoting my life to cataloguing, displaying, restoring, warehousing. But my chances of getting a research job, slight enough with a Ph.D., were nil with only an M.S. The girl I was going with said (I had not told her about Redadu) that if we married she would work as a nurse to support me while I went through law school; I was tempted by the opportunity to fulfill my original ambition, and probably I would have done it had she not pressed too hard; she wanted me to leave anthropology, she wanted me to become a lawyer, she wanted to support me, but what she did not want was to make my intentions, whatever they might be, her own. So when a new grant gave me the chance to return to the Dangs I gladly seized it; not only would I be asserting myself against Velma, but also I would be paid for doing the research for my Ph.D. thesis; besides, I was curious to see the Congo-Maryland-Dang bastard I had left in Redadu's belly.

My assignment was to make a general cultural survey but especially to discover the *content* of the vatic experience—not just the technique, not even the hallucinations and stories, but the qualities of the experience itself. The former would get me a routine degree, but the latter would, if I did it, make me a name and get me a job. After much consultation I decided against taking with me any form of magic, including medicine; the antibiotics had not been invented yet, and even if there had been a simple way to eradicate the fever endemic among the Dangs, my advisers persuaded me that it would be an error to introduce it since the Dangs were able to procure barely enough food for themselves as it was and since they might worship me for doing it, thereby making it impossible for me to do my research with the proper empathy. I arrived the second time provided only with my knife (which had not seemed to impress these stone-agers), salve to soothe my sores, and the knowledge of how to preserve fish against a lean season, innovation enough but not one likely to divinize me.

I was only slightly worried how I would be received on my return, because of the circumstances under which I had disappeared. I had become a fairly decent hunter—the women gathered grain and fruit —and I had learned to respect the Dangs' tracking abilities enough to have been nervous about getting away safely. While hunting with a companion in the hills south of our valley I had run into a couple of hunters from an enemy tribe which seldom foraged so far north as this. They probably were as surprised as I and probably would have been glad to leave me unmolested; however, outnumbered and not knowing how many more were with them, I whooped for my companion; one of the hunters in turn, not knowing how many were with me, threw his spear at me. I side-stepped it and reached for my darts, and though I was not very accurate with a blowpipe I hit him in the thigh; within a minute he was writhing on the ground, for in my haste I had blown a venomous dart at him, and my comrade took his comrade prisoner by surprise. As soon as the man I had hit was dead I withdrew my dart and cut off his ear for trophy, and we returned with our captive. He told our war chief in sign language that the young man I had killed was the son and heir of their king and that my having mutilated him meant their tribe surely would seek to avenge his death. The next morning a Dang search party was sent out to recover the body so that it might be destroyed and trouble averted, but it had disappeared; war threatened. The day after that I chose to vanish; they would not think of looking for me in the direction of Sorish's tribe, north, but would assume that I had been captured by the southern tribe in retribution for their prince's death. My concern now, two years later, was how to account for not having been maimed or executed; the least I could do was to cut a finger off, but when it came to the point I could not even bring myself to have a surgeon do it, much less do it myself; I had adequate lies prepared for their other questions, but about this I was a bit nervous.

I got there at sundown. Spying, I did not see Redadu about the village. On the chance, I slipped into our hut when no one was looking; she was there, playing with our child. He was as cute a little preliterate as you ever saw suck a thumb, and it made me chuckle to think he would never be literate either. Redadu's screams when she saw me fetched the women, but when they heard a man's voice they could not intrude. In her joy she lacerated me with her fingernails (the furrows across my shoulder festered for a long time); I could do no less than bite her arm till she bled; the primal scene we treated our son to presumably scarred him for life—though I must say the scars haven't shown up yet. I can't deny I was glad to see her too, for, though I felt for her none of the tender, complex emotions I had been feeling for Velma, emotions which I more or less identified as being love, yet I was so secure with her sexually, knew so well what to do and what to expect from her in every important matter that it was an enormous, if cool, comfort to me to be with her. *Comfort* is a dangerous approximation to what I mean; being with her provided, as it were, the condition for doing; in Sansom I did not consider her my wife and here I did not recognize in myself the American emotions of love or marriage, yet it seemed to me right to be with her and our son was no bastard. *Cool*—I cannot guarantee that mine was the usual Dang emotion, for it is hard for the cool to gauge the warmth of others (in my reports I have denied any personal experience of love among the Dangs for this reason). When we emerged from the hut there was amazement and relief among the women: amazement that I had returned and relief that it had not been one of their husbands pleasuring the widow. But the men were more ambiguously pleased to see me. Redadu's scratches were not enough and they doubted my story that the enemy king had made me his personal slave who must be bodily perfect. They wanted to hear me prophesy.

Redadu told me afterward, hiding her face in my arms for fear of being judged insolent, that I surpassed myself that night, that only the three high prophets had ever been so inspired. And it was true that even the men most hostile to me did not oppose my reëntry into the tribe after they had heard me prophesy; they could have

swallowed the story I fed them about my two-year absence only because they believed in me the prophet. Dangs make no separation
between fact and fantasy, apparent reality and visionary reality, truth
and beauty. I once saw a young would-be prophet shudder away
from a stick on the ground saying it was a snake, and none of the
others except the impressionable was afraid of the stick; it was said
of him that he was a beginner. Another time I saw a prophet scatter
the whole congregation, myself included, when he screamed at the
sight of a beast which he called a cougar; when sober dawn found
the speared creature to be a cur it was said of the prophet that he
was strong, and he was honored with an epithet, Cougar-Dog. My
prophesying the first night of my return must have been of this caliber, though to my disappointment I was given no epithet, not even
the nickname I'd sometimes heard before, Bush-Hair.

I knew there was a third kind of prophesying, the highest, performed only on the most important occasions in the Cave-Temple
where I had never been. No such occasion had presented itself during my stay before, and when I asked one of the other prophets
about that ceremony he put me off with the term Wind-Haired
Child of the Sun; from another I learned that the name of this sort
of prophesying was Stone is Stone. Obviously I was going to have to
stay until I could make sense of these mysteries.

There was a war party that wanted my support; my slavery was
presumed to have given me knowledge which would make a raid
highly successful; because of this as well as because I had instigated
the conflict by killing the king's son I would be made chief of the
raiding party. I was uneasy about the fever, which had got rather
worse among them during the previous two years, without risking
my neck against savages who were said always to eat a portion of
their slain enemy's liver raw and whose habitat I knew nothing of.
I persuaded the Dangs, therefore, that they should not consider
attacking before the rains came, because their enemies were now
the stronger, having on their side their protector, the sun. They listened to me and waited. Fortunately it was a long dry season, during which I had time to find a salt deposit and to teach a few women
the rudiments of drying and salting fish; and during the first week of
the rains every night there were showers of falling stars to be seen
in the sky; to defend against them absorbed all energies for weeks,
including the warriors'. Even so, even though I was a prophet, a

journeyman prophet as it were, I was never in on these rites in the Cave-Temple. I dared not ask many questions. Sir Bewley Morehead had described a temple surrounded by seventy-six poles, each topped by a human head; he could hardly have failed to mention that it was in a cave, yet he made no such mention, and I knew of no temple like the one he had described. At a time of rains and peace in the sky the war party would importune me. I did not know what to do but wait.

The rains became violent, swamping the villages in the lower valley and destroying a number of huts, yet the rainy season ended abruptly two months before its usual time. Preparations for war had already begun, and day by day as the sun's strength increased and the earth dried the war party became more impatient. The preparations in themselves lulled my objections to the raid, even to my leading the raid, and stimulated my desire to make war. But the whole project was canceled a couple of days before we were to attack because of the sudden fever of one of the high prophets; the day after he came down five others of the tribe fell sick, among them Redadu. There was nothing I could do but sit by her, fanning her and sponging her till she died. Her next older sister took our son to rear. I would allow no one to prepare her body but myself, though her mother was supposed to help; I washed it with the proper infusions of herbs, and at dawn, in the presence of her clan, I laid her body on the river. Thank heaven it floated or I should have had to spend another night preparing it further. I felt like killing someone now; I recklessly called for war now, even though the high prophet had not yet died; I was restrained, not without admiration. I went up into the eastern hills by myself and returned after a week bearing the hide of a cougar; I had left the head and claws on my trophy in a way the Dangs had never seen; when I put the skin on in play by daylight and bounded and snarled only the bravest did not run in terror. They called me Cougar-Man. Redadu's younger sister came to sleep with me; I did not want her, but she so stubbornly refused to be expelled that I kept her for the night, for the next night, for the next; it was not improper.

The high prophet did not die, but lay comatose most of the time. The Dangs have ten master prophets, of whom the specially gifted, whether one or all ten, usually two or three, are high prophets. Fifteen days after Redadu had died, well into the abnormal dry spell, nearly all the large fish seemed to disappear from the river. A sacrifice was necessary. It was only because the old man was so sick that a high prophet was used for this occasion, otherwise a captive or a woman would have served the purpose. A new master prophet must replace him, to keep the complement up to ten. I was chosen.

The exultation I felt when I learned that the master prophets had co-opted me among them was by no means cool and anthropological, for now that I had got what I had come to get I no longer wanted it for Sansom reasons. *If the conditions of my being elevated,* I said to myself, *are the suffering of the people, Redadu's death, and the sacrifice of an old man, then I must make myself worthy of the great price. Worthy*—a value word, not a scientific one. Of course, my emotions were not the simple pride and fear of a Dang. I can't say what sort they were, but they were fierce.

At sundown all the Dangs of all the clans were assembled about the entrance to The Cleft. All the prophets, masked, emerged from The Cleft and began the dance in a great wheel. Within this wheel, rotating against it, was the smaller wheel of the nine able-bodied master prophets. At the center, facing the point at which the full moon would rise, I hopped on one leg, than the other. I had been given none of the vatic liquor, that brew which the women, when I had first come among the Dangs, had been preparing in the small-throated pots, and I hoped I should be able to remain conscious throughout the rites. However, at moonrise a moon slave brought me a gourdful to drink without ceasing to dance. I managed to allow a good deal of it to spill unnoticed down with the sweat streaming off me, so that later I was able to remember what had happened, right up to the prophesying itself. The dance continued for at least two more hours, then the drums suddenly stopped and the prophets began to file up The Cleft with me last dancing after the high prophets. We danced into an opening in the cliff from which a disguising stone had been rolled away. The people were not allowed to follow us. We entered a great cavern illuminated by ten smoking torches and circled a palisade of stakes; the only sound was the shuffle of our feet and the snorts of our breathing. There were seventy-six stakes, as Morehead had seen, but only on twenty-eight of them were heads impaled, the last few with flesh on them still, not yet skulls cleaned of all but hair. In the center was a huge stone under the middle of which a now dry stream had tunneled a narrow passage; on one side of the stone, above the passage, were two breastlike protuberances, one of which had a recognizable nipple in the suitable place. Presently the dancing file reversed so that I was the leader. I had not been taught what to do; I wove the file through the round of stakes, and spiraled inward till we were three deep about The Stone; I straddled the channel, raised my hands till they were touching the breasts, and gave a great cry. I was, for reasons I do not understand, shuddering all over; though I was conscious and though I had not been instructed, I was not worried that I might do the wrong thing next. When I touched The Stone a dread shook me without affecting my exaltation. Two moon slaves seized my arms, took off my mask, and wrapped and bound me— arms at my side and legs pressed together in a deer hide—and then laid me on my back in the channel under The Stone with my head only half out, so that I was staring up the sheer side of rock. The dancers continued, though the master prophets had disappeared. My excitement, the new unused position, being mummied tightly, the weakness of the drug, my will to observe, all kept me conscious for a long time. Gradually, however, my eyes began to roll up into my head, I strained less powerfully against the thongs that bound me, and I felt my breathing approach the vatic rhythm. At this point I seemed to break out in a new sweat, on my forehead, my throat, in my hair; I could hear a splash, groggily I licked my chin—an odd taste—I wondered if I was bleeding. Of course, it was the blood of the sick old high prophet, who had just been sacrificed on The Stone above me; well, his blood would give me strength. Wondering remotely whether his fever could be transmitted by drinking his blood I entered the trance. At dawn I emerged into consciousness while I was still prophesying; I was on a ledge in the valley above all the people, in my mask again. I listened to myself finish the story I was telling. "He was afraid. A third time a man said to him: 'You are a friend of the most high prophet.' He answered: 'Not me. I do not know that man they are sacrificing.' Then he went into a dark corner, he put his hands over his face all day." When I came to the Resurrection a sigh blew across the people. It was the best story they had ever heard. Of course. But I was not really a Christian. For several weeks I fretted over my confusion, this new, unsuspected confusion.

I was miserable without Redadu; I let her sister substitute only until I had been elevated, and then I cast her off, promising her however that she and only she might wear an anklet made of my teeth when I should die. Now that I was a master prophet I could not be a warrior; I had enough of hunting and fishing and tedious ceremonies. Hunger from the shortage of fish drove the hunters high into the foothills; there was not enough; they ate my preserved fish, suspiciously, but they ate them. When I left it was not famine that I was escaping but my confusion; I was fleeing to the classrooms and the cool museums where I should be neither a leftover Christian nor a mimic of a Dang.

My academic peace lasted for just two years, during which time I wrote five articles on my researches, publishing them this time under my name only, did some of the work for my doctorate, and married Velma. Then came World War II, in which my right hand was severed above the wrist; I was provided with an artificial hand and given enough money so that I could afford to finish my degree in style. We had two daughters and I was given a job at Sansom. There was no longer a question of my returning to the Dangs. I would become a settled anthropologist, teach, and quarrel with my colleagues in the learned journals. But by the time the Korean War came along and robbed us of a lot of our students, my situation at the university had changed considerably. Few of my theoretical and disputatious articles were printed in the journals, and I hated writing them; I was not given tenure and there were some hints to the effect that I was considered a one-shot man, a flash-in-the-pan; Velma nagged for more money and higher rank. My only recourse was further research, and when I thought of starting all over again with some other tribe—in northern Australia, along the Zambesi, on an African island—my heart sank. The gossip was not far from the mark—I was not a one hundred per cent scientist and never would be. I had just enough reputation and influential recommendations to be awarded a Guggenheim Fellowship; supplemented by a travel grant from the university this made it possible for me to leave my family comfortably provided for and to return to the Dangs.

A former student now in Standard Oil in Venezuela arranged to have me parachuted among them from an SO plane. There was the real danger that they would kill me before they recognized me, but if I arrived in a less spectacular fashion I was pretty sure they would sacrifice me for their safety's sake. This time, being middle-aged, I left my hunting knife and brought instead at my belt a pouch filled with penicillin and salves. I had a hard time identifying the valley from the air; it took me so long that it was sunset before I jumped. I knew how the Dangs were enraged by airplanes, especially by the winking lights of night fliers, and I knew they would come for me if they saw me billowing down. Fortunately I landed in the river, for though I was nearly drowned before I disentangled my parachute harness I was also out of range of the blowpipes. I finally identified myself to the warriors brandishing their spears along the shore; they had not quite dared to swim out after so prodigious a being; even after they knew who I said I was and allowed me to swim to shore they saw me less as myself than as a supernatural being. I was recognized by newcomers who had not seen me so closely swinging from the parachute (the cloud); on the spot my epithet became, and remained, Sky-Cougar. Even so no one dared touch me till the high prophet—there was only one now—had arrived and talked with me; my artificial hand seemed to him an extension of the snake tattooed onto my skin, he would not touch it; I suddenly struck him with it and pinched his arm. "Pinchers," I said using the word for a crayfish claw, and he laughed. He said there was no way of telling whether I was what I seemed to be until he had heard me prophesy; if I prophesied as I had done before I had disappeared I must be what I seemed to be; meanwhile, for the three weeks till full moon I was to be kept in the hut for captives.

At first I was furious at being imprisoned, and when mothers brought children from miles about to peek through the stakes at the man with the snake hand I snarled or sulked like a caged wolf. But I became conscious that one youth, squatting in a quiet place, had been watching me for hours. I demanded of him who he was. He said, "I am your son," but he did not treat me as his father. To be sure, he could not have remembered what I looked like; my very identity was doubted; even if I were myself, I was legendary, a stranger who had become a Dang and had been held by an enemy as captive slave for two years and had then become a master prophet with the most wonderful vision anyone knew. Yet he came to me every day and answered all the questions I put to him. It was, I believe, my artificial hand that finally kept him aloof from me; no amount of acquaintance could accustom him to that. By the end of the first week it was clear to me that if I wanted to survive—not to be accepted as I once had been, just to survive—I would have to prophesy the Passion again. And how could I determine what I would say when under the vatic drug? I imagined a dozen schemes for substituting colored water for the drug, but I would need an accomplice for that and I knew that not even my own son would serve me in so forbidden an act.

I called for the high prophet. I announced to him in tones all the more arrogant because of my trepidations that I would prophesy without the vatic liquor. His response to my announcement astonished me: he fell upon his knees, bowed his head, and rubbed dust into his hair. He was the most powerful man among the Dangs, except in time of war when the war chief took over, and furthermore he was an old man of personal dignity, yet here he was abasing himself before me and, worse, rubbing dust into his hair as was proper in the presence of the very sick to help them in their dying. He told me why: prophesying successfully from a voluntary trance was the test which I must pass to become a high prophet; normally a master prophet was forced to this, for the penalty for failing it was death. I dismissed him with a wave of my claw.

I had five days to wait until full moon. The thought of the risk I was running was more than I could handle consciously; to avoid the jitters I performed over and over all the techniques of preparing for the trance, though I carefully avoided entering it. I was not sure I would be able to enter it alone, but whether I could or not I knew I wanted to conserve my forces for the great test. At first during those five days I would remind myself once in a while of my scientific purpose in going into the trance consciously; at other times I would assure myself that it was for the good of the Dangs that I was doing it, since it was not wise or safe for them to have only one high prophet. Both of these reasons were true enough, but not very important. As scientist I should tell them some new myth, say the story of Abraham and Isaac or of Oedipus, so that I could compare its effect on them with that of the Passion; as master prophet I should ennoble my people if I could. However, thinking these matters over as I held my vatic squat hour after hour, visited and poked at by prying eyes, I could find no myth to satisfy me; either, as in the case of Abraham, it involved a concept of God which the Dangs could not reach, or else, as with Oedipus, it necessitated more drastic

changes than I trusted myself to keep straight while prophesying—
that Oedipus should mutilate himself was unthinkable to the Dangs
and that the gods should be represented as able to forgive him for
it was impious. Furthermore, I did not think, basically, that any
story I could tell them would in fact ennoble them. I was out to
save my own skin.

The story of Christ I knew by heart; it had worked for me once,
perhaps more than once; it would work again. I rehearsed it over
and over, from the Immaculate Conception to the Ascension. But
such was the force of that story on me that by the fifth day my
cynicism had disappeared along with my scientism, and I believed,
not that the myth itself was true, but that relating it to my people
was the best thing it was possible for me to do for them. I remember
telling myself that this story would help raise them toward monotheism, a necessary stage in the evolution toward freedom. I felt a
certain satisfaction in the thought that some of the skulls on the
stakes in the Cave-Temple were very likely those of missionaries who
had failed to convert these heathen.

At sundown of the fifth day I was taken by moon slaves to a cave
near The Cleft, where I was left in peace. I fell into a troubled
sleep from which I awoke in a sweat. "Where am I? What am I
about to do?" It seemed to me dreadfully wrong that I should be
telling these, my people, a myth in whose power, but not in whose
truth, I believed. Why should I want to free them from superstition
into monotheism and then into my total freedom, when I myself
was half-returning, voluntarily, down the layers again? The energy
for these sweating questions came, no doubt, from my anxiety about
how I was going to perform that night, but I did not recognize this
fact at the time. Then I thought it was my conscience speaking, and
that I had no right to open to the Dangs a freedom I myself was
rejecting. It was too late to alter my course; honesty required me,
and I resolved courageously, not to prophesy at all.

When I was fetched out the people were in assembly at The Cleft
and the wheel of master prophets was revolving against the greater
wheel of dancers. I was given my cougar skin. Hung from a stake, in
the center where I was to hop, was a huge, terrific mask I had never
seen before. As the moon rose her slaves hung this mask on me; the
thong cut into the back of my neck cruelly, and at the bottom the
mask came to a point that pressed my belly; it was so wide my

arms could only move laterally. It had no eye holes; I broke into a sweat wondering how I should be able to follow the prophets into the Cave-Temple. It turned out to be no problem; the two moon slaves, one on each side, guided me by prodding spears in my ribs. Once in the cave they guided me to the back side of The Stone and drove me to climb it, my feet groping for steps I could not see; once, when I lost my balance, the spears' pressure kept me from falling backward. By the time I reached the top of The Stone I was bleeding and dizzy. With one arm I kept the mask from gouging my belly while with the other I helped my aching neck support the mask. I did not know what to do next. Tears of pain and anger poured from my eyes. I began hopping. I should have been moving my arms in counterpoint to the rhythm of my hop, but I could not bear the thought of letting the mask cut into me more. I kept hopping in the same place for fear of falling off; I had not been noticing the sounds of the other prophets, but suddenly I was aware they were making no sounds at all. In my alarm I lurched to the side and cut my foot on a sharp break in the rock. Pain converted my panic to rage.

I lifted the mask and held it flat above my head. I threw my head back and howled as I had never howled in my life, through a constricted, gradually opening throat, until at the end I was roaring; when I gasped in my breath I made a barking noise. I leaped and leaped, relieved of pain, confident. I punched my knee desecratingly through the brittle hide of the mask, and threw it behind me off The Stone. I tore off my cougar skin, and holding it with my claw by the tip of its tail I whirled it around my head. The prophets, massed below me, fell onto their knees. I felt their fear. Howling, I soared the skin out over them; one of those on whom it landed screamed hideously. A commotion started; I could not see very well what was happening. I barked and they turned toward me again. I leaped three times and then, howling, jumped wide-armed off The Stone. The twelve-foot drop hurt severely my already cut foot. I rolled exhausted into the channel in the cave floor.

Moon slaves with trembling hands mummied me in the deerskin and shoved me under The Stone with only my head sticking out. They brought two spears with darts tied to the points; rolling my head to watch them do this I saw that the prophets were kneeling over and rubbing dirt into their hair. Then the slaves laid the spears alongside the base of The Stone with the poisoned pricks pointed at my temples; exactly how close they were I could not be sure, but close enough so that I dared not move my head. In all my preparations I had, as I had been trained to do, rocked and weaved at least my head; now, rigidity, live rigidity. A movement would scratch me and a scratch would kill me.

I pressed my hook into my thigh, curled my toes, and pressed my tongue against my teeth till my throat ached. I did not dare relieve myself even with a howl, for I might toss my head fatally. I strained against my thongs to the verge of apoplexy. For a while I was unable to see, for sheer rage. Fatigue collapsed me. Yet I dared not relax my vigilance over my movements. My consciousness sealed me off. Those stone protuberances up between which I had to stare in the flickering light were merely chance processes on a boulder, similes to breasts. The one thing I might not become unconscious of was the pair of darts waiting for me to err. For a long time I thought of piercing my head against them, for relief, for spite. Hours passed. I was carefully watched.

I do not know what wild scheme I had had in mind when I had earlier resolved not to prophesy, what confrontation or escape; it had had the pure magnificence of a fantasy resolution. But the reality, which I had not seriously tried to evade, was that I must prophesy or die. I kept lapsing from English into a delirium of Dang. By the greatest effort of will I looked about me rationally. I wondered whether the return of Halley's comet, at which time all the stakes should be mounted by skulls, would make the Dangs destroy the Cave-Temple and erect a new one. I observed the straight, indented seam of sandstone running slantwise up the boulder over me and wondered how many eons this rotting piece of granite had been tumbled about by water. I reflected that I was unworthy both as a Christian and as a Dang to prophesy the life of Jesus. But I convinced myself that it was a trivial matter, since to the Christians it was the telling more than the teller that counted and to the Dangs this myth would serve as a civilizing force they needed. Surely, I thought, my hypocrisy could be forgiven me, especially since I resolved to punish myself for it by leaving the Dangs forever as soon as I could. Having reached this rational solution I smiled and gestured to the high prophet with my eyes; he did not move a muscle. When I realized that nothing to do with hypocrisy would unbind me desperation swarmed in my guts and mounted toward my brain; with this question it took me over: *How can I make myself believe it is true?* I needed to catch hold of myself again. I dug my hook so hard into my leg—it was the only action I was able to take—that I gasped with pain; the pain I wanted. I did not speculate on the consequences of gouging my leg, tearing a furrow in my thigh muscle, hurting by the same act the stump of my arm to which the hook was attached; just as I knew that the prophets, the torches, the poisoned darts were there in the cave, so also I knew that far far back in my mind I had good enough reasons to be hurting myself, reasons which I could find out if I wanted to, but which it was not worth my trouble to discover; I even allowed the knowledge that I myself was causing the pain to drift back in my mind. The pain itself, only the pain, became my consciousness, purging all else. Then, as the pain subsided leaving me free and equipoised, awareness of the stone arched over me flooded my mind. Because it had been invested by the people with a great mystery, it was an incarnation; the power of their faith made it the moon, who was female; at the same time it was only a boulder. I understood Stone is Stone, and that became my consciousness.

My muscles ceased straining against the bonds, nor did they slump; they ceased aching, they were at ease, they were ready. I said nothing, I did not change the upward direction of my glance, I did not smile, yet at this moment the high prophet removed the spears and had the moon slaves unbind me. I did not feel stiff nor did my wounds bother me, and when I put on my cougar skin and leaped, pulled the head over my face and roared, all the prophets fell onto their faces before me. I began chanting and I knew I was doing it all the better for knowing what I was about; I led them back out to the waiting people, and until dawn I chanted the story of the birth, prophesying, betrayal, sacrifice, and victory of the most high prophet. I am a good mimic, I was thoroughly trained, the story is the best; what I gave them was, for them, as good as a vision. I did not know the difference myself.

But the next evening I knew the difference. While I performed my ablutions and the routine ceremonies to the full moon I thought with increasing horror of my state of mind during my conscious trance. What my state of mind actually had been I cannot with confidence now represent, for what I know of it is colored by my reaction against it the next day. I had remained conscious, in that I could recall what happened, yet that observer and commentator in myself of whose existence I had scarcely been aware, but whom I had always taken for my consciousness, had vanished. I no longer had been thinking, but had lost control so that my consciousness had become what I was doing; almost worse, when I had told the story of Christ I had done it not because I had wanted to or believed in it but because, in some obscure sense, I had had to. Thinking about it afterward I did not understand or want to understand what I was drifting toward, but I knew it was something that I feared. And I got out of there as soon as I was physically able.

Here in Sansom what I have learned has provided me with material for an honorable contribution to knowledge, has given me a tenure to a professorship—thereby pleasing my wife—whereas if I had stayed there among the Dangs much longer I would have reverted until I had become one of them, might not have minded when the time came to die under the sacrificial knife, would have taken in all ways the risk of prophecy—as my Dang son intends to do—until I had lost myself utterly.